Seven Days

Daniel Alexander

ISBN: 1492765317
ISBN-13: 9781492765318

CHAPTER ONE

2:00am - Wow, it's only 2:00am. Based on how refreshed he feels William would have guessed it is 5:00am, his normal time to get out of bed. He laughs to himself as he listens to Geneviève snore like a sailor. If he had the inclination he'd record her to refute her claim that she doesn't snore and prove she not only snores but she snores like a world champion. Still, as he looks down on his wife fast asleep, he thinks to himself that she is, by far, the most beautiful thing he has ever seen. He'll never say it out loud but every once in a while she'll say something, or do something, or just look at him, and he'll think to himself, "How'd I get so lucky?"

The projection report for Monterey Point, a 250 unit apartment community in Scottsdale, Arizona is calling his name. His intention was to complete the spreadsheet with the last set of figures he got from the city and several vendors in the morning, but now that he's awake and there's no time like the present. William eases out of bed and tip toes out of the bedroom and into the hallway, for the room at the end of the hallway to his left, a small bedroom he uses as his home office.

1

He turns on his computer with the joy of a five year old at Christmas. He got this deal from one of his fraternity brothers, who brought it to him before taking it to market. William needed all of ten minutes to know, due to the low rents, this deal is better than a homerun. It's a grand slam. The way his firm underwrites deals is very conservative. He's sure he can beat the five year projection in one year and, given the improving economy and the competition, rents should go straight up from there.

Just as he opens the excel file that houses the projections he hears a noise that sounds like it came from downstairs. William remains absolutely still and he listens. When he doesn't hear anything else, he tells himself it was nothing. The notes he needs are not on his desk where he thought he left them. After scanning his office he realizes they're in his briefcase, which he must have left in his bedroom. To put himself back in stealth mode he gets up quietly from his desk. He gently squeezes and turns the doorknob on the door leading to the hallway. As soon as he steps out into the hallway all of his blood drains from his body and for a split second he's absolutely frozen.

At the top of the stairs, at the other end of the hallway, is a man dressed in all black, including a balaclava, with a gun in his hand. He has just enough time to yell, "Genny!" before the intruder levels the gun at William and fires. William is hit in the left shoulder but, more troubling than that, the momentum spins him around. He trips over his own feet and, as he falls, he hits his head on his desk. He tries to get up, but the blood rushes to his head. Even though his eyes are open he can't see anything, but he hears Genny scream, "William!" just before everything goes black

Three Days Later

10:00am - It's a cold, blistery night in Paris. The temperature is a frigid nine degrees Celsius, with a wind chill that makes it feel like negative one. On any other night, there wouldn't be anyone on the street that didn't absolutely have to get from one place to another. Even then they would be so wrapped up in gloves, scarves, and hats they would be unrecognizable to their friends and family. Tonight, however, is New Year's Eve, and there isn't an empty space on the entire Champs-Élysées from the Arc de Triomphe to the Place de la Concorde. More than that, everyone is deliriously happy. Maybe the density of human bodies on the street is keeping everyone warm or maybe it's the anticipation of the New Year, and the hope and promise that comes with it, that is helping everyone ignore the cold. Whatever it is, there isn't one person on the Champs-Élysées that isn't smiling, and laughing, and celebrating. That includes William and Geneviève, who are middle of the street, just off Rue Balzac, and surrounded by couples in various displays of affection, and families with parents desperately trying to keep an eye on all of their children, and young adults who are smoking and drinking and kissing and partying as if there is no tomorrow. To say the atmosphere is electric and positive would be an understatement. Just one ounce of this energy, if it could be contained, would supply the City of Lights with all the energy she needs for a year. Now, with just two minutes left before the clock strikes twelve, all eyes are on the countdown clock in the center of the giant Ferris wheel just in front of the Obélisque.

William is standing behind Geneviève with his arms wrapped around her. She turns her head to speak to William because if she didn't he wouldn't hear her. "I had forgotten how much fun it is to be here. Merci, mon amour."

William exclaims, "This is better than I imagined and I wouldn't be here if not for you. So, merci a toi." Geneviève asks, "Can you say all of that in French?"

William gives it a shot, "C'est mieux que ce que j'imaginais et je ne serais pas ici si ce n'est pas pour vous."

"Très bon mon amour. Votre français est de mieux en mieux."

Suddenly, the crowd around them bursts into a countdown and William and Geneviève join in.

"Dix, neuf, huit, sept, six, cinq, quatre, trois, deux, un, Bonne Annee!"

As everyone around them turns to the people they are with or to the people just standing next to them to kiss them and hug them and celebrate the New Year, Geneviève turns around to face William. But, when she does William drops to one knee and reaches into his coat pocket for something.

Geneviève asks, "Qu'est-ce que vous faites?"

William declares, "À partir du moment où je vous ai rencontré tous les autres femme sur terre est devenu invisible pour moi et chaque jour depuis, a été mieux que la veille. Je t'aime et je veux passer le reste de ma vie avec vous. Je veux que l'on nous les parents ensemble, et les grands-parents ensemble et meilleurs amis à jamais. Veux-tu m'épouser?

Geneviève is truly surprised. She admits, "I thought you might do this when you first told me we would be spending New Year's Eve in Paris, but you didn't show me any other sign, so I didn't allow myself to expect it. Oui, mon amour! Oui! Oui! Oui, je vais t'épouser!"

At that moment everyone surrounding them, who noticed William taking a knee, explodes in hearty applause and congratulations. As William and Geneviève hug and kiss, the couples, the parents and their kids, and the young adults take turns hugging them. The moment is punctuated by a particularly loud set of fireworks, which turns into a loud noise that sounds like someone tapping on glass.

William hears the loud tapping noise again and it brings him back to reality. He's sitting alone, in the back of a town car, and it's his Aunt Ernestine, using her cane to tap on the door window to get William's attention. William takes a deep breath and opens the door. His Aunt Ernestine is in her late sixties and she's been blind for twenty years as a result from her battle with diabetes. Yet, it is his Aunt Ernestine who takes a hold of William, and keeps him steady, as she leads him up the pathway to Geneviève's burial site, where the rest of their family and friends are waiting for him.

Three Months Later

7:00pm - Letting go of the house is both hard and easy. William and Geneviève found this two story, four bedroom, two and a half bathroom craftsman house on 17th Street in Santa Monica when they were on their way to a friend's house for a Super Bowl party. Geneviève became obsessed with the house the minute she saw it. While the guys were watching the game, she was on the phone with the listing agent trying to set up an appointment. Somehow, she got him on the phone and convinced him to leave the Super Bowl party he was attending, at halftime, to show her the house. By the time she came back the house they were previously interested in, but lost to someone who outbid them, became classified under "when one door closes another opens," or "everything happens for a reason," or any other cliché that explains how not getting what you want is, sometimes, a blessing. Her enthusiasm for this house lead the other guys at the party to joke with William that if he didn't get that house for her, their marriage would be over. So, the very next day they made an offer on the house subject to inspection. After the inspection they had a laundry list of things that needed to be renovated or replaced, but Geneviève saw past that laundry list and thought, "if the price can be made right, this is the house for them." There was no doubt in her mind that this is the house she wanted them to raise their family in. Luckily, the price was made right and they got the house. Once they took possession, the first thing they did was remodel the kitchen. Then they embarked on a bunch of painting projects. They planted new grass and flowers and bushes in the front yard and around the perimeter of the backyard. William took one of the bedrooms for his home office, while Geneviève cordoned off a section of the backyard for her garden. Upon meeting William, the first thing Geneviève liked about him was his smile. The second thing, however, was his last name, Flowers. Though she never admitted it, she imagined that her name was Geneviève Flowers the first night they met. So, once the front yard was done she got a plaque that read Flowers and she proudly hung that by the front door. As agreed, that was supposed to be the last thing they spent money on until they saved enough to continue with renovations. Of course, the following week, they had to replace the boiler unexpectedly, and a month later they needed a new washing machine. Still, even William had to admit the house was great.

Now, William rarely goes upstairs. He hasn't slept in a bed since that night. Rather, he's been sleeping on the living room floor, and living between the living room and the kitchen for the last three months. Given the house's location and all the work they put into it, getting interested parties, once the house was put up for sale, was easy. Selling a house where someone was recently murdered was another story. After three months and dozens of showings, with no takers, William considered lowering the price. After instructing the listing agent to do exactly that, but before the agent could, an offer came in at full asking price with no contingencies. William and his agent jumped at the offer and the house sold. The sale closed earlier today.

Detective Javier Morales is a twenty year veteran of the Los Angeles Police Department. He quickly rose to a detective in the Homicide Division, and he's been a homicide detective for fifteen years. He is the detective assigned to the Geneviève Flowers murder case. Unfortunately, his investigation has been less than fruitful. William was unable to give the detective a workable description of the intruder, as the intruder was covered from head to toe. Accordingly, the intruder didn't leave any finger prints, nor did he leave any fibers or foot prints inside or outside of the house. There were no eye witnesses or any reports of strange cars or strange people in the neighborhood in the days and weeks leading up to the murder. There were shell casings found at the scene. Tracking their lot numbers lead to the store where they were purchased, but that store's video cameras haven't been operational for over a year. On top of that, the store's records indicate that box of bullets were purchased with cash. In short, Javier doesn't have anything that could be used to determine the intruder's identity. It is always frustrating for a police officer to have to report to a victim's family and friends that there are no new leads and no new developments in their case, but that time comes every once in a while and Javier knows it's time to have that conversation with William.

On his way home, Javier finds William at his house. When he gets there William is in the garage, packing the few remaining boxes of his possessions into the trunk and into the back seat of his car. As Javier walks up the driveway he announces his presence with, "Hey."

William mirrors, "Hey."

Javier asks, "Do you need help?"

"No, I can handle it. I'm almost done anyway."

"I want to say congratulations on selling the house but I know that isn't appropriate."

William stops packing to address Javier directly. "I appreciate that. Don't worry about it, I know what you mean. So, what do you want to talk about? I can tell from your demeanor you're not here to tell me there's a break in the case."

Javier concedes, "You're right about that. Actually, I'm here to have an upfront conversation with you." William goes back to packing as Javier continues, "The first thing I want you to know is that I will never give up on the case. I have to tell you, however, that you may not hear from me as regularly as you have." Again, William stops so he can listen to Javier more attentively. Javier explains, "I have some, more recent, cases that I have to turn much of my attention to. More recent, was probably not the best words to use. It has more to do with leads. I have cases with more evidence to follow, and I am just as committed to solving those homicides as I am to solving Genny's."

Maybe it's the emotion of the day that leads William to respond uncharacteristically when he says, "LAPD. . . Let me go through a stop sign at a half a mile per hour, at one in the morning, and two squad cars will come out of nowhere to give me a ticket, but let someone break into my house, shoot me, and murder my wife, and you guys got nothing. You guys are useless."

Having said what he wanted to say, William goes back to packing. Javier has seen this emotion, unfortunately, a few times before. He knows it isn't William talking as much as it's William's frustration. So, he lets William get that one in without addressing it. Instead he mentions, "I see your arm is better."

"Yeah, there's still a little soreness and stiffness in the mornings but, for the most part, I'm OK." William loads the last box in his car and turns to Javier to ask, "So, is that all you have to say?" Again, Javier takes the verbal jab without responding. He asks William, "Where are you moving to?" "Don't worry about it. My number is still the same; not that you'll have any reason to use it."

"You know as well as I do, how hard I worked on this case. You know how much I want to find the person who did this and bring him to justice. I understand how . . ."

"Whoa, whoa, whoa, you understand what exactly? Has anyone ever broken into your house and murdered your wife?"

Javier inquires again, "I need to know where you'll be living. Where are you moving to?"

"I'm moving to the Copenhagen on Second Street, until I can figure out what I want to do."

"But, your cell number isn't changing, right?"

"Like I said, Javier, what do you care? Maybe I've seen too much television, but with what I know you know, which is nothing, you won't be calling me anytime soon. You and your whole department are completely useless."

"William, don't forget who you are talking to. I'm a police officer."

Williams jumps at that, "What is that, some sort of threat?"
Almost out of thin air comes, "Is there a problem gentlemen?"
William and Javier turn to see who is talking to them. William
recognizes the man but Javier doesn't, so he asks, "Who are you?"
The man answers, "I'm Cyrus Dabney, the new owner of this
house."

—

CHAPTER TWO

Day One

4:30am - It took some trial and error for Doug to get his routine perfected, but once he did it made every day, especially Mondays better. He always starts with a cup of coffee before he leaves his house. He always takes the same route to work. He always takes the same truck, number 2897B2993. He always gets to the starting point of his route early so he can park his truck and go to the 7Eleven just two blocks away. He always get a medium sized French Roast Blend Coffee with Hazelnut flavored cream. Then he walks back to his truck, where he enjoys the coffee while reading an actual newspaper before starting the day. Doug is a front load truck driver for Roma Trash Removal. He has been for five years and he loves his job. He loves the simplicity of it and he loves the routine. He also loves all the people he works with, including Sting, his scout driver. In fact, the morning call from Sting could be considered part of his routine and it usually comes somewhere after Doug has scanned all of the headlines and before he finishes reading the first article he wants to read. Today is no different.

Half way into his first article, Sting's voice comes over the walkie-talkie, "Dude, are you there?"

Doug replies "When am I not here?" There it is. That's how they say hello and that's the official start of the work day.

Sting goes on, "Dude, I gotta tell you about this weekend!"

"What happened?"

"OK, so it's Friday night and I'm at Dukes. My boy Rick is behind the bar, so the drinks are strong and every other one is free. Yeah baby! All of the usual suspects are there. After the Hula girls do their thing we are all just drinking, talking smack about each other, and watching the Laker game. Then, these five ga ga gorgeous girls came in. Dude, like the whole bar stopped talking to watch these girls walk by the bar on their way to a table outside on the patio."

Doug interrupts, "Don't tell you went and talked with those girls. Where was Diane?"

Sting answers, "I'm getting to that and Diane was out with her girlfriends in West Hills. No, I didn't go and talk with the girls but Big Bob did. Somehow he convinced all five of them to give up their table and join us at the bar. It turns out they are all Pepperdine girls and Dukes was just their first stop for the night. They had a party to go to later that night, another party to go to Saturday night, and they had a barbecue to go to on Sunday."

Doug interrupts again, "And let me guess, you hung out with them all weekend?"

"Damn right!"

"OK, where are you?"

"I'm on your six in ten seconds." Sure enough, ten seconds later Sting's scout truck zips by Doug and disappears in the parking garage in front of him. One minute later, Sting's scout truck reappears with the first dumpster. Doug and Sting jump out of their trucks to help each other position the dumpster on the fork for dumping. Their conversation continues there with Sting saying, "Dude, nothing happened." After getting the dumpster positioned, Doug activates the fork to dump the trash into the truck and, while doing so, he says, "If you keep playing around you're going to lose Diane."

While watching the contents of the dumpster spill into the truck Sting continues, "I told you nothing happened. All I did was drink, smoke a little weed, and party all weekend, but I didn't do anything with any of those girls or with anyone I met at the parties."

"Yeah, but how long do you think your relationship with Diane will last if the two of you are always socializing separately?"

"Dude!"

Doug cuts him off, "No, you need to listen to me."

"Dude!"

Doug cuts him off again, "I'm telling you, you need to settle down and you're not going to find a better girl than Diane."

"Dude!" This time when Doug tries to cut him off, Sting cuts him off and says, "Dude! I think we just dumped a dead body into the truck."

5:30am - Officer Anthony Isaac is the arriving officer at the alley between third and fourth streets in Santa Monica. At six feet two inches tall with a naturally athletic build, above average intelligence, and chiseled good looks Officer Isaac could have been anything there is to be. As the quarterback and captain of his high school football team he demonstrated that, along with his physical attributes, he has the qualities to lead. So, when he informed his family and friends he was leaving Bakersfield to move to Los Angeles everyone, except his parents and his closest friends, assumed he intended to try his hand at modeling, maybe even acting. Those who know him, knew different. Tony wrestled with the idea of joining the Marines but his true passion won out in the end. He has always wanted to be a homicide detective, and, maybe one day, Chief of Police. After a year on the force as a patrol officer the closest he has come to a murder investigation was when Mrs. Burke tried to bring charges against Mr. Burke for running over her cat intentionally, which, incidentally, turned out to be unintentional and a tragic mistake. So, when he got the call of a reported dead body in a dump truck he jumped at the opportunity enthusiastically. As soon as he arrived he quickly surveyed the scene. He confirmed that, indeed, there was a dead body in the dump truck. He took statements from Doug and Sting, the two individuals who reported the incident to the police. He made sure they stayed close by so they could talk with the detectives that would arrive soon to take the lead. Then he sectioned off the entire alley so anything that might be considered evidence remains at the scene. His one break with protocol was to tell his girlfriend, Lisa Becker, about the dead body. He only did that because he knew she'd be interested. Lisa is a budding crime beat writer and a blogger on criminal investigations. She, like Tony, has a propensity for murder investigations and she arrived at the scene just as Tony was about to put up the yellow crime scene tape at the far end of the alley. He told Lisa she could talk with Doug and Sting, but that she had to stay away from the dump truck. Then he turned his back and walked to the far end of the alley to put up the crime scene tape knowing that Lisa was probably on top of the truck taking pictures of the dead body. When he completed that task he turned around to walk back to the truck and he saw that he was right. He found Lisa right where he thought she would be. By the time he got back to the truck he figured she had enough time to get what she needs. Now it is time to protect his career. So he made sure she got down and, for public perceptions, he pretended to be upset that she didn't follow his directions. To really sell it, he escorted her to the outer perimeter of the crime scene. When they got to the tape at the near end of the alley he held the tape up so she could walk beneath it. It turns out their timing was impeccable because just as she walked beneath the tape two detectives arrived at the scene. The older of the two detectives, sensing that more than meets the eye is going on here, asks, "What's happening here officer?"

Before Tony can respond Lisa asks, "Are you the detectives assigned to this case?"

The older detective asks, "Who are you?"

"My name is Lisa Becker. I'm a writer for the Malibu Journal and I'm trying to get a jump on this story." In an effort to continue their charade she looks at Tony's name badge before she continues, "Officer Isaac here, won't tell my anything and he won't allow me anywhere near the body. I just want to get a couple of pictures and some information so I can break the story."

The older detective explains, "Officer Isaac is doing his job and he's right. It's too early for you to be gathering information."

Lisa is an exceptionally attractive young woman. She knows it, and she knows how to use it. Satisfied that the detectives no longer have any questions about Tony she turns her intention to making friends. Lisa says, "I really want to be the one to break this story, can you guys help me?"

Never one to deny a pretty woman of a request, if he can help it, the older detective introduces himself, "I'm Detective Eddie Roberts and this is my partner Detective Bobby Mallory. If you give me your card, I'll be happy to bring you up to speed after we've had a chance to get up to speed ourselves." Sensing that she should quit while she's ahead, Lisa happily gives each of the detectives one of her cards and asks, "When can I expect your call?"

"Maybe later today but probably in the morning."

"Can I get your cards?" Eddie gives her one of his cards. Lisa forewarns the detectives, "If I don't hear from you I'm going to call you. I hope you remember me. I hope we can work together on this case and maybe other cases in the future. It can't hurt a crime beat writer to have friends that are detectives."

Eddie tells her, "I like your style. We'll talk when we can. Have a good day."

Lisa knows that means enough is enough and she doesn't push it. The two detectives turn their attention to Officer Isaac, who's been watching their interaction with Lisa, his amazing girlfriend. As the three of them walk away she can hear Tony telling the detectives about Doug and Sting and she can hear Tony giving the detectives his description of the body.

6:30am - Rosa Lieberman pulls her Volkswagen Jetta in the parking lot on Mansfield Avenue and parks in her assigned space. It isn't surprising that there are only two other cars there at this time in the morning. Work officially begins at 9:00am but most of the employees at Equity Growth Partners arrive between 8:00am and 8:30am. The first car she sees in the lot is parked in the first and best space. It belongs to David Hughes, one of the two brothers that own and run the business. Seeing David's car in the lot gives Rosa a sense that all is right in the world. She's been working at the firm for two years and she has seen his car parked in that same space every single morning she's arrived for work and it's always there every night when she leaves. The rumor is

David is the inside man, the one who manages the people and the day to day activities of the business. His brother, Matthew, is the outside man, the one who meets with city officials, brokers, bankers, and investors to garner new business. The second car she sees is parked in the space adjacent to hers and it belongs to Cindy, David's assistant. Most of the employees at the firm have mixed emotions about Cindy. One on hand they feel sorry for her because it isn't easy working for David. He's the epitome of a never satisfied micro-manager. Since he demands that she be there whenever he's there, Cindy works exceptionally long hours, especially for someone who isn't a partner at the firm. On the other hand, however, she is envied and, maybe, a little despised by most of her co-workers at the firm. Though no one knows what her compensation package is, it is obvious she is extremely well paid. She's always dressed in designer clothing, she drives a silver Mercedes C250 Sedan, and it is common knowledge she lives in a great house in the Hollywood Hills that has a pool, a Jacuzzi, and a view that overlooks the entire city. Though she can be friendly, one of the first things a new employee learns from the employee underground is, beware of Cindy. As David's assistant she sits in a position of power at the firm and she wields that power unapologetically. Rosa has never had a bad experience with Cindy, but everyone knows if you get on her wrong side it won't be long before David is questioning your performance at work.

No matter how many times Rosa enters the building she is always more impressed each time. It's easy to drive by the building and not see it altogether. On the outside it's a plain white building with frosted windows. If it wasn't for the parking lot, filled with cars during the day, the building could easily be mistaken for an abandoned warehouse. Once you enter, however, you are blown away by the interior design. The first thing you notice is, it's just one super large room, sectioned off into offices, work stations, and a lounge area. There is a massive two story loft in the middle of the building. The first level up is where Cindy and Roger, Matthew's assistant, have their offices. High above their offices there is a space that looks like it could house another four offices, but it's just one large office that David and Matthew share. The whole interior is a modern mixture of marble tile, cedar wood, and steel. There are exactly thirty skylights that almost cover the entire ceiling. On a sunny day there is so much light from the skylights the use of electrical lighting is almost unnecessary. One of the best things about working for David is he's a technology junkie. Every office and every work station has the latest, greatest computers with the latest, greatest software. Even the coffee maker, the microwave, and the dishwasher in the employee lounge, the phone system and every copier in the building are so modern and advanced they would send a PhD from MIT scrambling for the instruction manuals. In fact, a large part of a new employee's orientation is devoted to how to work the machines found around the office.

Today Rosa is in early because she has to leave early. Rosa is, naturally, a sunshiny person but today she is beside herself. She met Elton, her boyfriend, two years ago, right after she got the job at the firm. They had a blissful first year together and then they hit a rough patch. Elton did something that negated her feelings and when he refused to acknowledge what he had done, Rosa refused to continue dating him. If she had a dollar for every time she wanted to pick up the phone to tell him that what he had done wasn't a big deal and she wanted him back, she'd be a very rich woman.

She didn't though. She held her ground. A week later Elton came to her ready to acknowledge that he was insensitive and promising never to make that mistake again. She took him back happily and the remainder of their second year together was better than their first. Lately, he's been hinting at marriage. He even asked her if she had a favorite cut of diamond. When she asked why, he gave her some story about just wondering. If she remembers correctly, he said something about reading an article that claimed to give insight into a woman based on what type of jewelry she liked. Rosa played along because she knew different, or, at least, she hoped she did. About a month after that conversation Elton was promoted to Vice President of Television Development at Fox, and since then he's mentioned the idea of marriage not frequently but regularly. It is obviously on his mind and Rosa has given him every indication, short of saying yes, that she's interested. In fact, she's more than interested. Elton is handsome, funny, smart, and successful and it is apparent to all of her friends that he's head over heels for her. She loves him just as much. Yesterday he asked her to take off work early so they could have a "special" dinner together at Spago, hands down Rosa's favorite restaurant of all time. In short, she's sure tonight he'll pop the question. So, as Rosa makes her way to her work station, she's walking on air.

The first thing she does when she gets to her desk is the first thing she always does, she goes through her inbox to determine what absolutely has to get done today. She puts those things in a pile on her desk and then she logs onto the network. Just as she inputs her password, Stephen from accounting walks by, and they talk for a minute. Then she checks her emails paying special attention to the ones that are really for William, her direct boss, that she's cc'd on. There are a couple of matters she'll need to get an answer from William on today, so she can take the next appropriate action. She prints those emails to put them on William's desk, so they are the first thing he sees when he gets in. She opens the door to William's office and she screams at the sight of a man that seems to be lunging for her. It takes a few seconds for her to realize the man is William and he wasn't lunging for her. It appears the sound of his door opening startled him out of his sleep on the couch in his office. The next thing she notices is that William smells of alcohol. He obviously slept there last night and he's a mess.

"Oh my God, William, you nearly scared me to death." William doesn't have anything to say. Rosa closes the door behind her so no one else can happen upon this scene. She asks the obvious, "Did you sleep here last night?"

"Yeah, I guess," says William.

"We have to get you out of here so you can wash up before anyone sees you." Unfortunately, it's too late for that. David heard the scream and he raced down to where the sound came from. While Rosa is trying to get William on his feet, David enters William's office.

Everyone at the firm has been trying to understand what William is going through. Losing a person you love must be horrible, but to lose that person in such a violent and senseless way must be indescribably gut wrenching. So, everyone, especially Rosa, has been trying to be what William needs at the time. That includes David. It's obvious, however, from the look on his face and his body language David is a little fed up. David can see that William is in no state to talk so he asks Rosa, "What's going on here." Rosa explains, "Everything is OK. I didn't mean to scream. I'm sorry if that's what caused you to race here. I was just startled. I didn't see William's car in the lot so I wasn't expecting him to be here." David says to William, "Clean yourself up and be in my office at 9:00am."

7:00am - Captain Upton, the captain of the Santa Monica Precinct, the precinct Eddie and Booby belong to, has heard about the dead body found in the dump truck. Since it's just a little bit out of his way to the office he decides to make the detour to see what's happening there in person. Eddie is standing on top of the truck when he notices Captain Upton's car making a u turn, probably looking for a place to park.

Eddie tells Bobby, "I think the Captain just pulled up. I'm going to climb down to meet him."

Bobby replies, "I just have to roll his left hand for prints, I'll join you in a minute."

By the time Eddie climbed downs the Captain is on scene. The Captain asks, "What have you got so far?"

Eddie answers, "Dead white male, approximately twenty-five years old, shot once in the back of the head. It's still early but no witnesses so far."

"Who called it in?"

"Those two guys over there called it in. They work for Roma Trash Removal and this alley is on their route."

Bobby joins them and says, "Hey Cap."

The Captain asks, "How are you feeling Bobby?"

"Better today."

"Good." Then he continues his conversation with Eddie. "I bet you thought you were going to have an easy last week."

"I was hoping."

"Unless we can get an ID on this kid or some other lead materializes, this may take longer than a week. Are you sure you want to spend your last few days before retirement chasing down a lead?"

"Yeah, I'm pretty much set up for retirement. I'd rather stay engaged and keep the juices flowing than sit around, doing nothing, until Friday."

The Captain says to Bobby, "If push comes to shove, you may have to carry this investigation for a couple of weeks, on your own, until we get you a new partner. Do you think you can handle that?"

"Sure. Why not?"

"Have you heard anything new from your doctor?"

Bobby answers, "I have to call him later today, but I feel fine. I'm sure everything is OK."

The Captain turns back to Eddie, "I wish you were staying in town long enough to take me out fishing on that boat of yours."

Eddie tells the Captain, "Yeah, I would hang around if I were getting younger. You can always come to Costa Rica."

"If I could think of a cover story to tell my wife, one that she'd believe, I would." The three men laugh. Bobby says, "If you can, you should stop the Marina to see the boat. I'm not a boat kind of guy and even I think she's a sight."

The Captain says, "I have until Friday. I'll try to find the time."

Eddie adds, "If you can, that would be great, but you are always welcome to visit me in Costa Rica. If you make it there, I'll make sure you have a great time."

Knowing Eddie the Captain has a good idea of what he means by "a great time." With that in mind he admits, "Do you know why I don't keep any ice cream in my house? Because, I'll eat it and I'll eat all of it in one sitting. In other words, I stay out of trouble by avoiding temptation all together." Again, the three men laugh.

Then the Captain leaves but not before saying, "Now, get back to work you lucky bastard, and you too Bobby."

9:00am - The fact that Roger, Matthew's assistant, a normally friendly and gregarious guy, didn't look up from his desk when William got to the first upper level of the loft was some indication. If that wasn't enough, the look on Cindy's face told William everything he needs to know. This isn't going to be a good meeting. David and Matthew, who are notorious for making employees wait to meet with them, were waiting for William and he was directed to go right in. A single chair was positioned directly in front of David's desk and William was instructed to take that seat. David is sitting in his chair behind his desk and Matthew is sitting on the edge of David's desk, approximately two feet from William. David begins, "I thought you would, at least, go home, wash up, and change your clothes."

William explains, "I had to go back to the restaurant I was at last night to get my car. By the time they located my keys, I didn't think I would have enough time to go home and make it back here by nine." Matthew says, "Tell us what happened last night."

William starts with, "First, I apologize for this morning. Last night I felt I had to get out my hotel room, so I went for a drive. I don't know how I made it all the way to Hollywood from Santa Monica but when I looked up I was just down the street from here. I went in the restaurant with the intention of getting something to eat but one drink led to another and then another. Ultimately, I ended up not eating anything. All I did was drink."

David says, "Ultimately, you passed out drunk in your office."

"Yes, I guess that is what ultimately happened."

David continues, "Couple that with all of the unscheduled time you've taken off over the last couple of months and your absence even when you're here, things don't seem to be getting better for you, they're getting worse."

Matthew turns to his brother and tells him, "Take it easy David." Then Matthew turns back to William and says, "Listen, none of us can possibly understand what you're going through, but we have a business to run. We've asked you to take some time off and we understand why you've resisted that idea. Again, I don't understand what you're going through, but if I were in your shoes I would want to keep working as well. I assume you are trying to maintain so sense of normalcy."

"That's exactly right. Right now, work is all I have. Again, I'm sorry about last night and I'm sorry if I appear not to be here even when I am,, but I am here and I'm getting things done. What happened this morning, I assure you, won't happen again. I'll also make a better effort at controlling my emotions, at least, while I'm at work."

David says, "No."

Again, Matthew looks at David but this time he doesn't have to say anything. David knows he needs to let Matthew do the talking. Matthew says to William, "The thing is, people are talking. Your behavior has become too disruptive to the atmosphere here. This time we aren't asking, we're insisting you take some time off."

"I understand. Let me just work through the acquisition of Monterey Point and then I'll take some time off."

David says, "No."

Matthew says to William, "No one will forget that you brought that deal to us. All of the hard work is already done. As you know, the inspection is done and the financing is in place. There's just a few minor deal points to work out and then the takeover."

"I know. That's why I think it's best if I just work through the takeover. After that, you won't get any more resistance from me. I'll take a week off and I'll come back with a clear head."

David says "No."

Matthew says, "We don't think that's a good idea and, frankly, we think you're going to need more than a week. Let me be straight with you, we've already decided this. We want you take a month off. We'll pay you during your time off and it won't count against your sick time or your vacation time."

David chimes in, "Wait a minute we agreed to pay him for the month but we didn't agree that it wouldn't count against his sick time."

Matthew doesn't acknowledge David. He tells William, "It won't count against your sick time or your vacation time, don't worry about that."

David asserts, "But, you need to come back to work ready to work."

Matthew extends his hand to William and William stands up to shake it. William goes to shake David's hand but David doesn't stand up to shake his. They do shake hands even though David is unable to find the grace to hide his frustration. As William turns to leave their office Matthew says, "Take care of yourself and try to find some peace. If you need to speak with someone we can make some recommendations."

10:00am - Abbey Marie was born Anja Morozov in the Bronx, New York to Andrei Morozov and Mila Morozov, her Russian immigrant parents. At an early age Anya showed exceptional skill in two things, math and acting. When she was ten years old, against her father's wishes, she auditioned for a kids show being produced by the Disney Studios. Against all odds she got the part. Her family had to move to Burbank, California so she could be on the show. The fact that she was making more money in one year than her father made in ten years didn't make her being on the show a hard pill for her father to swallow, though it did bother him on some level, at least, at first. What made it a hard pill to swallow was that the show's producers insisted that she change her name. Eventually, her father came around to accepting her being on the show and all that came with it, as long as she agreed to continue her studies and graduate from college. He didn't have to fight for that concession because Anya always wanted to continue her studies and graduating from college was always a goal of hers.

Abbey Marie was born and she had a great seven year run on that show. When the show was finally canceled Abbey's agent wanted her to audition for another show, but she wanted to take a few years off so she could attend USC. Four years later she graduated from USC with a degree in Economics. When she went back to acting getting a role on a show didn't come as easily as it did eleven years ago, but that didn't bother Abbey. Somewhere along the way her entrepreneurial spirit had been awakened in her and, now, more than anything she wanted to create her own business and find success in that endeavor. Though she did go on a few more auditions, she even landed a very lucrative national commercial, she gave up acting when she bought a title and escrow business from a lady who lived two doors down from her parents. She renamed the venture Sun Country Title and Escrow and in less than one year of owning the business she made a deal with Wells Fargo to handle their home mortgage business. She never looked back at acting again.

Over the last ten years her business has grown. When she bought the business she had four employees, now she has twenty. When she started she was only doing single family residential properties, but along the way she picked up a commercial property. Then she a got an entire office building on Wilshire Blvd, in the mid-Wilshire area of Los Angeles. Eventually she earned a good reputation in the Los Angeles business community and soon the revenue from her commercial property business surpassed the revenue from her residential property business. That's when she met Pete Jefferson, one of LA's most successful but enigmatic developers. She handled the escrow and title closing on two of his office buildings sales. Both transactions went so well, she developed a personal relationship with Pete, and he made sure she got more business. There are people, in the industry, who believe she was awarded the 300 store Forest Canyon Mall mega-deal escrow and title business because of her relationship with Pete, the principal of that deal, but anyone who knows Pete knows that's not how he does business. She was awarded what will be the largest deal in her company's ten year history, and the deal every title company in Los Angeles salivated over, because she and her staff earned it.

On her drive to the office this morning Abbey thought of how much she's been consumed by the Forest Canyon Mall deal for the last three weeks. The good news is the buyer and the seller have all of their ducks in a row. The negotiations have all been settled and all of the corresponding paperwork has been submitted. For the most part, all that's left is for the bank to fund the loan. She's very pleased that everything is set for the closing this Friday, in four days. The bad news is her company is overseeing six other closings this week, and she barely has any idea of where each one is in the process. So, the first thing she did when got to the office this morning was tell Julia, her assistant, to tell everyone they are going to have a staff meeting in the conference room at 10:00am.

Now, Abbey asks Julia, "Jules, is everybody in the conference room?"

Julia replies, "I'll make sure they are. Also, I just got off the phone with Mr. Yee. He says there are changes to the settlement statement. I asked him to email the updated settlement statement to me right away. He said he'll email it in the next ten minutes."

"Oh boy, well, we'll see what the changes there are when the statement gets here. In the meantime, tell everybody to be ready to update me. I'll be in the conference room in five minutes."

By the time Abbey finished responding to the email she was working on and stood up from her desk to head to the conference room Julia had the updated statement in hand and she gave a copy to Abbey. Julia says, "There's only one change. It looks like one of the partners is, perhaps, starting a new venture with a portion of his pay out."

"Great, that isn't a big deal at all." Abbey follows Julia out of her office but before she gets to the conference room the receptionist tells her she has Mr. Jefferson on line one for her. Abbey tells Julia, "Give me a couple of minutes to take this call. I'll be in right after." Abbey goes back to her office to take Pete's call. Five minutes later she hung up feeling a little frustrated. She really wanted to catch up on some of the other business her office is engaged in, but Pete's call wasn't personal. It was business. Even though they have a personal relationship Abbey knows she's no different than anyone else. When Pete wants to talk business she, like most people, will make the time to accommodate him. He invited her to his office for brunch to go over the closing. So, Abbey calls Julia and tells her, "We have to reschedule our meeting. I have to go to Pete's office."

11:00am - William wants to make it out of the building without calling too much attention to himself. He gathers his things and comes out of his office to talk with Rosa, but she is already in David's and Matthew's office. He's sure they are filling her in, so he leaves a note for her to call him and he leaves without saying word to anybody. As he pulls out of the parking lot he is struck by how aimless he feels. He doesn't know what to do or where to go. He still feels the effects of his drinking binge so he thinks the best thing to do is to get something to eat. Even then he can't decide what he wants to eat, so he doesn't know where to go. He points his car west and drives. He figures if he can't decide what he wants by the time he gets back to the hotel he'll just order something from room service when he gets there. On the way back to his hotel he passes a Ralph's supermarket and he decides to pull in and pick up a few things there.

The Copenhagen is a two story, thirty room courtyard style boutique hotel on Second Street, a quiet, tree-lined street in Santa Monica just one block away from Ocean Drive and the Santa Monica bluffs. The courtyard resembles a rainforest in that there are plants, and bushes, and trees everywhere. Small but well lit paths lead to the various rooms on the first floor, while four huge palm trees span the entire height of the property. The hotel, itself, sits on the east side of Second Street, nestled between a single family residence to the north and a small apartment building to the south. The rest of the east side of Second Street is a mixture of single family houses and apartment buildings. The entire west side of Second Street is a collection of small and medium sized apartment buildings. Even though the Copenhagen is the most modern building on the street, it blends in so well with the rest of the community it is one of Los Angeles' best kept secrets. Some say the Copenhagen is there and it isn't there at the same time, while others describe it as hiding in plain sight. Despite its location it has a well-earned reputation for quiet and privacy; and despite every room being a suite it has an equally well-earned reputation for affordability. That's exactly why William chose the Copenhagen.

Now back in his suite, number 107, William hangs up his suit jacket and unpacks the items he bought at Ralph's. He puts the pre-made sandwiches, the milk, the Vodka, the soda, and the instant coffee in the refrigerator; and he puts the chips and the sugar in the cabinet above the countertop to the right of the sink. He still hasn't had anything to eat and he can't bring himself to eat anything. Instead he mixes a vodka and soda, plops down in a chair, and turns on the television. As he takes a big gulp of his drink he pretends to watch TV, which is on less for the content and more to be another voice in the room to keep him company. After another big gulp of his drink the effect of the alcohol is doing the job he wants it to do. He closes his eyes and sinks deeper into the chair. It isn't long before he isn't there anymore. He can see Genny. She's in the kitchen cooking. Then she's coming back from meeting the broker for the house and she's telling William how much she loves it. Then she's in Home Depot talking with a sales assistant, trying to pick out the perfect color for their bedroom. Then she's back in the kitchen in her sweats and a tee shirt. She has dirt on her knees, and on her hands, and on her face. She's having a drink of iced tea, while she takes a break from working in the front yard. Even though Genny is talking to him William can't hear her, but he can see her again. He can see her smile, he can see the twinkle in her eyes, and he can see how animated she gets when she's excited about something. He can see that she's happy, and that makes William happy. On some level William knows this isn't real, but he keeps his eyes closed, takes another gulp of his drink, sinks deeper into the chair, and happily allows himself to stay right there, with Genny.

12:00pm - The Santa Monica Precinct is state of the art, at least as far as police precincts go. The second and third floors of the building are occupied by the uniformed officers, including the K-9 officers, both dog and human. The basement is divided into two separate and secure sections, and each section is further divided into two sub-sections. The north section of the basement has an outer section and an inner section. The outer section is an office manned by three uniformed officers and the inner section houses the holding pens. None but the top brass, and the three uniformed officers on duty, and the detainees, of course, are allowed in the north section's inner section. The south section of the basement is made up of two, side by side, storage rooms. The first is for the storage of evidence, which includes almost everything one can think of that is small enough to fit in that room. The second is for the storage of everything that isn't evidence, which includes paper files, old uniforms, old furniture, and out of date computers. The first floor of the precinct is reserved for the detectives. The front entrance, which all visitors use, is inviting and comfortable even though the two officers that greet each visitor sit behind a desk that spans the entire east side of the room, with bullet proof glass that starts at the top of the desk and extends to the ceiling. There are several interrogation rooms in the hallway between the front entrance and the inner waiting area. On the other side of the inner waiting area is a staircase that leads to the upper and lower floors and then there's the main room, which houses all of the detectives and the Captain's office. While all visitors must enter the precinct through the front entrance, ninety nine point nine percent of the precinct's personnel enter the precinct, ninety nine point nine percent of the time, through the back entrance. At the southeast corner of the main room another hallway begins which leads to the second staircase in the building, and past that is the door to the back entrance which opens out to the parking structure which is directly behind the building.

Eddie's and Bobby's desks face each other in the southwest corner of the room. Their combined desks are the closest to the Captain's office. Bobby is sitting at his desk on the telephone with his doctor, and Eddie is standing at another desk talking with one of the other detectives about his boat and his plans for retirement.

Doctor Jones is the doctor Bobby's general practitioner referred him to. Bobby's symptoms, and the fact that they come and go, baffled his general practitioner, and he thought Bobby would be better served by seeing an Internist. Unfortunately, Doctor Jones hasn't been able to diagnose the source of Bobby's condition either.

Doctor Jones says, "I'm happy to hear that you're feeling better. For the time being I want you to keep taking Lexapro. Remember, let me know, as soon as you can, if you experience any cramping or any nausea or any vomiting or any blurriness in your vision."

"I will. Do you think it's just anxiety?"

"It's too early to say for sure but since you are responding well to the Lexapro I want to keep you on that. If you experience any of the side effects we've talked about we'll either lessen the dosage or we'll have to take more aggressive tests."

Eddie is telling another detective, "From what I hear Costa Rica is a surfer's paradise. They say the waves are perfect in form and they roll in relentlessly. Supposedly each wave looks exactly like the one before it."

The other detective says, "It sounds like paradise, though I can't picture you surfing."

"Me either but you never know." Eddie's cell phone rings. As soon as he sees who's calling he excuses himself from the conversation to take the call. He answers the phone and says, "Hold on, let me get somewhere so we can talk." Eddie walks out of the back entrance of the building to an open air space between the building and the parking lot. Confident that he's out of everyone's earshot he takes the call. "What's up? Where are you?"

"On the 5 Freeway, headed south. I just heard you guys found the package I threw away," says Breck.

"Yeah, good work. I'll keep an eye on it."

Breck replies, "That's two down and one to go."

"What do you mean one to go? I thought you already sent that package."

"Yeah, I did send that package but I need to drop it off."

"When are you going to do that?"

"My bus doesn't leave until 5:30pm. So, when I get to town I'll think of something to do until 4:00pm. Then I'll drop it off and catch my bus."

"Do you think it's a good idea to hang out in town?"

"Don't worry about it. I won't be seen."

"I still don't think that's a good idea."

"If it makes you happy, I'll hang out in the town before the town. Then I'll drop it off and be on my way. How's that sound?"

"I think that's a better idea." Out of the corner of his eye Eddie can see figures coming his way. He turns and sees two patrol officers heading directly for him. He's acquainted with both so they could be coming to talk with him, or they could just be walking in his direction. Either way Eddie decides to use them to get off this call, which he feels has gone on too long already.

"Listen, there are a couple of people walking over to me. I gotta get off the phone. I'll see you in about a week in Costa Rica."

"Yup, and you'll have my money, in cash, right?"

As the two patrol officers walk by Eddie says to one of them, "Hey Tom! Yeah, OK, let me just finish this call." Then he says to Breck, "Yes, I agree. I gotta go. I'll see you next week."

After Eddie hangs up Tom asks, "What's up?"

Eddie says, "Oh, I thought you wanted to talk with me."

Tom says, "No, I was just saying hi."

Eddie smiles and replies, "Sorry about that."

1:00pm - Although he exists in the Age of Information, with the internet and numerous search engines and countless reference sites, very little is known about Pete Jefferson. The simple explanation is, that's how Pete wants it. The hidden explanation is, even though Pete is fifty five years old, Pete Jefferson didn't exist thirty years ago. What few people know is that Pete Jefferson was born Pavel Hurynovich in Minsk, Belarus. His father, Aleksey, was a carpenter and his mother, Sveta, was a cook. His family was poor and they struggled to survive. So, young Pavel took to the streets, at an early age, in an effort to bring in more money for his family. He started by forming a gang with four of his friends. They made their first money by hijacking a shipment of denim jeans and reselling it on the black market. Over the next two years they stole and resold everything they could get their hands on. When Pavel was sixteen his gang of five stole a shipment of American cigarettes. It was their biggest score. They made more money on that one score than they had in all of their other scores combined. Finally, the world started to become a better place for Pavel and for his family. Unfortunately, one member of their gang was arrested for something completely unrelated, and in his effort to negotiate a lighter sentence he rolled over and gave the police the details on how his gang stole the shipment of cigarettes. Two days later, to his surprise, the police dropped all of the charges against him and set him free. Two days after that his bullet ridden and headless corpse was left in the middle of the street in front of his parent's home. His family was devastated but everyone assumed, given that he was a hothead, he got mixed up in something bigger than himself and paid the price for it. One month after that another member of Pavel's gang went missing. When his body was dropped off in front of his family's home, Pavel and the two remaining members of his now disbanded gang started to worry.

Through his contacts in the black market Pavel found out that the shipment of American cigarettes they stole was part of a larger shipment of items that CETKi, a Belarusian crime organization, purchased from their Russian counterparts, which was being shipped to them in Belarus. Even though the shipment they stole constituted a tiny fraction of the worth of the shipment in whole, the heads of CETKi ruled that allowing that theft to go unpunished made them a weaker outfit. When Pavel told his father what he had learned, his father knew there was only one thing he could do. It took every penny his family had and a few they didn't have to send Pavel to England, but that was the only thing he could do to save his son's life. Aleksey knew if Pavel stayed in the country he would surely be found and killed.

Pavel couldn't stop crying as he said goodbye to his mother and father. A big part of his pain came from not knowing if he would ever see them again. He worried that if CETKi couldn't find him, they would exact their punishment on one or both of his parents. The larger part of his pain came from the fact that his actions had now caused his family to become more destitute than they had ever been. Through his tears he vowed to become a success in England, then he would send for his parents, and they would live out the rest of their days in the lap of luxury. After one last hug and kiss and with three hundred dollars in his pocket, Pavel boarded a train that would take him through Poland, through Germany, and through the Netherlands all the way to Amsterdam, where he would board a ship that would take him to England.

In London, not wanting to give up his heritage completely but in need of changing his name, Pavel took the name Paul Kurylovich. He found work as a busboy in a Russian restaurant, but it didn't pay him enough to have the smallest of lives. Still, he was thankful for the job, he worked seven days a week, and he saved every penny he could. A few years later the restaurant shut its doors, and Paul found himself without work. He decided to take his savings and go to America, the land of opportunity.

He landed in New York and found work in a Russian restaurant owned by the cousin of the owner of the restaurant in London, who spoke very highly of Paul, particularly of his work ethic. This time, however, Paul decided to reinvent himself entirely. With the help of an older gentleman who took a liking to Paul and was happy to do what he could to help him, Paul took the name Pete Jefferson. One year later he convinced the owner of the restaurant to lend him fifty thousand dollars so he could buy a house, down the street from his apartment in Queens, which was being sold at auction. After he sold that house and paid off all of his loans Pete walked away with a seventy five thousand dollar profit. He sent twenty five thousand dollars to his parents in Belarus and he reinvested the rest. After a few years of doing real estate deals relentlessly Pete decided to leave New York and to move to Los Angeles, where he felt there was even more opportunity.

One of the things Abbey admires most about Pete is his humility. Though he surrounds himself with the best of everything she can't recall one time she's ever heard him brag about himself or about any of his possessions. They were supposed to have a working brunch, but when the catered meal arrived Pete took a call. He was on the telephone, discussing other business, for so long he instructed her to go ahead and eat without him. On one hand, Abbey feels a little frustrated because had she known this was how brunch would play out she could have had her meeting at her office and come to Pete's office after. On the other hand, the baked salmon with mango salsa was fantastic and, in truth, whenever she was around Pete and listening to how he talked with people, she became a better businesswoman.

Now that Pete is off the phone he gives her his full attention. "I'm sorry about that."

Abbey says, "You should eat. Let me fix a plate for you. The salmon is fantastic."

Pete comes from around his desk to join her at the small conference table in his office just as she places a plate of food where she's sure he'll sit. "I'll try not to speak with food in mouth but you'll forgive me if I do. I just wanted us to go over everything once again. I wish I could say this will be the last time before Friday but I'd just be lying. Why don't you start from the top and walk through everything. I won't interrupt unless I have a question."

"I'll be happy to do that but let me tell you right now, we have a revision for the settlement statement. Outpost, LLC is taking its full pay out payable to Outpost less two and a half million dollars, which is now payable to 24th Street, LLC."

Pete asks, "That's Carl Davis' entity, right?"

Abbey answers, "Yes. We figured he's starting and funding a new venture."

"Maybe. But, Carl hasn't mentioned it and that doesn't sound like a company he named. I want you to find out who owns 24th Street, LLC."

"No problem," replies Abbey. The two of them continued walking through the deal and, at the end, both of them were satisfied that everything was buttoned up and ready to close.

2:00pm - Today was supposed to be a simple day. Come in, get a few things done, and then leave early to prepare for tonight, which was supposed to be a great night. Instead Rosa has been bouncing between catching David up on all of the things William was working on and answering the questions of her co-workers about William all day. She was hoping she'd be leaving the office around this time but, instead, she's been bogged down with going through all of William's emails and she hasn't even started to create the spreadsheet David asked her to prepare. Furthermore, she probably won't get to that for, at least, another hour.

Helen, a co-worker, knocks on the door to Williams's office so as to not startle Rosa and says, "I brought you a Cobb salad."

Rosa says, "Thank you. I haven't even thought about eating, but this is perfect. I'm actually starving."

Helen asks, "Have you spoken with William yet?"

"No. I left a message for him but he hasn't called back. I tried him a few more times but he didn't pick up. I'm starting to worry about him."

"Maybe he just needs some time."

"Maybe. Still, I can't get the picture of him, from this morning, out of my head. I've seen him sad but this morning he looked worse, he looked lost and broken."

Helen says, "I can imagine. It's so sad. I thought he and Genny were the perfect couple and they always looked so happy and so in love with each other."

Just then Stephen, from accounting, knocks on the door to the office, enters, and asks. "Have you heard from William yet?"

Rosa says, "No. I was just telling Helen that I'm really starting to worry about him."

Helen says, "I'm sure he'll be all right. Maybe not having to worry about work will give him the time to find peace."

Rosa says, "I don't think so. William loves his work. I'm worried he'll feel even more alone."

Stephen adds, "I agree with that. I think a guy needs to be working just to feel normal, and I think he needs to work now more than ever."

Rosa asks, "If I get in contact with him would you guys be willing to take him to dinner tonight?"

Helen asks, "Aren't you supposed to go to "dinner" tonight with Elton?"

"Yeah, but I'm sure he'll understand. He thinks William is the best. Besides I just need to know that William is OK."

Helen says, "Sure, I'll go."

Stephen adds, "I'm in."

Helen says, "I'll ask around. I'm sure we can a few other people to come along as well."

Rosa says, "That will make me feel better and I'm sure the show of support will make William feel better too. Thanks for the salad, but let me get back to work. David has me doing a million things all at once and if I don't keep going I won't get out of her until midnight."

Helen asks, "Can I help?"

"No, but thanks. It all a bunch of stuff I have to do; but see who you can get to join us tonight. I'll keep trying William. I'm sure I'll get him on the phone so let's plan on taking him to dinner."

Helen and Stephen leave the office. Rosa pours the dressing on the salad, closes the container and shakes it up. She takes one hearty forkful, and then puts her head down and gets back to work.

3:00pm - After getting a call from Javier, Eddie and Bobby pull up and park in front of the Desert Palms Apartments, an old and rundown apartment building on North Sweetzer Avenue in West Hollywood. Bobby doesn't know why Javier would ask them to meet him here. Eddie knows why but he's not saying. Bobby wonders out loud, "I wonder what's going here? I didn't expect to see squad cars."

Eddie says, "You're the one who wanted to come. I told you this would be a waste of our time."

"Come on, Javy's a good guy. Maybe he needs our help."

Eddie replies, "Well, there's only one way to find out. Let's go in."

Upon a closer look the Desert Palms isn't as bad as it immediately appears. In fact, it's a quaint building with a lot of character. Maybe it seems worse than it is because the entire building has been painted in different shades of grey, and it looks like it hasn't been repainted in years. The chips in the paint, the dirt caked on the walls, and the half alive half dead shrubby combined give the impression that this building is neglected, but a new paint job in a vibrant color would go far to bringing this building back to life. Like many of the properties in this neighborhood, this one is a two story building with a courtyard design. From the billboard in front of the building we know this one has twenty four units that are all studios or one bedroom apartments. Currently there are no vacancies, which means the building is probably under rent control. Judging from the condition of the building one would guess the rents are low as well. As Eddie and Bobby approach the entrance they look on the intercom for the name of the occupant in apartment 18, the apartment Javier told them to come to. There isn't a name next to the number 18, just a word, "vacant." Judging from the collection of insects that found their way into the call box but couldn't find their way out and died there, the list of names hasn't been updated in months, maybe years. The courtyard itself, however, is clean and well-kept except for several sconce lights that have obviously burned out and haven't been replaced. In the middle of the courtyard is a small flower bed that contains a collection of Aster X frikartiis, and

Coneflowers, and Heucheras surrounded by Catmint. It is obvious that someone cares for this flower bed because, unlike some of the other features of this property, these flowers are alive and vibrant and doing well. Just off both sides of the flower bed are staircases the occupants, and their visitors, use to get to the second floor. Even if Eddie and Bobby couldn't see the numbers on the apartments they would know where to go because there is police tape that extends from the wall of the building to the railing on both sides of one door on the second floor.

Eddie and Bobby cross beneath the police, knock on the door for apartment 18, which is slightly ajar, and they walk in. The first thing that hits them is the stench. Being seasoned officers they are familiar with that smell. Someone died here. The apartment itself is spartanly bare. There is a television in the living room sitting atop of eight cinder blocks, and the only other thing in the living room is a futon couch that faces the television. The carpet in the living room is tattered and torn and there's a worn out section that begins in the living room and goes through the hallway leading to the bedroom. The kitchen is bare except for numerous used bags from a variety of fast food restaurants and empty cans and bottles of soda and alcohol. There's a parade of ants coming from the floor underneath the baseboard, leading to one of the cans of soda and returning from the soda can across the countertop, down the cabinets, and disappearing beneath the baseboard. An occasional roach can be seen scampering from one of the fast food bags to another and then disappearing behind the dripping faucet of the kitchen sink.

Javier comes out of the bedroom and says, "Thanks for coming." Bobby says, "No problem. What's going on?"

Javier asks them both, "Do you recognize this place?"

Bobby speaks for the both of them when he says, "No."

Javier says, "Come in the bedroom."

On their way to the bedroom they pass the bathroom but one look in there is all they need. It's filthy. If the stench of a dead body didn't fill the apartment the stench from the bathroom would have. Javier picks up a picture that is sitting on the night stand next to the bed and gives it to Bobby. Bobby immediately recognizes the guy in the picture and he says his name, "Teddy." Bobby hands the picture to Eddie who looks at it only because he's expected to. Bobby asks, "Is this Teddy Gallo's apartment?"

Javier answers, "Yes."

Bobby follows that with, "Did he die here?"

Javier answers, "Yes. He apparently overdosed almost a week ago. One of the neighbors reported a smell coming from this apartment two days ago. The resident manager went in and found Teddy lying in bed with a needle sticking out of his arm."

Eddie finally contributes to the conversation with, "That's too bad for Teddy."

Javier asks, "What can you guys tell me about this?"

Eddie says, "Nothing. What would we know about Teddy?"

Javier says, "Everybody knows he was one of your informants. I was hoping you'd have some insight into his recent associations or activities."

Bobby says, "Yeah, we did use him for information every once in a while, but we haven't talked with him or seen him for, I don't know, maybe a year, more or less."

Javier turns to Eddie, "What about you?"

Eddie says, "What about me?"

Javier asks, "When was the last time you saw or spoke with Teddy?"

Eddie says, "It's like Bobby said, we used him from time to time, but it's been a long time since we've seen him or talked with him or even heard anything about him. Why are you asking us about him?"

Javier explains, "The investigating detectives told me they have reason to believe Teddy was still working as an informant. I didn't mention your names but I thought it might be you guys."

Eddie says, "Well it isn't."

Javier concedes, "I know that now. I was just hoping that because Teddy is, or was, associated with one of my other cases. Do you remember the woman who was murdered in her bedroom about three months ago?"

Eddie asks, "What woman?"

Javier says, "Remember the couple that was living on 17th Street. The husband was shot and the woman was murdered in the middle of the night." Neither Eddie nor Bobby react to the additional information. Javier continues, "Anyway, it turns out Teddy dated that woman many years ago. I know it's a long shot but I was hoping to uncover something in Teddy's background that could be helpful in the investigation of her murder."

Eddie suggests, "It sounds to me like it's just a coincidence. I mean, maybe there is something there but I know I can't think of anything to tell you."

"Unfortunately, me either," says Bobby.

Javier says, "Well, thanks for coming. I really appreciate it. Like I said, I knew it was a long shot but I would really like to solve her case so I thought I'd ask."

In parting Eddie tells Javier, "Listen, if you want, please tell the investigators they should feel free to contact us about Teddy, but like we told you, I don't think we'll be much help. Teddy must have been working for some other detective because he hasn't worked for us in over a year."

4:00pm - William wakes up on the floor in the living room in his hotel suite. The last thing he remembers is fixing a drink and sitting down in front of the television. Obviously, a lot has happened since then because his drink is gone, the television is off, and he woke up on the floor underneath a blanket, but he doesn't remember doing any of those things.

By this time he's been in the same clothes for almost two full days. His socks are bunched up around his ankles, his underwear and his pants are riding up in places where they shouldn't be, his shirt is drenched in sweat and sticking to his chest and underarms, his mouth is dry and pasty, his breath is atrocious, and his scalp is dry in some places, sweaty in others, and itchy everywhere. All of these things motivate William to shake his malaise, at least long enough to take a shower, brush his teeth, and change clothes. It takes another minute before William talks himself off the floor but he does. He starts to undress as he walks to the bedroom. Just before he takes off his pants he empties his pockets. In a pile on the bed he places his car keys, the card key to his suite, his wallet, some loose change, and a couple of receipts. Looking down on this pile it dawns on him that he hasn't seen his smartphone in a while. Though not Earth shattering, it does come as a surprise that he doesn't have his smartphone close by. After all, he's in the habit of telling people they can always reach him, night or day, because he's had his smartphone surgically attached to his hip. That always gets a laugh and, like most things that are funny, it's funny because, in a sense, it's true. In fact, the surprise doesn't come because he doesn't have his smartphone in the pile with the other things. The surprise is coming from the fact that he has absolutely no idea where it is. He looks for it in the living room, but it isn't there. He looks for it in the kitchen but, it isn't there. He checks the inside pocket of his suit jacket, but it isn't there. He calls his own number from his suite telephone, but he doesn't hear it ring or vibrate. It has to be in the car, but he can't think of how. To the best of his recollection he didn't use it in the car, which means it must have fallen out of his pocket, but that hasn't happened before and he can't think of how it might have happened now. Still, it obviously isn't in the suite, so it must be in the car. Unless, God forbid, he left it in his office. William starts to put the same clothes he had taken off back on, but when he puts on his suit jacket it feels heavier than normal. There, in the left hand outside pocket on his suit jacket he finds his smart-phone. Strangely enough, it was on silent. William can't recall putting his phone in that pocket nor putting it on silent. Both things are somewhat baffling to him, but more than anything, he is happy he doesn't have to go back to the office.

He has twenty seven emails and eleven voicemail messages. He scans the emails and all but three of them are work related. The three that aren't work related aren't important in the scheme of things. The twenty four that are work related are, as of this morning, beyond his control. He knows Rosa will retrieve them and whoever is doing his job will handle them. He dials voicemail and puts the phone on speaker so he can get undressed and listen to his messages at the same time. Five of the eleven messages are from Rosa. The other six are like the three emails, not important. However, unlike the twenty four emails, he feels bad about not returning Rosa's calls. First of all, he left a message for her asking her to call him, and second, he adores Rosa. If she needs his help in any way he wants to be there for her. Accordingly, as soon as he listened to all of the messages he calls Rosa. First he calls the office. He makes polite chitchat with the receptionist, who recognizes his voice, and then he asks her to put him through. She does but he gets Rosa's voicemail. He leaves a message apologizing for missing her calls and asking her to try him back. Then he tries her cell but he gets voicemail again. He leaves the same message there.

Now, down to his boxer briefs William turns on the lights in the bathroom and stares into the mirror that spans from the top of the marble countertop surrounding the sink to the ceiling. Besides the redness in his eyes William doesn't see any change in his face. There is the wound on his shoulder from where he was shot, and the resulting soreness and stiffness that comes and goes, but besides that he doesn't see in change in his body either. His legs are still as muscular as ever and so are his arms. He has gained a little weight around his midsection and he laughs to himself when he thinks of how Genny used to describe his abs as "a four pack on ice." Yet, he feels so unlike himself. He continues to stare in the mirror as if staring long and hard enough will reveal whatever it is that is causing him to feel like a stranger in his own skin. When he's finally convinced that whatever it is won't show itself, he turns to the shower and turns on the water. Just as he's about to take off his boxer briefs his cell phone rings.

Just as he thought, it's Rosa. William picks up the call and starts with, "Hey Rosa, I'm sorry I didn't pick up your calls earlier. I didn't mean to but I guess I took a nap."
Rosa says, "I was really worried about you. Are you OK?"
"Yeah, I'm fine."

"You don't sound fine."

"You haven't been working we me that long, how do you know me so well? Really, I'm not fine today but I'll be better tomorrow. Everything will be OK."

"Listen, a few of us would like to take you out for dinner tonight."

"That sounds great and I appreciate the thought but not tonight. I don't have it in me tonight."

"I'm not taking no for an answer, so pick your favorite place and let us take you out to get your mind off things, if only for a minute. You won't believe this but Matthew said I can use my company card and expense the whole thing."

"You're right. I don't believe that. What did David have to say about it?"

Rosa laughs and says, "Yeah, I know. Matthew made me promise not to tell David. He told me to give the receipts to him in the morning and he'll take care of it from there. You can't pass up an offer like that. Even if you wanted to, think about the rest of us. How often do we get carte blanche for any restaurant in LA.? Come on, you have to say yes."

For the first time in what seems like a long time William feels light again and he can't help but smile and be moved by Rosa's gesture, and Matthew's for that matter. Still, he says, "I simply adore you Rosa. You have been a great co-worker and a good friend."

"I know. So, you're saying yes, right?"

"No. If it were any other night then maybe but not tonight. I just don't have it in me to be social tonight."

"I didn't want to have to go here but you are leaving me no choice. Did you ever wonder why I was in so early this morning?"

"No. Now that you mention it, you were in early, but that didn't register until just now."

"Well, I was in early because I needed to leave early. Do you want to know why I needed to leave early?"

"I'm sure you're going to tell me."

"Like I said, I didn't want to play this card but you're leaving me no choice. I needed to leave early because I am sure Elton was going to propose to me tonight. By the way, he says he hopes you feel better and if there's anything he can do for you don't hesitate to call him."

"Tell him I said thank you and I will if I need to. How do you know he was going to propose?"

"Just trust me, I know. Instead, I called him and asked him if we could have our "special" dinner tomorrow night instead. He tried to convince me that he had special plans all laid out and tomorrow night was no good, until I told him why I couldn't go tonight, namely because I was taking you out to dinner. Only then did he agree to try to arrange everything for to-morrow night instead. So, you see, I postponed the night I've been waiting for all of my adult life just so I could have dinner with a friend, you. So no is not an option. Put your party dress on, we are going to dinner tonight. We don't have to stay out all night and there aren't a whole bunch of us going. You have some friends here that care about you and we want to cheer you up, like I said, if only for a minute."

William laughs and says, "OK, I'm in."

"Good, I have to go so I can hurry up and finish a spreadsheet for David but I'll call you back in an hour. Think about where you want to go and let's go there."

William says, "OK."

Rosa reiterates, "I'll call you back in hour an hour, answer your phone. Please don't let me have wasted what was supposed to be a great night for me and Elton."

"I promise I won't. I'll be ready to make plans when you call."

"Great. I'll speak with you in an hour. Bye."

William disconnects, lays the phone back on the bed, and returns to the bathroom. This time when he looks in the mirror he sees someone he recognizes and, more than that, that person is smiling back at him. He thinks to himself: "Rosa is crazy." Then he takes off his boxer briefs and steps into the shower.

5:00pm - Breck Sullivan shot his first gun, a .22 caliber, single shot Crickett Rifle, when he was four years old. Northerners are usually appalled by that fact, but in Ardmore, Tennessee, a small town close to the Tennessee Alabama border, where he was born and raised, he was considered a late bloomer. Even though he had been walking for two years before he took his first shot, Breck made up for lost time. By the time he was fifteen years old he was an excellent shot with both pistols and rifles. He grew up listening to his grandfather, Craig Sullivan, a Vietnam War veteran, tell stories about Carlos Hathcock, from Arkansas. As far as Craig was concerned Carlos was the greatest sniper in American history. Every night, Breck went to sleep dreaming of joining the Marines and following in Carlos' footsteps. By the time he was seventeen Breck had competed in dozens of marksman tournaments from Alabama to Kentucky, and he either won or placed in the majority of them. While school was never what he did best he did graduate, and the day after graduation he enlisted as a 0311 rifleman in the Marines. Even though he excelled in boot camp he started to show signs that he could easily be goaded into losing his temper. After boot camp he completed infantry training as a volunteer for the Scout/Sniper Platoon, but during that training he, again, demonstrated a lack of emotional control when he started a fight with another volunteer over who was the better shot. Unfortunately, that fight may have cost him his dream. The volunteer he fought was not only a better shot but he was well liked and considered the leader among his battalion. When it came time to vote for the candidates who would be sent to Scout/Sniper School Breck was left off that list. Breck continued to let his emotions get the best of him and he ended his military service OTH discharged. He returned to Ardmore bitter and defeated.

Bitter and defeated became happy and prosperous once Breck got back to Ardmore. His family and friends welcomed him home with open arms. They didn't see him as a failure. They saw him as someone who tried to accomplish a very difficult thing and came up just a little bit short. The owner of the Big Sky Shooting Sports Club, in, coincidentally, Ardmore, Alabama, the firing range where Breck often practiced, offered him a job, which Breck was happy to take. He sold firearms and ammunition, and he made extra money giving shooting lessons. On the weekends he traveled with the owner to trade shows from Alabama to Kentucky and from Texas to North Carolina, to buy, sell, and trade guns.

At a trade show in Raleigh, North Carolina he met a gentleman who said he had a friend in Panama who could use the services of someone with Breck's skills. Breck met many people who approached him with a similar pitch. He did what he always did. He made polite conversation with the gentleman and he gave him his card, but he was sure that would be the last time he hears from him. This gentleman, however, stayed in contact with Breck for months via email. With each email the gentleman made the offer again, and each time he did, Breck politely declined. It wasn't until the gentleman offered Breck an all-expenses paid trip to Panama for a week, in return for a ten minute meeting with his friend, that Breck showed any interest. Ultimately, he took the gentleman up on his offer. That trip to Panama changed Breck and his life forever. He returned to Tennessee with a dossier on a known drug trafficker operating in Oaxaca, Mexico. One month later he traveled to Oaxaca. He shot and killed that trafficker from one hundred yards away. Then he traveled to Panama to pick up twenty five thousand dollars before returning to Tennessee. Breck did four more jobs like that, one in Colombia, one in Nicaragua, and two more in Mexico, over the next year. After each job he drank more, his personality became darker, and he distanced himself further and further away from his family and friends. When he was fired from his job at Big Sky he decided to take a month off to vacation in Panama. While he was there his contact was killed in a car accident. To avoid any contact with the police he immediately left Panama for Costa Rica. His intention was to finish his vacation there and then return to the States, but one month turned into two and two turned into four. Ultimately, he decided to stay in Costa Rica.

That's where he met Eddie Roberts, who was in Costa Rica on vacation. They met at the bar in the Del Rey Casino in San Jose. The two of them became quick friends. Eddie gave Breck the impression that he was an investor in Costa Rica looking for a good time, and Breck gave Eddie the impression that he was ex-military disenchanted with post military life in the States and living the good life in Costa Rica. Breck offered to show Eddie around the country and Eddie took him up on his offer. That was over five years ago. Since then the two stayed in contact, and as their friendship grew they both filled in the other with a little more detail as to who and what they really are. As each of them learned more about the other their friendship grew less passionate, but their usefulness to each other intensified. When Eddie got the call from Carl Davies, he knew immediately who he could call to help them with their problem. Given the pay, Breck was more than happy to help.

As promised, Breck had spent the last hour and a half outside of town, but now it is time to drop off the package and make his way to San Diego. No one noticed him as he pulled his silver Honda Accord into a space in the small parking lot just north west of Tabitha Park, off Orinda Drive in Cardiff By The Sea. He retrieved his small suitcase from the back seat and then he opened the hole he cut out in the back seat that led to the trunk. He lit the fuse, calmly walked away from the car, and towards the Golden Valley Resort. By the time he took his seat on the shuttle bus to the San Diego International Airport he imagined that the car was probably noticeably smoking by then. When the shuttle bus left the resort he could see black smoke billowing skyward and he saw fire engines, with their sirens screaming, speed past his bus on their way to put out the car fire, which was roaringly ablaze due to the amount of accelerants he employed.

6:30pm - Everyone from the office was there by the time William arrived. They chose to meet at Salvador's Cantina, one of the newest, hippest, and best rated restaurants in Venice on Abbot Kinney. Rosa gets up from the table when William arrives and gives him a big hug. They have a short and private conversation followed by another hug, and then they walk to the table to join the others. Rosa is seated in the chair to the left of the head of the table. John, the company's controller is seated to Rosa's left. Norma, from accounts payables is seated to John's left, and Stephen, from accounts payable is seated at the other end of the table. To Stephen's left is Samantha, the receptionist. Vince, from acquisitions is seated to Samantha's left and Helen, Vince's assistant is seated to Vince's left, just to the right of the head of the table, the seat reserved for William. Everyone greets William warmly.

As soon as William takes his seat at the head of the table he says, "Listen you guys, I didn't want to come here tonight. It was hard for me to imagine having a good time. Someone at this table, however, can be very persuasive." Everyone looks and smiles at Rosa.

Rosa smiles and proudly exclaims, "I'm a Puerto Rican Jew, what do you expect?" That makes those who were grinning, smile, and those who were smiling, laugh.

William continues, "Well, I want to thank you, Rosa, for forcing me to come here, and I want to thank all of you, for being here. I am thankful that you all cared enough to be here and I'm really happy I came."

Before anyone else could react, Stephen, at the other end of the table says, "Hey William, I don't know what you're talking about man. I heard free dinner and free drinks and I just followed the crowd." Everyone, including William, laughs and the night gets off to a great start.

By the time everyone got their drinks and placed their food orders the general conversation had broken down into several mini conversations. Rosa hesitated to discuss her probable engagement because she thought William might be sensitive to that discussion, but when William raised the topic it opened the door and she walked right through it. Of course he was delighted for Rosa, but she and Helen discussed everything from the venue, to the wedding dress, to the bridesmaids and their dresses, and there was only so much girl talk William could take. So, while Helen and Rosa continued their conversation William spoke with Vince about the Monterey Point deal and who was taking over the work he would normally do. Norma knew that sitting next to John was going to be trouble. She likes him and she likes working with him, but he has a one track mind. True to form while they were at what was supposed to be a festive night out, away from work, John was grilling her on the accounts that remain outstanding, and on what payment arrangements had been made to satisfy them. Norma is a margarita girl and, usually, she's good with one. As John fired question after question at her she thought of telling him that it's OK to take a night off, but she knew she'd only have that type of courage after two margaritas. So, she downed her first one and hoped everyone would quickly finish their first drink so she could order another. Stephen was doing what he always does, cracking jokes and hitting on Samantha. Samantha enjoys Stephen's company, after all he is funny and he is cute, but he's also very young. If she were to date anyone in the company, it would be Vince. She was happy to be seated next to him but, so far, she hasn't been able to get his attention. So, she continues to play along with Stephen and while doing so it dawns on her that he might be more cute than he is young. When their waitress comes back to their table to check on them William orders another vodka tonic, Samantha orders another strawberry martini, and Norma wants to order two margaritas but she only orders one.

At some point Helen noticed that John had Norma cornered, so she signaled that to Rosa, who rescued her by asking Norma to take some pictures of her, Helen, and William. Norma seized the opportunity and offered to take pictures of everyone at the table, individually and in groups. By the time the food arrived everyone had spent a little time talking with everyone else. They all had pictures taken with each other, and they had a group shot taken by their waitress. It was a typical company dinner and everyone seemed to be having fun, especially William. Only Stephen noticed that William had three drinks before the food arrived, and he ordered another right after the food was served.

The food was every bit as flavorful, well cooked, and well presented as the reviews claimed it would be. After dinner some of them ordered dessert and the ones that didn't order a dessert took a bite or two of the dessert of the person sitting closest to them. After the check was paid John called it a night. So did Helen. Samantha, however, suggested they try a new place she heard about. It's supposed to be a lot of fun and it is just down the street. Since Samantha was going so was Stephen. Since John wasn't going Norma was in. Vince and Rosa were immediately in. William wasn't sure if he wanted to go but, by this time he isn't feeling any pain, so it only took one "Come on!" and he was in. Where Salvador's Cantina was well lit and, for the most part, a quiet restaurant, The Saloon, was a dark, packed, and loud bar. Tonight a local band, with a large and loyal following, was on stage rocking the house. At this point Rosa's only concern is David. She's worried that putting what everyone has to drink or eat on the company card is excessive. Vince agrees, and offers to buy the first round for everybody. Stephen dared himself to ask Samantha to dance, and he was over the moon when she said yes. Norma took a spot close to the stage. She fell in love with the band and was already planning to see them again. Mike's happiness turned to sadness when he and Samantha returned to their table and Samantha asked Vince to dance and he said yes. Not five minutes later his sadness turned back to happiness when he made eye contact with a beautiful girl standing next to the bar who smiled at him. He went over to her and twenty minutes later they were dancing. Maybe it was the lack of light, or the pounding music, or all of the drinks William had, or maybe it was a combination of all three, but Rosa noticed that William's speech was starting to slur. Even more frightening, she noticed that William was starting to resemble the William she had seen this morning. That's when she realized that this extra stop may have been a mistake. One by one she found everyone in her party and voiced her concern. They all agreed, it was to time to get William out of there, but before the movement could pick up speed and momentum, William had ordered and finished another drink.

8:30pm - Eddie and Bobby pull up and park in front of Tola's, a small, family owned Thai restaurant just a few blocks away from Eddie's apartment.

Bobby asks, "Do you want me to wait?"

Eddie says, "What do you mean?"

"Are you going to eat in the restaurant or are you going to order to go? If you order to go, do you want me to give you a lift home?"

"No, I'm going to order the food to go but I'll walk home. Let me ask you a question, what did you make of Javier today?"

"I thought it was odd that he insisted we go to Teddy's apartment to ask us what he could have asked us at the precinct but, other than that, I believe he was doing what he said he was doing. He was just looking for anything that could help him with, you know, that other thing."

"Do you think he believed us?"

"Why wouldn't he? We didn't tell him anything and what we did say was true, right?"

Eddie asks, "Speaking of that other thing, have you worked that out in your mind?"

"I really don't want to talk about it," says Bobby.

"We have to talk about it. The whole thing wraps up in four days. I gotta know if you are still with me." "I was never with you on that. I wish you never told me. I had a good day today and I think that's true because I didn't think it about all day, at least, until Javier mentioned that other thing."

"What are you worried about? You didn't have anything to do with it."

"Yeah, except I didn't stop you. If I had the balls I would have arrested you myself."

Eddie reminds Bobby, "Partners don't turn partners in."

Bobby reminds Eddie, "I'm your partner but I'm not your partner. It makes me sick to think about what you did."

"In four days you'll be rewarded handsomely. Just put it out of your mind and take that wife of yours somewhere nice, or put a down payment on a bigger house, or do something else with the money and forget about it."

"What good will the money do me if I'm too sick to spend it or, worse, dead."

"Come on, now you're just talking crazy."

"You know why the doctors can't figure out what's wrong with me?"

"Oh boy, not this again. You are not cursed."

"Yeah, this again and yes, I am cursed. The doctors can't figure it out because there isn't anything wrong with me. I'm sick from the stress of knowing what I know. This mystery illness started right after you told me."

"Why would you be cursed? I'm the one who saw to it and I'm not cursed."

"Maybe you are and you just don't know it yet. Maybe the person who watches and does nothing is guiltier than the guilty party. I don't know. All I know is I started to get sick right after you told me, and the doctors don't have a clue about what's wrong with me."

"You're over-reacting but this conversation isn't getting us any-where. I just need to know if you are still with me."

"It's too late to do anything about it and I'm certainly not going to say anything about it now. At this point, I'm just as liable as you are. The answer to your question is, no, I'm not with you but you don't have to worry about me saying anything. Just retire, get your money, set sail, and be happy."

"When you get paid you'll find a way to forget about it. Listen, you're not cursed. The doctors don't know what's wrong with you because they're idiots. There is nothing wrong with you. Maybe you are a little stressed out. Believe me, I regret telling you any-thing but, at the time, I thought it was the right thing to do."

Bobby thinks to himself: "The right thing to do, that's funny," but he doesn't say that. Instead he says, "It's better if we just don't talk about it. Like you said, in four days it will be over. Maybe I will take a long vacation. Maybe that would help."

Eddie says, "That's the spirit, buddy. You'll see, tomorrow will be better than today, and come Friday it will be a whole new world for the both us. I'll see you in the morning."

Bobby says, "Yeah, I'll see you tomorrow." Eddie gets out of the car, and Bobby pulls off.

Sirichai is happy to see Eddie, he's one of the restaurant's most loyal and favored customers.

Sirichai says, "As always, it's very good to see you Detective."

"It's good to see you too, Sirichai. Is Sarawut around tonight?"

"He should be back any minute now. Why? Do you need him or is there something I can do for you?" "I just wanted to say good bye. This may be the last time I'm here, at least, for a long time."

"That's right! You are retiring. I'll call Sarawut and tell him you are here. In the meantime, please allow me to prepare something very special for you. I am going to cook it myself, and your money is no good here tonight."

"Thanks Sirichai, I appreciate that."

"It will be my pleasure. That's the least I can do for a very good friend. You may have to wait an extra fifteen minutes but I promise you, it will be worth it."

"Take all the time you need. I'm looking forward to it."

"Good. I'll call Sarawut right now. I'm sure he'll rush back to say goodbye to his friend."

While Sirichai is in the kitchen preparing Eddie's special meal Eddie thinks back to the incident that earned him the respect of Sarawut, the owner of Tola's and of Sirichai, who at that time was just part waiter and part busboy. On a night like tonight, in a word, perfect, about seven years ago Eddie was enjoying his meal at the very same table he is sitting at now, when a young thug with a blood red Mohawk wandered in. He was drunk, loud, and rude from word one but he ordered his food and didn't make too much of a scene while he waited. All that changed when it was time to pay. The kid grabbed the food, refused to pay, and started yelling at Sarawut that not paying was his pay back for Vietnam, which if Eddie had to be truthful, he thought was pretty funny at the time. Before the kid noticed, Eddie was standing behind him waiting for the kid to turn around. He had seen and subdued several drunkards and he didn't think this incident would be any different. He would explain that he was a cop, flash his gun, and, if necessary, put the kid in a choke hold until he came to his senses. The worse that would happen is he'd have to arrest the kid, which he was hoping wouldn't happen since he had just gotten off work and he had plans for the evening that he had been looking forward to, especially since he didn't have to work the next day. Unfortunately, the kid hadn't resolved his youthful notion of anarchy and the fact that Eddie was a cop only incensed him further. Eddie was forced to subdue the kid while Sarawut called the police. When the kid appeared relatively calm Eddie went to place the cuffs on him. The kid wiggled free just long enough to hit Eddie right in the mouth with his elbow. That was the first and last time Eddie was ever hit by a suspect. Instead of trying to cuff him again, Eddie left him uncuffed and proceeded to beat that kid until he was unconscious. The viciousness of Eddie's attack surprised even him, but he didn't think about that at the time. All he thought about was how good it felt to hit someone repeatedly. By the time the police arrived the kid was conscious and cuffed and he looked like he was hit by a Mack truck. Several weeks later, Internal Affairs approached Eddie to make him aware that a lawsuit had been filed against him, and the LAPD, for police brutality. The matter, however, was quickly resolved based on the somewhat fraudulent testimony of Sarawut, Aom, his wife, and Sirichai, who all claimed that the suspect continued to fight with Detective Roberts until he was unconscious. They even added that they saw the suspect reach for the Detectives gun, a fact Eddie asked them to add for good measure. It came down to Eddie's word, which was corroborated by Sarawut, Aom, and Sirichai's word, against the word of a young drunk thug anarchist with a red Mohawk. The case was dismissed. Since then, Eddie has enjoyed preferred status at Tola.

Before the meal was prepared Sarawut had gotten back to the restaurant and he and Eddie had a chance to speak for a while. Sarawut told Eddie that he too was thinking of retirement. He spoke highly of Sirichai, who started as a busboy and has now risen to general manager. It didn't hurt that Sirichai married his daughter. That gave a lot of comfort to Sarawut and since the restaurant was doing so well under his guidance if not retirement than maybe he and his wife would take an extended vacation. Aom always wanted to take a trip South America. In particular, she always wanted to go to Brazil and Argentina, and Sarawut was starting to think now might be the time before they get too old to enjoy it. Sirichai came into the dining room and presented Eddie with Tom Yum Gung, or Spicy Thai Shrimp Soup, for his appetizer, and Kao Phad with shrimp, for his dinner. Eddie thanks Sirichai for the dinner and he thanks them both for their friendship over the years. They are just as appreciative to him for his friendship, and for his patronage, and protection over the years. Eddie promises to call Sarawut to give him his contact information in Costa Rica, and Sarawut promises that if he and his wife do take that trip to South America, they will find their way to Central America first, just to visit with him. They all wish each other well, and Eddie leaves the restaurant.

On the walk home Eddie thinks about the things he'll miss in Los Angeles. He'll miss places like Tola's and the friends he's made there and everywhere he frequents. He'll miss the Southern

California nights, like tonight. He's sure he'll make new friends, and he's sure the climate in Central America will be just as nice, but he's also sure there will be some adjusting to do. Since his divorce he hasn't been quite the ladies' man, though he has had his fun. Of course, there will be a night life and pretty girls in Costa Rica but he'll miss the laid back SoCal nightlife and he'll miss California girls. The streets of Santa Monica are alive tonight. There are young guys and girls on every corner making their way to the restaurant, or to the bar, or to the house party of their choice. Though he hasn't felt that care free in years, he likes being surrounded by it. It makes him feel younger. Case in point, just one block from his apartment, a new bar and restaurant, called Bar 121, just opened maybe six months ago. He has never passed that place at night and found it less than packed. Though he's never gone in he can tell from the outside it's for the twenty and thirty year old set. It's for the new young starlets, and the new athletes, and the new corporate executives. Everyone is young and beautiful with their whole lives ahead of them. As he passes by he looks into the windows and sees couples and groups of friends drinking, laughing and having the time of their lives. He thinks to himself that he may be too old for places like that, but come Friday he'll have all the money and free time he has ever wanted. Maybe he'll play a little catch up then. He's five steps past Bar 121 when it hits him. He thinks he recognizes one of the women sitting at a table next to the window. He turns around and walks back to take another look. He's right. Sitting alone at a table is the girl he met this morning. He can't remember her name so he searches his pockets for her card. Lisa Becker, that's her. For a split second he thought of going in and maybe striking up a conversation, but before he can complete the thought she's joined by some guy with a drink in each hand.

He gives her one drink and in return she gives him a kiss, the kind of kiss a girlfriend or a new wife gives her boyfriend, or her new husband. That makes Eddie smile and he turns to continue on his way home, but, again, he turns back to the window. There's something familiar about the guy she's with. Eddie recognizes him upon a second look. It's Officer Isaac, whom he met this morning as well. It's obvious this isn't their first date. Eddie thinks of how she pretended not to know Officer Isaac. He isn't worried about either of them at present though she could cause a problem if she gets too close. Eddie thinks to himself: "She's tricky, that one. I'll keep that in mind when I call her tomorrow."

10:00pm - "I think I had too much to drink," William says while he lowers the passenger side window.

Rosa asks, "You're not going to throw up are you?"

William says, "No . . . well, maybe . . . no, I'm OK."

Vince says, "Hang in there William, you're almost home."

"Vince, is that Vince?"

Vince laughs and says, "Yeah, it's me."

"Where are you Vince?"

Vince laughs again and says, "I'm in the back seat."

William turns to Rosa and says, "Vince is in the back seat."

"I know," says Rosa

William asks, "Where did . . . is everyone else go?"

Rosa says, "Norma, Samantha, and Stephen are in the car behind us."

William says, "Hey Vince, Norma, and Samantha, and Norma . . . I mean Samantha are in the car behind us."

Vince laughs again and says, "I know."

Samantha says, "I don't know, I think there is something romantic about a guy falling apart from the loss of his wife."

Stephen says, "OK, that is totally a girl thing."

"Maybe."

"I mean, I can totally understand, maybe not understand, but you know what I mean, that a guy falls apart from losing his wife the way William did. But, in general, I don't think a guy should fall apart over losing anything."

Norma says, "You just haven't been around the block yet. Haven't you lost a loved one, a parent, a sibling, a grandparent?"

"Nope. Everyone is still living."

Norma says, "That's good for you. You are a very lucky person, but that also proves there's a lot you don't know yet."

Mike asks, "What about you?"

Norma replies, "We don't need to discuss it, but believe me, I know what William is going through, and there's no shame in it."

Samantha asks, "Do you think he'll be all right?"

Norma says, "Sure. He's got a good head on his shoulders. It won't be easy, but he'll figure out how to get through it."

Both cars pull up in front of The Copenhagen. Samantha and Norma stay in Samantha's car, and Stephen gets out to help Rosa and Vince get William to his room. Rosa goes ahead of them to the front desk and says, "The car out front belongs to one of your guest, Mr. William Flowers, and these are his keys. Would you please park his car and hold on to his keys? He'll pick them up from you in the morning."

Gael, the front desk clerk and the concierge on duty after 7:00pm says, "I recognize the car and I'll be happy to have it parked, but who are you and where is Mr. Flowers?" Instead of answering Gael's question, Rosa turns her head towards the front door. There, Stephen is holding the lobby door open and trying to help Vince get William through it and into the lobby.

Gael says, "There must be a full moon tonight or something, because this is the second guest to return, let's just say less than sober, and the night is still young."

Rosa asks, "Can you direct us to his room?"

"Of course. Go through those glass doors and follow the path through the garden on your left. He's in room 107. It's about half way through the garden."

Rosa holds the inner glass doors open while Vince, who has William's arm over his shoulder and his arm across William's back and under his arm, leads William through the garden. Stephen is behind Vince and William just in case he's needed. While William was sitting in the car the effects of the alcohol weren't as pronounced as they are now that he's trying to walk. The four of them make it through the garden and to William's door. Vince retrieves William's key from his pocket and hands it to Rosa, who opens the door. Once inside Rosa asks Stephen to get a glass a water and put it on the night stand next to the bed. Vince helps William out of his suit jacket and then helps him to the bed. Rosa writes a note and leaves it on the dining room table. By the time she returns to the bedroom, William appears to be asleep already. Satisfied that he's OK, and that they have done everything they could, they turn off the lights and leave.

William lies there, not really asleep, but not really awake either. The darkness and the quiet are comforting. The pounding in his head, however, makes it hard for him to think of anything else. As long as he stays absolutely still, he still feels nauseous, but, at least, the pounding goes away. While he lies there, in the dark, he thinks to himself: "What am I doing?" He replays the night in his mind and he feels ashamed. Now he's more than nauseous, he's disgusted with himself and with what he's becoming. He decides then, he's done with drinking. This is not what he wants, but what he wants, he can never have again. Geneviève. She's gone and there's nothing he can do about it. William finds the strength to open his eyes so he can speak to her. "Genny, I miss you so much. I never wanted you to see me like this. I promise, you'll never see me like this again." Then he closes his eyes and falls asleep.

He slept just long enough to dream of them in happier times. He saw her smile again. He felt her touch again. They laughed together. They ate together. They made love again. He kissed her forehead before quietly getting out of bed. Then his dream turned into a nightmare. The intruder is standing at the top of the steps. He hears Genny scream his name. Then he hears only silence. He makes his way to their bedroom, he looks on the bed and the shock of what he sees startles him out of his sleep. He's sweating, he's nauseous, his head is throbbing now, more than ever, but he can't stay where he is. He doesn't even have the strength to sit up, so he drags himself to the side of the bed, and he lets himself fall to the floor. The room is spinning and every part of his body hurts, but, at least, he's not on the bed. It takes several agonizing minutes but he keeps his eyes closed and he stays absolutely still until sleep comes for him again.

———

Day Two

1:00am — The valet says, "Welcome back Mr. Davies."

"Thanks," says Carl. "Please park it up front. I don't intend to stay long."

Carl Davies is in the habit of getting what he wants when he wants it. He always has been. Growing up in Mountain Lakes, New Jersey, as the youngest of three kids born to Sherman and Miriam Davies, pampering is all he has ever known. Sherman was a door to door salesman for the Sears and Roebuck Company when he met Miriam. She was living with her parents at the time, and she was the only one home when he knocked on their door to interest them in buying the latest model Sears and Roebuck vacuum cleaner. He didn't make the sale, but he left with something much more valuable, a date with the most beautiful girl he had ever seen. Their first date went well and so did their second. On their third date he brought Miriam to his apartment, where she was surprised to see that there was hardly any room to sit down, much less enjoy a dinner together. Sherman's apartment was overrun with tools, raw materials, gadgets, and machines, all in various states of use and completion. That's when he confessed to his true passion. He explained that he used all of his spare time to work as an inventor. The two of them continued to date, fell in love, married, and settled into a one bedroom apartment on Pelham Parkway in the Bronx, New York. By the time they had their first child, Sherman had risen to the top salesman in his district. He was bringing in more money, but none of his inventions had come to fruition. One day Miriam nearly sliced off the tip of her finger chopping vegetables. Sherman hated to see Miriam in so much pain and he wanted to make sure that wouldn't happen again. So, he created a small device that she could use to chop and dice vegetables without having to use a knife. It worked so well Miriam convinced him that every housewife in America could use one of his "Veggie Choppers." He patented the idea and set out to sell it.

Naturally, he approached Sears and Roebuck first but they didn't see the value of it. Instead, they wanted Sherman to continue selling vacuum cleaners. Next, he approached two competitors of Sears and Roebuck, the Corvette's Department store and the Woolworth's Department store. Both allowed him to set up a station in the front of their stores, on weekends, to sell his invention. Both department stores noticed that his product was selling. When Woolworth's found out that he also sold his device at Corvette's they did something about it. They offered him an office, and a permanent station at their store; and in return for a percentage of his sales they offered to promote his product along with their own. Sherman took them up on their offer and sold his product exclusively through Woolworth's. Sales took off. He did that for a year, until sales started to slow. Sherman felt that selling exclusively through just one Woolworth's store, though a godsend at first, was now limiting his sales. So, just one month before their second child was born, Sherman, with Miriam's blessing, quit his salesman job at Sears and Roebuck and he stopped selling at Woolworth's to work on expanding the sales of the "Veggie Chopper" on his own. He traveled to almost every department store, from Connecticut to Florida, trying to convince the store managers to carry his product and many of them did. Five years after the birth of their second child, Miriam got pregnant again. By that time, however, the Davies were an affluent family with money to spend. They looked for a house to buy in their neighborhood, but they couldn't find one they liked. They tried different parts of Westchester County, the county just above New York City, but they weren't comfortable there. Then they heard about a new development being built in Mountain Lakes, New Jersey. For the same amount of money that would get them a three bedroom house on an acre of land in Westchester County, they could get a six bedroom house on five acres of land in a gated community in Mountain Lakes. They closed on the house one month before Carl was born, but they stayed on Pelham Parkway until after his birth so they would be close to the hospital where their other children were born. Officially, Carl was born in the Bronx but his family moved to their new house in New Jersey three weeks later.

By the time Carl came to consciousness his mother and father were pillars in the Mountain Lakes community. Sherman was away often, managing the sales of his expanding line of kitchen products, but Miriam was active socially. Carl had a nanny that took him to school and after school events, and his older brother and sister had a hand in keeping an eye on him as well. Though he had experimented with drugs since he was fourteen, he was seventeen when crossed the line between user and addict. He was sent to a rehabilitation facility in Malibu, California, where he got sober again and he completed high school while he was there. That summer he returned to Mountain Lakes. Since he wasn't sure what he wanted to do he took a year off from school, which his parents allowed him to do only if he agreed to work with his father. After a year of selling his father's latest invention, air tight containers to store food in, Carl was certain he wanted to return to school. He had fallen in love with California during the six months he was in Malibu, so he applied to Pepperdine and he was accepted. During his junior year at Pepperdine his parents were killed in a horrific traffic accident with an eighteen wheeler on the New Jersey Turnpike. Since he had recently turned 21 years old, he was able to access his inheritance. When he graduated from Pepperdine he decided to stay in California.

He watches the valet park his car in a space that is acceptable to him and then he turns and walks to the front door of The Essex. He hoped Jackson would be the doorman tonight and it turns out that he is. Jackson is even happier to see to Carl than Carl is to see him. Two months ago Carl hired Jackson to be a bouncer at a party he threw at his house in the Hollywood Hills, and he paid him handsomely. Jackson expressed his gratefulness that night when he got paid, but he made a mental note to thank Carl again the next time he saw him, which if the past is any indication of the future, would be when Carl visited the club again. The two of them greeted each other warmly, Jackson got his chance to say thank you again, and then the two of them got down to the business at hand. Carl asks, "What's the name of the Philippine girl you told I should try?"

Jackson says, "Desi, but she's not working here tonight. I can try her on her cell to see what she's up to."

"In that case, maybe next time. It's late and I'm not going to want to wait any longer than I have to. Is there someone else, who's here now, that will work? You know what I like."

"I have just the girl for you. She's tall, thin, and beautiful; and she has big breasts, and brown skin. She's new to the club. She's only been here for two or three weeks, but she's already made it clear that she's game for anything. She loves to party, and she loves nose candy."

"You never disappoint."

"Her name is Naja. Tell her I told you about her." Jackson told the cashier that he'll take care of Carl's admittance fee and she let Carl into the club.

The Essex is an upscale gentlemen's club. The girls that work there, at a minimum, speak two languages and, for the most part, are highly educated. The patrons go there less for the lap dances and more to make new and temporary friends. Carl spots Naja immediately. She is more beautiful than Jackson described her to be. The two of them talk and Carl is on his way home having been there less than twenty minutes. On his way out, he folds three fifties in his hand and then he shakes hands with Jackson and says, "She said she'll be at my house in an hour. Do me a favor, tell her how profitable it is to please me."

Jackson didn't need to look at the amount he was given. He knows when Carl is in the mood to party the sky's the limit. He says, "I'll make sure she's there in an hour and, don't worry, she'll be game for anything."

6:10am - Bobby lies in bed, with his back to Robyn, his wife, pretending to be asleep. Judging from the light shining through their bedroom window his guess is it is sometime after 6:00am. It can't be 6:30am yet because that's when their alarm clock is set to wake them up. He is happy that he slept through the night. He's hoping that's a sign that today will be better than yesterday. All day yesterday he felt great and he's happy that everyone seemed to notice, especially Captain Upton. What everyone didn't know was that he was awake for most of the night, the night before last, coughing and throwing up. That he was able to get up and go to work was a testament to his commitment to duty. That he felt fine and everyone noticed was evidence for his mind that he did the right thing. He toyed with the idea of getting out of bed early, but he decided against it for two reasons. First, in truth, he still feels tired, so he wants to get every bit of rest he can get. Second, and more importantly, he didn't want to wake up Robyn. She was up with him the whole time he was sick the night before last, and he couldn't bring himself to possibly waking her up early again. He also wants to appear strong to her. He wants her to think that he is getting better, and there's no better way for him to do that right now than to pretend to be asleep and to pretend that he would have continued to sleep peacefully if it weren't for the alarm clock and the call to duty.

Robyn lies in bed, with her back to Bobby, pretending to be asleep. She toys with the idea of getting out bed and making breakfast for him, but there will be plenty of time for that before he goes to work. More than that, if she gets out of bed that might wake Bobby up and she wants him to get all the rest he can get. She peeks at the clock and sees they have twenty minutes before their day begins. Another twenty minutes of rest for her isn't a bad idea either. When Bobby sleeps he sleeps like a rock. The fact that he seems fidgety lying next to her tells her that he's either awake or starting to wake up, but she decides to pretend that she doesn't notice.

The two of them lay there for another five minutes before Bobby starts to cough. He felt the urge coming on. It was so strong there was no way he was going to be able to suppress it, so he did the best he could to muffle it. A second urge came on almost before he was done muffling the first. This one, perhaps because it followed the first so immediately, was stronger than the first. He decided to let it out with the hopes the urge would leave his body and that would be the end of it. Robyn heard him muffle the first and, of course, she heard him cough thereafter, but her guess was the same as his, namely, there is nothing to be alarmed about yet. She knew that he was trying to hold it in so as to not wake her up and worry her, so she let him have that small victory. She continued to pretend to be asleep. The urge to cough, however, kept coming. Unable to muffle each one, Bobby coughed loudly and each one seemed stronger and more violent than the last. When Robyn heard enough she turned around to check on her husband. By that time he was sitting up on the side of the bed trying to get some control over his body. "Hey baby, are you OK?" she asks.

Bobby says, "I'm fine. I think I just have a scratch in my throat or maybe it's just my allergies."

"Did you get a good night's sleep?"

"Yes and I feel fine. Try to get some more rest."

"The alarm is going to go off in ten minutes away. I'm up now. Do you want me to get you a glass of water?" Before Bobby can answer that question another violent urge to cough takes a hold of him and this one isn't letting go. Robyn jumps out of bed and rushes to the kitchen for a glass of water. The whole time she's there she can hear Bobby coughing incessantly. By the time she gets back to the bedroom, however, he has stopped. Other than wiping the tears from his eyes, he appears to be OK. She gives him the glass of water and insists that he drink it anyway. While he drinks the water she says, "I don't care what Doctor Jones says, there has to be a reason for your coughing spells. Maybe it's time to get a third opinion." Even while she's saying that to him she knows what he'll say in return and she's right.

Bobby says, "Believe me, I'm fine. There isn't anything wrong with me except stress."

"You keep saying that but what stress do you have that could be causing this?" Again, she knows what he'll say and, again, she's right.

"It's just worked related stuff babe. It's nothing to worry about."

"Fatigue, being up all night throwing up and coughing up a lung every other day is nothing to worry about? This has been going on for months now. I think it is time to get more serious."

"I know it has been persistent but you have to admit I've been getting better for two weeks now. Besides, right now, I feel better than I have in a long time. That coughing spell was just a remnant. It's over. Thanks for the water."

Robyn knows that's Bobby's way of saying I don't want to talk about this anymore so she changes the subject. "What do you want for breakfast?"

"Whatever you want to make but make something light. I have a feeling today will be a busy day."

"Do you think you'll be home late again?"

"Maybe, but if so, not too late. Why? Is there something going on?"

Robyn snuggles up to Bobby from behind and whispers into his ear, "No but there could be, if you know what I mean. I know of a fun way to help you deal with your work related stress."

Bobby smiles and turns to face his wife, "Yes you do. I'll do my best to get home a decent hour."

Robyn kisses Bobby and, as she gets off the bed and searches for her robe, she says, "Good. If you do, that will be the only thing decent about tonight." As she walks down the hallway towards the kitchen she yells back at Bobby, "What we really need is a vacation. You've been promising me to take me to Europe for two years now. I swear Bobby, I'm starting to think you like being around murderers more than your wife."

That last comment would have been funny to Bobby if it weren't a reminder of last night's conversation with Eddie. Four more days, including today, of being his partner and then this chapter of his life is over. Bobby is convinced that he's been feeling better because this partnership is coming to an end. In fact, he's sure of it. On one hand, he loves Eddie. He always has. If there's anyone to have in your foxhole, so to speak, it's Eddie, and he's proven that time and again. The fact that they aren't great friends outside of work hasn't been a bad thing to Bobby. He's the kind of guy who believes good fences makes for good neighbors. He's never really cared about what Eddie does with his free time. Eddie's not a family man. He was married once but he's been divorced longer than they have been partners, so other than work and sports, Bobby's guess has always been that they don't have a lot in common. Now, knowing what he knows, he's sure of it. Bobby has been a cop long enough to know that most cops lose their idealism after being on the force for a few years. That some cops abuse their power and that some cops cut corners in ways that would get civilians arrested is par for the course, but to be an accessory to a murder is something Bobby never saw coming. More than that, he still isn't sure if Eddie is more abhorrent than himself. After all, he decided to keep his mouth shut out of some false sense of loyalty and for the money. Four more days, including today, and this partnership is over. That's what Bobby keeps telling himself. Maybe Robyn is right. It appears, even to him, that he likes being around murderers more than his wife. Well, in four days he'll change that perception. He'll use some of the money to take his wife on the vacation he's been promising her for years. He has enough vacation time to make it an extended holiday, he'll have the money for them to visit several major European cities, and he'll have enough money for them do it all in first class. His final thought before pushing himself off the bed for the shower and then work is: "In four days I'll put this whole thing behind me, my health will get better, I'll take my wife on vacation, and from there, we'll go on with the rest of our lives."

7:30am - Heidi, the receptionist at Viking Motor Yachts in Marina Del Rey, says, "I bet you can't wait until Friday."
Eddie replies, "Friday is going to be a great day, but I've been looking forward to today as well."
Heidi says, "They finished her up last night. I got a chance to see all of the changes. I'm sure you are going to be very happy."
"I'd be happier if I could convince you to sail away with me."
"You are nothing if not persistent Mr. Roberts. Help yourself to some coffee and pastries. Mr. Carlsson knows you are here. I'm sure he'll be right down."

Eddie goes into the conference room and helps himself to a cup of coffee and a Cheese Danish. He takes a seat and thumbs through Yachting World magazine while he waits for Piers. Five minutes later Piers Carlsson, the General Manager of Viking Motor Yachts, enters the conference room. "We received the papers from the escrow agent yesterday. Congratulations Mr. Roberts! You must be very excited."
Eddie says, "I am. How did everything go?"
"Perfectly. I'm sure you will be very pleased, but don't take my word for it. Let's take a look."

Heidi buzzes the two gentlemen into the shipyard. As they walk towards the slip that houses Eddie's boat Piers says, "Before you leave today make sure Heidi gives you the access code for the side entrance. That way you can come and go as you please."
Eddie says, "Thank you."

"It's our pleasure. I know you intend to push off Friday night. This way you can start stocking up on supplies and get everything you need onboard before Friday. Ahh, here she is."

No matter how many times Eddie sees her, each time is better than the last. "Miss Behavin" is a 58' Hatteras Motor Yacht. The perfect boat for someone who is looking to live aboard, like Eddie is, at least temporarily. Piers found her in Hilton Head, South Carolina. He negotiated the sale on Eddie's behalf and had her shipped, over land, to Viking. The two men board the boat on the starboard side of the deck. Piers points out the wet bar and the new table and chairs Eddie ordered. They continue through the patio doors into the salon. Pursuant to Eddie's instructions, the wicker furniture has been replaced with built in couches covered in a medium brown faux leather. The lamps have been replaced with sconces, a high definition flat screen has been added in the corner of the salon to the right of the patio doors, and the old fashioned thermostat has been replaced with digital controls. The large windows on both sides of the salon have been tinted just enough to provide some shade but not enough to lose their transparency or subtract from the magnificent views. Luckily for Eddie he didn't have to spend any money updating the upper galley or the lower galley. The previous owner saw to that. The upper galley features a refrigerated stainless steel Subzero wine cooler, marble countertops with teak edge moulding and teak-wood cabinetry and accents with a satin finishes. There is a four burner cook top, with a stainless steel range hood and oven, a stainless steel Subzero pull-out refrigerator and freezer, a stainless steel microwave oven, two deep stainless steel sinks with a spray nozzle to the right of the faucet, and a stainless steel dishwasher. The lower galley features another stainless steel Subzero freezer and a laundry area with a stacked washer and dryer combination unit, and a built-in ironing board. The three staterooms are the same as the galleys, in that the previous owner updated them during his ownership and, accordingly, Eddie didn't have to spend a penny for any changes in any of them. The master stateroom has a queen size bed, a lounge area, several shelves for a small library, a high definition flat screen television, and plenty of closet and storage space. The second stateroom has two twin beds, a flat screen television, and plenty of storage space underneath both beds, and the third stateroom has two bunk beds in a 90 degree upper and lower formation, a flat screen television, and just a little less storage space than the second stateroom. All three staterooms have their own private head, but only the master has a full bathtub and shower. From the staterooms the two men continue up into the lower helm area, which features Morse controls and Glendinning engine synchronization, a Garmin 3210C Radar and Plotter, a Bottom Machine, Icom VHF, a Ritchie Compass, a Depth Meter, a spotlight, a rudder angle indicator, and updated engine gauges. Before heading up to the fly bridge, Piers directs Eddie's attention to the new plush cushioning on the bow deck, a feature Viking threw in to thank him for his business. From there the two men take the companionway to the upper deck fly bridge area, which is a completely open air area with shading over the two helm chairs, but without shading over the deck to aft and the L-shaped couch bordering it. As far as electronics go, this upper helm area has the exact same set up as the lower helm, but the majesty of the fly bridge is twofold: it isn't enclosed in any way, and the view from this upper deck is 360 degrees, and limited only by what the eye can see.

During the tour Eddie and Piers discuss almost everything about the boat, from the anchors and the engines, to the decking and the navigational equipment, but the tour ends purposefully on the fly bridge because Piers knows no part of the boat generates as much pride of ownership, at this stage, as sitting in the helm chair on the fly bridge. Without any direction from Piers, Eddie eases himself into that very chair at the end of the tour and Piers pounces on the opportunity. He asks, "Tell me what you think."

Without a moment's hesitation Eddie's response is, "If I could make love to her, I would."

That's all Piers wants to hear. Finally, Piers excuses himself to attend to other business, but he invites Eddie to relax and get used to his new boat, and he reminds him to see Heidi for the access code on his way out. After standing, only to shake Piers' hand, Eddie eases himself back into what he has already been labeled, "The Captain's Chair," as soon as Piers takes his leave. "Ten years in coming," that's all Eddie can think. "Ten years in coming." Eddie had no way of knowing that the events of that night, ten years ago, would lead to this, but it has and here he is, sitting on top of his wildest dream. His happiness turns only slightly towards melancholy when he thinks of the three. Bobby, Breck, and Carl are the only three people, alive that is, who can implicate him. As he repositions himself in the Captain's Chair he does the math. Carl won't say a word because he's just as guilty. Breck won't say a word because he's looking forward to the money. That leaves Bobby. Eddie decides he's not really worried about Bobby because Bobby is too weak. Still, he'll keep an eye on him. Melancholy returns to happiness as Eddie leans back in the Captain's Chair, puts his feet up on the console, and thinks to himself: "I just have to make it to Friday."

8:30am - On most days you can count on an accident or a stalled car or just pure congestion to bring the east bound traffic on the 10 Freeway to a crawl, at least once, between Santa Monica and Downtown, but not today. This morning traffic was surprisingly light and free flowing. It usually takes Lisa 40 to 45 minutes to get from her house to the parking lot on the corner of West 3rd Street and South Spring Street, where she always parks when she's meeting Russell for breakfast. Today it took 10 minutes. Normally she gives the keys to the parking lot attendant and sprints to the Los Angeles Times Building, or to whatever restaurant they've agreed upon. Today she left extra early so she wouldn't have to sprint and wouldn't you know it, now she has over thirty minutes to kill before they are supposed to meet. Instead of giving the keys to the attendant she parks her car herself, with the intention of sitting in the car and checking her email, or scanning the news, or getting started on her blog for the day, but she's having a problem concentrating. She can't stop thinking about Tony. More accurately, she can't stop thinking about last night.

Every summer Leslie Blue, one of Lisa's girlfriends and the owner of a web hosting company, throws her annual Summer Salsa Fiesta for her friends and her clients. Normally Lisa is a fixture at these parties since she's both a friend and a client. Last year, however, Leslie had to talk Lisa into attending and it wasn't an easy thing to do. Lisa had just broken up with Tony, coincidentally the name of the boyfriend she had before her current boyfriend with the same name. Lisa decided to pass on last year's Fiesta for two reasons: she didn't want to run into old Tony, for fear that he would chase her around the party trying everything he could think of to get her back, and she just didn't feel like partying. Leslie's Fiestas always starts on Saturday at 1:00pm with a pre-party cookout. Leslie converts her entire backyard into a dance floor and by sundown the party is raging, with food, drinks, a DJ spinning loud Latin music, and couples dancing the Salsa on every inch of the dance floor for every minute the music is playing. Leslie's close friends and clients know the party doesn't end around 1:00am when the neighbors have had enough. It just winds down to a more intimate gathering that lasts until Sunday afternoon when Leslie has another cookout. The only thing that's different about Sunday's cookout is there is no DJ. By that time, the party planners have broken down the dance floor and the DJ station. Still, there is food and drinks everywhere and the music is contained inside Leslie's house, emitting from her sound system. There is always a couple or two still dancing Salsa or, at least, practicing the moves they picked up the night before, but, for the most part, by then the party is a collection of friends who are mostly eating, drinking, talking, and laughing with each other. After each of Leslie's Fiestas Lisa always needs a day or two of rest, and one or two gallons of water to run through her system before she's recovered. Last year she just wasn't up for all of that, but Leslie convinced her to come anyway. Now, she's happy she did because that's where she met new Tony.

Their eyes first met while Tony was standing in the backyard watching everybody dance. Lisa was dancing with one of her girlfriends and every time she glanced over at him he was admiring her. When she took a break he walked up to her and immediately admitted that he didn't know how to dance the Salsa and he asked her to teach him. It turned out he didn't know anybody at the party and he wasn't invited. He was just passing by, he heard the loud music, and he just walked in. A new boyfriend was, at the time, the very last thing Lisa had on her mind or wanted, but from the moment she and Tony danced their first dance together they have been inseparable. She was impressed by his boldness, she was impressed that he had just joined the police department, she was impressed by his wit and intelligence, and by how it seemed they could talk all day without a moment of empty space. It didn't hurt that he was tall, well built, and extremely handsome too.

After dating for seven months they moved in with each other. Last night, however, was the first time he told her he loved her. Before she knew it she had told him she loved him too. There was no use in being embarrassed by the admission because the truth is she wouldn't have agreed to move in with him if she didn't feel that way, though she never said it until last night. Hearing him say it and hearing herself say it changed everything. Before last night, the two of them were just playing house, for lack of a better description. She didn't allow herself to imagine a future with him. She thought it was better to take it one day at a time and she stuck to that strategy. Now it's as if a damn broke. Now her mind is flooded with thoughts of marriage and kids. Well, maybe just a dog at first but, still, she wants and can't stop thinking about a committed relationship with Tony, and all that comes with it. As she sits in her car thinking about all of this, it all boils down to one thing. She's madly in love with Tony, he's madly in love with her, and they are both really happy.

Lisa thinks to herself: "There I said it. I'm in love with Tony and I want to get married. Me, the girl who didn't want to get married, not at least until I had a solid career. Me, the girl who doesn't need anybody. It's crazy or I'm crazy or the world is a crazy but the truth is I do love Tony and I do want to get married." Having admitted that to herself out loud and allowing her herself to think of a future with someone other than herself feels liberating and it makes Lisa feel happy. She checks the time. "Damn!

I'm ten minutes late!" Lisa jumps out of car, throws her keys to the attendant, and sprints to the Los Angeles Times building.

9:00am - William flirted with consciousness two or three times before this time, but each time, until now, he fell back asleep. Right now, he wishes he could go back to sleep but he can't. Now he's awake and he's going to have to deal with it. His head is throbbing as if there is something inside his skull that is trying to get out. All he can think of now is pain relief. Besides the throbbing, his head feels as heavy as a bowling ball. He brings himself to his knees in an effort to get his body underneath his head, to support the weight, so he can use his legs to stand erect. Having done that he labors into the bathroom in search of aspirin. He doesn't find any in the leather pouch he keeps his toiletries in and he knows he hasn't purchased any recently, but he also knows he has seen some somewhere in his suite. The pain of the throbbing is so intense it makes his focus blind to everything except relief and that leads him to the box of toiletries that the housekeeper refreshes every day. There he finds one packet containing two aspirins and with a handful of water from the sink he swallows them down as if they are food found after not eating for a week. While he waits for the pills to take effect the next thing he wants to do is get out of his clothing and take a shower. He turns on the shower and makes his way to the chair in the bedroom. When he leans forward to take off his socks he quickly realizes that was a mistake. He feels light headed and faint and he immediately breaks out into a cold sweat. He forces himself to lean back, sit still, and ride out this wave of nausea. He sits there for what feels like twenty minutes before he can continue taking off his clothing, all the while being careful to keep his head upright this time. By the time he makes it to the shower he is nauseous, dizzy, and completely out of energy. The better thing to do is turn off the shower, and go to the bathtub, and sit in there until it is full enough to wash his body, but he doesn't even have the strength for that. So, he sits in the shower stall, completely motionless, underneath the shower that is still running.

After sitting there for a few minutes the luke warm water starts to bring his mind and body back to life. The aspirin is doing its job, or at least, the throbbing has diminished enough for him to think. He had a friend who used to always ask, "What's really going on with you?" That's the question he's been asking himself for days, if not weeks. That's the question that needs to be answered. Yes, he's devastated by Genny's murder. Yes, he misses her more than any words can say. The reality is she's gone forever. There'll be no more birthdays, no more anniversaries, no more Christmas', no more Thanksgivings, and no more vacations for them to spend together. There'll be no children, no little league outings, no PTA meetings, no family holidays, no weddings, and no grandchildren for them to share together. Every single dream he shared with Genny is gone, with her, forever. Yes, the pain is, at times, unbearable. Still, that's not it. There's something else. Sitting there naked and close to hopeless, finally, the answer to the question comes to him. He's angry. Sure, life is unfair. Everybody knows that good things, sometimes, happen to bad people and bad things, sometimes, happen to good people, but what's been eating away at him is Genny's murder wasn't a random and tragic accident. If it were, the pain wouldn't be any less severe but, at least, he could, given enough time, reconcile it. The fact of the matter is their bedroom was ransacked but nothing was taken. There were plenty of valuables lying around for the murderer to take, but he took nothing. Detective Morales is a good man. William doesn't have a doubt in his mind that he investigated the murder to the best of his ability, but that doesn't change the fact that he came up empty. William isn't buying the official LAPD stance, that the murder was a burglary gone horribly bad. He has absolutely no clue as to why someone would want to murder Genny, but it appears to William that once that was done, the murderer had no other business in their house. Ransacking their bedroom was done to give the impression that it was a robbery. The murderer could have finished William off if he chose to, but he didn't. His mind says he's crazy to think there's more to it, but his gut tells him there is. Pretending that life will just go on is what's driving William to drink and it will drive him to worse if he allows it to. The thought that whoever murdered Genny might be thinking that they can get away with it makes William angry. The thought that someone can purposefully take, from him, what he cherished the most, in their house no less, makes William angry. Out of two days of self-pity and self-destruction comes the clearest thought William has had since the incident. "Someone has to answer for Genny." Before William can lift himself off the shower stall floor a moment of self-doubt follows the moment of clarity. What if he's wrong? What if it was just an accident? More than that, what if he's right? If he is, truthfully, he's no match for someone who can kill someone else or hire someone to kill someone else for reasons other than self-defense. But, with that thought, there it is again, the knot in his stomach. William decides there and then that he's only going to allow himself to think about what he believes is true. Genny was murdered by someone for some reason, and he has to know who and why, no matter what that means. His mantra now is, somebody has to answer for Genny. Just to make sure he isn't crazy he knows he needs to talk with somebody, and he knows exactly who that somebody is. Now, feeling just slightly less nauseous but filled with purpose, William lifts himself off the floor, washes his body, gets dressed, and thanks to the note left behind by Rosa, he knows where is car is. He heads for the front desk to retrieve his car keys.

9:30am - To the best of Lisa's recollection that day started like every other day. Her father, Sigmund, had gotten up at his normal time, 5:00am, and gone for his morning jog. She never knew how far he jogged or what route he took, but she did know he would return home sometime before 6:30am because every week day morning at exactly 6:30am he would gently knock on her door, sit on the edge of her bed, and wake her up for the day. His first words to her every morning were, "Good Morning Princess." Being the daddy's girl that she was, even if she was awake before her father came to her room she wouldn't get out of bed until she heard him say, "Good Morning Princess." On that day, as usual, he knocked on her door at exactly 6:30am.

Lisa remembers that on that day she was particularly excited to go to school. It was Wednesday during the last week of eighth grade. School had effectively ended on the Friday before. This last week of middle school was filled with arts and crafts classes, long lunches, and more arts and crafts. Since she was a member of the graduating class at Stevenson Middle School, she was royalty for that week. On that day she couldn't wait to get to school. She loved arts and craft, especially painting, but, more importantly, she couldn't wait to meet up with her friends and catch up on the latest gossip. Her father had to leave early that morning, so he yelled goodbye while she was in the shower and when she was ready for school her mother, Gita, drove her there.

Sigmund Becker was an engineer for the Bridgewell Company. His home office was in Century City, on Avenue of the Stars just down the street from Fox Studios, but on that day he had a morning meeting with The Stavros Company, a company based in Van Nuys that his firm was using as a subcontractor. As he drove around the Van Nuys neighborhood looking for parking he noticed two guys standing next to a car looking into the driver's side window and talking. He didn't think anything of it. He thought even less of it as he drove by and smiled back to one of the guys who turned to smile at him. He was determined to find street parking since The Stavros Company didn't provide parking and parking on the main thoroughfare would have cost money. On his second pass down that same street he saw the same two guys still standing next to the same car. As he drove closer one of them got in the car and started handing things to the other guy, the one who smiled at him. Broken glass littered the street next to the car. His first instinct was to stop and back up, then he thought he'll just drive by and pretend not to have noticed anything. What he did, however, was pull up next to the car and ask, "Hey, what are you guys doing?" The guy who smiled at him must have told the other guy that someone was coming because no sooner did he finish that sentence than two shots rang out and the two of them took off on foot down the street.

It wasn't Russell Armstrong's story. He read about it in a column by his counterpart at Los Angeles' other major newspaper, The Daily News. Though he was touched by the senseless death of, by all accounts, a hard working family man, who left behind a wife and a thirteen year old daughter, that wasn't why he chose to get involved. He had lived in that Van Nuys neighborhood for many years and he still had friends there. He chose to get involved because he was sure he could help. It took two months of calls and visits but he finally came up with the name of someone who had been heard bragging about being the shooter. He fed that information to the police. They dug a little deeper and ultimately they came up with enough evidence to arrest that guy and his accomplice.

During his two month investigation Russell got to know Gita and Lisa. Their relationship started simply with him introducing himself and interviewing them for a follow up story he decided to write. It continued with him giving them updates on his investigation. Though Gita appreciated all that he was trying to do, it was Lisa who would call him for an update whenever two or three days passed by without her hearing from him. After both men pleaded guilty and were sent to prison, it was Lisa who insisted that she and her mother have Russell over for dinner. A few weeks later Lisa insisted again that they have Russell over for dinner. Before this dinner, however, Russell called Gita to speak about Lisa. During that conversation he informed Gita that Lisa had called him several times just to say hi and to ask about what he was doing. Naturally, he asked her about school and music and her friends; and the more he asked the more Lisa happily told him about those things and more. Gita admitted she knew about those calls and she admitted that Lisa spoke about him frequently. The two of them determined that since Russell wasn't married and had no children, and since Lisa lost her father, perhaps she felt they were kindred spirits. Russell confessed that if he did have a daughter he would consider himself the luckiest guy in the world if she was just like Lisa. By the end of their second dinner together Russell was a confirmed family friend and, with Gita's permission, a budding surrogate father to Lisa.

Lisa is a rock star at the Los Angeles Times building or, at least on the fifth floor, where Russell has his office. Everybody knows her as Russell's not so little anymore little girl. After she made her rounds to say hello to everyone and after she and Russell caught up, Lisa gently eases into what she had come there to discuss. Russell has always been flattered that Lisa wants to follow him into the world of crime reporting, but he tried several times, over the years, to dissuade her. His thinking is that Lisa, a beautiful, smart, and ambitious young lady, could be anything in the world she wants to be. Why would she want to spend her time writing about the low lifes in society? Somewhere along the way, after it became apparent that that's what she is determined to do, he changed his tune from discouragement to support. After looking at the pictures Lisa took of the victim in the dump trunk he changed his tune back to discouragement. This time, however, he didn't try to discourage her from being a writer, he just doesn't want her to pursue this story. "Why?" asks Lisa.

While still taking in the picture Russell says, "This guy wasn't killed in a bar fight or by a jealous lover. This guy was killed by a professional. I just think it is a little too much for you to bite off and chew at this point in your career."

Lisa doesn't buy that for a minute. "No it isn't. You're just worried about me."

"You're right. I am worried about you. Suppose you go digging around and you get close enough to whoever did this for that person or persons to start worrying. Worst case, they're not going to ask you to stop, they're going to stop you themselves."

"I understand that you're worried. So far, I've only written about petty robberies and drunk driving cases. I know this is my first murder case, but this could help me make a name for myself. I was on the murder scene before the police were. I have the lead on this one. I don't know when, or if, I'll get another opportunity like this. Besides, if you help me, it will be like we are doing it together. That way you can keep track of me."

Russell knows trying to talk her out of it is useless. More than that, she's right. She does have the lead and, based on the way this kid was killed, it would be career making story to break. "OK, here's the deal. You don't do anything until I find out what the police know about this guy already. Also, you have to keep me up to speed every step of the way."

Lisa says, "Deal!" as they shake on it.

"I'll try to have some information for you later today but, more likely, I'll have something for you sometime tomorrow morning."

Lisa says, "OK."

Russell smiles and says, "So, let's get back to why you were late."

"Since you didn't react I thought you didn't hear me."

"I didn't react because you said it and then you changed the subject so quickly."

"I know. I'm still trying to work it out in my mind. Maybe I was just hoping you didn't hear me."

"You should know better than that. So, you think you're in love with Tony, huh?"

"Yeah, I am."

10:30am - As Lisa walks back to the parking lot to get her car she can't shake the bitter sweet feeling from her sit down with Russell. On one hand she's elated that he saw, as she did, the potential of breaking this story as it relates to her career. She was even more elated that he agreed to help by using his contacts in the LAPD to get information that might lead to the greater story. At the same time she knew Russell was right. Clearly the kid wasn't killed by an amateur. What if he was killed for seeing something he wasn't supposed to see or for knowing something he wasn't supposed to know? What if she discovers what he saw or what he knew? Would the same person or people come after her? Then it dawned on her. Sure she's a little nervous of what she's getting herself into, but she's more excited than nervous. She reminds herself that this is the very feeling she's been craving since she decided to write for a living. Besides, she isn't going to get anywhere by writing about petty crimes or by playing it safe.

By the time she got to the parking lot the bitter was gone and all that was left was the sweet, but now another dilemma presents itself. What to do with the rest of her day? That turned out to be an easy decision for her to make. Her first official investigation will begin tomorrow, so there's nothing to do there today. Couple that with the fact that she's feeling a little tired from the dinner, and the drinks, but, mostly, from the two sessions of love making she and Tony shared last night. Add to that, the fact that she's craving more of Tony tonight, and she knows exactly what she is going to do today. The plan is first, take a nap. Second, pamper herself a little. A manicure and a pedicure and a little shopping, including some new lingerie, sounds good to her. Finally, she'll have a romantic candlelit dinner ready for Tony when he gets home and, hopefully, that will lead to love making session number three. Knowing Tony that will lead to love making sessions three and four. As she starts her car, a smile widens across her face and she thinks to herself: "Now that's what I call a good day."

11:00am - Sitting atop one of highest peaks in the mountains and valleys between Malibu and Calabasas, overlooking the Pacific Ocean to the west, and the whole San Fernando Valley to the east, is The Center For Recovery. Established in 1991, this faculty serves the needs of those who suffer from debilitating mental disorders, from severe anxiety and depression to substance abuse. Besides the obvious mandate of providing the most professional care possible in the most caring way possible there is another mandate that ranks just as high, and is enforced just as stringently. This second mandate is anonymity. The entire staff, each client, and every guest, indeed everyone allowed on the property, are contractually prohibited from discussing or revealing the identity of any of the clients or any of the methods employed at the facility. Today, however, is different. There are a handful of television cameras and reporters from the local news outlets on the property. As well, there are over two hundred guests on the property. They have all been invited to mix and mingle not with any of the clients but with selected members of the staff and with certain dignitaries from the cities of Malibu and Calabasas. Today they have all gathered to celebrate the architectural rendering of a new wing to be added to The Center, the construction of which is scheduled to start in the spring. So far the assembly has listened to ninety minutes of testimonials, from doctors, nurses, counselors, former clients, the Sheriffs from both cities, and the Mayor of Malibu, all of whom have gushingly expounded on the short term and the long term benefits to be derived from the addition of the new wing. It is the distinct pleasure of the Mayor of Calabasas, once he's contributed to the praise worthiness of the new wing, to introduce the man who made the twenty five million dollar donation to The Center that made all of this possible.

In summation Mayor Rogers says, "The scores of jobs that will be created will benefit those lucky enough to get the employment and it will benefit the local economies as well. That alone is wonderful news, but what is truly wonderful about the new wing is that it will provide The Center with the facilities it needs to help more people than ever before. As many of you know, the fees The Center collects, in part, allows it provide help on a pro bono basis for those in need who lack the resources to pay for the help themselves. I could go on and on about how thankful and how proud I am to have The Center, its staff, and all the good work they do there as a member of our community, but I think the more important thing to do now is to invite, to the podium, the man whose twenty five million dollar donation made this new wing possible, and to ask him to give us his thoughts on and his hopes for the new wing. Please join me in a thunderous round of applause for Mr. Pete Jefferson." All of the cameras are rolling, every flashbulb is going off, and everyone rises to their feet and loudly applauds Pete as he makes his way to the podium.

Pete's aversion of publicity is legendary. Customarily whenever he has acquired or disposed of a large property or done anything considered newsworthy, he has sent a member of his organization to meet with all forms of the media to answer any question they may have. The only time Pete speaks publicly is when it is on behalf of his son, Ricky. So, today he has agreed to be seen and to speak openly about the new Ricky Jefferson Wing. Now, as he stands at the podium, ready to speak, the cameras continue to roll but the flashbulbs have gone silent as has the applause, and everyone has retaken their seat. "First, I'd like to thank each and every one of you for being here today. The Ricky Jefferson Foundation was created after the death of my son and in light of his battles with drug addiction. You have listened to several people, this morning, talk about The Center and the wonderful work done here. You have heard several people talk about the benefits of having a facility like this to the surrounding community and to the community at large. What, or who, you haven't heard enough about is the director of The Center, Miss Marguerite Best. This entire facility is the realization of a dream she had over twenty years ago. If I say she created The Center For Recovery single-handedly that would be incorrect. She has certainly had help. Yet, all of us who have worked with her, or for her, would agree that she is the force behind the creation of this facility. Marguerite started her fight for The Center two years before it opened. Since then, and every day, she fought for and forged, with her own relentless tenacity, this dream of love, patience, and hope. As far as my donation goes, it's only money. If my donation prevents just one parent from going through the pain of losing their child to drugs, every penny spent would be beyond worth it. Still, if one child and one parent is to be sparred it won't be because of my donation. It will be the result of the work Marguerite and her staff do here. You were all very kind to welcome me so warmly, if I have any influence here allow me to ask you to be even more generous with your applause as we welcome Miss Marguerite Best to this podium." As asked, the entire assembly rises, again, to their feet and their applause is even more thunderous for Miss Best.

Miss Best gave an inspirational and rousing speech detailing the birth of The Center, its journey to date, and the ambitious mission of The Center into the future. At the end of her speech Pete stood next to her and ceremoniously handed her the check. Then the architect unveiled the rendering, which evoked the ooo's and ahh's that echoed from the people sitting close enough to see it clearly to the people sitting in the back, for whom the rendering was out of view. The new Ricky Jefferson Wing will have several rooms to be used for medical evaluations, group and staff meetings, and research in the fight against drug addiction, but it will also have amenities that can and will be used by everyone on the property. In the southeast corner there will be ninety foot by thirty foot pool enclosed in a glass room with a roof that will retract partially. In the northeast corner there will be a full length basketball court with pull out bleachers on one side of the court. That makes it, officially, the largest assembly room on the property. And, finally, there will be twenty additional one bedroom, one bathroom mini-apartments that can be used for staff or client housing. The architect beams with pride, Pete smiles and nods his head with satisfaction, and Marguerite cries tears of joy as she sees another one of her dreams turning, slowly but surely, into reality.

After every news camera and reporter captured the story along with the visuals, the remaining guests were invited inside for a private reception. Abbey stood by Pete's side during most of the reception, especially during the first twenty minutes while Pete and Marguerite huddled in a corner of the room. The reception went on for another hour and a half. During that time, Pete spoke, if only briefly, with everyone who wanted to speak with him. By the end of the reception, by both Pete's and Abbey's count, every one of Pete's business partners had showed their support by attending with the exception of one, Carl Davies.

11:30am - William pulls up in front of a one story pink house with a terracotta tiled roof on Orange Avenue in Long Beach.

Every time he returns to this house a flood of memories come back to him, and every time they do he tells himself he should visit more often. He tried calling her before he arrived but she didn't answer the phone. He would have tried her cell phone but she doesn't have one. The driveway is empty but that's no surprise since she doesn't own a car or drive. From the sidewalk he can't see any lights that are on in the house but he opens the front gate anyway. The chain linked fence that starts at the front gate in the center of the property, and runs along the front of the house and the sides of the house in both directions is less for protection and more for decoration. The entire fence is lined with 3 foot hedges that are intertwined with the fence and, as always, perfectly manicured. Once he passes through the front gate he has to follow a slightly winding gravel filled path to get to the front door. The lawn extends, on both sides of the house, from the hedges to the row of flowers just before the porch. On each side of the walk path is a row of Dymondia Margaretae dotted with pink Echeveria, and behind the Dymondia Margaretae is a row of Agave Attenuata. The front of the porch is bordered on both sides by a collection of African Daisies, Lobelia, Sea Lavender, and Silvery Dusty Miller. Each and every flower, in each arrangement, is perfectly cared for and blossoming beautifully. It has always been this way and, it appears, it always will be this way. To the left of the left side of the path, in the middle of the lawn, there's a four foot high birdbath. For a period of time, when William was young, there was a Bluebird that would show up at that birdbath every morning. That went on for weeks, every day. Then one day, just as abruptly as it began, it ended. The Bluebird stopped coming. From that day to this, whenever William sees that birdbath he can't stop himself from expecting to see that Bluebird again. On the front porch there's the same swing built for two that's been there for, what must be, twenty years. Now, on the front porch he looks through the front window and, upon a closer inspection, he still doesn't see any lights that are on in the house. He pushes the doorbell anyway. He looks through the front window again for any sign of movement, but there are none. He gives it a minute and then he pushes the doorbell again.

After another minute of waiting without seeing or hearing any signs of movement William resigns to the thought that she must not be home. He takes one last glance inside the house and then turns and heads back down the gravel path towards the front gate. Just as he's about to pass the hedges, he hears the front door unlocking. By the time he turns around his blind Aunt Ernestine is standing on the porch. "William," she yells.

From his position next to the hedges William asks, "How did you know it was me?"

Aunt Ernestine says, "Oh Honey, you know I can smell your sweet scent from a mile away. Come on in and spend some time with your Aunt Ernestine."

12:00pm - Naja got to Carl's house at 2:30am exactly. Twenty minutes later Carl was sitting in the Jacuzzi naked and Naja handed Carl her glass of champagne so she could take off her bra and panties to join him. Carl pretended that she was just another girl but, in truth, he was blown away by her beauty and sexiness. The first thing he noticed about her, when they met at the club, was her build, tall and lean. Carl's guess is she's 5'9" to 5'11". The second thing he noticed was her full and long brown hair, which she wore naturally, just parted in the middle. Even when curly, it reaches to the middle of her back. While they talked in the club she used her hand to pull her hair away from her face and that aroused him then. After handing her glass of champagne to Carl she did it again, and again he felt his sense of arousal heighten. Lit only by the stars and the lights from the pool and the Jacuzzi, Carl watched Naja take off her black laced bra. He was memorized by her flawless light tan skin and if he has ever seen more perfect breasts he couldn't remember when. They are full and her nipples sit atop her fullness, perfectly. Carl was particularly turned on by her large areolas, which are two or three shades darker than her skin. More than that, he's turned on by her nipples themselves, which at that point were fully erect. Carl followed her fingers as they went from squeezing her own breasts, down her muscle toned mid-section, past her diamond navel ring, and to the sides of her hips. He watched as she grabbed the sides of her panties and slowly slid them down the length of her long slender legs. When she stood erect again she called Carl's attention to her pubic area, which had been waxed clean except for a small section right above her labia which was closely cropped and in the shape of a heart. Once she got into the Jacuzzi they had another sip or two of champagne. Carl, pretending to be interested, asked her a few get to know you questions, but what he was really thinking about was the picture of her, standing before him, just a moment ago, with nothing on except a diamond navel ring. Even as she was answering his last question, he was noticing the bubbles dancing on her breasts, he was noticing that her areolas had become just a shape darker from the water, and, most of all, he was noticing that even in the warm water of the Jacuzzi her nipples were still erect. Carl was kind enough to let her finish answering his last question before he lifted himself out of the water to sit on the edge of the Jacuzzi. He pulled her closer to him and he positioned her between his legs. Then he guided is erect cock into her mouth and she gave him head.

Their cocaine and Viagra fueled party lasted the rest of the night and all morning. Around 4:30am they stopped to take a dip in the pool, and then they sat in the Jacuzzi, and then they started up again. Around 5:30am they stopped to watch a movie, and listen to music, and talk about furniture and cars, and then they started up again. Around 10:00am they stopped and Carl made an omelette with toast and coffee for Naja. While she ate, he did more cocaine and took another Viagra and then they started up again. At noon, Carl's doorbell rang. At first he planned to ignore it, but the doorbell rang again and again. That's when Carl remembered who it is. He checked the video feed from the camera at his front door and he was correct. He totally forgot that he asked Eddie and Bobby to stop by today at noon.

Carl explains to Naja that a couple of his business partners stopped by to talk with him, but it should only take a minute. Naja thinks this is probably a good time to leave. She says she needs to get some rest because she has to be back at the club tonight at 7:00pm. Carl isn't done with her yet so he asks her to stay. She says she will but she needs another line and she'll need him to give her some candy to take with her so she can get through her shift later that night. Carl agrees. Carl unlocks the front door from his bedroom and over the intercom he tells Eddie and Bobby to wait downstairs. While he searches for some pants and a robe to put on he tells Naja again that this meeting will only take a minute. He splashes some cold water on his face and before he goes downstairs he tells Naja that he is going to close the door behind him and he wants her to stay in the bedroom. In fact, he wants her to just stay in the bed.

"You look like shit," is the first thing Eddie says to Carl when he gets downstairs.

Carl says, "I was out partying last night, you guys woke me up."

Eddie asks, "Did you bring someone home? Is there anyone else here?"

"No, just me."

"We have a lot to do today, so what's this all about?"

"It's about you insisting on putting your company on the closing statement."

"I told you, I had to. Viking wanted to make sure the money would be where I said it would."

"That's bullshit. They were fine with the way we handled the down payment and the transport fees. Why don't you just admit it, it was all about the Eddie Roberts ego."

Before Eddie can respond, Bobby says, "I don't want to be here any longer than I have to, so why don't the two of you get to it so we can leave."

Carl explains, "Any changes to the closing statement is exactly the type of thing Pete will notice and ask about. I just want us to go over our story so we're on the same page." Then the three of them hear something large hit the floor. The sound comes from upstairs.

Eddie says, "I thought you said we're alone."

"Don't worry about her, she's no . . ." Before Carl can finish his sentence Eddie slams his fist into the left side of Carl's head, sending him crashing into his refrigerator and then falling to the floor. Eddie has wanted to do that for a long time. Carl gave him a reason and Eddie seized the opportunity.

12:30pm - The two sisters were close their entire lives. Even when Evelyn, William's mother, married Perrigold, William's father, Ernestine and Evelyn never strayed far from one another. Ernestine was at Evelyn and Perrigold's house so often, the three of them developed a skit that William and Denise, his younger sister, loved to hear. Perrigold would come home and find Ernestine and Evelyn talking in the kitchen and he'd say, "You're still here!?! I feel like I married both of you but I'm only getting the benefits from one." Each time Perrigold delivered his lines the sisters, in unison, would say, "Oh shut up Perry." Neither William nor Denise really understood the joke until they got older, but they found it funnier each time the adults performed it nonetheless.

Perrigold was the love of Evelyn's life and she was the love of his. Everyone who knew Perrigold, including Ernestine, loved him and had nothing but respect for him. No one, however, loved Perrigold as much as William. His father was his idol. He walked like his father, he talked like his father, and to hear him speak of his father would leave one with the impression that Perrigold could walk on water. So, it was particularly hard on William when Perrigold passed away, but his mom and Aunt Ernestine kept Perrigold's memory and spirit alive in William every day.

Ernestine was fifty five years old when she began to lose her sight from her battle with diabetes. At the same time, Evelyn was battling breast cancer. By the time Evelyn succumbed to the disease Ernestine was blind. Despite her affliction Ernestine was by her sister's side every day during her final days. When Evelyn sensed that the end of her Earthly journey was near she said goodbye to William and goodbye to Denise, and then she asked to be alone so she could speak with Ernestine. The doctors, the nurses, William, Denise, and a few other family members watched, through the window to Evelyn's room, as the sisters held hands and talked to each other. When want needed to be said was said, Ernestine kissed her sister on the forehead and Evelyn stopped fighting. The doctors and the nurses rushed in to resuscitate her, but Ernestine told them that her sister was ready and she asked them to let her go.

From that day to this and into the future for as long as she lives, Ernestine has and will fulfill her promise to her sister. Namely, she'll keep the memory of their parents and the spirit of their family alive in both of her kids. Denise has since moved to New Mexico. She's married now with three kids. She and her family are doing well. William, on the other hand, now sits in front of her devastated, hurt, and confused. First things first though. Aunt Ernestine won't allow William to get into what drove him there today until he has had something to eat. Together they prepare a hearty breakfast for William. While he eats Ernestine sits across from him at her kitchen table sipping tea. Along with the alcohol Ernestine can smell, as it evaporates off his skin, she can also feel pain and confusion coming from William. Now that his belly is full, Ernestine asks, "What's eating away at you Little Perry?" That's Ernestine's nickname for William. He tells her about his job, his two nights of drinking, and of how much he misses Genny. Finally, he tells her of what he's thinking of doing. Ernestine can't hide the fact that she thinks it's a bad idea. She sites all of the reasons William is already familiar with. Namely, if he's right he'll be dealing with people who are far more ruthless than he'll ever be. William listens to her words and advice but he doesn't hear her. Nothing she says makes him feel better. In fact, he feels worse. Ernestine tries a different tactic. She likens what he's thinking of doing to someone on safari who gets out of the truck so he can get a better view of that pride of lions, in the distance, staring at him. This time Ernestine's words sink in. They discuss it a little more until William finally admits, out loud, that nothing she has said makes him feel any different. Ernestine finally gets a sense of what's really going on with William, so she says, "Let me tell you a little story your mother told me about your father. When Perry was sixteen years old he took twenty five dollars to the bank to open his first bank account. Somewhere during that transaction the lady who was helping him said something that offended him. Now, you know your father. It took a lot to get under his skin. No one remembers what she said exactly but it was enough to make Perry demand an apology. The lady refused to apologize and the bank manager refused to make her apologize, so Perry took a seat at that ladies desk determined to sit there until she did. The bank manager forced him to move so that lady could help other customers, so Perry took a seat in the waiting area. He sat there all day until the bank was closing and, even then he refused to leave. The security guard, literally, picked Perry up and threw him out of the bank. Your father went home that night with a cut on his forehead and with bruises and cuts on his hands. The next day, at 9:00am sharp, Perry walked back into the bank and took a seat in the waiting area. During the day the manager tried to convince Perry to leave and so did the security guard, but Perry wouldn't leave without an apology. They even called the police. Once they heard Perry's story the police determined he wasn't breaking any laws. They tried to convince the lady, and the manager, to apologize and be done with it, but neither of them would. At the end of the day, the security guard again, literally, picked up Perry and threw him out of the bank. The next day, at 9:00am sharp, Perry walked into the bank and took a seat in the waiting area. That went on for seven days until the manager forced the lady to apologize. Listen, I'm going to be worried about you because I don't want to see you wrestling with lions but, on the other hand, David did slay Goliath. I guess what I'm trying to say is I love you, and I want you to be smart and take care of yourself, but if this is something you have to do, then do it."

1:00pm - "I'm not worried about him," says Eddie as he merges into the westbound traffic on the 10 Freeway headed to Santa Monica and back to the precinct. "There's nothing he can do to hurt me now." Bobby says, "I still don't think you should have hit him, and, by the way, there's plenty he can do to hurt you."

"No there isn't. Now that I'm on the settlement statement my money comes directly to me. He may be a coke addicted spoiled rich boy, but he isn't stupid. Anything he can think of doing to me will hurt him twice as much at the end of the day. Believe me, our business association is effectively over and done with."

Bobby asks, "Who's the Pete he's talking about?"

"Pete Jefferson."

"The Pete Jefferson?"

"Yeah."

Bobby asks, "How is Pete Jefferson mixed up in all of this? And, why is Carl worried about Pete finding out that the two of you know each other?"

Eddie looks over his right shoulder and merges right preparing to get off at Lincoln. He also takes a moment to take a good look at Bobby. Then he says, "You know what I need you to do? I need you to stop worrying. You already know more than you need to know, and you blame me for your stress. Stop worrying about me and Carl and don't think about Pete. Carl doesn't even have a reason to worry about Pete. Me and Pete are not going to meet. I don't need to meet Pete and I don't want to meet Pete. That's the drugs scrambling Carl's thinking." Now, Eddie pulls into his parking space at the precinct. He turns off the car but before he and Bobby get out he tells Bobby, "Just find a way to relax. Take the money and do something nice for yourself and that wife of yours. Everything is going as planned. Don't worry about anything."

The two of them get out of the car and walk towards the building. Another detective is on his way to his car. When he sees Eddie and Bobby he shouts across the parking garage, "Hey, Captain Upton is looking for the two of you. I think he has an ID on your dump truck victim."

2:00pm - More and more these days Russell finds himself reflecting on the decades of work he's put in. He thinks of all the murder cases, the corruption scandals, the rape cases, the DUIs, the burglaries, the robberies, and the arsons, all of it. He's been around the block enough to know that he hasn't seen everything. He thinks about how many times he's had that thought only to be surprised by some new low, more often than not, the very next day. He leans back in his chair and looks at the walls in his office. He surrounded by plaques and awards he's won, and by pictures and newspaper clippings of stories he's worked on, some of which were resolved and others weren't. Sometimes he's at a loss for what it all means, and this is one of those times. Truth be told, the fire that used to burn in his gut is no longer as strong as it used to be. Sure, he's done some wonderful things. At the top of that list is helping the police find Sigmund Becker's murderers and the subsequent bond he's developed with Lisa and Gita. If there's one bright spot in his decades of work, it isn't the plaques, the awards, or the commendations. It's Lisa. She's as close as he's ever come to having a child of his own and at this point she's as close as he'll ever get. He can't help but wonder, sometimes, how different his life would have been if he chose to do something else. There certainly wouldn't have been Lisa, but maybe he would have married again and had kids of his own. Maybe his point of view wouldn't be as cynical as it is. Maybe he would have seen more beautiful things and not so much death, crime, and corruption. Thirty years ago he would have never thought this way. Thirty years ago he was a lot like Lisa is today, a crime fighting avenger. He thinks to himself that he's just being silly. He loves his work, there's absolutely no doubt about that. Still, that doesn't change the fact that he's having "what if" thoughts more and more these days.

As he usually does when feels this way, he snaps himself out of it and gets back to work. As he sits up and pulls his chair closer to his desk, preparing to get back to writing, a call comes in. It's his contact in the LAPD returning his call. The two of them chitchat for a minute and then Russell explains why he called. His contact takes the information and promises to get back to Russell as soon as he can. After they hang up Russell is confronted with mixed emotions. On one hand, he's excited for Lisa. Every time he thinks about her wanting to follow in his footsteps, he feels so blessed from the love and admiration she's given him all of these years. She's right, if there's a good story to be told here, it's great that she was the first one on the scene. It's great that she made contact with the investigating detectives. She's making all the right moves to further her budding career. Despite his objections, if he can help her, in any way, he'll certainly do that. On the other hand, given his concerns, for the first time in his entire career he's hoping his contact comes up empty.

2:30pm - Traveling south on the 101 Freeway, during the middle of the day, is always a bit of a pain. Being stuck in traffic has always been one of Abbey's pet peeves, but traffic is moving. Albeit at a crawl but, at least, it's moving. The slow pace is giving her time to reflect on the unbelievable morning she's just experienced. She always feels renewed when she's reminded that anything is possible. Everything about this morning is proof that if you have a dream, and if you don't take no for an answer, somehow, some way, you'll get to yes. Who would have thought that Marguerite Best would have achieved the things she has. By her own admission, not even Marguerite Best thought that she could or that she would. And, who would have thought that Pete, a guy who came to this country with nothing, would be in a position to donate twenty five million dollars to a charity. As for herself, she has to admit there were days when she was crippled with self-doubt. Everyone told her she was crazy to give up acting to own a tiny title and escrow company. Even though she had success immediately, there were lean years that made her wonder if she did the right thing. Still, she stuck with it and because she did she got a few lucky breaks here and there. Now, she couldn't be happier with her choices and with her career. Days like today are more than inspirational. They are like God or the Universe telling her that she's right where she's supposed to be.

Speaking of being right where she's supposed to be, she isn't. She should have been back at her office by now, but what was a crawl has now become a standstill, and despite the positivity of the morning, traffic is now a buzz kill that's starting to get on her nerves. It's time to stop reflecting and get back to work. When she calls her office, she asks Dylan, the receptionist, to put her through to Julia, her assistant.

"So, how was it?" asks Julia.

Abbey says, "It was truly unbelievable. I'll tell you more about it when I get back. By the way, put Marguerite Best's name on the list of possible speakers for the next Women In Business Conference." Julia says, "OK, I will."

Looking down in the passenger seat Abbey realizes there is something she can tell Julia, right now, that will make her happy. "I'm bringing a box of pastries back to the office."

"Did they have my favorite?" Abbey knows there a few things in this world that makes Julia happier more than chocolate does. And she knows that Julia's weakness is chocolate chocolate chip muffins.

"When I saw them I grabbed two for you."

"You're the best boss I've ever had."

Abbey smiles and asks, "What's going on there?" Julia fills Abbey in on the day's events. As usual, there's a problem here and there, one closing has been postponed, and another has been confirmed. In other words, besides the fact that this is a particularly busy week, it's all par for the course.

Regarding the Forest Canyon Mall closing, everything remains on track and, thankfully, there's no new developments there except, "I have the information you asked for," Julia tells Abbey.

Abbey says, "Excellent. I want you to tell me what you've learned now and I want you to email it to me right away."

Pete is having better luck with traffic. He has a meeting in Santa Monica so his driver took Kanan Dune Road over the mountains and now they are driving south on Pacific Coast Highway. He too is on the phone with his office, but he's taking part in a conference call with a couple of people from his office and a couple of people from a brokerage firm in Phoenix, Arizona. When his cell phone rings he interrupts the conference call to say, "Excuse me guys, I have to take another call. Keep discussing the deal, I'll rejoin the call in a minute." He picks up the call coming into his cell. "Hey, what's going on?" Abbey asks, "Are you busy?"

Pete says, "Yeah, I'm on a conference call."

"OK, I'll be quick. I'll also email this information to you as soon as I get back to my office. I have the information you asked me to get. The owner of the 24th Street, LLC is a man named Edward H. Roberts. I'll send you his address and his other information in the email. I just wanted you to know that I have what you asked for. By the way, Mr. Roberts is a Homicide Detective for the LAPD, Santa Monica Division."

Pete says, "Interesting. Thanks for getting that so quickly. I'll check in with you later."

Before Pete rejoins the conference call he thinks to himself, "A homicide detective? Why would Carl be transferring two and a half million dollars to a homicide detective?" Unable to come up with a plausible explanation right away, Pete decides to give it some thought later. He pushes the mute button and says, "OK guys, I'm back. What have I missed?"

3:00pm - Javier knows it's a long shot, but he can't escape the thought that maybe there's something he missed. That's what has driven him back to Teddy's apartment. As he enters the apartment he's hit, again, with the stench of a dead body, but, at least, it's a little less pungent than it was yesterday. There isn't much to look at or go through in the living room, nor in the kitchen, nor in the bathroom, so he walks directly to the bedroom. He begins by searching through Teddy's clothing. He goes through the pockets of every item of clothing he finds in Teddy's dresser draws and closets. He finds nothing. Then he goes through every item on the shelves above the hanging clothes in Teddy's closets. The drug paraphernalia: the shoe box with three small scales, the two boxes of zip lock bags, the zip lock bags with trace amounts of marijuana in them, and the aluminum foil with what appeared to be a trace amount of cocaine in it, were all collected when the body was discovered. What's left are several old pairs of sneakers and shoes, some hats, some books, some Playboy and Hustler magazines, and some feature film and some porn DVDs. Javier goes through each of them but, still, there's nothing of any significance found in or among any of them. Javier is feeling a little discouraged. That Teddy overdosed isn't hard to believe, and if that is the case, then there won't be any signs of an intruder. So far, that explanation is consistent with what's been found in his apartment, and consistent with what he knows of and with what he has found out about Teddy. The nagging feeling that causes Javier to push on comes from the fact that Teddy was linked to Geneviève Flowers and now they are both dead. William told Javier about Geneviève's former relationship with a gentleman named Teddy Gallo, but he also mentioned that it ended years before he met Geneviève and he had no reason to believe that the two of them were in contact. Javier's investigation supported that. After he went through Geneviève's emails and cell phone records there was no evidence that she and Teddy were in contact with each other. He didn't pursue that lead any further than that. Javier thinks to himself maybe that's why he's here. Maybe he should have tried to speak with Teddy when he had the chance. Maybe that's it. Maybe his guilt is the source of the nagging feeling he's having. The only thing left in the room to go through is the small three drawer dresser next to Teddy's bed. The bottom drawer is filled with extension cords and phone recharger wires. The middle drawer is empty because more drug selling supplies were found there and already collected. So, Javier only goes through the top drawer, which is filled with scraps of paper. All of his receipts and anything that had a name or a telephone number on it has already been collected, but there a bunch of random pieces of paper left in the drawer. Javier went through each one. There is nothing there that will be helpful. There is something, however, that he didn't see yesterday. In one of the folded pieces of paper are two tickets to a Dodgers game from last season. The date of the game strikes Javier but not for investigative purposes, rather for personal reasons. Javier remembers that game. The Dodgers were down by three in the bottom of the ninth. They had three men on base, two outs, and the count against the hitter was three and two. On the eight pitch of the at bat the Dodgers won the game with a walk off grand slam. It was great. Javier remembers this game because he was there with his son and that was a great game and a great day the two of them shared. The memory gives Javier pause. He was at the same game he assumes Teddy and probably a friend of his were at as well. Again, he is amazed by the human theater. It baffles him that people can be so alike and so different. At least now he feels better about not following up on the Teddy lead. It's obvious to him that Geneviève's death and Teddy's death are completely unrelated. Now, he's satisfied that it's just a coincidence.

As he takes one last look around the room he hears someone knock on the front door. Javier walks to the front door and looks through the peephole. He can't see the face of the person on the other side because he has his head down and he's trying to jiggle the door open. Javier takes a step back and draws his firearm. He waits for the person to try the door again and then in one move he unlocks the door and swings it open, keeping his gun drawn and pointed at the person on the other side. The person on the other side is too surprised to speak and it takes Javier a second to realize who it is. Javier asks, "William, what the hell are you doing here?"

4:00pm - Eddie and Bobby are sitting in Captain Upton's office taking notes as the Captain gives them updates on the various cases and assignments they are working on. Finally, the Captain gets to their most recent case. He tells them the dump truck victim's name is David Waverly. His identity is confirmed through his fingerprints, which match those of a David Waverly from Colorado Springs, Colorado where he was arrested for drug possession four years ago. Pursuant to his DMV records, his current address is on Clarissa Avenue in Los Feliz. While in Bobby's and the Captain's presence Eddie pretends to be pleased that a positive ID came up for their victim. In truth, he's furious that the victim was so easily identified. While he carries on his conversation with Bobby and the Captain, he's thinking that he can't wait to speak with Breck to find out what went wrong. He told Breck that he wasn't to use someone with a record so many times Breck literally said, "You don't have to repeat yourself so many times. I'm not an idiot." Well, it turns out he is an idiot and, what's worse, Eddie is in bed with him. Eddie tries to calm himself down by remembering that the link between David and Breck is certainly dead. If Breck carried out the rest of the plan successfully, his body has already been found, and it won't matter if an ID is made on him. Even when it is, it will take an overly ambitious detective to tie the two together. The chance of that happening is unlikely, not because there's a lack of overly ambitious detectives. Rather, with the number of cases the department has to handle, murder cases of convicted felons often go unsolved so detectives can focus their energy and limited resources on solving cases of law abiding citizens. Still, he's furious with Breck but, given the big picture, nothing has really changed. After the meeting breaks Eddie and Bobby discuss going to David Waverly's last known address to see what they can turn up. Before they can come to a decision about that, Eddie tells Bobby he needs to make a few phone calls. Bobby has a few things he needs to do as well so they agree to circle back to the idea in thirty minutes.

Breck is completely unaware of the time. His best guess is he checked in around 7:00pm and played until 1:00am. He took a nap to catch up on some sleep and to sleep off his drunk. Then he went back to the tables. He has no idea how long he slept, he has no idea when he got back to the tables, and he has no idea what time it is now. All he knows is he's up two thousand dollars, he has a nice buzz on, and he wants to keep both things going. The river card is the ace of spades. That's exactly what Breck didn't need. That ace pairs with his ace, but with four spades showing, and with only the five of spades in his hand, he has to fold. If he had gotten any other ace he would have stayed in and the chances were good that the pot of thirty five hundred dollars would have been his. Not to mention, that was the pot amount before the last round of betting. That's lost now along with the five hundred dollars he put into the pot. Now, he's only up fifteen hundred dollars. As he watches the last round of betting his cell phone vibrates. It's Eddie. Breck figures this is as good as time as any to take a break. He tells the dealer he'll be right back, and he excuses himself from the table to take Eddie's call.

"What the hell are you doing in San Diego?" asks Eddie.

Breck replies, "What do you care. I did what I had to do. By the time you get to Costa Rica, I'll be there."

"They ID'd the kid."

Breck asks, "What are you talking about?"

"What? Am I not speaking English? We have a name and an address for the kid. Now, I have to investigate."

"So what, it's you who's doing the investigating. That's exactly why I used Ronny, and he isn't going to talk to with anybody ever again."

"That's not the point. The plan was not to use anybody with a record. We went over that a million times. Next you were supposed to get rid of Ronny and then get out of the country. I'll tell you what, keep playing cards. Enjoy yourself. I'm coming down there right now. When I get there I'm packing you up and then I'm putting you on the plane myself."

5:00pm - Javier had enough of the stench and the whiff William got when Javier opened the door was enough for him, so they moved their impromptu meeting to the sidewalk in front of the building. Javier explains, "Of course I would have told you, especially if I uncovered a link between the two deaths. Let's get back to why you're here."

"From what you've said I am here for the same reason you are, except I expected to talk with Teddy." "So now you're investigating your wife's homicide?"

"I would have preferred to leave it to the professionals but . . . that didn't come out the way I meant it. I know you've done what you could. And I appreciate that you're here today following up on your gut feeling. I have that same gut feeling and, like you, I needed to do something about it."

"I can't condone you taking part of an official investigation. The case is still open and, obviously, I'm working on it. If you have any additional information I need you to give it to me and let me do the work."

"I don't need you to condone anything I do and I'm not breaking any laws by asking questions. Think about it. Here we are, in the same place, at the same time, for the same reason."

"That doesn't prove anything."

"You're wrong. The two men who care the most about Genny's murder independently came up with the same suspicion. Where there's smoke there's fire. Maybe we need to learn more about Teddy. Who were his friends? Where was he working? We can talk to his neighbors. We can talk to anybody and everybody who knew him. Maybe we can turn up something."

"There won't be a 'we,' but I'm open to talking with you more about this. I've had a long day and I'm going home after this. Can you meet me at the precinct in the morning at 10:00am?"

"Yeah. I can meet you there at 10:00am."

"Good, I'll see you in the morning. Until then don't do anything." The two men shake hands and go their separate ways.

As he walks back to his car William feels a sense of excitement that's almost foreign to him. It's been a long time since he's felt excited about anything. He's sad about Teddy's death for two reasons. First, he isn't harboring any ill will towards Teddy, so the news of his death is saddening. Of course, that will change if it turns out that he had anything to do with Genny's death, but, for today, that's where he stands. Second, and more importantly, now he can't speak with Teddy. Still, William feels alive, and excited, and filled with a sense of purpose because Javier had the same feeling he had. That may mean very little to Javier, but to William that means everything.

6:00pm - There hasn't been a homicide in Cardiff-by-the-Sea in over ten years. Even then it was adjudicated as a negligent homicide, a grossly irresponsible accident. Cardiff, as it is known by the locals, is about two hours south of Los Angeles and about a half an hour north of San Diego. It's a small, quiet, utopian beach and surfing community. So, it is no surprise that the talk of the town is about the car that was set on fire in the parking lot just off Orinda Drive and the dead body found in the trunk.

The brothers and sisters have made it a tradition to have dinner with each other, at one house or the other, once a week. Tonight Steven Silva, the town's medical examiner and his wife, Stella, are having dinner at Dominic and Rebecca's house. Dominic Silva is Steven's older brother and the town's Sheriff; and Rebecca is Dominic's wife and Stella's twin sister. While Rebecca and Stella are putting the finishing touches on dinner, Dominic and Steven continue their conversation as they set the table. Dominic says, "Clearly the car was set on fire to destroy evidence. We found out today that the car is a rental from a Budget Car Rental based in Burbank. It was reported stolen two days ago."

Steven says, "I'm 95% sure the gunshot to the back of the victim's head is the cause of death. Did you find anything that could identify the victim?"

"No, we found remnants of a wallet in the victim's back pocket, but it and everything in it was burned to almost complete destruction. There wasn't anything else in the car that appeared to be personal property."

"Do you think it could have been someone from town in the trunk of that car?"

"I don't think so. No one has been reported missing. I think who-ever it turns out to be was killed in Los Angeles and driven here. I still don't know why someone would drive the body here of all places. That doesn't make any sense to me. Right now my only guess is the killer drove the car here, and he or she is either still in town or they got another car and took off. No one has reported that their car has been stolen, so I'm thinking they had a car here or they rented one; and I guess it's possible that a third party could have followed them in a different car and driven the killer back to Los Angeles or wherever he or she wanted to go. Tomorrow I'll have a list of all the car rentals that went out yesterday from the surrounding neighborhoods, maybe that will lead to someone."

"I think you are going to have a bunch of nervous residents on your hands, especially if everyone thinks the killer is still in town."

"You might be right. I'll tell everyone to keep their eyes open but I really don't think the killer is here. "Do you think you'll be able to identify the victim, if we can't?"

"If you can't match his dental records we'll have to rely on DNA, but that could take weeks, even months, and it's possible we could come up with nothing."

Before the brothers can go any further Rebecca comes out of the kitchen and says, "OK boys remember, there's no talking about dead people during dinner and dinner is served."

8:00pm - The altercation Carl had with Eddie earlier in the day was both a curse and a blessing. It was a curse because it exposed Carl's true feelings for Eddie, namely he's afraid of him. Ten years ago, when he needed him, Carl was happy he came through with the money. He knew almost immediately, however, that his over excitement led him to making a lopsided deal with the detective. Over the years, as the value of his investment grew, Carl grew angrier over the amount he promised to give to Eddie. Carl had no way of knowing his investment would balloon the way it did. Now, based on their agreement Carl owes Eddie two and a half million dollars. It was a blessing because it sobered Carl up. He had totally forgotten that he had a date with Debra Carr tonight.

Debra Carr is the only daughter of Reginald Carr, the automotive entrepreneur and philanthropist. The Carr family's net worth is estimated to be between nine hundred million dollars and one billion dollars. Carl met Debra at her father's annual Polo Match for Charity. She was attracted to him immediately. He found her attractive but not necessarily his cup of tea. That is, until he found out who she is. Then he thought of her as extremely attractive and he hatched his plan to marry her to get at her money. They have been dating for almost a year, and so far he's been able to hide his extracurricular activities. At some point he knows he'll have to give them up. His thinking is with the money he gets from the Forest Canyon Mall deal he'll have enough to impress Debra's father, who, as of now, only sees Carl as just another one of Debra's boyfriends. His plan is to squeeze in a few more nights of cocaine and hookers, and then he'll sober up and close what he calls the Carr deal.

As soon as Carl learned that Debra's favorite restaurant in Los Angeles is Mr. Chow's in Beverly Hills he made it his mission to get to know everyone there. Now, he's just as well-known as any of the captains of industry or celebrities that eat at Chow's regularly. When the two of them pull up for dinner tonight they are greeted warmly by the valets. Carl holds the door open for Debra and the two of them go in. Estelle, the gorgeous Maître D, says, "Mr. Davies and Ms. Carr, it's so nice to see the two you again. Will it be just the two of you for dinner tonight?"

Carl says, "It's nice to see you too. Yes, just the two of us, but I didn't make a reservation. Will that be a problem?"

Carl knew the answer to his question before he asked it. He's already eaten here several times without Debra, and each time he's gone out of his way to spread the wealth around enough to have earned elite status. In short, he knows he doesn't need a reservation at Chow's to be seated and that is an impressive sign of status to be played out for Debra to see. Estelle answers, "We are booked solid tonight but we can always find a way to make room for you. Just give me a minute or two to see what I can do."

As if on cue Debra demonstrates her appreciation by spinning Carl around so she can look into his eyes and give him a quick kiss. After the kiss Carl looks over Debra's right shoulder and makes eye contact with Miguel, the bartender. Carl holds two fingers in the air. Miguel waves hello and nods in acknowledgment of the request. Two fingers means two apple martinis stat. Miguel knows as long as he keeps them coming quickly, flavorful, and strong he will be rewarded handsomely. Estelle returns and says, "We're in luck. I will have a table ready for you momentarily. Would you like to order a drink while you wait?"

"I already have. Will you bring them brought to our table after we're seated?"

"Of course."

On their way to their table Estelle and Debra walk ahead of Carl. He hears Estelle compliment Debra on her shoes and her handbag, which is right up Debra's alley. Debra is a serious woman. She doesn't take her family's wealth lightly. She doesn't work for money because she doesn't need to. Instead, she works tirelessly on behalf of two charities. She is completely dedicated to the fight against breast cancer and she is completely dedicated to children. Whether the fight is against homelessness, starvation, or a lack of educational opportunities, no one has to ask Debra twice before she finds a way to give of her time and her money. Still, when she isn't doing charity work she is just as dedicated to her other true passion, fashion. She has a room in her house that is entirely devoted to her collection of shoes and handbags. So, when Carl heard Estelle compliment Debra on both he knew dinner had gotten off to a perfect start. On the way to their table Carl passes a friend of his who is having dinner with his family. Carl stops briefly to shake hands and say hi before he turns to join Debra, who is already seated and talking with the two gentlemen at the table next to theirs. He takes one step towards Debra and then stops to collect himself. The same thing happened several months ago when he came to Chow's to have lunch with a friend. At that time it was a pleasant surprise and a stroke of luck because he was able to overhear their conversation, which set in motion the unpleasant but necessary event. This deja vu, however, will be awkward at best. As he approaches their table Debra, thinking it will make Carl happy, is delighted to point out who they are lucky enough to be sitting next to. It's Pete Jefferson and little does Debra know that his guest is the same man Pete was having lunch with, several months ago, when coincidentally Carl was seated next to them.

9:00pm - The Sycuan Golf Resort and Casino is a beautiful and plush property located in the Dehesa Valley, about 40 miles east of downtown San Diego. The hotel is situated on the golf course so that every room has a view of the magnificent fairways and greens. The casino is just a short shuttle ride away from the hotel. The casino is huge and spacious and it features almost every game a gambler might want to play. It took Eddie and Bobby a few minutes to find Breck. By the time they did he is up three thousand dollars and he's still winning, so he refuses to get up from the table.

The whole ride down to San Diego was done in near silence except for the radio. Bobby insisted on coming along as soon as he figured out that Eddie's trip had something to do with that thing he knows about. Though Eddie claims otherwise, it is clear to Bobby that his plan is coming apart and now Bobby is more worried than he's ever been. He doesn't want to know any more than he already knows, which is good because Eddie feels he knows too much already, but if putting Breck on an airplane out of the country is the thing that has to happen next, Bobby wants to be there to make sure that it does. Eddie, on the other hand, had nothing to say during the ride south because he can't stop thinking about killing Breck. During the drive he fantasized about killing Breck right there in San Diego. That would solve two problems. First, Breck is one of two people left alive that can tie him to Geneviève Flower's murder. So, killing him would mean that Eddie was that much closer to getting away with it. Second, Eddie wouldn't have to pay Breck for his services. The amount he owes Breck isn't significant given the whole, but it is significant enough that Eddie would rather keep it. Now that Bobby has insisted on coming along there's no way he can kill Breck. Truthfully, he wouldn't have done it in San Diego anyway. That's far too risky, especially when he can wait a week, and figure out a way to kill him in Costa Rica. There it will be easier to dispose of the body and his chances of getting away with it are much greater.

"Breck, come on, let's go. You're going to make us late," pleads Eddie.

Breck plays along, "We have plenty of time. Let me play a few more hands."

Eddie and Bobby are standing over Breck trying to coax him away from the table. Neither of them want to draw too much attention to themselves so they ask, he refuses, and then they back away for a hand or two before they ask again. That goes on for forty minutes until Breck finally agrees to leave. Finally, they escort Breck to the car and they make the short drive to the hotel. Once they get to Breck's room the conversation opens up, but even then there isn't much detail discussed because Bobby's present. Besides there isn't much for them to discuss anyway. What's done is done and there's no use complaining about it. Now what needs to be done is to get back to the plan and that means getting Breck out of the country. It isn't easy to corral Breck and get him to pack because he has been drinking and, more than that, he still doesn't want to leave. When Bobby has had enough of the gamesmanship happening between Eddie and Breck he takes it upon himself to start packing Breck's things. That was what it took to get Breck to accept his fate and stop dragging his feet. While Breck packs, Bobby excuses himself to use the bathroom.

Daniel Alexander

Once he's behind the closed and locked door he unbuttons his collar and splashes cold water on his face. He doesn't need to use the bathroom, he's just trying not to pass out. He started feeling faint while they were standing over Breck in the casino. He could have taken off his suit jacket then, but that would have exposed how much he's sweating. Now, behind the closed door he does take off his jacket and he sees he has sweated so much his shirt is almost drenched. The splash of cold water has helped so he does that again and then he sits on the edge of the bathtub with his head between his knees, hoping this wave of nausea will pass quickly. Now that he's out of the room he can hear Eddie and Breck engage in a heated argument but he tries not to focus on that. Right now, he just needs to stop feeling dizzy. He splashes some more cold water on his face and neck and he sits there until Breck knocks on the door. He wants to come in so he can get his toiletries, the last things he needs to pack and then he'll be ready to leave. Bobby tells Breck to give him a minute. Another minute is all he needs. The cold water and the time sitting down has helped. Bobby feels strong enough to stand. He still feels a little dizzy, but he feels a lot better than he felt just five minutes ago. He puts his suit jacket back on and straightens himself out as best he can. When he comes out of the bathroom Breck goes in to collect his stuff. Eddie asks Bobby if he's alright and Bobby tells him that he's fine. He says his stomach is just a little upset probably because of the fish he had for lunch. Breck has finally packed everything and the three of them leave.

Eddie, Breck, and Bobby make it to the American Airlines terminal at SAN just in time for Breck to buy a boarding pass for the 11:55pm flight to Panama City, Panama. From there he'll catch a connecting flight that will get him into San Jose, Costa Rica at

124

9:30am. Eddie and Bobby flash their badges and pass through the security check point to accompany Breck to the gate. During the walk from the check point to the gate Bobby starts to feel nauseous again. This time the sweat is impossible to hide because he is sweating not only from his torso but also from his forehead. Luckily, Eddie and Breck don't notice because they are walking ahead of him and they are engaged in another heated conversation. By the time they get to the gate Bobby needs to sit down. He takes a seat in the waiting area while Eddie and Breck check in. Just as the ticket agent tells Breck that the flight is scheduled to leave on time, but he'll need to wait before she knows whether she can upgrade his seat, the noise of a small commotion comes from the waiting area directly behind them. They turn around to find Bobby lying face down on the floor and unconscious.

10:00pm - William's suite at the Copenhagen looks like a bomb hit it. There are open boxes on the counters and on the table in the kitchen. There are open boxes on the floor and on the couch in the living room; and there are three open suitcases on the floor and on the bed in the bedroom. Though he's been living at the Copenhagen for almost three months now, until tonight he hasn't had the desire nor the strength to unpack anything. Since his talk with Aunt Ernestine he has tapped into a source of energy. Running into Javier has also provided him with a boost. After he had dinner he couldn't sit still. He thought of going out for a walk. Maybe, he thought, it would be relaxing to walk up and down the 3rd Street Promenade and watch a performer or two. He entertained the idea of seeing a movie. Instead he chose to unpack his belongings and try to rejoin the world of the living. While he unpacks his mind is racing a mile a minute about the connection between Genny and Teddy. In an attempt to organize his thoughts, he calms himself down and starts from the beginning.

How did Genny and Teddy meet in the first place and what did she see in him? It's been a while since they talked about Teddy but to the best of William's recollection the two of them met at a party in Hollywood. Genny had come to the States twice before for modeling gigs, but when she met Teddy she had just moved to Los Angeles permanently. William remembers her telling him that she found Teddy handsome and he seemed like a fun guy. While she didn't consider their relationship exclusive she wasn't seeing anyone else and neither was Teddy. William remembers Genny telling him that Teddy was a struggling actor, but that he had done a few national commercials so he had money coming in. Next he remembers that Genny discovered that Teddy was also selling drugs to make money. She confronted him and he denied it at first, but eventually he confessed that he was selling, what he called, harmless drugs: marijuana, xanax, ecstasy, and small amounts of cocaine; and for the most part he was only selling the drugs to his friends. She said that's when she started to lose respect for Teddy but she continued to see him. Next he remembers her telling him that a couple of months later Teddy disappeared for three days. When she finally heard from him he confessed that he had been arrested for possession and he was in jail, but he assured her it was all a mistake. As proof that it was a mistake he told her he walked away from the arrest without any further jail time and even without any probation. Still, she stayed with him until it became apparent to her that Teddy was smoking marijuana more regularly, and as a result he was relying less on acting and more on selling drugs to make money. He remembers

Genny saying that it took her so long to discover Teddy's other life because other than smoking marijuana, she never saw Teddy do any other drug. She never saw him take a pill other than aspirin and she definitely never saw him do any cocaine. She said she never saw him looking like he had done any of those things either. In fact, even though his weed consumption was at an all-time high by the end of their relationship, she was confident that other than for the purpose of selling, he avoided drugs. That thought causes William to stop unpacking and think for a minute. Does a guy who smokes weed eventually overdose on heroin? Maybe. In truth, all he knows about Teddy is what Genny told him and she, obviously, didn't know everything. When he thinks of someone who overdoses on heroin he pictures an addict. It's possible that Teddy could have become an addict. It's also possible that he could have overdosed the first time he tried it. That happens too.

The last time they saw Teddy was over a year ago. They ran into him in the street. He was with his new girlfriend, who was very attractive, and they seemed happy to be together. After some small talk the two couples went their separate ways. Genny told William that Teddy was obviously still smoking weed, but William remembers thinking he looked OK to him. Maybe he just wasn't paying attention. That was the last time they saw or spoke about Teddy. William thinks maybe he is grasping at straws. Maybe Javier is right. Maybe it is just a coincidence. If the person who murdered Genny had taken anything maybe he could find a way to think differently. There was plenty to take but he took nothing, and, more than that, he left him alive. William thinks that the murderer could have easily finished him off but he didn't. He killed Genny and then he left. William would think that he's crazy if it weren't for his gut feeling. In the face of absolutely no evidence, somehow he's sure that Genny was murdered for a reason. William thinks to himself that if he isn't crazy now he will drive himself crazy with all of these thoughts. He's had enough of unpacking for now. It's late. The stores are probably closed or closing and most of the street performers are probably wrapped up for the day, but he still can't sit still and he's certainly not ready for bed. He decides to take that walk anyway.

11:00pm - By the time the ambulance arrived Bobby was drenched in sweat but he was conscious and sitting up. While the emergency medical technicians were putting Bobby on a stretcher Eddie made sure Breck understood that he better board his flight, and he instructed Breck to call him when he lands in Costa Rica. The ambulance took Bobby to UC San Diego Medical Center and Eddie followed them there.

Abasiama Martins is the newest and brightest star of the UC San Diego Medical Center's staff and personnel. Abasiama was born in Lagos, Nigeria. He is the second son of Boseda and Adanya Martins, both medical doctors themselves. As a child Abasiama had visions of himself as a midfielder for the Super Eagles, Nigeria's National Football Team. He had posters on every wall in his room. He had posters of the 1994 team, who won the Africa Cup of Nations and then went on to become the first Nigerian National Team to play in the World Cup. He had posters of the 1996 team that won the gold medal in the Summer Olympic Games in Atlanta. And, he had posters of Rashidi Yekini, Austin "Jay Jay" Okocha, and Nwankwo "Papillo" Kanu, his favorite players. Though he excelled in school, football was his passion. If he wasn't studying, he was playing football. He held on to that dream until he left Lagos for London to attend the King's College London. That's where his genetics took over and he became interested in the family business, medicine. After his four years there he wanted to leave London and continue his studies in America. He applied to several schools and he chose to attend The School of Medicine at University of California, San Diego. He chose that school because he developed an interest in Neuroscience while studying at King's. He decided to become a neurosurgeon and the program at UCSD is internationally regarded as one of the best. Abasiama graduated at the very top of his class. That combined with his 6'2" athletic frame, his dark skin, his chiseled good looks, and his easy going manner, makes him one of the most talked about and highly regarded residents on campus. Now, even though he's only in his first year of residency, nurses, both male and female, sometimes switch to the graveyard shift just to work with him, and other doctors already refer to him as Doctor Aba. He met Bobby and Eddie in the waiting area right after the emergency medical technicians wheeled Bobby in. After a short discussion Abasiama had Bobby taken into the emergency room where a nurse measured Bobby's vital signs.

When Doctor Aba returned he started with, "Let me take your blood pressure again. It looks like all of your vitals have returned to normal. You say this is the first time you've fainted?"
Bobby answers, "Yes."
Doctor Aba asks, "Have you taken any medication recently?"
"Just the anti-anxiety medicine you already know about."
"Have you experienced any kidney or liver problems?"
"No."
"Have you been experiencing any abnormal pain or swelling?"

129

"No. I really think it's just the fish I had for lunch."

"Yeah, I don't think that's what it is."

Eddie asks, "He's not going to have stay overnight is he?"

Doctor Aba turns to Bobby and says, "No, I'm going to release you but I want you to give me a blood sample and I want to know how I can contact your physician in Los Angeles."

Eddie says, "Listen Doc, can we keep this between us?"

Doctor Aba thinks that's a curious request, especially coming from the person who isn't the patient, but Bobby doesn't seem to object. "If you're asking me not report this to your department, that's not something I would do as a matter of course anyway, but when I get the results from your blood tests I am going to want to talk with you and your physician. Agreed?"

Bobby says, "Agreed."

"Great, the nurse will be back in a minute to take your blood. After that you guys are free to leave."

11:59pm - Eddie and Bobby walk to the car in silence. Bobby sits in the passenger's seat, reclines, and closes his eyes. He's disgusted with himself for being a part of this mess and he's exhausted. Eddie couldn't care less about Bobby. All he can think about is that Breck better be on his way to Panama. "What a friggin day," is what he thinks next. It started out great with a tour of his boat but then there was Carl, and then the kid's identity was discovered, and then Breck, the idiot, is in San Diego playing poker when he's supposed to be on a flight to Costa Rica, and finally Bobby's episode, which Eddie is sure Bobby will blame on him. Eddie noticed that the Doctor found his question odd. Thankfully, he assumed they just didn't want the department to find out about Bobby's fainting. In truth, he doesn't want anyone to find out that they were in San Diego. He knows he can come up with a story, but he is afraid that Bobby will crack under questioning. Looking back on his career he can't count how many times he's arrested someone because someone else talked. In that way, their trip to San Diego has served a purpose. Before tonight, despite what he's told himself, there was a chance he'd get to Costa Rica, have a good time with Breck, and decide to give him a pass. After speaking with Breck tonight Eddie knows he can't afford to let him live one minute past his usefulness. If there was a shred of doubt about killing Breck, now it's gone for good. And then he thinks, "That leaves Bobby." Almost as if he heard Eddie's thoughts Bobby says, "Karma."

Eddie asks, "What?"

Bobby, without opening his eyes, says, "Karma. That's what this is."

Eddie says, "Don't be ridiculous. If it was Karma, I'd be the one in the hospital. I told you not to come. I told you it was nothing to worry about and that I'd take care of it. If you had listened to me you'd be home, in bed and fast asleep right now. None of this had to happen."

"I'm cursed. You should have never told me about the girl or I should have arrested you right there and then."

"Your right, I should never said anything. Just try to get some sleep. This whole episode will be behind us in the morning and everything, from here on, will go exactly as planned."

"I'm cursed," says Bobby and then he did his best to fall asleep, which turned out to be easy. Eddie kept his eyes on the road for a few minutes in attempt not to betray what he's thinking. When the moment passed he looks over to Bobby, who is finally asleep. He knows if Bobby gets weak enough he'll talk. He knows the District Attorney will happily cut Bobby a deal in exchange for his testimony. Most of all, he knows if any of that happens, he'll spend the rest of his life in prison if he's that lucky. In truth, Eddie has always felt sorry for Bobby. He has always cared more for others than he has for himself. As a public servant that trait translates into potential greatness. As an individual that trait translates into weakness. It was that weakness that Eddie relied upon when he told Bobby what he did. He thought Bobby would do what he always does. He would suffer through it in silence. Then, when he got the money and Eddie was retired and out of his life, he would forget it. Now, Eddie has reason to fear that Bobby's weakness may backfire against him. Eddie never thought Bobby would associate his illness with what he was told. Now that he has, he may not suffer through it in silence. He may seek salvation by asking for forgiveness. Eddie glances over at Bobby once again. This time, however, he has a message for Bobby. He won't say it out loud in case Bobby is listening. He thinks it but he means it just the same. "I love you. I truly do. We've been through a lot together as partners and friends over the years. I won't take any pleasure in it like I will when I kill Breck, but if you continue down this path, if it comes down to me or you, if you leave me no choice, I will find a way to kill you too."

Day Three

12:30am - William's walk takes him down the 3rd Street Promenade from Wilshire Boulevard to Broadway. From there he makes a right and follows Broadway across Ocean Avenue. Then he makes a left and walks to the overpass that crosses Pacific Coast Highway, close to where it ends and becomes the 10 Freeway. He takes that overpass to the Santa Monica Pier.

Just as he suspected, the rides and the stores are closed for the night, though there are a few artists still selling their paintings, and jewelry, and mixed CDs. The night air cooled by the salty sea breeze feels refreshing and the exercise itself helps William clear his head. For the moment he isn't thinking about Genny and feeling sad. Nor is he thinking about Teddy or Javier. His thoughts are centered on how wonderful it feels to be alive. His sadness is replaced with a sense of joy and with feelings of thankfulness. He's thankful for the very air he's breathing, for the cool breeze whispering across his face, for the smell of the salt water, for the sight of the stars illuminating the dark sky, for the sound of the waves crashing into the shore, and for the sound of conversations and laughter coming from the people around him. Standing at the end of the pier and looking out at the Pacific Ocean William finds a moment of mental silence and peace, and oneness. Though he grabbed and enjoyed a grande latte from the Starbucks on the 3rd Street Promenade at Santa Monica Boulevard he's finally feeling fatigued and he decides it's time to go back to the hotel and get some rest.

There are noticeably less people on the pier now. In just the few moments William spent gazing out over the ocean all of the artists have packed up and left. There are just three people on the pier, a single man walking towards Ocean Avenue and a couple holding hands headed the same way. When William gets to Ocean Avenue he decides to walk along the bluffs to get back to the hotel instead of walking through the streets. There are fewer people along the bluffs than there was on the pier. Ahead, in the distance, William can see what appears to be two people playing. It looks like a girl running in a zig zag pattern and a guy right behind her in hot pursuit. William continues along the bluffs stopping every once in a while just to take in the activity across the street. The restaurants that line the east side of Ocean Avenue are winding down. The last few patrons are either finishing their meals or standing outside waiting for the valet to retrieve their cars. The windows to the hotels that line that same side of the street, above the restaurants, form an imperfect checkerboard pattern. Some of the rooms are dark, while others are illuminated by the overhead lights or by the flickering blue glow from the televisions. So far William has walked past Broadway, past Arizona Avenue, and now he's at Wilshire Blvd. He's enjoying the walk and the ocean air so much he decides to continue along the bluffs for one more block to California Avenue and he'll take that back to the Copenhagen. He heard them first and the familiar sounds caught his attention. They must be close because he can hear them clearly but he still can't see them. After a few more steps he can finally see them. Shielded by a palm tree so that they can't be seen by anyone on the east side of Ocean Avenue are a couple. The woman is holding on to the tree and the man is standing behind her. The woman has her sweater pulled up above her breasts and both of them have their pants and their underwear down around their ankles. The man has his hand over the woman's mouth and he's thrusting in and out of her from behind. William's first instinct is to pretend not to notice and quietly walk around them. Then he wonders if this is the same couple he saw earlier. If it is, was he mistaken in believing they were playing? Maybe she was trying to get away from him but he caught her and now he's having his way with her. William can't stop himself from staring at them. Now, on his second look the guy's thrusts seem violent and the fact that he has his hand over her mouth is cause for concern. Again William thought he should pretend not to notice. Instead he says, "Hey, what are you doing?"

He expected the couple to stop, even if only for a moment, out of embarrassment, but that didn't happen. Instead the man continues to thrust in and out of the woman all the while keeping his hand over mouth. Only now he's stopped telling her how much she wants it and how much she likes it and he tells William, "Get the fuck out of here. Mind your own fucking business."

When the guy spoke the woman turned her head towards William and she looks frightened. William charges the man, knocking him off the woman and to the ground. The woman screams. Out of the corner of his eye William sees the woman scrambling to get dressed. The man pulls up his pants and he is back on his feet in a second. He charges William, knocking him to the ground and falling on top of him. William is on his back and the man is sitting on top of him. Their arms are flailing trying to punch each other and block each other's punches simultaneously. The man lands a solid punch to William's left eye blinding him momentarily. William knees the man in the back knocking him off of him. William quickly rolls over on top of the man. He has his knee in the man's back and he's throwing punches. It isn't until the man turns his face to the right that William lands a punch to the side of the man's head right between his right cheek and his right temple. Again, the woman screams but this time she screams, "Stop!" William continues to hold the man down with his knee in the man's back and his left hand pushing the man's face into the dirt. The man has his arms covering his face, but William is still throwing punches that are striking the man's shoulders and the back of his head. The woman pushes William off of the man and she screams, "Stop it!" Instead of running away or screaming for help, she goes to the man William was on top of and she consoles him.

It turns out they are a couple and they were acting out a fantasy of theirs. The woman and the man are both angry with William, though the woman's anger is tempered by understanding. The man's anger isn't, nor does it become tempered even after William apologizes profusely. He tries to explain what he saw and why he did what he did, but neither the man nor the woman wants to hear it. The fight is over. Now, the man and the woman just want to leave and so does William. The walk back to the hotel seems to happen in an instant. William feels embarrassed, which is understandable, but he also feels scared. He can't make sense of that emotion since the fight is over but he can't deny it, he feels scared. More than anything, however, he feels excited. Alive is the word that keeps coming to mind. William hasn't had a physical fight with anyone since high school. He hasn't thought about that day in years but, at this moment, it's as if it happened yesterday. He remembers having the same feeling then as he has now, scared but excited at the same time.

7:00am - Robyn turned off the alarm clock so Bobby could get some extra sleep. As far as she knows, he and Eddie were on a stake out last night until 3:00am. Robyn was sure that with the lack of sleep Bobby would wake up not feeling well, but the exact opposite happened. Bobby woke up feeling rested and great and even a little randy. He snuck up behind her while she was in the kitchen on her laptop and kissed her on the neck. Robyn turns around and gives Bobby a passionate kiss and says, "That and more was waiting for you last night."

"If I had known that I would have found someone else to sit in a car for hours doing nothing. What about now?"

"Tempting but we can't now. You've got to ready and so do I. I have a busy day planned." Bobby is visibly disappointed so Robyn continues, "But, I'll tell you what, if you can find your way home tonight before 3:00am, I'll be waiting for you in your favorite lingerie."

"The pink bra and panties with the lace?"

"Just bring yourself home, and save your strength. You're going to need it."

On his way to the bathroom, he asks, "Are you still planning to go to your mother's this weekend?" "Yes, if it's still OK with you."

"Sure it is. I'll miss you but you'll be back on Monday, right?"

"Yup, that's the plan."

Bobby closes the door to the bathroom behind him. He will miss Robyn but, truthfully, he's looking forward to some time off work and some time alone. Bobby hates lying to Robyn, but in this case he won't be hard on himself. If there's one thing he knows for sure, it's that she doesn't need to know anything about his deal with Eddie. He still hasn't figured out how he'll explain the money, but he figures he'll cross that bridge when he gets to it. Just three more days, including today, and then Eddie will be gone and hopefully so will the stress. Bobby takes a good look in the mirror and then he snaps into his routine. After he showers and comes out of the bathroom to get dressed, Robyn goes in and closes the door behind her. She also takes a good look in the mirror and then snaps into her routine except she doesn't use the toothpaste next to both of their toothbrushes. Instead, she squeezes some out into the sink, washes it away, and puts the tube of toothpaste back where it should be. Then she reaches into the cabinet beneath the sink and pulls out her travel bag. She squeezes some toothpaste from the tube in her travel bag onto her toothbrush and, before she brushes her teeth, she returns the toothpaste to the bag and she returns the bag to its hiding place underneath the sink. While she's brushing her teeth she opens the bathroom door and steps out into the bedroom to check on Bobby. She tells him how much she loves the tie he has chosen. He winks at her. She goes back into the bathroom to rinse the toothpaste out of her mouth and then she jumps in the shower. By the time she's out of the shower and has dried her hair Bobby is ready to leave. Bobby says, "OK Babe, I'm outta here."

Robyn asks, "Did you eat something?"

"No. I don't have an appetite right now. I'll get something to eat later."

"Mr. Mallory you are pushing it sir. First, you only get four hours of sleep and now you're not having breakfast. I'm glad you seem to be feeling better but, I told you before, you're going to need all of your strength today."

"I promise, I'll get a bagel or something once I get to the office."

"Before you leave, at least take your vitamins."

"Nag, nag, nag, that's all you do."

"If you like, I can stop." Bobby walks to Robyn, takes her in his arms and says, "Don't you ever stop, not for a minute."

Robyn gives him quick peck on the lips and says, "That's what I thought." She spins Bobby around and pushes him towards the kitchen. She tells him, "Take your vitamins before you leave and take them with water or orange juice, not with soda or coffee."

"Nag, nag, nag. I love you baby. Have a good day."

"I love you too. Call me when you're on your way home and, don't forget, save your energy. You're going to need it."

8:00am - There are very few things remaining in Eddie's two bedroom, two bathroom apartment. Most of his belongs have been given away or put in storage in preparation for his move to Costa Rica. Besides his bedroom which still houses his bed and a dresser, the room with the most items remaining in it is the kitchen. There he has a few pots and pans, some plates, bowls, utensils, a coffee maker, and a television, which is turned on and tuned in to CNBC, as it always is at this time in the morning.

"At least for now I remain bearish on the price of crude oil. I can't argue with the fact that Russia and Saudi Arabia remain the world's dominate suppliers of crude. The Arab Spring, however, has unleashed all kinds of chaos throughout the Middle Eastern region, which could impact the production and sale of crude for those countries as well as have a negative impact on their partners. If the price for crude were to decline for a substantial amount of time, or worse, for the foreseeable future, that would devastate the economies that are now relying on the high price of crude to make up short falls in their budgets. For Americans, at least, the new supply coming from the enormous reserves recently discovered in Montana, means less reliance on foreign suppliers resulting in lower prices and greater economic stability. I still think we are a long way away from seeing the changes I'm speaking about but we can already see a shift in American political policy as it relates to Saudi Arabia and, more noticeably, as it relates to Russia."

CNBC's Maria Bartiromo says, "OK, that was Marcos Dmitriyev, Head Analyst for Global Venture Capital. When we return we check in with Jim Cramer for his thoughts on Apple's latest innovation and what it will mean for the shareholders."

Eddie pours another cup of coffee and has just positioned himself in front of the television to make sure he's present for the next segment when his cell phone rings. He checks the caller ID with the intention of letting the call go to voicemail but he takes the call because it's Breck. He begins the call not with hello but with, "Where are you?"

Breck says, "Stop it with the worrying. I'm in Panama. My connecting flight starts to board in a few minutes. How's your partner doing?"

"By the time he got to the hospital he was stabilized. The doctors checked him out and released him. He's OK."

"How much does he know?"

"He doesn't know anything."

"He must know something. Does he know about me? Should I be worried about him? And, what about the kid? Does he know who the kid was?"

"He might have his suspicions about you but he doesn't know anything for sure. Don't worry about it. I'm taking care of him. None of us would've had to worry about the kid if you had done what you were asked to do. Everything here is under control. All I need you to do is stay in Costa Rica and keep your phone on and close by in case I need to talk with you."

"You're still planning on be there by Monday night right? I guess what I'm asking is when do I get my money?"

If Breck could see the smile on Eddie's face he would know he has a problem. Eddie thinks, "You will never see that money," but he says, "Yeah, I'll be there Monday night at the latest. We'll go to the bank together on Tuesday and I'll do the transfer."

"They're calling my flight. I have to go. I'll call you later."

The first thing Eddie thinks when he hangs up is how much he hates Breck. Not only has he made things more perilous, but now he caused him to miss the Cramer segment. He has to catch it on YouTube or someplace else later. He thinks of calling Bobby just to check in with him, but decides to let him have a little space. Besides, Eddie knows if Bobby wasn't going in today he would have called him by now. The fact that there's an ID for the kid really doesn't mean anything, especially since he's heading that investigation. All he has to do is keep Bobby in the dark about any other clues and he's home free. Unless, of course, Breck screwed that up too. On his way out the door Eddie grabs his keys and his money from the table next to the entrance. Next to his money clip is Lisa Becker's business card. He grabs that too. He stares at it for a while and it reminds him of what he saw the night before last. He isn't overly concerned but he thinks it's a good idea to talk with her today.

9:00am - The day off, the rest, the pampering, and another romantic night with Tony did Lisa good. She woke up feeling refreshed, excited, and eager to attack the day. In fact, she got to her office two hours early, just because she couldn't wait to get back to writing. Lisa saw the potential in the position while others were mocking the idea. Who would want to write a blog about crime in Malibu? What crime? Statistically speaking, Malibu is one of the safest places to live in the entire country. Others thought, besides the occasional hit and run on PCH what is there to report? Lisa bet, given Malibu's residents, writing a blog on celebrity transgressions could lead to her being on television. Though the bet hasn't paid off yet, she knows it's just a matter of time before TMZ or E! comes calling. The first story she updates in her blog is about one of the stars on ABC's highest rated comedy. This actress, a Malibu resident, turns out to be a kleptomaniac. Though she makes over two hundred and fifty thousand dollars per episode, she was caught, for the third time, stealing bottles of fingernail polish from the CVS Pharmacy just up the street from Cross Creek. The update is she is getting off with a slap on the wrist. She got six months' probation during which time she has to go for counseling once a week, and she's not allowed in that store for a year. The second story Lisa updates in her blog is about another Malibu resident. This nineteen year old recording artist is having a hard time managing his success. Twice during the last year he was pulled over for racing his brand new Ferrari up and down Pacific Coast Highway. Both times he was clocked at speeds exceeding ninety five miles per hour. Three months ago, at 3:00am, he crashed that Ferrari into a bus waiting area bench. There was a rumor that alcohol was involved, but that allegation quickly disappeared. The update is his driver's license has been suspended for a year. Just as Lisa posted her second update Iris, the owner and the publisher of the Malibu Journal, arrives at the office. Iris likes to meet with all of her writers, one on one, each morning if they are in the office. Lisa's scheduled time is at 9:15am so she decides to take a break and get a cup of coffee before her meeting. After her meeting she'll start to write her story on David Waverly.

If you were to pass Iris Abrams in the street, you would guess that she works in a thrift shop specializing in everything from the 60's. She wears her long hair in two braids, one on each side of her head. She wears baggy pants and baggy shirts, and 360 days out of each year she wears Birkenstock sandals on her feet. If you met her casually you might find out that she publishes a newspaper but you would still walk away with only the tip of the iceberg on her story. If you visited her in her office, then you would get an idea of how serious she is. On her office walls hangs an undergraduate diploma from Syracuse University in Journalism, and a Master's Degree diploma in Business Administration from Harvard University. There are also dozens of pictures, on the walls in her office, of her with celebrities from film, sports, and television, as well as pictures of her with the two former Mayors of Los Angeles, a picture of her with the current Mayor of Los Angeles, a picture of her with a former Mayor of New York, a picture of her with a former Mayor of Boston, and there are pictures of her with two former Presidents of the United States. If you ask her what she cherishes most she'll tell you it's the Andy Warhol painting of Elizabeth Taylor that hangs on the wall directly behind her desk.

It has already been a busy day for Iris. She had her first meeting this morning at 7:00am over breakfast. Now, she drops her carry-bag on her desk and heads to the kitchen to get her second cup of coffee. Lisa is there with the pot in her hand. She pours some coffee into Iris's cup and then, taking Iris's direction, she follows her back to her office. Settling into her chair Iris asks, "I haven't seen anything on the news about the murder in Santa Monica yet, so how did you find out about it?"
Lisa says, "I was just in the right place at the right time."
"Are you sure you didn't get a tip from your boyfriend?"
Lisa hesitates and then says, "Maybe I did, and maybe I didn't."
"The right answer to that question is no. Let's try again. Are you sure you didn't get a tip from your boyfriend?"
"No. I didn't."

"Good. Now tell me what you know so far." Without mentioning that Tony did give her the victim's name, David Waverly, and without mentioning that Russell confirmed the victim's name and gave her more information, Lisa tells Iris that she's learned the victim's name, his current address, that he has a record for drug possession back in Colorado Springs, Colorado, where, apparently, he's from given his parent's address, which she also has. She tells Iris that she plans to visit his address with the hopes that he has a roommate she can speak with or at least she hopes to speak with his neighbors. Iris asks, "Do you think you're ready to cross the line? It sounds like you taking an investigative approach to writing this story."

Lisa says, "You said it yourself. You haven't heard anything about this story yet. Breaking this story might be good for my career."

"I appreciate your chutzpah but, given the manner of death, it's likely that you'll come into contact with some dangerous people. It might be better to let the police handle the investigation and then report the story from what they tell you."

"I'll be careful. In fact, I did exchange business cards with the two homicide detectives that arrived at the scene. If I find out anything that appears dangerous I'll feed the information to them. They have already agreed to give me the exclusive."

"Really? That's good. What are their names?"

Before Lisa can respond to the question, Iris's receptionist interrupts their meeting over the intercom. "I'm sorry to interrupt your meeting but Lisa asked me to find her if Detective Edward Roberts or if Detective Robert Mallory calls, and I have Detective Roberts on the line asking for Lisa."

9:30am - Bobby has been gone for an hour but Robyn is still walking around the house in her robe. The first thing she did was make the bed. Then she cleaned the bathroom and the kitchen. Since then she's been cleaning things that are already clean and moving things around that don't need to be moved just to burn off nervous energy. When the doorbell rings it startles her though she knew it would ring and she expected it to ring exactly when it did. Instead of answering it she stays in the bedroom hoping the person at the door will get the message. When the doorbell rings for a second time it didn't startle her, instead, in response, she took a deep breath. Still, she doesn't take one step towards the door. She's certain, this time, that if she doesn't answer it the person at the door will get the message.

The house looked vacant when he approached it. There isn't a car in the driveway and none of the lights appear to be on. He rang the doorbell twice just to be sure. Then he walked around to the side of the house peering into the windows as he did. Still, he doesn't see any lights on and he doesn't see any movement inside. When he gets to the back of the house he can see the entire kitchen through the glass patio doors. There are no plates or cups on any of the countertops or on the kitchen table. There aren't any pots or pans on the stove either. He knows none of the neighbors can see him standing where he is but he takes one look around just to be certain that no one is looking. He tries to open the sliding glass patio door but it appears to be locked. He gives it a second try, harder this time, and he finds that it wasn't locked. It just needed a good jerk. The popping sound the door made when he jerked it open caused him to freeze in his tracks for just a second. Since no sound came from inside the house he slid the door open, walked in, then closed and locked the door behind him. He made his way through the kitchen and into the living room. He stopped there to take a look around. He thinks to himself that they have a nice set up. The living room is warm and inviting. There are expensive looking leather couches and chairs, a built in bookcase with books in every space except those spaces filled with framed pictures. There's a large flat screen television hanging on the wall and next to it are built in shelves that house the components of their sound system as well as a few CDs and their extensive collection of DVDs. Oddly enough, the only thing that seems cold is the fireplace. There's a stack of wood on the left side of the fireplace and there is a tripod on the right, from which hangs a poker, a small shovel, and a brush. Even with all of that the fireplace is so immaculately clean it looks like it hasn't ever been used. He reminds himself that he's not here to look around so he continues through the living room to the foot of the stairs that lead to the second floor. Now he is no longer worried about being discovered. In fact, he takes each stair confidently one by one, and with each step his excitement builds. When he gets to the top of the staircase he sees that the doors to each room on the second floor are open except for one. He knows that's the one he wants. A wave of guilt flows through his body. He takes a deep breath and thinks to himself that he didn't come this far to turn away now. He walks to the door, opens it, steps across the threshold, and finds Robyn lying on the bed. The opening door gets Robyn's attention and she recognizes him immediately. It's Romario, their representative from the landscaping company they employ. Romario closes the door behind him and stands there. Robyn gets off the bed, unties her robe, and let's it fall to the floor, revealing her naked body. She was attracted to him from the moment they met. It has taken some time, some planning, and some maneuvering to get him here but, now that he's here, she's happy he came. Judging from the growing erection bulging in Romario's pants, he's likes what he sees and he's happy he came also.

9:45am - When William agreed to meet Javier at the precinct it meant he was taking action, getting somewhere, and that made him happy. Now, that he's there all he feels is the frustration. He has to remind himself that this time is different. Before, they were in control and he was hopeful that they would help. This time, despite what Javier says, despite his own feelings of fearfulness and uncertainty, he's in control and this time, though he has no idea how, he's going to find a way to make something happen. He walks into the lobby and is greeted by the same officer he had gotten to know during the days when he would go to the precinct two or three times per week. After the customary small talk, the officer tells William he'll have to wait for a little while. At the moment, Detective Morales is in a meeting with the Captain. William takes a seat.

In fact, Captain Upton has Javier, Eddie, and Bobby in his office. Captain Upton is saying, "The Chief is getting some pressure from the merchant coalition in Santa Monica. Even though the evidence, so far, leads us to believe that David Waverly was singled out and killed, as opposed to being the victim of a random murderer, the merchants don't want the bad publicity. There's nothing they can do to avoid having the news of the murder reported to the public, but they feel, and rightfully so, with an arrest the tension will be diffused. Javier, I asked you to be a part of this meeting because if we don't get an arrest this week I'll need you to partner up with Bobby after Eddie retires. Eddie, let me ask you if you think Javier should start getting involved now. It's your last week on the job, some cops like to work until the end and others use their last week to tie up loose ends and prepare for what's next."

Eddie says, "No, I'm here and I'm working. I'd like to finish up with the arrest of whoever did this."

The Captain replies, "That's fine with me but if we don't have our guy by the end of the week I want you and Bobby to bring Javier up to speed."

Eddie looks at Javier and says, "I'll be happy to."

The Captain continues "Good. Let's go over what we know so far. I know we haven't turned up any eye witnesses so far but we have some uniforms interviewing all of the people who were working in the area at the approximate time of David's death. I'll let you know if we get a lead. You already have his current address or, at least, what we think was his current address from his DMV records. We know the kid was from Colorado Springs, Colorado. In your packet you have a copy of his arrest record and his parent's names and address. We don't know where he was working, though given his build and good looks it's probably safe to say he was trying to make his way in entertainment. I guess the first thing you guys need to do is talk with his parents and then see if he lived where we think he lived and see if you can get something out of his neighbors and friends."

Bobby asks, "Have we had any luck finding the bullet?"

"No, as you know it appears that he was shot with a 9mm but the bullet exited his forehead. We still haven't turned up the shell and, at this point, I'm fairly sure we won't. I don't think we'll find the bullet either. His body is still with the coroner but, as you know, there was no sign of struggle so we aren't hopeful that we'll find any DNA evidence under his fingernails. I know you don't have a lot to go with, and on top of that, we're under some pressure, but I have a meeting with the Chief in two days. Try to turn up something I can report to him. Javier, if you didn't have the caseload you have I'd pull you and put you on this today. For the time being, Bobby and Eddie, I need you guys to dig in and get something."

Eddie adds, "If we get close, I'll stick around next week and keep on working."

William is patiently waiting in the lobby reading the latest copy of Sports Illustrated. The article he's reading is so interesting he's almost lost track of time. He's oblivious to the comings and goings around him until the sound of men laughing loudly, coming from down the hall, causes him to look up and in that direction momentarily. Then he turns his attention back to the article.

To Eddie's surprise Captain Upton, Javier, and even Bobby broke out in spontaneous and loud laughter after his last comment. The Captain says, "How many times have you told everyone who would listen that you'll be somewhere in the Pacific an hour after your retirement? Besides, you know once you're off the force, you're off the force. I can't, officially, allow you to work on anything. Thanks for the laugh though. That's a good way to get this day started. That reminds me, I have to make it to the Marina before Friday. I want to see that boat of yours."

Eddie says, "Whenever you want Cap."

Captain Upton finishes with, "Good. OK, let's break up this party and get to work."

10:00am - When the meeting breaks Captain Upton asks, "Eddie, can you stick around for a minute?"

"Sure Cap." Eddie turns to Bobby and asks, "Where are you going to be?"

Bobby says, "I'm feeling thirsty all of a sudden. I'm going to get some water and then I'll meet you at the desk."

When Javier gets out of the Captain's office one of the other detectives tells him he has someone waiting for him in the lobby. Javier makes his way to the lobby and finds William there reading. His first words to William are, "What happened to your eye?"

William says, "It's nothing."

Javier asks, "What happened to your eye?"

William concedes, "I got into a little skirmish last night. It wasn't serious, it was just a silly misunderstanding." Wanting to change the subject William asks, "So, are we going to talk in conference room one, two, or three?"

"Actually, we are going to talk in the Captain's office. I told him about our encounter yesterday and that you were coming in today, and he said he wants to be in on our meeting. He's wrapping up a meeting we just had, I'm sure he'll be ready for us in a few minutes."

Bobby left the Captain's office first, followed by Javier. Captain Upton closed the door to his office after the two men left. Captain Upton asks, "How's Bobby doing?"

Eddie says, "Much better. He hasn't had an incident for a few days now. I keep telling him there's nothing wrong with him, he just needs a vacation."

"Is he well enough to work this case, especially after you leave?"

"Sure. If we get this one solved this week maybe you can suggest that he take some time off. Or, if the case isn't going anywhere, after a couple of weeks, maybe you should make the same suggestion. Javier is really smart, he could probably handle it by himself until Bobby gets back. Maybe, when Bobby gets back from vacation, you can put him on something else. At the end of the day, he's all right Cap. He just needs a break."

"Remember what I told you about my meeting with the Chief. Let's not think about this case going nowhere. The two of you need to get out there and bring something in that I can report to the Chief." "You got it, Cap."

By the time Eddie is leaving the Captain's office, Javier has gotten William to tell him how he got a bruised eye. William says, "I thought the guy was raping her. What was I supposed to do, call the police?"

"That's very funny."

"I didn't mean that the way it sounded. I'm just saying I was standing right there, while it was happening, and no one else was around."

Javier sees Eddie leaving the Captain's office and says to William, "Wait here." After checking with the Captain Javier waves to William to come into the office.

After William takes a seat in the Captain's office and they exchange the pleasantries of seeing each other again, the three men get to the purpose of the meeting. Captain Upton begins, "I asked to be in this meeting for two reasons. First, as I'm sure Javier has already told you, we are still very sorry about your wife's death. We haven't forgotten about her or you. I'm sure you know that Detective Morales still includes the murder of your wife among his cases. Second, however, it has come to my attention that you've taken on the investigation of your wife's murder for yourself. You're not the first person to do something like that, and I understand where you're coming from, but I am strongly advising you against doing that. If there were any new leads we'd be on top of it."

William says, "You have a new lead."

Captain Upton exchanges a glance with Javier before he continues. "Tell me how you think Teddy Gallo is a new lead in your wife murder case."

"For one thing, Teddy was my wife's former boyfriend."

Captain Upton says, "I'm sure your wife wasn't Teddy's only former girlfriend and I'm sure he wasn't her only former boyfriend. So what does that prove?"

"You're right, that proves nothing. Let me tell you what I know. I don't have any enemies that I know of and neither did Genny. Someone came into my house, killed her, and took nothing."

"What that says to me is that it was a botched burglary. The intruder got so freaked out he left without taking anything."

"In that case, why didn't he leave after shooting me? If it was a burglary, maybe he assumed the house was empty. After finding me there he had to think there could other people there as well. Or, if he was convinced, somehow, that I was the only person there, why am I here today? I was lying on the floor, shot, and unconscious. He could have put a bullet in my head and then he would have had all night to take whatever he wanted. Let's just agree, right now, that you are never going to get me to believe that it was a botched burglary. Genny was murdered intentionally and Teddy was the only person we knew who has the type of friends who could and would do something like that. I believe Genny's murder can somehow be traced back to Teddy. I know Javier thinks I'm crazy and maybe you do too. Maybe I am. I just have a gut feeling. Maybe I'm believing the only thing I have to believe, but I believe it nonetheless."

"You do know that Javier found Teddy dead of an apparent overdose? So, even if we bought into your gut feeling, he's not around for us to talk with."

"Yeah, I know. That's a problem, but that's not the end."

Captain Upton hesitates before he says, "Please don't take this the wrong way, I'm not trying to sound glib, but why don't you throw yourself into your work. It will help you take your mind off things and it will help you get through this."

"I don't have any work. I was forced to take a leave of absence. Without saying it, they thought I had become a zombie. They were wrong. For lack of a better word, I was constipated, but I'm not anymore."

"I'll tell you what, I'll ask Javier to ask around about Teddy. If we come up with anything I'll make sure he lets you know what that is. Let me be clear, however, we don't want to find you back at Teddy's apartment or anywhere else pursuing your wife's murder. You need to agree to leave it to us. Do I have your word on that?"

The three men look at each other without saying a word. Captain Upton's fixes his stare on William but the most William can do is stare back. Before Captain Upton can repeat his question there is a loud crashing noise followed by someone yelling, "Call an ambulance!" All three men turn to find out what has happened. Captain Upton can see people rushing to one side of the room. Javier sees it too. Captain Upton comes from around his desk to rush to the event. Javier tells William to stay in the Captain's office and then he follows the Captain.

Bobby is white as a sheet and lying unconscious on the floor. Eddie and all of the detectives in the room are surrounding him. William can't see what, exactly, is going on, but he couldn't care less. His thoughts are on the conversation he just had with the Captain. The answer to the Captain's question is no but he's happy he didn't have to say it. He looks around the Captain's office.

From the pictures, awards, and commendations, it's obvious that the Captain is well liked and good at what he does. That too means nothing to William. He turns to see what's going on. The Captain is directing the action and he doesn't see Javier. The man down must be named Bobby because he heard that named yelled twice already. For a moment he wonders what happened to him. He didn't hear a gunshot or anything. Whatever happened, it doesn't concern him. He waits patiently looking around the Captain's office until something on the Captain's desk catches his attention. He looks back to see what the Captain is doing. He's still directing traffic and William still doesn't see Javier. While he looks for them he's also trying to talk himself out of what he's going to do. Since the coast is clear and with the thought, "What's the worst that could happen to me?" he reaches on the Captain's desk and grabs the file labeled "Teddy Gallo." With the file in his hand he turns again to see where the Captain is, then he sits back down and starts to read the file's contents. Teddy has a list of arrests but William can't find any judgments against him. Nowhere in the file does it say that he has served any time in prison. There's other information, like addresses and known associates, and then William sees the word "Informant." William tries to memorize as much as he can, but now he's feeling he better put the file back before he gets caught. Once again he checks the action in the outer room and then he places the file back on the Captain's desk right where and how he found it. No sooner did he take his hand away from the file than did Javier come in the room to tell him to just stay where he is. For a moment William thought he was busted, but Javier didn't give any indication that he had seen anything. William tells Javier, "I have another appointment this morning and I can't be late for it. Let me call you later today and we'll pick up where we left off."

Javier says, "I guess that's OK, but make sure you call."

"I will." William walks back to the lobby and is about to walk out, but first he has to step aside to make room for the paramedics, with a stretcher, who are rushing in.

10:45am - Detective Melvin is kneeling next to Bobby, pumping his chest with his hands, and counting out loud. "Twenty-five, twenty-six, twenty-seven, twenty-eight, twenty-nine, thirty." Then he tilts Bobby's head back, lifts his chin, pinches his nose, covers Bobby's mouth with his and breaths in until he sees Bobby's chest rise. Then he does that again. Bobby vomits. Detective Melvin turns Bobby's head to the side and wipes all the vomit out of Bobby's mouth with his hands. Once all of the vomit is out of Bobby's mouth and off his face the Detective starts to pump his chest again. When the paramedics arrive the Detective is just getting to thirty. They stand by for just a moment to allow the Detective to breathe twice into Bobby, who still isn't breathing. The first paramedic takes Detective Melvin's place pumping on Bobby's chest, while the second paramedic starts to assemble a defibrillator. While he sets up the portable AED he asks, "What event led up to this?"

One of the detectives offers, "He was just sitting at his desk and he just keeled over."

The paramedic asks, "Do you know if he is a diabetic?"

The Captain says, "No, he isn't.

"What about allergies?" No one knows if Bobby has allergies.

"What about medications? Is he taking any heart or blood pressure medicine?" The other detectives look to Eddie to answer this question. Eddie says, "I think he's taking something for anxiety but I'm not sure."

Finally the paramedic asks, "Does he have a history of this?"

Eddie answers by saying, "No, he has never passed out before."

By the time Eddie answers this last question the first paramedic has completed the cycle of pumping the heart and breathing and Bobby still isn't breathing. The first paramedic removes Bobby's shirt and attaches the defibrillator pads. When the AED signals that it's ready, the paramedic yells, "Clear," and pushes the button to administer a shock to Bobby's heart. Still, nothing. They wait for a minute and, again, when the AED gives the signal the paramedic pushes the button. This second shock gets Bobby heart beating again and revives him. The two paramedics try to make Bobby more comfortable while they give him a minute to regain consciousness. The second paramedic asks Bobby what his name is. He answers correctly. Then he asks if he knows where he is. Bobby answers correctly. The paramedic asks, "What day is it?"

Bobby says, "I don't know. Wait a minute today is Tuesday, no, Wednesday."

The paramedic asks, "What happened to you?"

Bobby answers, "I don't remember. I remember feeling thirsty and getting a drink of water but I don't remember anything after that."

The first paramedic shines a light into Bobby's eyes to see if they are both equal in size and if they react to the light. They are and they do. Then they get Bobby on the stretcher and hook him up to an IV and a heart monitor. Eddie and the Captain tell Bobby not to worry, that everything will be all right and the other detectives voice their support for Bobby as the paramedics wheel him to the ambulance.

After the ambulance has gone and the other detectives have returned to what they were doing before, as much as could be expected, Eddie finds himself back in Captain Upton's office. The two of them are wrestling with the seriousness of Bobby's condition and there is no longer any question as to whether or not he can carry on with the investigation, or with any police work for that matter. While the Captain is saying that he hopes Bobby will be all right and that he needs to contact Bobby's wife to let her know what's happened, Eddie is nodding, feigning interest, but in his head one thought keeps repeating itself, over and over again. "This can't be happening."

11:00am - William and Genny pull into the parking lot at the Century City Mall. Genny says, "We have an hour before the movie starts."

William says, "I know. I thought there'd be more traffic. What do you feel like doing?"

"Really? Do you have to ask?"

"I know. Silly of me wasn't it?" The mall in Century City is Genny's favorite. It has an excellent variety of stores and restaurants, a large multiplex movie theater with luxurious seats, and an extensive food court with delicacies from all over the world. Besides the fact that her favorite shoe store is in this mall what makes it her favorite is that the mall is open air. There are few better places to saunter around on a lazy Friday night with seventy degree weather and not a cloud in the sky. They got their tickets for the movie and then, following Genny's lead, they made a bee line to the shoe store.

"What do you think about these?" asks Genny.

"I like those too but I like the first pair you tried on more." They went back and forth like that over three more pairs of shoes, including one pair of boots. Ultimately, the choice came down to the first pair of shoes she tried on and the boots. William could see that Genny was agonizing over the decision so he suggested that she get both.

"No, I don't need both right now." Genny has countless qualities that William adores but one of his favorite is that she's really good with money.

William whispers in her ear, "Let's be crazy tonight. Go ahead and get both."

Genny, sensing a deal coming on, asks, "OK mister, what's in it for you?"

"I'm thinking a fashion show, later tonight, starring you in the boots and nothing else."

Ten minutes later they walked out of the store with one big bag that held a pair of shoes and a pair of boots. They thought about getting something to eat but they only had twenty minutes before the movie and they didn't want to eat in a rush. They decided to take the scenic route back to the movie theater.

"Genny?" They both heard the male voice coming from their left and they turned to face it simultaneously. "Genny." he called again.

Genny said, "Teddy?" The name sounded familiar to William but he couldn't remember how or why. As he watched and listened to Genny and Teddy get reacquainted he figured out this must be the Teddy she dated and told him about on a couple of occasions. Genny introduced Teddy to William, and Teddy introduced Megan Smith, his current girlfriend, to both William and Genny. The two of them talked briefly about what they've been up to since the last time they saw each other and William and Megan made small talk as well. Then the two couples went their separate ways. Genny made a comment about Teddy not looking well, but William hadn't noticed. That was the last time she ever mentioned Teddy.

"Megan Smith," William now thinks to himself as he drives aimlessly but away from the precinct. He tried to remember the names in Teddy's file under "Known Associates" but with such a quick glance and without writing them down he knew that wouldn't be likely. In his effort to remember them, however, the memory of the night he met Teddy came right back to him, and with that came the name of his girlfriend. William remembered one other thing about Megan. During their brief conversation she mentioned that she lived in Venice. She even mentioned the street, but William can't remember that, he only remembers Venice. As William continues to drive he ponders the fact that Teddy was an informant. Ultimately, he figures that may come into play at some point, but for now he can't think of how that piece of information can help him. He certainly can't bring that up to Javier because there's

no way William should know that. A sense of frustration starts to build in William. The police want him to stay out of it. The Captain took time out of his day to tell William that personally. Teddy, his one lead, is dead. As hard as he tries he can't remember, with certainty, any of the names in Teddy's file. Even if he did there were only names found therein, not one of them had a corresponding address. "Think William think," is what he's been telling himself since he rushed out of the precinct. Besides the memory of meeting Teddy, he has come up with only one idea, "Try to find Megan Smith." Since that's all he has, he decides to go with it.

12:00pm - Captain Upton got the call right after he got off the phone with Robyn, Bobby's wife. Bobby's blood pressure dropped in the ambulance on the way to the hospital and he stopped breathing again. He had to be resuscitated for a second time today. That news made Bobby more important than any work, at least for the time being. Captain Upton, Eddie, Javier, and a few other detectives rushed to the hospital. When they got there Bobby was still in the emergency room. Two minutes later Robyn arrived. She was greeted and consoled by the Captain, who filled her in on what happened to Bobby while he was on route. Robyn tries to get more information from the nurse's station but there isn't anything they can tell her that she doesn't know already. Like her, they are waiting to hear from the doctor attending to Bobby. Robyn turns from the nurse's station and she sees all of the detectives standing in a circle, talking. She's sobbing now and in no mood to talk with them, so she takes a seat at the end of the bench in the waiting area. One of the newer nurses gives Robyn a box of tissues and introduces herself. She tells Robyn that she'll be close by, and if there's anything she needs or wants, all Robyn has to do is call on her.

The detectives are being led in prayer by Captain Upton. When the prayer breaks there's a moment of silence that is broken when the Captain says, "This is unbelievable. He looked fine just a couple of hours ago." The other detectives nod and voice that they agree.

Eddie goes further by saying, "There's no way he's going to die. He's too good a man to go out this way." Again, the other detectives voice their concurrence. Each of them are showing particular sympathy towards Eddie, Bobby's partner and longtime friend. Eddie accepts their sympathy graciously, but secretly he's hoping that Bobby does die. Sure, it would be a sad loss, but then he wouldn't have to worry anymore about Bobby talking. More than that, he'd get to keep the money he promised to Bobby. Again the men fall into a moment of silence. There isn't anything to say. All they can do is wait. Eddie sees Robyn sitting by herself at the far end of the room. He excuses himself and walks over to her. She sees him coming and braces herself for the conversation. He starts by telling her that he's sure Bobby will be all right. She tells him she knows he will. Before their conversation can go any further Eddie gets a call on his cell phone. He checks the caller ID, and much to Robyn's relief, he excuses himself to take the call. "What's up Carl?" asks Eddie.

Carl says, "We have a problem."

"Whatever it is, I can't talk about it now."

"If we spoke about it yesterday, we wouldn't have a problem."

"Well, I can't talk about it now."

"I'm not calling to speak about it now. It's a conversation we need to have in person. I'm calling to figure out a time and a place we can meet today."

"I can't give you a time."

"You're not seeing the gravity of this situation. It's all right if you don't want to, but I do. We are going to deal with this today. You will thank me later. You better give me a time. If I have to I'll come to the precinct and ask for you."

"Where are you?"

"At the house."

"OK, I'll try to be there at 3:00pm."

"I'll try isn't good enough."

"Calm down. There are things happening that are out of my control. I'll try to be there at 3:00pm. If not, I'll be there later today. I'll either be there at 3:00pm or I'll call you at 3:00pm to let you know when I'll be there." Eddie doesn't wait for Carl's response. He hangs up as soon as he's done talking.

When he walks back into the emergency room waiting area he sees that the Captain and the other detectives have moved closer to Robyn and they are all talking with each other. Just as he is about to join them Doctor Gagosian comes out of the emergency room. They all stand up and walk towards the doctor. Doctor Gagosian tells them that Bobby is in stable condition, for the time being, but his system is weakening. Frankly, he can't say for sure what's wrong with Bobby but it is life threatening. Doctor Gagosian tells them they are welcomed to stay but Bobby is asleep right now and it's better if they allow him to get some rest. The plan is to monitor him closely for another hour or so and, if he stays stable, they will move him to a room upstairs. That's all he can tell them right now. He promises to tell them more when he has more to tell.

12:30pm - William is back in his suite at the Copenhagen on the internet. He starts with the simplest of things, a Google search. None of the pictures that show up for search "Megan Smith" are the Megan he's looking for. Next he checks the social network websites, Myspace, Facebook, LinkedIn, but again none of the Megan Smiths found on those sites are the one he's looking for. William paces the floor in his suite, walking from the living room into the kitchen into the bedroom and then back into the living room. He made this circuit four times before his next idea hit him in the head like a V8 commercial. He picked up the phone and tried 411 information. The operator gave him the telephone number and address for three Megan Smiths that live in and have a land line in Venice. He tried the first number and Megan answered the phone right away. He suspected it isn't the Megan he's looking for based on her voice. They spoke for a minute before she confirmed that he had the wrong number. He tries the second number but he gets an answering service. He can't tell if this is the Megan he's looking for because the voice on the service is a robotic voice that just repeats the number he dialed. He tries the third number but the line just rings. No one answers and no service takes the call.

After thirty minutes William tries both numbers again and gets the same results. His thinking now is that it's likely that both Megans are at work or out with friends and, in either case, he'll probably have better luck trying them in the evening. If that's the case, he figures he has two options. He can sit in his suite, pacing the floor, and trying the numbers every half an hour until he speaks with them, or he can go to their address and hopefully run into them. Even if he doesn't run into them maybe he can meet a neighbor who can give him some indication that he's on the right track. The idea of sitting in the hotel all day is not going to work. He knows that will drive him crazier than he is right now. So, he grabs the paper with the numbers and addresses on it and he heads to Venice. The Megan with the robotic answering service lives on Navy Street and the Megan with the line that just rings lives on San Juan Court. Off the top of his head he doesn't know where either address is but they are both in Venice so they can't be far from one another. He decides to try Navy Street first.

1:00pm - "Six in one hand, half a dozen in the other," was Lisa's thought after speaking with Detective Roberts, who insisted she call him Eddie. When they spoke earlier they agreed to meet for lunch around 1:00pm, but he just called to postpone their lunch and he said he isn't sure when he would be able to get back to her to reschedule it. In truth, the postponement took a little of the wind out of her sails. She was looking forward to their meeting. She was hoping to establish her first contact inside the LAPD, besides Tony, and Russell indirectly.

After their conversation this morning she went back into Iris's office to finish their meeting. After that she posted her first story about David Waverly's murder on her blog. Though no one could tell by looking at her, with that posting came an almost over-whelming sense of accomplishment. It was a moment she im-mediately wrote about in her journal and it was a moment she would remember forever. The excitement she felt came from being the first to break a story. It didn't matter that it was just in her blog, which is just a small section in the Malibu Journal, which relatively speaking, is a small publication with a relatively small following. What mattered was she crossed the line. She was no longer a journalist just regurgitating what others have already written about, or just putting into story form what could easily be found in public records. Now, officially, at least in her mind, she is an investigative reporter. She ended the description of the event in her journal with the words, "Today is Day One," and she couldn't have been more proud of herself.

After that she tied up some loose ends in her office and she chat-ted with some of her co-workers. At noon she left the Journal and headed to Santa Monica. She and Detective Roberts hadn't picked a place to meet but she figured it would be better to be in town when they spoke again. While she waited for his call she returned to the alley behind 3rd Street where David's body was found. As to be expected, the Promenade was packed at this time of the day. As Lisa arrived at the alley she wondered how many people knew that a person was murdered, or at least, dumped here just two days ago. It was business as usual for most people. Nothing appeared to be out of place and a dozen people were using the alley as a short cut, or to get to their parking space just as they do every day. The likelihood of finding anything that could be considered evidence was almost non-existent, given the police probably took everything they found when they sectioned off the alley. Also, it's been two days since David's body was found. That's two days of heavy traffic through and up and down the alley. Still, with time to spare, Lisa decided to walk the alley not knowing what she was looking for but looking for something anyway. By the time Detective Roberts called she had already walked up and down the alley twice. It was obvious to her when she told him, given the moment of silence, that Detective Roberts was surprised to hear she was doing that. Other than the pause, he didn't react to that bit of information, and she wondered what he was thinking. She hoped it signaled to him that she was a serious reporter and she hoped that would lead to him taking her seriously. When they met she saw that twinkle in his eye that men often have when they meet her. She knew he was attracted to her. That didn't bother her. She is used to that and, more often than not, that is a good thing. She knows how to turn on the charm when dealing with some men, and some women too, in order to get what she wants. This time is different however. This time she wants to be seen and heard not for her beauty but for her professionalism. To that extent, she had planned to share with the Detective some of the things she learned about David but not everything. Principal among the information not to be shared is David's last known address. Lisa figures he already knows that but, if he didn't, she wasn't going to tell him. Not, at least, until she got a chance to ask around herself. "Six in one hand, half a dozen in the other," is how she's taking the news that they aren't going to meet just yet. Since the Detective couldn't tell her when they would speak next, much less whether or not they would even meet today, Lisa decided to do, now, what she planned to do after they met. She got back to her car and jumped on the 10 Freeway headed east towards Los Feliz and the Elysian Gardens Apartments, David's last known address.

1:30pm - Southern California can be tricky. The sun is always shining, flowers are always in bloom, and there are pretty girls in bikinis and muscular studs in swim shorts riding their skateboards everywhere. It's easy to think you are in Utopia and far from danger, but that isn't always reality. What's true for Southern California is true for her neighborhoods. William remembers learning this lesson in his youth. He was driving through a neighborhood in Long Beach, not far from Aunt Ernestine's, on his way to pick up a girlfriend for their first official date. He had just gotten his driver's license six months ago and he still delighted in driving to new places. It was 10:00am on a Saturday morning and he was looking forward to spending the day with her at the County Fair. As he drove through her neighborhood he saw America. There were people in their driveways washing their cars. There were people standing in their front yards talking with their neighbors. Some houses had their sprinklers on, making sure their lawn and flowers got all the water they needed. In front of one those houses there were two kids playing with each other and stopping only to be sure they were in the right position to get drenched when the sprinklers rotated back to where they were playing. When he got to the corner of that block he came to a stop sign. Still the neophyte to driving, he came to a full stop and looked both ways, twice, before gently stepping on the gas to proceed. On the next street the houses were just as well kept. There were green lawns and flowers, and people talking on their porches. He looked for kids playing but there were none and then he heard three pops that sounded like firecrackers. He wouldn't have thought anything of it if it weren't for the young man who came running from the side of one of the houses and across the street with a gun in his hand. Seconds later another young man came running from the side of the same house and another one came running from inside the house. The two of them met each other in front of the house and took off chasing the first man through the street. Both of them had guns in their hands as well. The first young man crossed the street and disappeared behind a house about fifty yards further down the block and on the other side of the street. The two young men followed him and disappeared as well. When William got to his girlfriend's house she told him that he had driven down a street that was a known gang area. Being young, he didn't think much of it at the time. In fact, if he thought anything of it, he thought it was a kinda cool experience. The two of them went on to have a great day at the Fair. By the time they got back to her house it was dusk. They said their goodbyes but not before making plans for the next weekend. Then she gave him a sweet kiss on the lips and reminded him to take a different route home. As he drove home he thought about her and their day and how much he was looking forward to the next weekend, but he also thought of the three gunmen and how he would have never guessed that he would have seen what he did in that neighborhood just that morning.

Now, for the first time since that day he's getting that feeling again. He drove past what he thinks is the right house on San

Juan Court. On his first pass it was impossible to be sure if it was the right house because there were no numbers on the house and none on the curb. William doesn't want to call too much attention to himself so he decides to park his car around the corner and walk the block to be sure. While he was driving, it wasn't the street that gave him the feeling of possible danger, it was the house itself. It is the only house on that street without a green lawn and flowers. It is the only house on that street without numbers. It is the only house on that street with tinted windows. In short, it is the only house on that street that didn't look inviting. On foot, he can sense the stillness of the street, and the closer he gets to that house the denser the stillness becomes. Just to be safe he doesn't walk directly in front of the house. He surveils the house from across the street. He's sure that that's the house because the houses to the right and to the left both have numbers and the address for this house falls right in the middle sequentially. Just as he comes to that conclusion something else catches his attention. There's a guy standing on the roof of the house watching William. Instinctively William waved hello since the two of them made eye contact, but the guy on the roof doesn't move an inch. Also instinctively, William turned his head to look straight ahead and he picked up his pace. He walked to end of the street and made a right around the corner. There was no way he was going to walk back down that same street to get to his car. He walks around the entire block instead. Even as he walks along an entirely different street he can't stop himself from looking behind him a couple of times to make sure he isn't being followed. When he gets back to his car it is easy to convince himself that he isn't going to find Megan there. He goes further than that. He convinces himself that Navy Street sounds familiar. He's sure of it now. The Megan who lives on Navy Street is definitely the Megan he's looking for. Navy Street is west of San Juan Court. William could have easily made a right on San Juan to get to Navy, but he doesn't. Instead he drives two blocks further east and he makes his right hand turn there.

1:45pm - Lisa pulls up in front of the Elysian Gardens Apartments on Clarissa Avenue in Los Feliz and finds parking. Given the picture and the information on David's driver's license, namely he was 6'2", 210 lbs., 22 years old, and strikingly handsome, Lisa's guess is that he was a model or an aspiring actor. Elysian Gardens is exactly where someone who fits that description would live. Los Feliz, itself, is one of Los Angeles' better neighborhoods. It's a perfect mix of location, trendiness, and stability. Nestled between Hollywood and Silver Lake, it is unlike its neighbors. While Hollywood and Silver Lake have B rated sections they both have C minus rated sections as well. Los Feliz is a solid B to B plus rated section of Los Angeles. It has great restaurants, art galleries, specialty bookstores, schools, and parks. The apartment buildings in Los Feliz are surrounded by well-kept and expensive single family homes, and Los Feliz's most well-known resident is the newly remodeled Griffith Observatory. It's obvious that this section of Los Angeles is a magnet to the creative types that are finding some success in their endeavors.

The Elysian Garden Apartments was named befittingly. Despite being the only apartment building on this block of Clarissa Avenue, which is otherwise occupied with beautifully landscaped single family homes, Elysian Gardens is, by far, the most beautiful property on the street. To stand directly in front of the property is to stand in front of a tranquil painting. There are two statuesque and perfectly pruned palm trees in front of the property, one on each side of the building. There is a row of small hedges that extends from each Palm Tree to the front staircase in the middle of the building. Behind both rows of hedges, in a built up flower bed, is a row of apricot California Poppies, behind the California Poppies, in another built up flower bed, is a row of Broadleaf Sedum, behind the Broadleaf Sedum, in another built up flower bed, is a row of pink California Poppies, and behind those is another row of taller hedges. The landscape design both captures the imagination and it draws the attention of the viewer to the center of the property, where through the glass entrance one can see that there is an even more elaborate garden in the courtyard of the property. When Lisa arrives at the property the gardener is wrapping up his work for the day, but the hose he is using is running from inside the courtyard to the front of the property keeping the front entranceway slightly ajar. Lisa walks on to the property and looks for apartment #16. She finds the apartment on the second floor and she knocks on the door. She waits for a moment before knocking again. This time a woman's voice from inside invites her to hang on for a minute. Almost exactly a minute later, Lisa can see someone looking through the peephole from inside the apartment and then the door opens. Lisa is a little a taken back by what she sees. Standing half behind the door and half in the open is a young, voluptuous, and stunning 5'10" blonde with green eyes, in her bra and panties. From her mannerisms and messy hair it's obvious Lisa woke her up. She asks, "Can I help you?" while she sweeps her hair behind her ears and rubs the sleep from her eyes.

Lisa says, "I'm looking for David. Is he home?"

"David doesn't live here anymore."

"When did he move out?"

"He moved out about two months ago."

"Do you know where he moved to?"

"No."

"When was the last time you saw him?"

"I'm sorry but who are you?"

"My name is Lisa Becker. And you are?"

"My name is Jessie."

"Jessie, are you David's roommate?"

"Up until he moved out. Why?" Now that she knows she's speaking to the right person Lisa explains that she isn't really looking for David. She tells Jessie that she a reporter for the Malibu Journal and she knows exactly where David is. With that, Jessie's mood changed as if she knew Lisa had bad news to tell her. Her first question is, "Is David OK?"

Not wanting to talk about it through the front door Lisa asks, "Do you mind if we talk inside?"

Jessie says, "No, come in," as she steps back to open the door so Lisa can enter.

2:00pm - William is right but not for the right reason. He is familiar with Navy Street, though he knows it as the street with the liquor store on the corner. Anyone who has visited Venice Beach knows that finding parking isn't easy. On one of his trips to Venice Beach he did the impossible, he found a perfect parking space in the middle of the day. On his next visit the same thing happened, and the same thing happened on the visit after that. Since then, however, he hasn't been as lucky. Still, when he and Genny wanted to stroll up and down the Venice Beach Boardwalk, he always turned right off Pacific Avenue, at the liquor store on the corner, and looked for parking on Navy Street. This time, like the last few times, he hasn't had any luck finding parking. He parks his car in a lot two blocks away and walks back to the address he's looking for. Even this search brings back memories. The address is for a condo community at the end of Navy Street, just yards from the beach. He and Genny walked past this building on several occasions and on one of those occasions that building inspired them to fantasize about having a place on the beach one day.

He tries the telephone number again, but he gets the same recording. Even though the likelihood is that Megan isn't at home he tries the intercom anyway. Again, he gets the same recording. Just as he pushes the button on the intercom to disconnect someone coming out of the community opens the front door. William says, "I'll be right there," to give this person the impression that he belongs there, and it works. William makes his way to unit number five and knocks on the door. He isn't surprised that there's no answer, but he isn't sure what to do next. Perhaps the best thing to do is to come back later in the day with the hope that this Megan is home by then and she's the Megan he's looking for. The thought of going back to the house on San Juan Court, in the meantime, crosses his mind but he immediately dismisses that idea. He walks through the common areas of the condo community trying to think of a better plan. He sees a middle aged gentleman walk from his condo to the parking area and William thinks of asking him if he knows the girl in unit number five, but before he can come up with a story to explain why he's asking, the man is in his car headed for the front gate. Unable to think of anything new William returns to unit number five and knocks on the door again. Of course, there's no response but that doesn't stop him from knocking one more time. Finally, he's resigns himself to coming back later, but as he turns to walk away the resident in unit number three comes out of his front door. This gentleman is probably in his seventies, though he has a youthful look about him and he appears to be in good shape. William isn't sure about approaching him, but he knows if he doesn't he'll spend the rest of the day kicking himself for not trying. He begins with, "Hi! Excuse me, do you know if a Megan Smith lives in number five?" William knew, right away, that wasn't the best question he could have asked. If he didn't know that for himself, all he has to do is look at the incredulous expression on the gentleman's face and that tells him all he needs to know. Namely, he's cooked.

The gentleman inquires, "Who's asking?"

William hopes the truth will help rehabilitate himself, so he explains, "I am an old friend of Megan's but I've lost her contact information over the years. I'm looking for her because she may have some information I need." It doesn't work.

The gentleman asks the follow up question, "How did you get in here?"

William asks, "Can you just tell me if this Megan is about 5'5" with long, dark brown hair?"

"I think you should leave."

"I'm not looking for any trouble. I just need to find the Megan I'm looking for. It's really important."

"I think you should leave before I call the police."

William concedes, "OK, OK."

"Good," says the older gentleman. "I'm leaving too, I'll walk you out."

The two men walk to the front door, step out on the sidewalk, and the gentleman keeps an eye on William until the front door closes. Then he goes on his way, walking up the block towards Pacific. Standing on the sidewalk, in front of the building, William thinks to himself that there's nothing left to do but wait.

He turns to watch the older man walk up the street and realizes he has a fondness for the old man. He stood his ground, unafraid. William starts to walk in the same direction to get back to his car and his cell phone rings. Though he doesn't recognize her voice, the caller says her name is Megan, and that she's returning his call.

They speak for a minute or two. It turns out to be the Megan who lives on Navy Street but she isn't the Megan he's looking for. William knows the answer to the question but he runs through the problem anyway. There are three Megan Smiths living in Venice. He's already spoken with two and neither of them were her. That leaves the one who doesn't answer the phone or have an answering machine or service, and lives in a dreary house with tinted windows and a man on the roof. On the walk back to his car William thinks about the strength the old man demonstrated.

2:30pm - Jessie took the news of David's death with mixed emotions. She was saddened but she wasn't surprised. Lisa asked if they could talk about David for a little while and if Jessie is OK with her taking notes. Jessie agrees. Lisa begins with, "How did you meet David?"

Jessie tells her, "We met two years ago. We were both hired as bathing suit models for a print campaign for Double XX Factor Nutritional Supplements."

"Tell me about him."

"I remember the first time I saw him I thought he was extremely handsome, but when he stripped down to his bathing suit all I could think was 'Wow!' Sometimes, when male models are that good looking they can be completely self-absorbed. David had a little bit of that in him but he was also very charming and funny.

At first, I thought he was a bore because he spoke a lot about jobs he had done and what they paid. Then I realized I was wrong. He wasn't bragging, he was sharing and gathering information on the employers who paid the highest rates. That's David in a nutshell, good looking and obsessed with making money."

"How did you become roommates?"

"During the shoot I was a little stressed out because my roommate was moving out, to move in with her boyfriend, in a couple of weeks and I hadn't found a new roommate yet. I overheard David tell the photographer that he was looking for a new place and I thought of asking him but decided against it. As the day went on I learned that David was from Colorado Springs. I moved from Boulder to Los Angeles to pursue modeling and acting about a year before I met David. So, we had that in common, and we talked and laughed about our experiences growing up in Colorado. The more we talked the more I liked him. Most important to me at the time was that he was a working model and, like I said, he was always thinking about making money. That made me feel confident that he would always pay his half of the rent. By the end of the day, I changed my mind and asked him if he wanted to be roommates with me. He came by that night to look at the place and said yes."

"He sounds like a good hard working guy, so why aren't you surprised that it ended this way for him?" "About three months after he moved in the drama started. I found out that he did drugs, mostly cocaine, on a regular basis. He would go away for the weekend very often, mostly to Palm Springs. At first, I thought that was great but then I found out that he was working as a bisexual escort and partying the whole weekend when he was there. The drug thing and the escort thing bothered me, but I didn't make a big deal about them because when he was here he was always respectful, and he always paid his rent in advance. We lived like that for over a year. Then, about five months ago, everything changed. The drug use started to catch up with him. What was normally confined to the weekend started to creep into the week. Eventually, he modeled less and partied more. We spoke about it and he told me not to worry, that everything was all right, but he was looking less and less like the David I met. He was still in great shape and looking good, but instead of being charming he was becoming dark and moody. Then, about three months ago, he told me to tell everyone who calls, or asks about him, that I haven't seen him and I don't know where he is. That's when I decided I couldn't live with him anymore, but every time I tried to talk with him about our arrangement he found a way to say let's talk about it later. He was still very nice to me but he stopped returning my phone calls and he seemed to know when I wasn't at home. That's when he would come home, but he never stayed overnight. About a month ago I came home and the place looked ransacked. I almost called the police because I thought we got robbed, but then I noticed none of my stuff was touched. It looked like someone had gone through his stuff in a hurry looking for something. Then I found a note he left for me. It said he had to move out and he only had time gather the things he absolutely needed. It said I could throw away or sell the rest of his stuff because he wasn't coming back. He apologized for everything and finally, in capital letters, he reminded me to tell anyone who asks that I haven't seen him and I don't know where he is. I was worried for a couple of weeks, but no one ever came around or asked for him. You're the first."

"Can you tell me where he worked last or who he worked for?"

"I really can't. I don't have any idea. For the last few months we rarely spoke to each other."

"What about where he hung out?"

"I really don't know."

"What about his friends? Can you tell me who they are and how I can get in touch with them?"

"I can give you the name and number of some of his old friends, but I've spoken with them and they've had the same experience with David as I did. He stopped calling them and he stopped returning their calls. The one thing I can tell you, though, is right around the time he started to change he was hanging out with a guy named Ronny. Ronny White was his name and there was another guy with them but I never met him and I don't remember his name. I think it started with a D or a B. Anyway, I did meet Ronny once and I didn't like him at all. He was a real slick looking guy and he always had something to say, like a used car salesman or something."

"Do you have a number or address for Ronny White?"

"No."

"Do you know if he and David hung out anywhere in particular together?"

"I don't remember David mentioning that, but I know he was spending a lot of time in North Hollywood around that time. The one thing I can tell you for sure is, out of David's friends I'm the only one who met Ronny. The others heard of him, but they never met him. And, if I remember right, they never heard of the other guy. But, none of us liked Ronny. We all felt he was leading David down the dark path he was taking."

"Knowing what you know, what do you think happened to David?"

"That's hard to say. If I had to guess, I'd say because of his escalating drug use he got weak and he stopped thinking clearly. Somehow he got sucked into a scam. I'm sure he thought he was going to make a lot of money. Apparently, he got mixed up with the wrong people and it cost him everything. It's sad but some of us saw this coming. In truth, David was living a double, maybe even a triple life before I met him. I realized, after he moved out and I had time to think about everything that happened, that I don't think I ever knew who he really was."

"OK, last thing. Take my card. If you think of anything else please call me."

"OK, I will."

3:00pm - Carl doesn't consider himself the outdoors type, though he likes to hike, play tennis, play golf, and deep water fish. He doesn't consider himself the adventurous type either, though he has white water rafted down the South Fork of the American River and he has skydived twice. So, when Debra asked and when Pete asked about the bruise on his face, he told them he tried kickboxing, and neither of them doubted it for a minute. The person standing in front of him now won't ask about the bruise because he's the one who gave it to him. In fact, they are both standing in almost the exact same places they were in when he did.

This time Carl promises Eddie they are alone and since Eddie is sure Carl knows what will happen if they aren't, so he believes him. With that aside, they pick up the conversation they couldn't have earlier. Eddie asks, "So, what did he ask you?"

Carl says, "He didn't ask me anything. He just mentioned that he noticed I planned to transfer a large part of my proceeds to 24th Street, LLC."

Since he doesn't see a problem with that Eddie's response is, "So what?"

"You don't understand Pete. Right now he's wondering, why? I'm sure he's wondering why I would do that as a part of the closing, when I could have easily done it after, without him or anyone else knowing."

"Again, so what?"

"There's more. On his way out he thanked me for doing my part to make the deal happen. He didn't mention the two hundred and fifty thousand dollars specifically, but that's what he was talking about." "Maybe he was simply thanking you."

"That's not how Pete operates. He doesn't make comments like that in passing. He's always thinking two steps ahead. He mentioned the transfer and he thanked me for a reason."

"I think the drugs are getting to you. You're being paranoid. I don't see anything suspicious in either of those comments. If he suspects something that means he doesn't know anything. If that's the case, he's trying to pressure you into spilling the beans. Keep your mouth shut. Avoid him if you have to. Just go about your business as you normally do. It will all be over in two days."

"That may be but I still think we need a cover story."

"OK, what do you think it should be?"

"If anyone asks, we met each other five years ago at a Yahoo, Inc. shareholder's meeting in Santa Clara and we've stayed in contact over the years. You pitched the idea of buying land in Costa Rica and developing it into a hotel and resort property. The money I gave to you is for a 30% stake in your company."

Hoping this will satisfy Carl, Eddie says, "Fine, done."

"Good. How's everything on your end?"

"I'll tell you but you have to stay calm. Everything is under control. The kid we used has been identified."

"So quickly? How'd that happen?"

"The kid had a record in Colorado Springs, Colorado, his hometown."

"I thought . . ."

Eddie cuts him off, "I know, I know, he wasn't supposed to have a record. It doesn't matter. Breck is back in Costa Rica and Ronny is dead."

"I assume Breck took care of Ronny, but wasn't Breck the one who was supposed to make sure we had someone clean to use? How do you know Ronny is dead?"

"I had the same concern. I checked Breck's story out this morning. I'm sure Ronny's dead. That severs the connection. The only thing that changes is I actually have to pretend to work for the next two days." "What about Bobby, and where is he, by the way?"

"He took the day off. We don't need to worry about him. Are you happy now? Everything is working out and we have a cover story."

"I'll be happy in two days."

"Quid pro quo," is what Lisa is thinking, or "one hand washes the other," as her mother likes to say.

The interview with Jesse went reasonably well. She came away with a few names and numbers for David's friends and, more importantly, with the name, Ronny White, whom she's sure the police would label as a person of interest. She's torn between waiting for Detective Roberts to call back and trying him again. She knows the information she has isn't earth shattering, but it might be enough to impress the Detective and help her form a partnership, of sorts, with him. At the risk of seeming pushy she decides to call. Eddie's cell phone rings and he tells Carl, "I gotta get this." Carl takes the opportunity to go to the bathroom, leaving Eddie alone in the kitchen. He starts the conversation with, "I was just about to call you. I'm sorry I had to postpone. Something came up."

Lisa says, "It's no big deal. Do you think you'll have time to meet today? Before you answer that let me tell you I met with David Waverly's former roommate and I know a few things that might be helpful to you."

"I was going to say yes anyway, but now I am particularly interested. Where are you?"

Lisa tells him where she is and what she has to do during the remainder of the day. They agree on a location and they agree to meet at 5:00pm.

4:00pm - William's mind is telling him to do one thing but his body is doing something else entirely, namely nothing. He's thinking to himself, "It's now or never. It's late in the afternoon and the last thing I want to do is be near that house at night. Get out of the car and let's go." This is the second time he's had that pep talk with himself and for the second time his body has done nothing. He hasn't even unfastened his seat belt, and both of his hands are still gripping the steering wheel. In his rear view mirror William sees a mother holding her daughter's hand as the two of them walk down the sidewalk. They pass William's car and stop at the corner. The mother is obviously taking this opportunity to remind her daughter to look both ways before she crosses the street. The daughter looks both ways and then says something to her mother. Her mother smiles, nods yes, and the two of them cross the street. Long after the mother and daughter have disappeared into the distance William remains fixed on the space the two of them occupied together.

It's a beautiful spring morning in Southern California. It's somewhere in the high 60's, there is a gentle breeze coming off the ocean, there are only whispers of clouds in the light blue sky, and the sun is peaking around the buildings to the east. William and Genny approach a crosswalk and stand behind a father and his daughter who are also waiting for the signal to walk. The man's daughter has two ponytails, multi-color leggings, and a denim dress on. And, she appears to be just as happy as anyone can be. Genny points her out to William and then says to the father, "She is absolutely adorable."

The father smiles and says, "Thank you."

Genny asks, "How old is she?"

The father says, "She's three." Then he looks down to his daughter and says, "Say hi Kayla."

Kayla smiles and turns to William and Genny and says, "Hi Kayla," and then she starts to laugh hysterically.

The father explains to William and Genny, "She does that on purpose. That's her latest thing. You can tell she thinks it's the funniest thing. Watch." Again, the father turns to his daughter and says, "Say hi Kayla."

Kayla has to find the strength to stop laughing from the first time, so she can do it again. She turns to William and Genny and says, "Hi Kayla," and then she goes right back to laughing. Her laughter is so genuine and hearty it's infectious. Soon Kayla, her father, William, and Genny are laughing like they just heard the funniest thing in the world. A moment later the signal turns from don't walk to walk. Kayla's father reminds her to look both ways. She does and then he sings, "OK, we can walk now. Walk, walk, walk. We can walk now. Walk, walk, walk. We can walk now. Walk, walk, walk."

Genny and William are mesmerized by Kayla, who continues to sing her song until she steps on the curb on the other side of the street.

Genny tells William, "I can't wait for us to have children."

"Me too," says William as he drapes his arm around Genny. A moment later, there's a loud and startling bang that came from William's right. In real time, he turned to see that the noise was created when a large crate fell off a vendor's hand truck while he was off loading. Now, however, the loud bang takes William back to crawling from the floor in his office to their bedroom. He can hear himself calling Genny's name without any answer. Then he lifts himself up to the top of the bed and sees Genny, lying in a pool of blood in their bed. The shock of what he sees snaps him out of his daydream and back to reality.

The next thing William knows is he's walking down San Juan Court towards the house. The lookout on the roof has spotted him and has watched him until he got directly across the street from the house. By the time he crosses the street and approaches the front gate the lookout has disappeared. He walks towards the steps leading to the porch, but before he reaches them a pretty young woman, probably in her twenties, in cutoff jeans and a tee-shirt, steps out of the house and holds the front door open so William can go in. He steps through the front door and into the living room. Without asking his name or introducing herself, she simply tells William, "Wait here," and then she walks to the other side of the room and through a curtain of stringed together sea shells. There are nine flat screen televisions, in three columns of three, on the wall in the living room. All of them are on, all on different channels, but all of them are muted. There is techno music streaming through the house just loud enough to be a distraction. There are chairs and couches throughout the living room and in between them are dozens of games, several game consoles, and DVDs. A moment later a young man comes from behind the curtain of sea shells. William isn't one to judge a book by its cover but he thinks, in this case, "the cover probably tells the story." The young man is bald with a goatee. He has on boots, jeans, and a tee-shirt; and from what William can see, tattoos cover every inch of his body, from his neck to his fingertips. He walks right up to William, but he doesn't say a thing. So, William begins with, "I'm hoping you can help me. I'm looking for a girl named Megan Smith.

"The young man asks, "Who are you?"

"My name is William Flowers. I'm a friend of Megan's. Actually, I'm not a friend. I only met her once, but I really need to talk with her. I think she may have some information that can help me. Does she live here?"

"What kind of information?"

"Does she live here?" The young man doesn't respond to that question, he simply continues to stare at William, waiting for his question to be answered. William continues, "Look, I'm not out to cause any trouble. I just need to talk with Megan. I need to know what she knows about a guy named Teddy Gallo."

Before William mentioned that name there was a chance, just a chance that he'd get out of the house unscathed. But, that name, in this house, turns out to be like a land mine. If you aren't being careful you'll step on it, and by the time you do, it's too late. Triggered, the young man punches William, in the gut, so hard and so unexpectedly, his legs turn to spaghetti. First, William buckles over, and then he drops to his knees.

4:30pm - Robyn wanted to be the first thing Bobby sees when he wakes up and when he opened his eyes she was standing over him holding his hand and stroking his hair. The first thing she says is,

"Baby, I am so sorry I couldn't get here sooner. They wouldn't let me in the emergency room to see you before you went to sleep."

Bobby says, "That's OK. I'm just happy to see you."

"Oh Bobby, I love you so much."

"I love you too."

"How are you feeling?"

"I'm fine, I just feel a little tired. What did the doctor say?"

"He hasn't really said anything. He's still trying to figure out what's going on with you. The only thing he knows for sure is that you need to stay here for a few days. Captain Upton, Eddie, and few other people from the department were here earlier. They said they'll be back this evening."

"See if you can find the doctor."

"He was just here about a half an hour ago to check on you. He said he'll be back before he leaves for the night. The nurses have been checking on you every hour also. What can I do to make you more comfortable?"

"I just want to speak with the doctor."

"Bobby, baby, I'll let everyone know you're awake, but I want you to relax. This may be hard to hear but maybe this is a good thing. Now that you're here they can find out what's wrong before it gets worse. I'll go look for the doctor. I'll be right back."

"No, never mind, I can wait. I want you to stay here." He reaches his hand out for hers. She takes it and sits on the bed next to him. Bobby says, "I know you had a lot you needed to get done today. I hope this hasn't messed up your plans too much."

"Oh Bobby, don't worry about me."

"I don't want you to worry about me either. I know I'll be fine. I think this is just my body's way of asking for rest."

"I think I should cancel my plans to visit my mother this weekend and my plans for next week."

"No, no, no, don't even think that way. Everything is going to be fine. Listen, don't tell anyone but, now that I'm here, it's OK. I could use the rest. If they try to send me home before Monday I'll just pass out or something." Bobby doesn't get the reaction he was hoping for so he has to admit, "That was a joke."

"That's not funny."

"Don't worry. All of this is stress related."

"What kind of stress are you under that would cause you to get sick like this?"

"It's work related. We don't need to get into it. Just believe me when I tell you that by Monday it will all be behind me. You'll see, by Monday I'll be a new man. I bet all of my symptoms will go away by then."

"I still think I should cancel my plans just so I can stay close to you."

"Robyn, trust me, everything will be OK. I'm just going to spend the weekend resting. I'll watch a few games, read a little bit, and take it easy. I'll let the nurses know how to reach you if anything happens, but nothing is going to happen. I don't know what you have planned for next week, but by then, you'll see, I'll be back home and feeling great."

Robyn kisses Bobby gently on the lips and caresses the side of his face. Robyn says, "I'm sorry to hear about the stress you're under. I wish you had told me about it sooner."

"I didn't want to make a bigger deal of it than it already is."

"Are you in any trouble or danger?"

"No, it's nothing like that. Everything is fine at work. It's just, sometimes we see things or hear about things that turns our stomachs. I chose to be a cop, you didn't. I never want to share that stuff with you." Robyn leans in to give him another gentle kiss. This time, as she backs away, he holds her close and says, "Visit your mom this weekend and have a good time. I'm going to stay right here, in this bed. Believe me, by the time you get back on Monday, I'll be a new man. Do you believe me?"

Robyn, with tears in her eyes, says, "I believe you Bobby."

"Then why are you crying?"

His guess is, she's crying because she's worried, but he doesn't wait for her to answer. He wipes her tears away and he gives her a hug. Robyn breaks from the hug and says, "I'm crying because I don't want to see you suffer."

Bobby smiles and says, "Then, give me another kiss."

4:45pm - The punch in the gut was just the beginning. Immediately after the first punch another man came from behind the curtain and the two men dragged William, kicking and flailing, down to the basement. William desperately tries to explain his intentions but nothing he has to say means anything to them. In fact, they aren't even listening. Once they get to the basement William uses a surge of energy to try to escape, but it's futile. The other man takes it as an opportunity to get in on the action and he delivers another blow to William's mid-section. The blow is so crippling the first guy compliments him.

William is stripped of his shoes, pants, and shirt; and tied to a chair placed in the middle of the damp, dark basement. The two men are so efficient at the strip, search, and binding move, it's impossible to believe this is the first time they've done this sort of thing. Once they are convinced that William isn't wired they begin to question him. From their interaction with each other William knows the guy who came out to greet him is Wade, and his equally bald and tattooed backup is KiKi, who appears to be the older of the two and the one in charge. KiKi asks William, "What are you doing here?"

Though he hasn't fully recovered from KiKi's punch, William tries to explain again. "I'm looking for a girl named . . ."

Before he can finish that sentence KiKi cuts him off. "I know that part already. What do you have to do with Teddy Gallo?"

Despite being stripped down to his underwear and tied to a chair in a place he could easily disappear from and no one would ever know what happened to him, William feels good about his situation and KiKi's question. The tone in KiKi's voice gives William reason to believe that KiKi knows both Megan and Teddy. He explains, "Teddy used to date my wife."

Wade jumps in with, "And you found out that motherfucker is still banging her so you're looking for him, right?" Now, it's clear to William that KiKi's in charge based on the look he gave Wade and on the way Wade backed down and shut up.

"No. My wife was murdered three months ago. It was made to look like a burglary but I don't believe that. I believe she was intentionally murdered, but I don't have any idea why. I don't even know that Teddy had anything to do with it or knew anything about it, but he is the only person I could think of who might."

KiKi asks, "So why aren't you just looking for Teddy? What does Megan have to do with it?"

"I know where Teddy is. He's in the morgue. He overdosed a few days ago. My wife and I ran into Teddy a couple of years ago and he was with Megan. I'm just hoping she can tell me something about Teddy that will help me figure out who killed my wife."

KiKi and Wade are left speechless. They look at each other and neither of them have any more questions. They leave William tied to the chair, but they step into the shadows on the other side of the staircase. William asks them both, repeatedly, if they know

Megan, and, if they do, will they please tell him where he can find her. William also asks that he be untied and set free to go. He even tries to bargain with them. He offers to just leave, without asking another question, if they just untie him. He knows both Wade and KiKi are still in the room because they didn't go upstairs, but neither of them say a word and neither of them come out of the shadow that covers them.

The door opens at the top of the stairs. Before William hears the heavy breathing of someone gasping for air, he hears the sound of something very large, or very heavy, land on the first step. The sound of the step creaking beneath the weight makes him think it might break under the pressure, but it doesn't. Nor does the next step or the next. William can see that the person, who is now half way down the staircase and coming his way, is extremely large and heavy, but he really has no idea just how large and heavy he is until he reaches the bottom of the stairs and walks over to William. Dressed in what had to be a custom made sweat suit, standing in front of William is, without a doubt, the largest and heaviest man William has ever seen in person. It's hard to tell if he is Latino or Native American or something else. William's guess he's about six foot five or six foot six and he must weigh, at least, three hundred and fifty to four hundred pounds easy. He has long straight hair that he wears in a ponytail and he has what William calls a Fu Manchu mustache, that's thin over his lip, and gradually gets more full as it winds down to his chin. He stands right in front of William, but he doesn't say a word. He just looks William in the eye without blinking for an extended period of time. William follows his instincts and he doesn't say a word either. He just stares back at this man hoping he'll see that he's telling the truth and he has nothing to hide. It's dead silent, except for this man's breathing. When he's seen enough he turns and walks into the shadow on the other side of the staircase where KiKi and Wade are waiting.

KiKi speaks first, "He's not wearing a wire and his ID says he is who he says he is."

Wade says, "We should fuck him up anyway, just for coming here." The heavyset man tells KiKi to ask William what his wife's name is. KiKi returns a few seconds later and says, "His wife's name was Geneviève. What do you want to do with him?"

William knew better than to say anything while the heavyset man was checking him out, but now his imagination is getting the better of him. He's convinced they are discussing what to do with him and, more than that, he's convinced it won't be good. In a desperate attempt to prove he's no threat to them he starts to yell out his name, where he lives, why he's there, and if they just let him go he won't ask any more questions and he'll never return. The heavyset man, KiKi, and Wade are trying to decide what to do with him, but William's pleas are getting on their nerves. The heavyset man steps from out of the shadow and walks up to William to say, "Shut the fuck up." William does and the heavyset man returns to the shadows. After what seems like an hour, but was really only ten minutes, the heavyset man stands in front of William again, with KiKi and Wade on either side of him. He tells William, "Because you brought me good news about Teddy, that rat motherfucker, I'm going to let you go. I ain't telling you shit about Megan, and it's in your best interest to forget you ever met her. If you ever come here again, I'll kill you myself. Then, I'll chop you up and grind you down to chum, and I'll feed you to the fish off the Santa Monica Pier. We clear?" William says, "Yes."

5:00pm - Eddie arrives at the Public Library in Santa Monica first and waits for Lisa in the courtyard, where they agreed to meet. He only had to wait for a couple of minutes before he spotted her waving and walking towards him. While extending her hand Lisa says, "Detective Roberts, thanks so much for taking the time to meet with me."

Eddie smiles, shakes her hand and says, "I thought we agreed that you would call me Eddie."

Lisa smiles and says, "OK, Eddie."

Eddie says, "What do you say we take a walk around the block while we speak?"

"That sounds good to me."

As they head out of the courtyard Eddie begins with, "So, tell me a little bit about yourself before we get down to business."

"Well, you already know that I'm a writer for the Malibu Journal."

"Yes, I checked out your blog the other night. I think you are a good writer."

"Thank you. That means a lot to me."

"How'd you get interested in writing?"

"I have always loved to write. If you met my mother she would tell you that I wrote my first book when I was five. It's actually a one page description, written in orange crayon, of the day I got my first pet, Swimmy, the goldfish. My mother framed it and hung it on a wall in our house and I remember feeling so proud of it. Since then I've always written. Anyway, to make a long story short, a few years later my father was murdered."

"I'm sorry to hear that."

"Thanks. It's been a while so I'm OK with it now. Anyway, the police were having some difficulty coming up with leads. Russell

Armstrong heard about my father's murder and where it happened, and decided to get involved."

"Russell Armstrong, why do I know that name?"

"He's a crime beat writer for the Los Angeles Times."

"That's right, I remember who he is now. He isn't just a crime beat writer, he's the best Los Angeles has to offer."

Lisa smiles and says, "You're absolutely right. I'll tell him you said that. It will make him happy."

"You do that, but I interrupted your story. Please continue."

"Russell asked around and came up with a few leads that led to the arrest of the men who murdered my father. I don't know exactly when, but at some point, I'd decided I wanted to be just like Russell. I still love and miss my dad, but I consider Russell my second dad. He came to all of my school events and he had dinner with my mom and me, at least twice a week every week, for several years. Of course, I've read everything he's written and he was the one who introduced me to Iris Abrams, the owner of the Journal. Now, I love doing research as much as I love writing. I consider myself an investigative journalist but I don't see it as a job. It's who I am. That's why this case is so important to me. It's my first meaningful story and I was on top of it first."

"You were there even before me."

"What about you? Do you mind telling me a little about who you are?"

"Well, I've been a cop for twenty years, and a detective for fifteen. I guess the most exciting thing about me is that I'm retiring on Friday."

"This Friday?"

"Yes. You sound disappointed."

"Sorry. I mean, I'm happy for you, but I was hoping we'd develop a working relationship."

"We can still do that. I'm still on the job for a couple of days. You met my partner Bobby. For reasons I can't explain, there may be other detectives taking over the case when I leave. I'll make sure to introduce them to you and I'll tell them that I promised you an exclusive or, at least, the lead."

"I'm sorry I won't be working with you but that sounds great."

"OK, so tell me about David's roommate."

Lisa tells Eddie everything Jessie told her. None of it bothers Eddie. If Lisa is right, none of David's friends met Ronny with the exception of Jessie. And, Jessie is the only one who heard of Ronny's friend, who is obviously Breck, but she never met him and she can't even remember his name. If Lisa is right, Jessie thinks that his name begins with a D or a B. There's a possibility that she might remember the name if she hears it again. Still, Eddie is happy with what he's hearing. At least, Breck and Ronny got that part mostly right. He makes a mental note to confirm everything that Lisa has told him with Jessie when he talks with her. Even if David's other friends did meet Ronny, it isn't a problem since Ronny is no longer a threat. The only thing that concerns Eddie now is Lisa. While she tells him about her meeting with Jessie, Eddie asks her if she remembers the name of the officer that was at the murder scene. Lisa says she doesn't. Of course, she could be lying about that just to protect her boyfriend, but that's the point. Her boyfriend is on the force and in Eddie's precinct for that matter. She's also connected to Russell Armstrong. Eddie wasn't kidding when he said Russell is one of Los Angeles' best journalist. Russell has a reputation for uncovering things that have escaped other people, including, sometimes, the police themselves. Most troubling, however, is Lisa's ambition. She already knows more about David than he does and it's obvious, she isn't going to stop digging. Given the mistake Breck and Ronny made with David, it's entirely possible that they made other mistakes. He thinks about how long he's waited for the payoff to come in just a couple of days. He thinks about all the things he's done, including all of the murders, to insure that his day would come. He didn't come this far and he didn't do all of the things he's done to become a man in prison instead of a man with two and a half million dollars, a yacht, and a life of leisure in Costa Rica. Before Lisa finishes telling him what she knows Eddie decides that he needs more insurance. Now that he and Lisa are back at the courtyard Eddie compliments her on her work so far and he assures her, again, that he and his successors will do everything they can to help her. They agree to check in with each other in a day or two, unless there's a reason to speak sooner. Eddie walks Lisa to her car and watches as she drives away. As soon as she is out of sight he takes out his cell phone and calls Costa Rica.

"What the hell are you talking about?" asks Breck. "You and your partner practically threw me out of the country and now you want me to come back?"

Eddie says, "I don't think I'm going to need you, but I want you here just in case. I need you to get on a plane right away. I'll make it worth your while. If I have more work for you I'll pay you double your rate. If not, I'll pay you half your rate just for coming. By the way, just buy a one way ticket. You can cruise with me on the boat back to Costa Rica. What do you say?"

"Pay me my full rate just for coming, and I'll be on a plane in a few hours."

"Done. Call me just before you board." Eddie hangs up and smiles to himself as he walks back to his car. He's thinking, "It's been a good day. I still have to worry about Bobby but I can handle him. Carl is happy. I have Breck coming back to take care of Lisa and/ or any of David's friends if they know more than they should, and I could have promised Breck ten times his rate if I had to. He'll never see a dime of the money because he'll never make it back to Costa Rica. Today has been a good day."

5:30pm - The danger is over but William's heart is still racing and his hands are shaking uncontrollably. Somehow, while he was in the house he found a way to stay as calm and as collected as could be expected, but now, sitting in his car, he's having a mini nervous breakdown. He doesn't even remember walking to his car. One minute he was getting dressed under the supervision of Wade and KiKi and the next minute he's in his car feeling more panic and anxiety than he's ever felt before. Driving away from the house isn't helping his anxiety go away. In fact, all of the people, traffic, stop lights, stop signs, street lights, and noise on Main Street are only serving to heighten his anxiety and nervousness. In addition to his uncontrollable shaking he is now starting to dry heave. Never in his life has he wanted to throw up except for right now. He thinks it will help him calm down, but he can't get himself to do it. He can only dry heave. On top of all of that his bladder needs to be relieved. The urge is so sudden but strong he realizes he only has two choices. He can relieve himself right there in the car or he can pull over and find a bathroom. There's no way he can hold it until he gets back to his hotel. He pulls his car into the first space he sees and jumps out, leaving the back of his car sticking out in traffic slightly. He heads for the Starbucks he sees on the corner in the distance, all the while telling himself, repeatedly, "If I just make it to the bathroom I'll be OK."

Luckily the bathroom is unoccupied so he walks in and locks the door behind him.

Relieving himself did help. His heart is still racing and he's still breathing visibly, but his hands have stopped shaking and so has the dry heaving. Standing in front of the sink and mirror he un-buttons his shirt to look at his mid-section. He's sore and there are two visible bruises, but he knows nothing is broken and he'll be OK. He splashes cold water on his face and chest and that helps him to relax. Still, he needs more time before he's ready to leave the bathroom. At first glance, in the mirror, he sees a man who's lucky to be alive. At second glance, however, he's not sure who or what he sees. More cold water helps him to relax more and now his breathing and heart rate are almost back to normal. At third glance, he laughs at the man's face starring back at him in the mirror, but after that, he has a question. "What the hell are you doing?" The only answer that comes to mind is, "Think. Now that you know you have the right Megan, there has to be a way to get in contact with her. Calling won't do any good. Neither will parking in front of the house hoping to catch her before she goes in or after she comes out. You could park down the street and try to catch her either walking or in her car before she gets to the house. Think William think." William paces in the bathroom for a minute or two before he decides he still doesn't have a good idea. Maybe it's time to get back to the hotel. Maybe he'll get an idea during the drive. If not, he'll take a walk along the bluffs and maybe he'll come up with something then. He looks in the mirror again and this time he likes what he sees. He tells the man starring back at him, "You were afraid to go in that house but you did it. You were afraid of being tied up in the basement but you survived it. You're a crazy bastard but I like you." He turns on the cold water again and let's it run for a few seconds so it gets as cold as it gets. He splashes his face and his chest one more time. This time, not to relax him. He already feels as calm as he normally does. This time he does it just because it feels so good. He dries himself off and buttons his shirt. He takes a deep breath and heads for the door.

Lexi has already ordered and paid for her tall Caramel Macchiato. Now she is standing by the Barista's station, which is next to the short hallway leading to the bathroom. Her drink should come up as the drink after next. The opening of the bathroom door caught her attention and she immediately recognizes William, but she doesn't say anything to him as he walks past her. Her first thought is to let him go and mind her own business. Her second thought is about the story she heard while she was sitting upstairs in the surveillance room and he was downstairs in the basement. Even though she is doing what she has to do to get by, she hasn't lost her dream of finding true love and having a family one day. She's feeling conflicted. She knows it's in her best interest to stay out of it, but she feels something for the man whose wife was murdered and who obviously loves her so much that he would risk his own life seeking revenge. The Barista says, "I have a tall Caramel Macchiato for Lexi," but no one claims the drink.

She catches up with William just before he gets to his car. He didn't know who she was at first. The last time he saw her she was in cutoff jeans and a tee-shirt and her hair was down. Now, she's in a sexy black dress, with sexy open toe heels. She has on makeup and her hair is up in an elegant bun. Once she has his attention she asks, "Do you have a pen and paper?"
William answers, "No, but I do in my car. Let me get it."

Lexi says, "No. I can't be seen talking to you. I'm going to tell you this once and then I'm walking away and you better not come after me." She gives William Megan's cell phone number and then she gives him hers and she tells William to call her only if he can't reach Megan, which shouldn't happen because she talked with Megan yesterday at that number. True to her word, Lexi told William what she wanted to tell him, and then she turned and walked away.

6:00pm - Sitting at her desk just outside Sheriff Silva's office, Phyllis Stafford, his assistant, yells into his office, "You're just trying to get my goat!"

Sheriff Silva smiles to himself because that's exactly what he's trying to do. He yells back at her, "Ty Murray is the greatest Rodeo Cowboy ever." Phyllis has been Sheriff Silva's assistant for the five years he's been the Sheriff. He inherited her from the previous Sheriff, whom she served for ten years. Though he doesn't tell her often, he does tell almost everyone else that having her as his assistant is one of the best things that's ever happened to him. She's more like family than a co-worker and as such, when time and work allow, Sheriff Silva takes some pleasure in pushing her buttons. If there's one thing that gets her going every time, it's saying anything that appears to besmirch the name of Larry Mahan, "the greatest Rodeo Cowboy to ever live," according to Phyllis.

Sheriff Silva piles on with, "Larry won the World All-Around Rodeo Champion title six times, Ty won it seven times and he won the World Bull Riding Championship title twice."

"So did Larry," says Phyllis. Now it's Phyllis's' turn to pile on with, "Oh, by the way, I'm sure you've heard of the Academy Award winning documentary film called "The Great American Cowboy."That's about Larry not Ty."

"Yeah, but Ty has done more commercials."

"Commercials? Who cares about commercials? You're comparing being memorialized in an Academy Award winning film to doing commercials?" Phyllis's' phone rings but before she answers it she has one more jab. "And let me tell you another thing, if they were competing at the same time, Ty wouldn't have more titles than Larry."

Sheriff Silva is smiling from ear to ear, thinking: "This never gets old."

He hears Phyllis tell the caller, "Yes, he's still here. I'm glad you called. He's in his office doing his best to get my dandruff up. Hold on." Sheriff Silva knows that Phyllis would only say that to one of two people, either his wife or his brother. He hopes it's his brother, otherwise he'll have to answer to his wife when he gets home for teasing Phyllis. Phyllis says, "It's Steven for you."

Steven says, "What's going on over there?"

Sheriff Silva says, "I'm just teasing Phyllis about Mahan again."

"What's wrong with you? You know she'd rather hear you say she looks fat, than to hear anything bad about Mahan."

"That's why I do it. It's the one thing that drives her crazy."

"So what's up? I'm returning your call."

"I just wanted you to know that we got lucky and got a match from his dental records. His name was Ronny White. He was a small time but career criminal. Apparently, he was arrested several times. Each time it was either for possession or assault. He did some time but got an early release due to overcrowding. Forensics confirmed, he was shot with a .45 caliber pistol."

"Just as I thought. What do you think happened?"

"My guess is he knew or did something that didn't sit well with others and they killed him for it."

"Is that good or bad news?"

"Probably both. It's good because that probably means it's an iso-lated incident and none of the town's folk are in any danger. It's troubling because I have to figure out why someone would dump his body here."

Steven asks, "Well, if . . ."

Sheriff Silva cuts him off because Phyllis is standing in his doorway trying to get his attention. "Hold on Steve. What's up Phyll?"

Phyllis says, "I have Bradley Koch on the line for you."

"The Bradley Koch?" "

Yes," says Phyllis.

Sheriff Silva says, "Steve, I have to call you back. Bradley Koch is on the line for me."

"Wow. Have you ever spoken with him before?"

"Never."

"Well, there's a first time for everything. Call me back."

Before picking up the call Sheriff Silva wonders why the Chief of Police for the Los Angeles Police Department would be calling him. There's only on way to find out. He picks up the line and says "Sheriff Silva speaking."

"Sheriff Silva, this is Chief Koch."

"Chief Koch, it's an honor to speak with you. What can I do for you sir?"

6:30pm - By the time William took out his phone, put the num-bers into his contacts, and looked up, Lexi was out of sight. He dials the number she gave him for Megan but gets another mechanical recording that tells him what number he dialed and prompts him to leave a message. He leaves a lengthy message explaining who he is, when and how they met, and how impor-tant it is that she call him back as soon as she gets his message.

William only had enough time to get in his car and get to the first stop light before his cell phone rings. The voice on the phone sounds familiar to him right away. William says, "Thanks for calling me back so quickly. I don't know if you remember but we met . . ." Megan cuts him off and says, "You don't to explain that again. I remember meeting you and your wife. I'm sorry about her death. I read about it online."

"Thanks. That's why I'm calling you."

"I'm glad you did. When I read about her death I thought about calling you, but I just couldn't bring myself to do it."

"What made you think about calling me?"

"I don't think your wife's death was an accident. I wanted to tell you what Teddy told me, but then I thought about it and I realized he didn't really tell me anything specifically. I just put two and two together and came up with a theory. I'll tell you now what I was going to tell you then. You need to talk to Teddy. I think he knows who killed your wife and why."

William is stunned by what Megan has said. So much so, his mind has gone blank and he can't think of what to say next. Megan says, "Hello. Are you still there?"

William snaps back to consciousness and says, "Teddy's dead."

"Oh my God! When? How?"

"The police found him a few days ago in his apartment. They're not sure if he died by accident or if he committed suicide, but he overdosed on heroin."

This time it's Megan who has gone silent. When she speaks, William can hear in her voice, that she's crying. Megan says, "I think they killed him."

"They? Who's they?"

"I don't know, but I can tell you that Teddy didn't overdose on heroin."

"How do you know that?"

"I guess I don't know for sure. I guess anything is possible, but I'm 99% sure he didn't overdose on heroin. Teddy was a pot-head. He did cocaine every once in a while, maybe some Ecstasy here and there. He tried Xanax once and, as far as I know, he never did it again. He said he didn't like how out of it it made him feel."

"Maybe he tried heroin for the first time and did too much."

"Maybe, but I don't think so. Teddy was terrified of two things, sharks and needles. He didn't swim in the ocean because he was convinced that a shark would get him, and he was afraid to go to the doctor because he might have to get a needle. I mean he was absolutely terrified of both of those things. I think someone else, probably someone he knew, shot him up with heroin to kill him."

"Can we meet to talk about what Teddy told you?"

"I don't know if that's a good idea. I broke up with him because I didn't want to be a part of the life he was living and I still don't want to have anything to do with it. Besides, I have problems of my own." "Just tell me what Teddy told you."

"Like I said, he didn't tell me anything. He didn't mention any names or anything that could help you." "Yeah, but you said it yourself. You put two and two together and you thought of Genny. He must have told you something that can help. You are right, I don't believe my wife was killed by accident. I've been fighting with the police because they are convinced it was a bur-glary gone wrong. You are the first and only person I've spoken with who believes what I do. Just tell me what you know and I'll go away and you'll never hear from me again. Please, I need your help."There's an extended silence on the phone and then Megan tells William where he can find her.

7:00pm - Lisa pushed through the doors of the Metropolis Diner and spots Russell immediately. Why wouldn't she? Every night, after work, Russell and his friends gather here to discuss the stories they are working on, sports, politics, and, occasionally, women. It's always a treat for Russell's friends whenever Lisa stops by, mostly because they've come to know her as Russell's little girl, but also because she's so pretty. The Metropolis doesn't serve alcohol, but the owner has given Russell and his old school crew permission to bring their own alcohol as long as they keep it on the down low, which they've managed to do for years. Their deal is, whoever's turn it is to bring the Vodka gets to sit on one side of the booth by himself. The others sit on the other side of the booth and at the table next to the booth. Lisa isn't privy to their deal, though she knows Vodka gets passed around at these gatherings. The guys at the table were the first to see her coming, followed by Russell, who's sitting on one side of the booth by himself, and finally by the two guys sitting on the other side of the booth across from him. After some small talk and laughs with Russell's friends, which always includes Ernie, the oldest guy at the gathering, asking Lisa if she has any friends who likes older old guys, the two guys on the other side of the booth scoot out and join the guys at the table, so Lisa can slide in to speak with Russell.

Russell asks, "How did your day go?"
Lisa says, "Great." She goes on to tell Russell of her meeting with Jessie and of the things they talked about. She tells Russell about the phone calls she placed to three of David's friends and what

she learned from the two who have returned her call so far. Then she tells him about her meeting with Detective Roberts and about the things the two of them discussed.

After she tells Russell everything his first comment is, "I wish you hadn't been so forth coming with Detective Roberts."

Lisa asks, "Why?"

"First of all, he has a reputation of being a do whatever it takes kind of detective. I'm not saying he's a bad guy. I don't know him well enough to say, for certain, whether he's a good guy or a bad guy. I just know his reputation, which is it isn't beneath him to bend the rules to get what he wants. Sometimes we need police officers like that to get justice and sometimes police officers like that go too far. More importantly, it takes time to build a working relationship with a detective. In general, they aren't looking for partners outside the force. In fact, some of them aren't looking for partners at all. You showed him all of your cards too early. In this case, I don't think it will hurt you. Just remember that doing that won't yield the results you want. Working relationships you can trust and rely on only come with time."

Lisa ponders what Russell has said and instinctively she knows he hit the nail on the head. She hadn't thought about it until just now but she got a sense from Detective Roberts that he is an Alpha Dog the moment they met. He has a way of walking and talking, as if he's in control of everything. Though she hasn't thought about it until just now, the truth is, she liked that about him. Maybe that's why she wanted to impress him so much. In hindsight, however, she can see how her judgment may have been clouded by his confidence. After all, everything she learned about David's murder, she learned from Russell and Tony. On top of that, Detective Roberts hadn't even spoken with Jessie yet, which means she was one step ahead of him. Now that she thinks about it, so far, she doesn't see why she needs him to get the story when she has Russell and Tony. She wants to kick herself for reacting the way a school girl would when the quarterback of the football team pays her the slightest bit of attention. Luckily, Russell brought her back to Earth. Lesson learned. She decides that she won't make that mistake again. Lisa says, "You're absolutely right. I'll be smarter from now on."

She and Russell continue to talk about her story and other things, and somewhere during their conversation Lisa notices something different about Russell. She asks, "Have you met someone who's giving you a little something something?"

Russell asks, "What do you mean by that?"

Lisa smiles and says, "You seem particularly happy and upbeat. What's going on with you? Have you finally taken my advice and met someone who's giving you a little happy."

Russell now knows what she meant by a little something something. Russell laughs and says, "Oh, a little happy. No, I am not seeing someone, so I guess I have to admit I'm not getting a little happy." "Well, you should. How long has it been since you've had a steady girlfriend? I'd love to see you with a nice woman who truly cares about you." Lisa leans forward and whispers, "Listen, I love the guy but you don't want to end up like Ernie, do you?" Though he doesn't say it out loud, Russell knows the answer to that question is no. Lisa continues, "Not only will you have friendship and company, but maybe she'll be a good cook too. And, you'll get a little happy and that'll make you happy too."

While the conversation was on the benefits of friendship, company, and good food Russell could have continued on with the conversation. Now that it's back to getting a little happy, he's too embarrassed to have that conversation with Lisa, though in the back of his mind he knows she's right. So, he responds in a way to acknowledge her but change the subject. "I'll keep that in mind, but if you see some pep in my step it's coming from a tip on a story I got earlier today."

"Can you talk about it?"

This time it's Russell's turn to lean in and whisper, "I have a friend in the department who tips me off whenever someone is killed in Los Angeles with a .45 caliber pistol. I've been waiting for a ghost to reappear for two years now, and the tip I got today suggests that there's a possibility he's back. The problem is the body was discovered in Orange County, but I'm told that the higher ups in the LAPD wanted the test results with priority. I'll tell you more when I know more, but that's what's got me so excited."

7:30pm - Megan has been crashing with her friend, Yesenia, in Yezzy's one bedroom apartment on Sanborn Avenue just off Sunset in Silver Lake. She knows how long it takes to get from the front door of the building to the front door of the apartment, so she positions herself in the open doorway just before William arrives. William looks just as she remembers him, except he is thinner now and his eyes don't seem to be smiling as they had when they met. Megan felt sorrow for him when she read about Genny's death, but now she feels it even more because he looks like a man who's lost his best friend. After they say their hellos Megan offers William a drink, which he refuses until she says she is going a fix a rum and coke for herself. He decides to join her. As she gives him his drink he compliments her on her apartment. Megan explains that the apartment isn't hers. She says, "Like I told you earlier, I have some problems of my own that I'm trying to deal with."

William says, "Let's talk about Teddy."

"I broke up with Teddy about a year ago. We stayed in contact mostly because he would call me two or three times a month to say hi and see how I was doing. About three months after we broke up I entertained the idea of getting back with him so I agreed to meet him for lunch. During that lunch I realized he was still getting high every day, and he was still selling drugs. In short, he wasn't doing anything or going anywhere good. After that he'd still call, but I wasn't as quick to return his calls as I had been in the past. Then instead of returning his calls I'd just send him a text telling him I got his message, and that I hope he's good. After doing that a couple of times he finally got the message and he stopped calling me. I guess I can tell you this now. We had a big fight the night I met you and Genny. Apparently, seeing her again completely destabilized him. He was quiet and distant for the rest of the night. It was so bad I had to call him on it. I accused him of still having feelings for her. He never denied it. He just kept telling me that I was crazy to feel that way. About two weeks before your wife was murdered I ran into Teddy outside of a convenience store just down the street. As usual he was high, but he was also really sad and depressed. I tried to talk with him, but he wasn't hearing anything I was saying and he didn't have anything to say. I had never seen Teddy that way. Teddy loved to talk and he always had something to say. I guess I felt sorry for him so I invited him back here. I told him I was about to cook dinner and he could have dinner with me if he wanted to and he did. He lightened up once we got back to the apartment. He even helped me prepare the food and he set the table just before we ate. Half way through the meal he had a nervous breakdown. He started crying and saying what a bad person he is. He started talking about how fucked up his life is and that he's lost all of his friends and family. He apologized to me for everything he had done wrong during our relationship. No matter what I said to him he just kept going on and on about how fucked up his life had become. On one hand he was starting to scare me but on the other he looked like a person who was hitting rock bottom. I really thought he was reaching a turning point, so I asked him what was going on and what was making him feel that way. At first he wouldn't say. He just kept going on and on about how worthless his life had become and how he had nothing to show for it and no one in his life that cares about him. Finally, he got tired of crying and tired of complaining and he started to open up. He said he got mixed up with some bad people several years ago, the kind of people that do the worst things. He said they had gotten back in touch with him recently and they asked about someone. He told me he told them that she didn't know anything but they forced him to give them her name. A few days later they had a picture of her and he told them that they had the right person."

William asks, "Did he say it was Genny?"

"No. He never said Genny or any other name."

"So what makes you think he was talking about Genny?"

"At that point I didn't think he was talking about Genny. Truthfully, at that point, I was wondering if he was talking about me, so I asked him if I was in any danger. He said no, but that I was smart to break up with him. And then he started to apologize again for times he hurt me, but this time he admitted that I was right about that night we had a fight, which, honestly, I had completely forgotten about. I asked him who he was talking about but he wouldn't say. I asked him if was so worried that something might happen to her why doesn't he get in touch with her and warn her. He said there was nothing he could do. If he did anything he was sure they'd find him and kill him."

"Did he say who they are?"

"No and I didn't ask. I didn't want to know. At this point I wasn't thinking about anything except getting Teddy out of the apartment and staying as far away from him as possible for the rest of my life. He went on to say that he hadn't been home for a week and he asked if he could stay with me for a couple of days. I explained that the apartment isn't mine and my roommate would never allow it. The truth is, even if the place was mine, he had to leave. That was the last time I saw or spoke with Teddy."

"I still don't understand what makes you think he was talking about Genny."

"The first time I thought it was Genny was when he admitted that I was right to accuse him of having feelings for her. He had already apologized to me for several things he had done during our relationship, but it wasn't until after I asked him who "she" is that he brought that incident back up. At that time it was just a fleeting thought I had. It lasted for a second and then I started to think that maybe he was talking about me. I never thought about Genny again until I read about her murder. Even then I read that story along with ten other stories that caught my attention that morning. As the day went on something kept haunting me about her story. Later in the day I realized I knew her name. I found the article again and it mentioned your name as well and my heart sank into my stomach. That's when I knew Teddy was talking about Genny."

William spends the next few minutes trying to help Megan jog her memory. The things she's told him gives him reason to believe what he's been feeling all along is right, but she hasn't told him anything that helps in an evidentiary sort of way. No matter how many times they go over the conversation Megan insists that Teddy never mentioned any names and he never gave her any indication of who "they" might be. The longer they talked, however, the more Megan started to feel something for William. He obviously loved and adored his wife and that endeared him to her. Where once she was resolved to not get involved, slowly her resolve softened and she came around to thinking of ideas to help William. By the time William left her apartment, Megan had agreed to put together a list of Teddy's friends and associates.

8:00pm - The entire three story, six bedroom, six and a half bathroom, Mediterranean Style house on Sea Vista Drive in Malibu, overlooking the Pacific Ocean is lit by candlelight. There is a roaring fire in the fireplace in the family room and another one in the fireplace by the heated pool and Jacuzzi. Adding to the mood is a mellow blend of Jazz Fusion coming through the sound system throughout the house and on the party deck outside surrounding the pool. Pete Jefferson's guests are greeted first by the valets. Once they are in the house they are greeted by the servers, each carrying a large tray with an assortment of finger foods. Though many of Pete's partners in the Forest Canyon Mall deal are in attendance, tonight's soiree is primarily for the support staff at Pete's company and their significant other or their date. Secretly, with the exception of family outings, Pete has been looking forward to this party more than any other party he's attended all year. While Pete makes a habit of knowing the name and a little bit about everyone in the company, it's a rare day when he says more than two words to anyone other than the top executives and his three assistants. The only thing that was a cause for concern was having this party at his house. The original plan was to rent out a small and intimate venue and have the party there. Abbey suggested having the party at his house. He's never had a company party at his house and, given his penchant for privacy, he wasn't immediately open to the suggestion Abbey knew that hammering him with the suggestion wasn't a good idea. Without telling him why she thought it was a good idea, she just put it out there. It took Pete a couple of days to understand the purpose behind the suggestion, mostly because he didn't give it much thought until it was time to pick a place and leave a deposit. Once he thought about it, however, he realized that she was right. Namely, if he really did love her and if he really does want the things he says he does, he's going to have to be open to more than his business partners and his immediate family. So, with the hopes that Abbey would see that he was doing this for her, he decided to open his house to the people in his company.

By the time most people had arrived Abbey looked for Pete, wondering if he was having a good time. She sees Pete standing by the pool talking with some of the younger people in the company, who weren't afraid to bring their bathing suits as the invitation invited them to do. The group Pete is talking with, two girls and three guys, are talking with each other and laughing. Then Abbey sees Pete push one of the guys in the pool. The rest of them laugh hysterically and ultimately the other four jump in the pool. Abbey can't take her eyes off of Pete, she's never seen him be so playful. As the night progresses, each time Abbey looks for Pete she finds him talking with someone new. Throughout the night Abbey keeps herself busy by mingling with the guests, giving tours of the house, and making sure the caterers and the bartenders have everything they need. At various times, during the party, Pete can be overhead asking his guests about themselves and their families. Even when he's heard speaking to his partners, though the conversation starts out about money, if you listen long enough you can hear the conversation turn to being about family. Every once in a while Pete and Abbey make eye contact and wink at each other, but that's about as much time as they have for the other. Invariably a guest, a caterer, a bartender, or a valet is in need of their attention, but that's OK. They are both having a surprisingly good time. Pete is enjoying entertaining and Abbey is enjoying entertaining as well but, mostly, she's enjoying looking at Pete.

There comes a time when Pete wants to say a few words to his guests collectively. He asks Abbey to turn down the music and once she has, he taps on a glass to get everyone's attention. Pete says, "I want to thank you all for coming and I really mean you all since everyone in the company is here. I'm going to take that as a sign that you're happy to be a part of the company and you're happy with the work I am asking you to do. If you aren't please let me know. Correction, if you aren't, let Dana know. She doesn't have enough work." Dana playfully rolls her eyes and everyone laughs and claps at her reaction, because everyone knows that Dana is one of the hardest working people in the company.

Pete continues, "Seriously, I am truly touched that all of you made time to be here. It's been a very special week. As you all know we had a commencement ceremony for the Ricky Jefferson Wing of The Center For Recovery just yesterday. We have tonight, and later this week we are closing on the Forest Canyon Mall deal." All of the guests applaud. "As I said in the invitation, I want to make an announcement about that deal tonight, so I'll do that now. As a direct result of all of our hard work and dedication, Forest Canyon will be the most lucrative deal in the company's history." Again, all of the guest applaud. "With that in mind, I want to say thank you. So, you all will receive a bonus check next Monday. It will equal 50% of your annual salary."

This time the applause is loud and accompanied by audible gasps and shouts of "Yeah!"

When the applause and shouts die down Pete says, "And, no James, this bonus isn't in lieu of your year-end bonuses."

Everyone looks and laughs at James, who is looking around and saying, "What? I didn't say anything." Pete says, "Tonight I got a chance to speak with all of you personally and I can't tell you how proud I am of each of you. God bless you all and your families."

Again the guests applaud but this time as the applause dies down Mrs. Traylor, the wife of one of Pete's partners, who has obvious had a little too much to drink asks, "What about Ricky?" Now there's a hush in the room and everyone's attention is on Mrs. Traylor. She wants to know so Mrs. Traylor isn't afraid to ask, "I mean, did you ever find the people who, you know?" Mr. Traylor tries to hush his wife but it's too late.

Abbey cringes because she knows that is one of the areas of Pete's life that makes him cling to privacy, but to Abbey's, and everyone's surprise Pete's comeback is, "Mrs. Traylor, come up here and stand next to me." Mrs. Traylor nervously makes her way through the gathered guests. Mr. Traylor is slightly pleased that she's been called out since she has a habit of drinking too much and saying too much when she does. When Mrs. Traylor reaches Pete he turns her around to face the guests and he puts his left arm around her. "For those of you who don't know, my son was murdered ten years ago. It's true that at that time I would have set the world on fire if it led to finding my son's killer. I even offered a large reward for anyone who could supply any information that lead to an arrest. That was ten years ago though. Over the years, however, I've learned to accept his death which was brought on, in part, because of his association with drugs." Looking directly at Mrs. Traylor Pete says, "No, I've never found the person or people responsible for his death. Why do you ask! Do you know something?"

Mrs. Traylor looks at Pete in horror. This time even she realizes she's gone too far. The silence in the room is deafening for a few moments. None of the guest know how to react until Pete hugs her enthusiastically, laughs, and admits, "I'm just teasing you." Finally all of the guest breathe again and some of them get the joke and laugh. Pete still has his left arm around Mrs. Traylor when he turns to his guests and says, "Tonight is not the night for such serious matters. Tonight we are gathered to celebrate our hard work, good fortunate, and the love of our friends and family. Having said that, let me conclude by saying thank you all again for your work and dedication. I see nothing but good things in our future as long as we keep it up." He turns to Mrs. Traylor and says, "Since you brought him up, I'm sure you'll be the first to join me in this toast." Pete turns back to his guest and says, "Here's to my son, who I miss, very much, and I will always love. To Ricky Jefferson."

All of the guests, including Mrs. Traylor, respond in harmonious synchronicity, "To Ricky Jefferson!"

9:00pm - "I can't believe you got to her before the detectives did," says Tony, who's lying in bed bare-chested and in his Calvin Klein boxers, sort of reading and sort of watching SportsCenter. Lisa is in the bathroom, in her bra and panties, finishing her nightly routine of removing her makeup and washing her face. As she walks toward Tony to join him in bed she says, "I have you and Russell to thank for that."

"Tell me what she said again."

"Basically, she said he was a good guy until he met a guy named Ronny White. She thinks he partied too much and she says he was working as a bisexual escort, but even with all of that she thought he was a good guy."

"I saw his driver's license picture. He was a good looking guy. I'm surprised he wasn't making enough money with modeling and acting."

"I got the impression that he was money hungry. Jessie made it seem like he would have done anything if he felt the pay was good enough."

"That's what got him in trouble."

"What do you make of this guy Ronny?"

"Well, from what you've said, my guess is Ronny either sold drugs to David or, more likely, he was the kind of person who always had drugs on him and he used them to make friends."

"Maybe he was more predator than friend. Maybe he used drugs on the weak minded to first befriend them, and then later to get them to do things for him."

"That's entirely possible and that makes sense."

"If that's the case, then Ronny probably murdered David so he could get away with whatever David did scot-free. I wonder what David did or knew that got him killed?"

"When drugs are involved you never know until you know. He could have killed someone, robbed someone, slept with someone's girlfriend or boyfriend, or, if Ronny is David's killer and if he's a user too, a dog could have told him that he needed to kill David and so he did."

"Yeah, but David was killed neatly and whoever did it tried to hide the body. That makes me think that there was less emotion and more purpose behind his murder."

"You're right."

"I'm going to try to find out who Ronny White is tomorrow. I'm sure there are several Ronny Whites in Los Angeles, but if I can get a picture of some of them, maybe Jessie can verify which one he is, if any."

"How are you going to do that?"

"I have a couple of ideas and I'm sure I can get some help from a couple of the other writers at the Journal"

"Whatever you do, just be safe."

Lisa gives Tony a kiss on the cheek and says, "I will."

A few moments later Tony starts to gather the papers and the book he has lying on the bed. Lisa asks, "What are you doing?"

"Your shows are about to come on so I'm going to watch the rest of SportsCenter and then the game in the living room."

"I don't want you to go."

"Yeah, but if I watch your shows my head will explode."

"Come on, they're not that bad."

"There's no way I'm watching the Real Wives of anyplace. There's nothing real about reality TV and I can't stand it."

"I know it isn't real. It's just entertainment."

"I'm not stopping you from having your fun. Those shows have a different effect on me than they do on you. You can see past them and you can see their entertainment value. I can't. They just make me feel like I'm killing brain cells. If I wanted to do that, I'd rather smoke a joint. At least that way, I'd get something out of it." Tony leans over to kiss Lisa on the forehead and says, "Have fun baby! I'll be in the living room."

Lisa let's him take two steps towards the door before she says, "What if I wanted to watch SportsCenter and the game with you?"

"What'chu talkin bout Willis?"

Lisa smiles and says, "I mean, I don't know about SportsCenter, but what if I wanted to watch games with you from now on?"

"What do you mean by from now on?"

"I just meant tonight." Tony walks back to the bed and says, "No you didn't. I heard it in your voice, you said from now on."

"Of course you heard it in my voice. I said it."

"You know what I mean."

"What?"

"I've been thinking about you watching games with me from now on too."

"And?"

"And, nothing in this world would make me happier. I'm going to be serious for a moment, OK?" "OK."

Tony continues, "I don't want you to feel like you have to answer me right now because I'm really not going to ask you anything right now. I just want to say something. I love you Lisa Becker. I have since the day we met and I always will. Before I met you, I didn't think I would be here this soon. Now I feel it would have been just fine with me if I had gotten here sooner as long as it was with you. I don't think that came out the way I meant it. I'm just trying to say, I have never been happier and I can't imagine my life without you. So, if you're wondering if watching games with me from now on is all right, I want you to know that that's exactly what I want you to do."

"Does that mean you'll watch the Real Wives of . . .?"

Tony cuts her off and says, "That's never going to happen."

Lisa stares into Tony's eyes and thinks to herself: "That's the right answer." She pulls Tony closer and the two of them exchange gentle kisses that become more passionate each time they touch lips. The television is still on SportsCenter and the anchor is talking about today's top ten plays, but neither Tony nor Lisa hear it and neither of them care. At some point they'll realize that the television is still on and they'll turn it off, but that won't happen for another hour or two.

10:00pm - Over William's objection, Aunt Ernestine put another plate of lasagna and green beans in the microwave, and then she asks, "So tell me again, who's Lexi?"

"She's the girl who gave me Megan's cell phone number."

"And Megan is the girl who used to date Teddy and who lives at that house?"

"Yes, she's the one who dated Teddy but she doesn't live at the house."

"I thought you told me you got the address for that house by looking up Megan's telephone number." "That's right. I did."

"Well then why doesn't she live at that house?"

"I don't know." Aunt Ernestine takes the plate out of the microwave and gives it to William. Then she pulls out the chair across from him, sits down, and listens to him eat as if he hasn't already had a full plate of food. She decides to give him some time before she asks her next question.

"Have you told Detective Morales any of this?"

William says, "No, not yet."

"Well, I think that's what you should do next. I think you have enough to go back to the police."

"I thought about that, but as of now I don't really have anything new to tell them."

"What concerns me the most is that Megan said Teddy used the word 'they.' You said Teddy was an informant for the police, do you think that's the 'they' she was talking about?"

"No."

"Well, what did she say when you told her that Teddy was a police informant?"

"She was kind of surprised and kind of not. She said that hearing it from me, especially knowing how I found out, meant she had to believe it was true, but she heard that before and at that time she didn't believe it."

"Who told her before?"

"She wouldn't say, but I don't think Teddy was afraid of the police and neither did she. If anything, I think he was afraid of the people who may have found out that he was an informant."

"If you ask me, that's all the more reason to go back to Detective Morales and tell him what you think. I really think you should let the police do their job. They are equipped and prepared to deal with the kind of people you ran into at that house. You're not. You're lucky to be alive after an incident like that. When I told you to do what you had to do, I didn't mean go out and get yourself killed."

"I need more information before I can go back to Javier. My conversation with Megan won't mean anything to him. If she comes up with a list of people Teddy knew and if one of them can fill in more details, then I'll have something to tell Javier."

"That sounds good except to get more details you'll have to find these people and get them to talk to you. If they are the criminal type, they don't have the same kind of conscience that you and I do, and they live their lives by an entirely different set of rules. You got a taste of that when you walked into that house. What makes you think they'll tell you anything?"

"I don't know. I haven't thought that far in advance."

"Maybe you need to. I'm not trying to stop you, I just want you to see that you may be out-matched. Do you have a way of protecting yourself other than with your fists?"

"No."

"I think you need to re-think what you're doing. I don't want to see you get hurt or worse, and I'm sure that isn't what Genny would want for you either."

Aunt Ernestine hasn't heard William use his fork for a while so she asks, "Are you done with your food?"

William answers, "Yes. It was delicious. Thank you."

She motions as if she is going to stand up to clear his plate but William tells her to sit down and relax. He says he'll clear the table and put everything either in the refrigerator or in the dishwasher. Neither of them say anything for a couple of minutes until Aunt Ernestine asks, "What are you thinking?"

"I'm thinking about what you said."

"Good. So you'll go to Detective Morales and let him do his job?"

"No. I was thinking that you're right. I don't have any protection."

"Oh Lord! William, you are as deaf as I am blind."

William adds the dishwashing liquid, starts the machine, and then sits back at the table. "I heard everything you said and you're right about all of it."

Aunt Ernestine knows a "but" is coming so she supplies it herself, "But?"

"But, I started this and I'm not going to stop now. Believe me, I know you don't want to see me hurt and I know Genny wouldn't want that. Frankly, I don't want that either. But, I had a hunch and I believed it and it turned out to be true. The people who should have believed me didn't. Not only that, they tried to dissuade and discourage me. What I don't think they understand and what I don't think you understand is how I feel. It isn't their fault or yours. I don't think anyone is capable of understanding until they are forced to stand in the shoes I'm in now. If I don't do something, if I don't find a way to fight back, I'll live the rest of my life as a victim. Every time I think of Genny, every memory I have of her will be dampened by the fact that I couldn't protect her, she was taken from me, and I did nothing about it. I would have rathered the police found her murderer, arrested him, and locked him away for the rest of his life, but that didn't happen. Instead they think I should just deal with it. I tried that too. I couldn't do it; I can't do it, and I won't do that. Bad things happen, I understand that, but I'm not going to live the rest of my life as a victim. If Megan is right, the person or people who did this did it for what? Because Genny might have seen something or knew something years ago? We just bought a house, we were planning for children, and we were minding our own business. Somebody took the other half of every hope and dream I had. I feel so angry all the time. I have to do something."

Aunt Ernestine reaches across the table and takes William's hand in hers. With her other hand she strokes the back of the hand that she's holding. She says, "I think you're right. I guess what you're feeling is like a lot of things in life that you just can't understand until you go through it. Just promise me that you'll be careful. Remember, you may have lost your wife but you still have family members, who are still living, and who want to enjoy your company for the rest of their lives. I think over time you would learn to live with your loss but I don't believe in being a victim. If you feel that's what it will come down to, then, again I say, do what you have to do. Keep in mind what you have already been through. You are going to be dealing with people who have a lot less to lose than you do. That makes them dangerous people. So, what are you going to do?"

"You said best. I need some protection."

11:00pm - It takes Russell thirty minutes to talk himself out of bed. The file he wants to read is in his office, somewhere, and it will be there tomorrow when he gets in. There are hundreds of crimes that Russell is aware of, if not more, that go unsolved every year, but this is different. Even though the chances that the two cases are related is remote, something gets him out of bed, into his car, and on his way to his office. On his drive in he tries to recall the specifics of the first case, but all he can remember is that each person was shot in the back of the head and each of them were shot with the same gun, a .45 caliber pistol. The voice that was telling him not to get out of bed is back. Again, it tells him that he's wasting his time. He doesn't even know the name of the person who was killed in Cardiff by the Sea. All he knows is, that person was shot in the back of the head with a .45 caliber pistol. At this point that doesn't mean anything. Dozens of people have been killed with a .45 over the years. Some were killed in domestic disputes, some in barroom brawls, some in gang on gang disputes, and some were killed by accident, either when cleaning the gun or when minors have found their parents gun and didn't fully understand the danger. The other voice in Russell's head says yes, that's true but none of them were shot in the back of the head. The voice that got him out of bed wins the argument when it reminds the other voice that the trump card isn't that this person was shot in the back of the head. The trump card is the attention this murder is getting by the higher ups in the LAPD. When Russell's inside contact called, he made it clear that what he had to say wasn't supposed to be said outside the room, but he thought of Russell as soon as he heard the details. The information cost Russell two LA King Playoff tickets, but even if nothing comes of this, they were worth it just for the excitement Russell feels.

The file he's looking for isn't where he thought it would be, but that's not a surprise. The question is, if not in cold cases, then where? Instead of going through his files Russell decides to sit down and relax and let the answer come to him. As he leans back in his chair Russell tries to think of the last time he was in his office at this time of night. He can't remember. It's been that long. He wonders if he enjoyed it then as much as he is enjoying be there now. Without all of the lights that are normally on, without all of the people scampering around, and without all of the noise, his office reminds him of church, a place he goes to reconnect with himself and find peace. His eyes drift to the picture of him, Gita, Lisa's mother, and Lisa. If one didn't know better it would be easy to assume that's a family picture. He wonders why he was never attracted to Gita. He certainly loves her. He loves her for the smart and beautiful woman that she is, he loves her for the devotion she displayed for her slain husband, he loves her for the strength she demonstrated as a single mother, and he loves her because together they love Lisa. Still, he has never felt a spark for her, though she has become and will always be one of the great loves of his life. Next to the picture of the three of them is a picture of Lisa and Tony. He doesn't recall the event they were at, but Lisa is dressed up and Tony is in his LAPD uniform. LAPD, that's it! Russell jumps up and looks for the file labeled, "LAPD Issued." He grabs the file, sits back at his desk and starts to read. Quickly he is reminded of why there was so much interest by the police over the three people murdered then and why the police are tight lipped now. Six years ago three people were murdered independently, but all during a two week period. A single shell casing was found at all three murder scenes, but the telling piece of evidence was a bullet that was found at only one of them. The police were able to match the gun even without retrieving the gun itself, because the gun was a limited edition Beretta 8045F originally made for the police department that somehow found its way outside of the system and into the hands of a killer. As soon as that fact was determined there was a news blackout and Russell never heard or read anything about those murders since. Now, it appears the police, at least, believe that same gun is in play and, most likely, the same killer. His contact must not have known the importance of the case to the LAPD, otherwise he would have never given Russell the information that he did. Russell considers that a sign that he was supposed to find out and, if he was supposed to find out, that means he is supposed to do something with the information. Now that he's read the file the only thing to do is to find out more about the person killed in Cardiff by the Sea. He doesn't know, off the top of his head, who the right person to call is and, right now, he's not in the mood to figure it out. The best he could do now is leave a message with who he thinks is the right person, which is inefficient in comparison to being back in the office in the morning and making a few calls to determine who the right person is. Once he knows who he needs to talk with he's sure he can get that person on the phone. With the file in hand he climbs back in his car and heads for home. The voice that told him to stay in bed returns. This time it says that driving to the office was a waste of time. He didn't learn anything or do anything that he couldn't have done in the morning. Russell waits to hear what the other voice has to say, but the other voice is silent. Still, Russell remains excited about the possibilities. More than that, he can't help himself from feeling excited in the way he used to in the good old days, the days when he would jump out of bed in the middle of the night, without a second thought, to follow a lead. That reminds him of the time he drove to Vegas, without thinking twice, because he had an idea. And then it hit him. Finally, without saying a word, the other voice speaks. Russell gets it now and the whole excursion to the office was worth it.

11:30pm - William is back at the Copenhagen lying on the floor in the living room, in between thinking about the day and falling asleep. His mind is bouncing from one thing to the next. Thoughts of Javier turns to thoughts of Teddy. Thoughts of Teddy turns to thoughts of Megan. Thoughts of Megan turns to thoughts of Wade, KiKi, and the heavyset man, which leads him back to Megan, then to Teddy, then to Javier, then back to Teddy and back to Megan. He can't hold a single thought in his mind for more than a few seconds. All he really wants to do is turn it all off and go to sleep. In the courtyard of the hotel, just outside his room, he can hear a group of young adults talking and laughing and gathering to go out. The more he focuses on them the less he thinks about anything else. So, he directs what little energy he has left into listening to every word they say. So far, he detects three distinct female voices and two male voices. Next, to take himself even further into their world, he tries to imagine what each of them looks like based on their voices. No one has ever looked like what William thought they would but, right now, he's enjoying playing that game more than ever. A minute later all of the friends have gathered and they are on their way to their festivities, but the few moments William had with them was enough for him to drift off to sleep on the sounds of their laughter.

Genny is standing in the room that William has claimed as his office. She has on a pair of old blue jeans, a tee shirt, and a handkerchief covering her hair. She has a paint roller in her hand and she's laughing hysterically at the story William is telling. William has on a pair of shorts, a tee shirt, and he has a paint roller on a stick in his hand because he's painting the ceiling. He's laughing too but he's doing his best to keep it together since he's the one telling the story.

William says, "So the minister says, 'Now, we'll have a song selection sung by Junior Jones.' This is the moment everyone in the family has been looking forward to. Up until a month before Uncle Lenny died, no one knew Uncle Andy was gay. But, everyone loves Uncle Andy so after we got over the surprise nobody cared what his sexual orientation is. But then, he, a 46 year old man, introduced his 19 year old boyfriend to the family, and that's when the fit hit the shan. Still, everybody was willing to support Uncle Andy and his relationship because he told everyone that they were in love and in a committed relationship, and that Junior was a church going young man." William, doing his best to hold back his laughter, continues with the story, "Nobody is looking forward to this moment more than Uncle Andy because he's convinced that once the family hears how beautifully Junior sings they will accept him with open arms into the family." Genny starts to laugh again, not at the thought of Junior being accepted into the family but because she's heard this story a dozen times and she knows what's coming next.

William continues, "So after a few seconds there's still no Junior. The minister steps back up to the microphone and says again, 'Now, we'll have a song selection sung by Junior Jones.' A few seconds later still no Junior. Now everybody in church is looking all around and mumbling to each other. Uncle Andy doesn't know what's going on, but he feels he has to do something. So, he steps up to the microphone and says in the quietest voice possible, 'Let me go look for Junior.'

Somebody in the back of the church screams, 'What?'"

Genny decides she can't continue painting right now because she's laughing to hard. William continues, "Uncle Andy leans in towards the microphone and says, again in the quietest voice possible, 'Let me go look for Junior.'"

William and Genny are both cracking up. "While Uncle Andy tiptoes towards the door of the church he is using a hand gesture as if to say, 'I'll just be one minute.' As soon as he gets out of the church and the doors close behind him he screams, at the top of his lungs, 'Junior! Where the hell are you?' Everyone in the church fell out. We could not stop laughing. A couple of minutes later Uncle Andy walks in with Junior who steps up to the microphone and sings beautifully."

Genny says, "This is the best part. Do it like he did."

William, in between laughs says, "OK. OK. So, it turns out that Junior had gotten so nervous he went out behind the church to smoke some weed to calm himself down. He did sing beautifully but he forgot some of the words and not the words he should have forgotten."

Again, Genny says, "Do it. Do it."

William takes a deep breath because he just has to get through this last part and then he can allow himself to laugh. "So, he goes, 'How great thou art, how. . . Damn it!"

Genny and William laugh so hard they both begin to cry. Genny says, "That's the kind of story that will be just as funny ten years from now."

"I know, right?"

"I think it's time for a margarita break."

"I'll make them. I'll be right back." He leans his roller on a stick against a wall and starts to walk towards the door.

Genny says, "Get back here Mister." William walks back to Genny.

She gives him a kiss and says, "I love you William Flowers."

"I love you too Geneviève Flowers."

Genny releases him with, "Hurry back."

William reaches for the doorknob and opens the door. There's a man dressed in black standing at the top of the stairs with a gun in his hand. He levels it directly at William and fires. Just before everything goes black William hears Genny scream, "William!" It takes a few seconds for William to realize he isn't dreaming. His head is pounding and his arm is numb. Before he attempts to stand up he pulls the phone off his desk and he dials 911. When he hears a voice on the other end he tells the voice that he and his wife have been shot and he gives his address. He doesn't stay on the line to answer any other questions. He puts the handset on the floor next to the phone and he tries to stand to get to Genny. When he stands up his head gets dizzy so he sinks to his knees so he can get to Genny. As he crawls to her he yells her name, but the only thing he hears is the voice on the other end of the call asking him to come back to the phone. He crawls as quickly as he can out of his office, down the hallway, and into the bedroom. He's still saying her name as he reaches the bed. He lifts himself up and sees her lying on the bed in a pool of blood with a bullet hole in her forehead. He wakes up violently, on the floor in the hotel, in a cold sweat.

———

CHAPTER THREE

Day Four

6:00am - Breck is standing in the American Airlines Terminal at LAX waiting for his checked bag at baggage return Carousel Three. He's thinking about the young man he met in Panama, during his layover, who would have been perfect for the job. The pros were he was homeless and desperate. If he suddenly disappeared nobody would notice and fewer people would care. The lure of a substantial amount of money would have definitely worked on him. The cons were he didn't have a passport, so that eliminated him immediately. Also, Breck didn't have enough time to get to know his weaknesses. It's one thing to say you can kill someone, and it's another thing to do it. Still, Breck is certain he could have trained that young man to do it. That he chose to pass on that young man came down to him not having a passport. Breck smiles to himself when he thinks that he wouldn't have killed Ronny if he knew he had to come back to the States so quickly. In a way he misses that dumb bastard. Ronny was always good for a few of laughs, he always knew how to get anything Breck needed, including girls and drugs, and, most of all, he didn't have any problem with killing someone for money. Best of all, it didn't take a lot of money to activate him. The fool fantasized about being a so called hitman, and since he was a high school dropout and the dullest tool in the shed, he was easily manipulated.

Breck spots his bag, grabs it, and heads for the curb to catch a taxi. For the first time since Eddie asked him to come back he wondered who he might have to kill and how many. With such short notice and with Ronny being dead, there's a good chance he'll have to do the work himself. When he thinks about that he realizes he has mixed emotions about it. The killing itself isn't a problem for him, it's the method that causes his concern. Shooting someone from a hundred yards away, packing up, and casually walking away involves very little risk as far as Breck is concerned. But, shooting someone up close without being noticed and getting away with it is infinitely more risky. The greater the risk the greater the chance of being caught, or worse, being killed. Breck thinks to himself that's the worst thing that could happen at this point in his life. Life has been good in Costa Rica, mostly because it doesn't take much money to have a good life there. The money he's made for arranging the girl's murder combined with the money he gets to keep because Ronny killed David and he killed Ronny, adds up to a sizable chunk of change. Now, even if he only gets his normal rate for this trip, combined with the money he's already made, it adds up to life changing money. He smiles when he thinks he might have enough to get his own boat. He won't have enough to get a boat as big as Eddie's but he will have enough to get a boat he can keep in the Marina and take out for deep sea fishing trips. He thinks, "Maybe that's what I'll do. Maybe I'll start a charter service for deep sea fishing and retire from the killing business." Again, it's not the killing that bothers him, it's the risk. He figures why continue taking so many risks when he already owns his home, free and clear. He already has enough money to live on for the rest of your life, not including the money Eddie owes him. Maybe it's time to do something that is actually fun to bring in more money. And just that fast, the decision is made. After this trip, he's out of the killing business, and he's into the deep sea fishing charter business. In truth, Breck would have come back even if the money wasn't as good. Once Eddie offered the chance to be with him on his boat on the trip from Los Angeles to Costa Rica, Breck was in. He's never been on a boat for more than a few hours at a time, and he's always wanted to take a long trip on one. A couple of days on the ocean sounded perfect. With that thought Breck put out his cigarette and walked over to the taxi stand. It's too early to go to the storage outfit to pick up his gun, some ammo, and some spending money. He's looking forward to seeing it again. Of all the guns he's owned over the years, this one is his favorite. When he has it in his hand he feels invincible. Their reunion will have to wait because the storage outfit doesn't open until noon. Breck tells the driver to take him directly to Marina Del Rey. He figures he'll settle in, catch a quick nap, and then he'll be in North Hollywood at noon.

6:30am - Javier knocks on the door and sticks his head into his fourteen year old son's room. He says what he always says at this time in the morning, "Time to rise and shine Jay Jay. Time to get ready for school."

Jay Jay does what he always does. He pulls the covers over his head and says, "Just a couple more minutes."

"It's Thursday. Just one more day and then it's Friday and the weekend."

"Good. Come back tomorrow and I'll get up then."

"Good try Jay. Let's go buddy."

"OK, OK, two minutes."

Angela, Javier's sixteen year old daughter, is already dressed and in the kitchen. She's on her laptop and talking with her mother, Cynthia, who's making breakfast, when Javier comes downstairs.

Angela says, "Julie said she heard that Kevin is thinking of asking Yvonne to the school dance."

Cynthia's response is, "Didn't you tell me that Kevin came up to you after last week's game and asked if you were going to Nancy's party? And didn't you tell me that the two of you talked and danced all night at Nancy's party and that you didn't see him dance with anyone else the whole night?"

"Yes."

"Well, that makes me think he likes you and that he's going to ask you to the school dance."

"But, he didn't try to kiss me at the end of Nancy's party."

Javier, with his head in the refrigerator says, "Good."

Angela rolls her eyes. Cynthia smiles and says, "Maybe he's just a little shy. I don't care what Julie says, I think Kevin likes you and I'd be willing to bet that he's going to ask you to the school dance." Javier says, "What do you see in that boy anyway?"

"Dad! He's tall, he's handsome, he's funny, and he's a star on the baseball team."

"Yeah but does he have good grades?"

"I don't know."

"See. If he had good grades you would know. Why aren't you interested in a boy like Christopher? He's a straight A student."

"Christopher is OK but have you seen his nose?"

Javier smiles and says, "He does have nose on him."

Cynthia chimes in with, "You know what, it's not right to make fun of a way somebody looks. Christopher is a great young man . . . but, I have to admit, that boy does have a nose."

Just as the three of them laugh together Jay Jay walks into the kitchen and asks, "What are you all laughing at?"

Angela says, "Your grades."

"Ha Ha, that's very funny."

"I know, that's why we are laughing at them."

"Well, at least, I'm not funny looking like you."

Javier's cell phone couldn't have rung at a better time. He sees that it's Captain Upton calling so he walks into the living room to take the call in private or, at least, away from Angela and Jay Jay who are still making fun of each other. The conversation is short, but by the time Javier walks back into the kitchen Jay Jay has gone upstairs to shower and Angela has her headphones on, obviously listening to music. Cynthia asks, "Is everything OK?"

"Yeah, that was the Captain. Something is going on. I have to get into the office a little early."

"Don't forget tonight is our date night, so I don't want to hear anything about coming home late."

Javier pretends that he's forgotten about tonight. "Date night, that's right. Of course, I didn't forget that."

"Yeah, right. I can't believe you forgot."

"I didn't forget. It just slipped my mind for a minute. I'm looking forward to it."

"You better not forget." Javier can tell she feels she has the upper hand for having to remind him about date night. That's exactly what he wants her to think and that's exactly how he wants her to feel. That means she still doesn't have a clue about the surprise he has planned.

7:30am - Eddie was waiting for Breck just outside of Viking. He rushed him into the shipyard through the secured side gate and then they quickly made their way onboard and below deck. Eddie showed Breck his stateroom, which has its own head, and asked him to unpack and meet him in the galley. When Breck comes out of his stateroom he finds Eddie sitting at a table drinking coffee. He takes the seat opposite Eddie and asks, "What's the plan?"

Eddie says, "The most important thing you need to remember is you can't go on deck." Eddie slides a piece of paper to Breck and continues, "If you need to leave the boat and when you come back, use the side entrance we just came through. That's the code for the gate. Whenever you're onboard you have to stay below deck. Between your stateroom and the galley you have everything you need to ride out the next two days. It is vitally important that you are seen as little as possible until we take off. You got it?" "Yeah, I got it."

Based on Breck's tone of voice, Eddie is sure Breck doesn't understand what he's trying to say. "Listen, there have been other things that we discussed that were supposed to be followed to the letter, but they weren't. We can't afford one more mistake. I know you're going to say that Ronny found David but you brought Ronny into this thing. That makes you responsible for everything he did. But, let's put that behind us. I'm telling you right now you have to avoid being seen for the next two days. Come and go quickly and through the side gate. When you are here stay below deck."

"No problem. I got it."

"OK, we have two potential problems. David's roommate has seen Ronny and she's heard about you, though she can't remember your name. I'm going to talk with her today. I'll find out how much she knows. At this point, I don't think we need to worry about her but I'll know for sure later today. Our other problem is a reporter for the Malibu Journal. If it appears that I am upset with what Ronny did, this is why. If he had done what he was asked to do, we wouldn't have either problem. Anyway, this reporter was on the scene when David's body was discovered. She's trying to make a name for herself so she's attacking this case. She has already spoken with David's roommate, so she knows about Ronny and she knows you exist."

"What do you need me to do?"

Before Eddie can answer that question his cell phone rings. Seeing that it's Captain Upton calling, he excuses himself to take the call in his cabin. A few moments later Eddie returns and continues his conversation with Breck. He says, "I don't want you to do anything for now except stay below deck. I think both of these problems are manageable. Like I said when I called you, I really don't think I'll need you to do anything but it's good to have you here just in case."

"You should know I need to run a couple of errands. If I knew you wanted me to stay completely out of sight I would have run them before I got here."

"Just tell me what you need and I'll get it for you."

"I can't do that. I have to run these errands personally. They should only take a couple of hours and then I can be back on the boat for good or until you need me to leave. If I can use your car I can run them quicker."

"I need my car today. My partner isn't working."

"What's going on with him?"

"Don't worry about him. You'll have to take a taxi to run your errands but don't call the taxi from here or from anywhere near this shipyard. Go across the street and over two blocks, there's a popular restaurant there. They may have taxis waiting. If not, you can call one from there without drawing any attention to yourself. When you return have the taxi drop you off there and walk back here and don't talk with anyone."

"What's the plan for tomorrow?"

"If all goes well, we'll push off around 9:00pm and we'll be in Mexican waters before sunrise."

"When do I get my money?"

"We should be in Costa Rica Sunday night or sometime Monday morning. We can go to your bank and I'll have the money wired to your account. You should have all of your money on Tuesday and no later than Wednesday."

"Just so we are clear, if I do any work while I'm here I get double my rate and, if not, I get my rate just for being here, right?"

Eddie smiles and says, "Yes, that's the deal. Don't worry about your money, if all goes well I will happily pay you all that I owe you."

"Great!" Breck extends his hand. Eddie reaches for his hand and the two of them shake on the deal. Eddie smiles knowing, again, Breck doesn't understand what he's saying. Finally, Eddie tells Breck that he has to finish getting ready for work. He says there's a remote for the television in the top drawer of the table be- tween the two twin beds. He also says he'll bring Breck a few DVDs before he leaves. Breck asks Eddie to leave them on the table they are sitting at. He plans on taking a quick nap before he leaves. Eddie is quick to remind him to come and go quickly, don't make eye contact or talk with anybody, and stay below deck until they leave. Breck likes Eddie and he appreciates the work for the money, but now Eddie is starting to get on his nerves again. It started at the casino. Breck wasn't fond of how he was treated and spoken to then. So far this morning he's had to listen to Eddie blame him for Ronny, which sounded like a thinly veiled threat. And now, he has to listen to this hypocrite talk to him like he's a three year old. It doesn't take much to set Breck off and Eddie is getting close. Still, Breck knows, until the money is in his account, he better keep his feelings to himself. For what he hopes is the last time, he tells Eddie, "I got it."

8:00am - It could have been the walk along the bluffs at 6:30am, but, more likely, it is the double espresso. Whatever it is, William, despite not being able to fall back asleep until 4:30am and then wide awake again at 6:15am, feels fresh, alert, and full of energy. With nothing on except a towel wrapped around his waist he stands in front of the bathroom sink watching himself shave his face. He turns on the shower and then turns back to the mirror to look at his body. His mid-section is still a little sore from yesterday but given how much better it feels now, he suspects this will be the last time he pays any attention to it. The wound from where he was shot has healed nicely. Every once in a while he feels a little tightness in his shoulder but that too is nothing to worry about any more. Overall, he's pleased. He looks good and he feels good and he's ready to push forward. He unwraps the towel and is about to step into the shower when his cell phone rings. He's already made a couple of calls this morning and he's hoping that this is someone returning his call. So, he wraps the towel around his waist again and grabs his cell phone off the dresser in the bedroom.

He can't stop smiling even if he wanted to. The sound of Rosa's voice feels like the comfort of putting on his favorite tee-shirt.

It's only been a couple of days since he's seen her or spoken with her or thought about the company, but he feels two worlds away. She gives him a few updates on some of the people in the company and on the projects he was working on, but she saves the best news for last. She's finally engaged. She was going to leave it at that but William gets her to tell him exactly how it happened. He can tell she is very happy that he asked. In turn, it makes him happy to hear her say that he sounds 100% better than he did the last time they spoke. At the same time, they both make a comment about that not being hard to do since he was drunk the last time they spoke. They laugh about that. They talk a little more about how they are still in sync and about how much they miss each other. When Rosa asks what he's doing to keep himself busy, William can't think of how to begin to explain. Instead he offers her a generic response. He tells her he's working on something and she seems happy with that. Ultimately, their conversation gets around to the reason he called and the reason she's returning his call. She found the name and number he is looking for. That's a relief to William since he hadn't thought about that person in over a year. He worried that, during one of his compulsive purging sessions, he had thrown out or deleted that name and number. He grabs a pencil and paper and takes the information from Rosa. Their phone call ends with William congratulating her again and with Rosa getting William to promise to call her if there is anything else she can do for him.

He puts the phone down on top of the piece of paper with the information on it. It's too early to make the call but he will as soon as he can. He starts to unwrap the towel and head for the shower but his cell phone rings again. He's sure it's Rosa, who has probably forgotten to tell him something, so he answers it without looking. His, "Hello," is met with, "Why have you been avoiding my call?" The truth is, William has been avoiding Javier's call. Javier called him three times yesterday, though he only left a message after the third call. William didn't answer or return the call because he doesn't have anything to say to Javier yet. More than that, he promised Javier that they would continue their meeting, which he didn't really mean. At the time, he was just saying what he thought would get him out of the precinct as fast as possible. To answer Javier's question William says, "I haven't been avoiding your call. I planned to return your call today. I just got tied up yesterday. I had a really busy day."

Javier says, "Really? What were you doing all day? I hope you haven't gotten into any more fights with strangers."

William wants to say, "It's not really a fight when you take all the punches without ever throwing one back," but, instead he says, "No, no, nothing like that. I just had some personal stuff to attend to."

"Just some personal stuff and you couldn't return my call?"

"What's going on Javier? What do you need me for?"

"I told you, before you left, we need to finish our conversation. Why don't you come in at 10:00am, it won't take long."

"I don't think I can be there at 10:00am, I have something else to do."

"Why don't you come in at 10:00am, it won't take long."

"I really don't think I can reschedule it. How about sometime tomorrow?"

"Why don't you come in at 10:00am, it won't take long."

"OK, I'll be there. I'll see you at 10:00am." William puts down the phone, unwraps his towel, and steps in the shower. As the warm water caresses his body from his head to his toes, he thinks of how strange it will appear to Javier that yesterday he was eager to discuss how Teddy's and Genny's murders are related, but today he won't have much to say about it. He grabs the soap and starts to lather and wash his body. He'll just have to cross that bridge when he gets to it.

9:00am - "Close the door behind you Eddie," says Captain Upton. Javier is seated in the Captain's office and the Captain looks like he's worked a full day already. Captain Upton says, "Eddie, if you meant what you said about working through tomorrow, here's your chance. I've been on a conference call with the Chief, and others, all morning. There's a few issues that are weighing on the Chief. The one that he's concerned with the most doesn't have anything to do with us for now, but he is getting some pressure from the Chamber of Commerce in Santa Monica to solve the David Waverly murder." Eddie says, "I did mean what I said and I'll be working on that exclusively today and tomorrow. I have a couple of leads. I didn't follow them up yesterday because of Bobby but I'll get to them double time today."

"That why I wanted to meet with the two of you. Since Bobby is on leave, I need to pull you, Javier, from the cases you're working on, and partner you up with Eddie to work the Waverly case. Eddie, I know you're not crazy about the idea but we need to get the Chief some results."

Eddie says, "Javier, you know it has nothing to do with you. I'm just better on my own. It took me a year to get used to working with Bobby. Cap, I have today and tomorrow. Just let me follow up on the leads I have."

"That's just it. After tomorrow, you'll be gone and Bobby will still be on leave. I won't have anyone working the case. Javier will have to bring himself up to speed on his own."

"I'll tell you what. Let me see what I can dig up today. I'll be sure to bring Javier up to speed tomorrow before I leave."

Javier says, "Cap, it's all right with me if I take the case tomorrow. I have a few loose ends I can tie up today. That way I can give my full attention to the case when I get it."

"Neither of you understand. I'm not asking either of you what you'd like to do. I'm telling both of you the way it's got to be. Javier, tie up any loose ends you need to and get up to speed with Eddie today. Eddie, fill Javier in on everything you know already and on your leads. It's OK if the two of you work independently this morning, but by the end of the day, today, I need the two of you on the same page. Like I said, we need to get the Chief some results. I have a meeting with him tomorrow afternoon. I need you both to get me something I can tell him. I'll leave it to the two of you to decide how to go about it."

Captain Upton's assistant comes through on the intercom, "I have your wife on line two."

Captain Upton says to Javier and Eddie, "Hang on, I have to take this call."

While the Captain speaks with his wife, Javier says to Eddie, "Listen, if you want to follow up on your leads on your own, that's OK with me, just as long as we meet later today. I have someone coming in at 10:00am to tell me what he knows about Teddy Gallo, and then I have a few other things to do this morning."

"Teddy Gallo? I thought that was determined to be a suicide."

"Yeah, it was but this guy seems to think it wasn't."

"Is it anyone I know?"

"You know of him but I don't think you ever met him. Do you remember, about three months ago I got a murder case. It was a woman in Santa Monica, shot dead in her house in the middle of the night. The case we discussed at Teddy's apartment."

"Vaguely. Wasn't that the burglary gone bad?"

"Yeah. The guy who's coming in is her husband. He doesn't believe it was a botched burglary. He believes she was targeted and murdered. More than that, he believes her murder and Teddy's death are connected."

Outwardly, Eddie is as cool as he always is, inwardly he's saying to himself: "This can't be happening."

He asks Javier, "I don't get it. How are the two connected?"

"I don't think they are, but he believes his wife was murdered over something that happened when she was dating Teddy."

"What do you mean by she was dating Teddy?"

"I told you before, she and Teddy dated several years ago, before she met William, the man who would become her husband. It's a farfetched connection, I know, but this guy is, if nothing else, persistent and he's determined to prove that he's right. I think he's reaching, but I feel bad for the guy for losing his wife, so I'm having him come in to hear what he has to say."

William walks through the front door of the precinct. The officer that has always been there when he arrives is there again today. The two of them exchange small talk and then he tells William Detective Morales is in a meeting. William knows the routine, so he takes a seat in the waiting area.

Captain Upton hangs up the phone and asks, "All right, is there anything else we need to discuss?" Neither Javier nor Eddie have anything more, so their meeting breaks. When Javier gets back to his desk he learns that William is waiting for him in the lobby. Eddie overhears Javier ask the front desk to buzz William in and he watches as Javier walks towards the conference rooms, which are between the lobby and the main Detectives room. Javier and William meet outside conference room number two. They talk, outside the conference room, just long enough to give Eddie the opportunity to walk by and say, "Javier, I'll catch up with you later this afternoon." Javier replies, "OK."

Eddie then turns to Javier's guest and says, "How're you doing? I'm Detective Roberts." And, it works perfectly.

William says, "Hi. I'm William Flowers. Nice to meet you."

Eddie turns to Javier and asks, "Is this . . .?"

Before he can finish the question Javier answers, "Yes."

Eddie turns to William and says, "We were all really sad to hear about your wife. I'm sorry for your loss."

"Thanks."

Eddie continues, "I understand you knew Teddy Gallo."

Javier jumps in and explains, "Detective Roberts was acquainted with Teddy as well."

William asks, "Oh yeah. How?"

Eddie says, "I arrested him on more than one occasion. You know, I'd be interested in what you know or have to say about Teddy too. Do you guys mind if I sit in?" Javier finds the request strange, especially since Eddie, just a moment ago, appeared to be headed somewhere. He reminds himself, however, that Eddie did know and work with Teddy, so maybe he's just interested. Javier doesn't object. As far as William is concerned, Detective Roberts will be just another person in the room who thinks he's crazy. On the other hand, there's a chance he'll say something helpful. William doesn't object either. The three of them go into the conference room.

10:00am - For only the second time in his entire life it is happening again. The first time it happened was over fifty years ago.

Russell and his friends were at the Orange County Fair. For three months before it opened the Fair promoted its newest ride, The Dragon, a high speed rollercoaster with more drops, turns, and tunnels than any rollercoaster before it. Russell and his friends got to the park early, about an hour after it opened, just so they could be among the first to ride the Dragon that day. The ride was so high they could see it from the parking lot, but it wasn't until they were standing next to it that they could really appreciate how high and scary the ride really was. As they got in line they could hear the clanking of the cars as they climbed the first and most massive hill. Then there was a moment of silence, followed by screams that were so high in pitch and blood curdling they could only come from people who were scared to death and loving every minute of it. Even when the coaster cars were out of sight you could still hear the screams. As the coaster cars got closer you could hear what sounded like rolling thunder approaching, and as the coaster cars whipped around a turn just above the line the thunderous noise and the screams were deafening. The only time Russell had heard a sound like that was during an earthquake, several years before, when it felt and sounded like the whole world was shaking. When their turn came around Russell was lucky enough to get in the first car with one of his friends, and his other two friends got in the car directly behind them. Russell was raised in the church, but, at that time he was in his teenage years, so he preferred sleeping in over going to church. Sure enough, however, as the car made what seemed like a never ending climb to the top of the first hill Russell was saying his prayers. When he got to the apex, high above all of the trees in the vicinity, Russell looked out over what seemed like all of Southern California, from Orange County all the way to the border with Arizona. While he was standing in line, waiting his turn, he told himself that he wouldn't scream like the riders before him, but when the coaster car started its descent, in that moment when he felt zero gravity, Russell screamed like everyone else, and he didn't stop screaming, not for a second, until the ride was over. When the ride came to an end Russell and his friends got right back on line. While they waited for their second ride they couldn't stop talking about the first drop, and how fast they whipped around turns, and how cool the rolling hills through the tunnels in the middle of the ride were. It was the most exciting thing ever and all they wanted was more, more, more. Russell and his friends were so engrossed in talking about the ride they didn't notice the pretty girls standing in front of them. When the next ride started its climb to the top Russell turned from his friends to look forward at the coaster car making its ascent. Just then she turned around to talk to one of her friends that was standing in line behind her. That was it. Russell was hit by the Thunderbolt. In that moment, he realized he didn't know her name, he didn't know where she was from, he didn't know anything about her, but what he did know was that he was in love, that he would do whatever it takes, for however long it takes, to be with her, and that he would love her forever.

Her name was Linda. Russell found a way to talk with her after the ride. Later they had lunch together. Later still they went on the Dragon again and together. From that day forward they were a couple. Just as he thought, from the moment he first laid eyes on her, he loved her like no other. They got married a few years later and they lived their entire lives together as best friends and lovers. She was everything he needed and all he ever wanted, and she felt the same way about him. It's been fifteen years since Linda lost her battle with Leukemia. When she died Russell was sure he would live the rest of his life alone. Over the years he thought about dating, he even tried it a couple of times, but he gave it up because no one came close and, in his mind, no one could ever replace Linda. Until now.

On his drive to Cardiff by the Sea he thought of nothing else besides the gun, the murder victim, and the idea that popped into his head on his drive home from his office last night. When he got to the Sheriff's office he was still thinking about those three things. When Phyllis Stafford stood up from behind her desk to welcome him and shake his hand, before she said a word, she smiled, and he was hit by the Thunderbolt for the second time in his life. It started last night when he allowed whatever it was to get him out of bed to drive to his office. It carried over to this morning when he jumped in his car and headed south. He felt young again. He felt the thrill of doing things just because he thought of doing them. Now, in his mid-sixties, he must still be riding that wave because he's thinking of all the things he can do to make sure he sees Phyllis Stafford again. Then reality hit him and he wonders if she was married. When he notices that she isn't wearing a wedding ring he is more than happy, he is downright giddy. When Phyllis tells him that he needs to give the Sheriff a few more minutes before he's ready, he tells her he doesn't mind waiting. He tells her that he's just happy that the Sheriff was able to make time for him on such short notice. When she offers him a cup of coffee, he thinks to himself that he's already had two cups of coffee during the drive there. The last thing he needs is another one, but he also thinks that is something he can do that could lead to a conversation, so he says, "Yes, please."

10:30am - The meeting with Javier and Detective Roberts is, thankfully, coming to an end. William reiterated his stance that neither he nor Genny had any enemies that would want to hurt them. Nor did they have any friends that could be involved in such heinous activity. Again, he explained the only person they knew with any links to the underworld was Teddy. He explained, for Detective Roberts' benefit, the relationship Genny had with Teddy. He explained why he thinks her death stems from that relationship, and why he thinks Teddy's death and Genny's death are related. Against his better judgment he told the detectives about his search for Megan. He even told them about the house on San Juan Court and what happened there. What he didn't tell them about was Lexi giving him Megan's number, and he didn't tell them that he found her, spoke with her, and that they are meeting later today. As far as the detectives know he went home and straight to bed right after washing his face in the bathroom at Starbucks. Javier's reaction to William's persistence was to be expected. He reminds William of the conversation he had with himself and Captain Upton yesterday. He uses William's experience at the house on San Juan Court as evidence that William is in over his head, and as evidence that if he continues down this road he will likely end up dead. Detective Roberts' reaction, however, was surprising. He appeared to be more supportive of William's suspicions and actions. Throughout William's explanations it was Detective Roberts who asked the most questions. He wanted to know what Genny could have possibly known that would have led to her being killed. Of course, William couldn't answer that question. He also wanted to know more details about her relationship with Teddy. Almost all of the things that Javier immediately dismissed as irrelevant, Detective Roberts found interesting. Still, after all of the information William cared to admit was on the table Detective Roberts joined Javier in his condemnation of William's continuing citizen's investigation. Even there, he seemed to come at William from a different place than Javier. While Javier appears to tolerate William, perhaps from his feelings of guilt stemming from his inability to solve Genny's murder, Detective Roberts appears to respect and support William's theories and actions, but condemn them at the same time more out of a genuine concern for William's safety. Purposefully, William leaves the detectives with the impression that the events at the house on San Juan Court served as a wakeup call. He tells them that experience made he realize that he is over his head. Detective Roberts seems to buy it, but not Javier. Javier sits back and lets Detective Roberts caution William on the perils of dealing with the criminal element. When Detective Roberts had his say, Javier adds a caution on the perils of vigilantism. He tells William he would hate to see William arrested, which could have happened if things got out of control yesterday. He warns William that an arrest and a charge, even if William is later found not guilty, could lead to William not only having to deal with life without his wife but also having to deal with a lengthy court process that could cost William time, standing, his employment, and tens of thousands, if not hundreds of thousands of dollars. As the three men stand up from the table in the conference room, William assures them he has heard all they had to say and that he's rethinking his actions. Detective Roberts, again, apologizes for the loss of his wife and wishes William the best of luck. Javier, again, promises William that the investigation into his wife's murder isn't over and that he'll update William as soon as he has any new information. William thanks Detective Roberts for listening and he tells Javier that he'll stay in touch.

As soon as William walks out of the precinct he calls Megan. She tells William that she has a list of people who knew Teddy, and who might know what he was up to over the last year. They agree to meet at 3:00pm to discuss the list. Then William makes the call he's wanted to make all morning.

"This is Jarrod," said the voice on the other end of the call.

"Jarrod, my name is William Flowers. I don't know if you remember me, we met at the Los Angeles County Museum of Art." William can tell Jarrod is trying to remember who he is because there is a moment of silence, but then Jarrod says, "William, of course I remember you. It's good to hear from you. How are you doing my friend?"

"I'm doing OK. How are you?"

"I'm good. I probably put on a couple of pounds since the last time we saw each other but I'm working on that. The wife is good, the kids are good, and business is good, so I can't complain. If I remember correctly you are married to a beautiful French woman, Geneviève, right? How are you guys doing?"

"Genny died three months ago."

"Oh my God! I'm so sorry to hear that. What happened?"

"She was murdered. Listen Jarrod, I'll tell you more when I see you, if you can make time for me. I'm calling because I need your help."

"Of course I can make time for you. I have to leave the shop in a few minutes but I'll be back here at 1:00pm and I'll be here for the rest of the day."

"Thanks Jarrod, I'll see you at 1:00pm."

"Do you know where the shop is?"

"I have the address. I'll be there at 1:00pm."

"William, I am so sorry to hear that news but I'll be here at 1:00pm. I'll see you then."

After William leaves the precinct Javier and Eddie discuss his case briefly. Then Eddie tells Javier that he isn't going to leave the office as he planned to do before he sat in on their meeting. Instead, if Javier has the time, he'd rather bring Javier up to speed on the Waverly investigation now. Javier tells Eddie he can make the time but he has a couple of things he has to do first. Eddie says that's all right with him because he has a couple of phone calls he has to make. They agree to meet at Eddie's desk in an hour.

11:00am - When Sheriff Silva came out of his office to meet Russell he felt bad. It has been a long time since he's heard Phyllis laugh like that. Still, based on the purpose of their meeting, he wants to talk with Russell, apparently, as much as Phyllis does. Their meeting starts off with the two of them being highly complimentary of the other. Sheriff Silva admits he has read a few of Russell's columns and special reports and that he was so impressed with them he would have made time for him just so the two of them could meet. Russell thanks for Sheriff for his kind words and thanks him for taking the time out of his schedule, at the last minute, to humor his idea. The Sheriff tells Russell that he's intrigued with this case. He admits to Russell that Chief Koch called him last night to discuss the case. Then he corrects himself. The Chief didn't call to discuss the case. He called to ask the Sheriff about the facts and about anything else he's learned since Monday. Now, one of LA's best writers is here asking about the same case. The Sheriff asks Russell what is it about this homicide that has everyone so interested. Russell promises to tell the Sheriff, but first he asks the Sheriff to allow him to ask a series of questions. The Sheriff agrees. First, Russell wants to confirm that the cause of death was a gunshot to the back of the head and not the fire. The Sheriff confirms that is true. Next, Russell asks if the weapon was a .45 caliber pistol and the Sheriff confirms that as well. Russell asks if the Sheriff has confirmed the identity of the victim and, if so, what does he know about him. Sheriff Silva says he has. He tells Russell the victim's name was Ronny White and that Mr. White was a petty criminal. He hands Russell Mr. White's file and Russell takes a moment to read through it. Now, Russell is ready to tell the Sheriff what he knows and, given that Chief Koch called the Sheriff last night, he's confident that he's right. He explains that the story started six years ago. Three petty criminals, like Ronny White, were killed on three different but consecutive nights. At the time, none of three homicides garnered much attention. With so much crime, including homicides, which happen to well-meaning citizens, it was easy for the police to dismiss crimes, including homicides, which happen between the criminal types. However, three things linked those homicides together and collectively they made those three murders different. First, all three happened to petty criminals. Second, all three were killed with a single shot to the back of the head. Finally, and most interesting to the police, a single spent shell casing was discovered at all three crime scenes and one bullet was discovered at only one of the crime scenes. Because all three shell casings came from the same box of shells the police reasonably suspected that all three murders were done by the same person, who was probably using the same gun. That raised a big, bright red flag, but that sort of thing happens in big cities. What took those three cases over the top was the gun itself. The police were able to determine that the murders were committed with the same gun from matching the forensic ballistics of the bullet with those they already had on record. Given that, they were able to match that gun with one that was manufactured for and used by the Los Angeles Police Department. In other words, somehow, a police issued gun had found its way out of the system and into the hands of a killer. Once that was determined there was a black out of all information fed to the media. Russell tells the Sheriff that the killer's trail went cold after that. There was no follow up discussion about the homicides and there were no other killings with the same gun. Russell explains that he's followed every homicide in LA that was committed with a .45 caliber pistol since then, and none of them match the ones six years ago either in M.O. or in forensic ballistics. Accordingly, he believes the Chief's interest in this case is the same as his own. There are two out of three matching characteristics, namely the victim is a petty criminal and the victim was shot in the back of the head. Russell knows the answer to the next question but he asks it anyway. Sheriff Silva confirms no shell casings were found in or around the car, spent or otherwise and the bullet wasn't recovered.

The two men continue to talk for a while. Russell's enthusiasm is infectious and the fact that he's hunting not only a killer but also a gun is intriguing to the Sheriff. After last night's talk with the Chief, the Sheriff would have been content to let the LAPD handle the investigation from wherever they wanted him to leave off. What was most important to him was to be able to inform the citizens of Cardiff by the Sea that a killer is not residing among them. He is confident that whoever committed this crime had simply chosen their small town as an ideal place to dump the body. That, in and of itself, is somewhat troubling, but with the killer gone he knows the townspeople will find that fact more peculiar and less worrisome. After hearing Russell's idea, however, the Sheriff has had a change of heart. It's like he's gotten a shot of adrenaline directly from Russell's exuberance. On top of that, thoughts of breaking this case before the mighty LAPD does are creeping into his head. He's in. Now, as the two men prepare to leave the Sheriff's office together, the Sheriff asks Phyllis to clear his schedule for the rest of the day. On their way out Russell tells Phyllis what a pleasure it was to have met her and to have talked with her for a short while. He tells her that he hopes to get a chance to do it again soon. What he doesn't know is that Phyllis feels the same way. What he does know, however, is that he will see her again, and soon, because he's already decided to do whatever it takes to make sure that happens. The two men leave the station and jump into the Sheriff's car, off on their mission.

11:30am - The meeting with William changed everything. Eddie thought of calling Breck but he abandoned that idea. In fact, now he's sorry he asked Breck to return to Los Angeles. After giving it some thought, Eddie decides the best thing to do is to take himself out of the equation. There's no one alive who can tie him to anything except Carl, Bobby and Breck. Carl won't say anything and neither will Bobby because they have as much to lose, and in Carl's case, more, if they talk. Breck won't say anything because he wants to be paid. The three people with less to lose than Eddie, David, Teddy, and Ronny, are all dead and any investigation into any of their murders will only lead to a dead end. In just a little over 24 hours he'll have more money than he ever thought he would have, and a few hours after that he'll be cruising down the Pacific Ocean on his way to Costa Rica. Eddie's sure of it now. The better thing to do is not to get deeper but to get out. Once he comes to that decision the stress he was feeling, just an hour ago, has all gone away. He feels light on his feet again. Now he just needs to tell Captain Upton and Javier that he made a mistake.

When Javier meets Eddie at his desk, Eddie explains to Javier that he thinks he has bitten off more than he can chew. He explains that he has so many things to do before he leaves to-morrow night, that on second thought, it doesn't make sense for him to be as involved in this case as he said he would. Javier isn't surprised by Eddie's admission. For the last few months Eddie has talked about nothing except retiring, his boat, and moving to Costa Rica. The only thing that was surprising was Eddie's sudden desire to keep working. Eddie gives Javier David's case file and the two of them discuss the details. Eddie tells Javier, how, when, and where David was found and who was there. They discuss where David is from and his last known address. Eddie gives Javier Lisa Becker's business card and explains where they met and what they talked about yesterday. He tells Javier everything Lisa told him about her meeting with Jessie, David's roommate. He explains that was the lead he was eager to follow up with, but he's already called her and told her another detective will contact her to follow up instead. He even tells Javier of the deal he has with Lisa, which Javier agrees to honor. Eddie has to admit he's not giving Javier much to work with. There were no witnesses to the murder or, at least, none have turned up yet. There were no fingerprints found on the victim's clothing, nor was the spent shell case or the bullet located. All Javier has is what Lisa told Eddie: that the victim was last known to be hanging out with a Ronny White and some other guy, whose name she can't remember but she thinks it starts with a D or a B. On top of having nothing, the Captain is being pressured to get results, which means the pressure is on Javier alone now that Eddie has decided he doesn't want to work the case. It's no wonder that Javier thinks, "Great. Thanks." Since he has to start somewhere Javier calls Jessie to make an appointment to talk with her, but he gets her voicemail, so he leaves a message. Javier thinks they should talk with the Captain just to fill him in on how the two of them have decided how to handle the case. Captain Upton, however, has stepped out of the office, so they agree to hang around the office so they can fill him in when he returns.

12:00pm - Lisa's plan for today was to write follow ups and post them on her blog and then meet with Jessie again. Thanks to one of her co-workers with contacts in the DMV, Lisa has photocopies of the driver's licenses of eleven men named Ronald or Ronny White. She knows not to get her hopes up to soon but she's hopeful that Jessie will pick one of them as the person she saw with David. However, half way through writing the follow ups Lisa got a call from Iris. She dropped her blog for the time being, grabbed the photocopies, jumped in her car, and headed downtown. She parks her car in the lot she was told to, she walks up the street she was told to, and just as she was told she would, she spots the black Ford with black tinted windows and CA Exempt plates. She opens the back passenger side door and gets in the back seat as instructed. Iris is seated in the passenger side front seat and she introduces Lisa to Bradley Koch, the driver and the Chief of Police for the LAPD. Immediately after the introduction, they pull out of the parking space. Iris says, "I want you to tell the Chief everything you told me about the David Waverly case." Without to many specifics Lisa recounts how she stumbled across the crime scene. Without saying how, she tells the Chief that she learned of David's last known address and had a talk with his former roommate. While Lisa spoke about the crime scene and David's history according to Jessie, the Chief didn't take his eyes off the road for a minute, nor did he ask any questions. When she got to the part of David's last known associates, namely Ronny White and some other guy whose name starts with a D or a B, she gets the Chief's full attention.

It quickly becomes apparent to Lisa that the Chief's main interest is in the other guy. Unfortunately, Lisa tells the Chief that Jessie says she never saw him. She couldn't even remember his name. Lisa tells the Chief that she's spoken with some of David's other friends and none of them even heard of the other guy. Lisa thinks about telling the Chief that she has plans to meet with Jessie later, when she'll try to get her to ID Ronny White and when she'll try to jog Jessie's memory on the other guy's name, but she decides not to give her hand away too early. Instead she tries to get some information from the Chief. She asks why he seems so interested in the other guy. The Chief doesn't answer. Instead, Iris turns around and gives Lisa a look, obviously trying to discourage her from asking questions. Lisa backs down and the Chief asks her to think if Jessie or if any of David's other friends said anything that could be a lead to finding out who the other guy is. Unfortunately, Lisa can't tell the Chief anything about him that she hasn't told the Chief already. Lisa says, "If I can't ask you about the other guy or who he is, can you, at least, tell me what's going on?"

Iris looks at the Chief, as if to ask him to give her something. The Chief explains, "If this other guy is who we think he is, we believe he has killed other people besides Mr. White."

Lisa asks, "Do you think he killed David?"

"No, not directly."

"What does that mean?"

Lisa hasn't been paying attention to where they have been driving but the Chief has. Instead of answering her question, he pulls the car over directly in front the parking lot Lisa's car is in and he says, "I really appreciate your help. I hope to see you again."

Iris adds, "Thanks honey. I'll talk with you later."

That's when Lisa looks around and recognizes where she is. More than that, she recognizes that's her cue to get out of the car. She does, but before the Chief and Iris have driven a block away Lisa is on the phone with Jessie.

12:30pm - Captain Upton isn't happy to hear the news, but like Javier, he's not surprised. More troubling is the evidence and leads, or lack thereof, for this case. After the three of them discuss everything they know, the Captain is inclined to agree with Javier. Namely, he may need to lower the Chief's expectations. The Captain considers partnering Javier with another detective but that won't make a difference. First of all, they are short-handed already. And, more than that, the problem isn't a lack of manpower. It's a lack of new information. So, for the time being, the Captain tells Javier the case is all on him. As for Eddie, the Captain is open to him running a few personal errands on company time, just as long as he's available to Javier. To that end, he suggests that Javier spend most of the day with Eddie just in case Eddie remembers something.

All three men feel relieved of some pressure, each for their own reasons. Eddie is more relaxed now because all he has to do is stay out of everyone's way and wait for tomorrow. Javier was worried because he has very little to go on and with so little to work with it is unreasonable to believe he'll solve the case in a day. His worry, however, is mitigated somewhat because the Captain agrees. Captain Upton is more relaxed because, while the Chief is a driven task master, he can also be a reasonable man. When the Captain reports to the Chief on what they have, what they know, and what they are working on, he knows the Chief will keep pushing but he also knows the Chief will understand their limitations. In this moment of levity, the conversation turns to Eddie and his plans, a topic Eddie is all too happy to talk about. He explains to the Captain and to Javier that he intends to push off tomorrow night around 9:00pm or 10:00pm. He explains that he would leave earlier but Viking is having a wine and cheese celebration for him tomorrow night, where he will officially be given the keys. He goes on to say that his plan is to cruise down the coast very slowly tomorrow night. He's looking forward to his first sunrise on the water and he hopes to be just south of San Diego for that. He says he plans to stop in Cabo San Lucas to refuel and restock supplies and from there he plans to step on it and make to Costa Rica as soon as he can. Javier and the Captain listen to Eddie ramble on about his plans with mixed emotions. On one hand they are happy for him and, on the other hand, they are as happy as anyone would be for a co-worker who has hit the lottery. In his exuberance Eddie made the mistake of telling the Captain and Javier that he would spend a part of the day getting the few remaining things he needs onboard his boat. That statement, of itself, seemed harmless at first, but the Captain followed that up by asking Javier if he had ever seen Eddie's boat. Javier said he hadn't found the time and nor has the Captain. So, the Captain tells Javier to go with Eddie to his boat and get some pictures they can put up on their bulletin board. Eddie immediately tries to downplay his boat, but the Captain tells him he's being modest just a little bit too late. This time the Captain tells Javier to make sure he gets some pictures of Eddie's boat today. Eddie knows he has no choice now but to play along so he does the only thing he can think of doing. He tells Javier that he needs to make a few stops before he gets to his boat and he asks

Javier to meet him there in an hour or so. That should give Eddie enough time to make sure that Breck isn't there.

1:00pm - As a young adult Geneviève spent hours in Musée d'Orsay. Growing up in Paris she had access to many great museums and to hundreds of great paintings, sculptures, and artifacts. She enjoyed them all. It's fair to say she spent as much time in Musée du Louvre as she did in Musée d'Orsay, but that was because Musée du Louvre is so much bigger and there is so much more to see there. The first time she went to Musée d'Orsay was to see a joint showing of the works by Andy Warhol and his protégé Jean-Michel Basquiat. Warhol's paintings were fun, Basquiat's were haunting, but it was the paintings by Vincent van Gogh that captured her imagination. She would return again and again to see van Gogh's paintings. Sometimes she would see different ones but even if she saw the same ones she would always see something in them that she hadn't appreciated before. So, when William surprised her with tickets to the Los Angeles County Museum of Art's showing of the works by van Gogh she was excited to go. While they were at LACMA William returned from the restroom to find Geneviève talking with another woman in French. It turned out that that woman was Swedish but she moved to Paris in her teenage years to pursue a modeling career. Somehow the two women got to talking and found out that they had both seen, for the first time in Musée d'Orsay, some of the same paintings they were admiring now in Los Angeles. Geneviève introduced William to the woman and to her husband. They all had a pleasant conversation for a few minutes and then they went their separate ways. A few months later David and Matthew Hughes, the owners of the firm William works for, threw a party, at their office, for their employees and their investors. William saw a man he thought looked familiar talking with David Hughes but he couldn't place him. When that man's wife joined her husband, William remembered where they had met. Together, with Geneviève, William made his way over to where they were talking. Though they had met before that's when William got to know Jarrod Macey and his wife, Deirdre. Jarrod and Deirdre were investors in David's company and David was a client of Jarrod's. Jarrod owns a shooting range, among other things. He taught David how to shoot and he sold several guns to David, and to his brother, over the years. Now, as William pulls into Jarrod's parking lot, he's less concerned about his request and more concerned about David and Matthew learning of it. As he gets out his car he makes a mental note to be sure to get Jarrod to keep their business to themselves.

Without going into too much detail William tells Jarrod about the night Geneviève was murdered. He tells him what the police have determined so far and what they think is at the root of the murder. Though he feels bad about the deception, he gives Jarrod the impression that he feels his life is in danger. William knows that he could wait a week to go through the registration process of buying and owning a gun but his plan is to walk out of Jarrod's shop with a gun in hand. The idea of skipping the registration process doesn't sit well with Jarrod, and William can sense the change of tone in their conversation. Instead of backing down he adds to his request. What he wants is a gun and ammo he can leave with today and, on top of that, he needs Jarrod to give him a quick tutorial on how to load, shoot, and take care of it. The tutorial isn't the problem for Jarrod, it's giving William an unregistered gun, but he hasn't said no yet. William continues to press. Finally, after giving it some thought, Jarrod offers William a deal. William needs to buy a gun and complete the registration form. If all goes well, and there's no reason to believe that it won't, William can come back in a week and pick up the gun he's paid for. In the meantime, Jarrod will teach William how to load, shoot, and care for a gun, and he'll give William a gun and some ammo he can take with him today. The caveat being, if anything happens with the gun William gets today Jarrod will report it stolen. Jarrod leans forward to talk with William about that part of the deal to make sure William completely understands what he's saying. To protect himself and his business, he has to report the gun stolen, and once he does, he can't go back on that claim. William has to sit through an earful of Jarrod complaining about the position William is putting him in. Rightfully so, William knows he's asking for a lot. He assures Jarrod the gun, today, is purely for protection. He has no plans of ever firing it. He just wants it now so he feels better. Jarrod asks William to stay in his office. A couple of minutes later he returns with the forms William needs to complete and with a .22 caliber pistol and some ammo.

1:30pm - Breck couldn't sleep, though lying in bed while the boat gently rocked, back and forth, on the swells was very relaxing. At 11:30am he exited the boat and slipped quickly through the side gate. He walked a couple of blocks away from the Marina and saw an Applebee's Restaurant. He had every intention of calling a cab from there, as Eddie suggested, but next to the Applebee's was an Avis Car Rental. The few hours he spent below deck were nice but the thought of having to stay below deck for the rest of the day and possibly all day tomorrow wasn't very appealing. It would be OK to hang out on the boat for a couple of days if he could come and go as he pleased. It would be nice to sit on the top deck, to get some sun and to read. It would be nice to chitchat with people as they came and went. Since none of that was possible, he would rather not stay on the boat all day. Seeing the Avis gave him an idea. As he climbed into his rented car he thought to himself that, at least this way, he could do other things. A few moments later he was on his way to North Hollywood.

JT, as always, got to O'Reilly's at exactly 12:00pm. Officially, he is the bar's main bartender and day manager. Unofficially, he is the organization's gatekeeper at this location. He was surprised to see Breck, not because Breck was waiting for him when he got there, but because he had just put his gun and other items back in storage, and it was usually months, if not more, before Breck would visit again. Normally there would be a lot to catch up on when they saw each other again, but since Breck was there just a couple of days ago, they exchanged pleasantries and then got down to business. Once inside JT retrieved Breck's safe box and unlocked the back room so Breck could have some privacy. As always, Breck was happy to see his buddy, a Beretta Cougar 8045f .45 caliber pistol. He also had an Ithaca 1911 and a Colt Commander there in storage but he hadn't used either of them in years. For a moment he thought of using the Colt Commander on this trip but then he remembered that, if all goes well, this will probably be his last go round. The more he thought about his Charter Fishing business the more he was in love with the idea. So, if this was the last time he was going to lend himself out for a contract killing, he is going to go out with his old friend, the Beretta Cougar. Along with the guns and the ammunition he kept in his box he also kept five thousand dollars in cash, just as spending money and as a backup in the event of an emergency.

Normally he'd take a grand or two and replenish the money on his next visit. This time he took the entire amount with him. Again he thought, if this is going to be his last job there's no reason to leave the money there. When he was done he left his safe box locked on the desk. JT was breaking down the tables and chairs in the bar area when Breck left. Breck's plan, after his stop at O'Reilly's, was to grab a bite to eat somewhere he can sit outside, and then head back to the boat.

Eddie has been trying to reach Breck since he left the precinct. All of his calls went straight to voicemail so Eddie figures Breck's phone isn't getting reception below deck or the phone is turned off. He was surprised not to find Breck on the boat but then he remembered that Breck said he had an errand to run. This time he called Breck again and left a message telling Breck to stay away from the boat until he called again to tell him the coast was clear. Then he took Breck's belongings and put them in closets so they would be out of sight just in case Javier wanted to look in each of the staterooms. Since he hasn't gotten in touch with Breck, Eddie's plan is to show Javier around and get him off the boat as quickly as possible.

As Javier drives through the Marina Del Rey area he passes Tony Roma's and thinks of all the times he and his friends gathered there on Sunday mornings to watch football games, eat hamburgers, and drink pitchers of beer. Those are good memories for Javier. He tells himself the next time he takes the family out for dinner he plans to bring everyone to the Marina. He spots Viking and pulls into the parking lot. Heidi, the receptionist, tells him that Eddie is expecting him. She directs him to Eddie's boat and she buzzes him into the shipyard. As Javier passes one boat after another he thinks it might be nice to own a boat one day, but with two kids, on their way to college, it will be a few years before he can seriously entertain that idea. Still, maybe one day, who knows? Then he spots her, "Miss Behavin". In a word, impressive. She's a beautiful boat and everything on her is shining like new. Javier gets the shots he needs for the bulletin board and then Eddie gives him a tour. They started on the fly bridge and worked their way down to the staterooms and galleys. Eddie didn't have to worry about rushing Javier off the boat. Javier enjoyed seeing the boat but he told Eddie that he had other things to do, so he had to make his visit short and sweet. As Eddie and Javier were taking the companionway up from below deck, Breck was stepping onto the boat. Eddie takes the lead and makes the introductions. He tells Breck that this is Detective Morales, one of the precinct's finest detectives, and he tells Javier this is Breck, the owner of a boat just down the slip. The two men shake hands. Javier says goodbye to Breck and he tells Eddie that he'll see him later. As Javier leaves, Eddie and Breck stare at each other without saying a word. Eddie is thinking, "What an idiot! I can't wait to kill this guy." Breck is thinking, "Detective Morales has seen my face."

2:00pm - They started in the parking lot where the car was discovered. They stood in the very spot the car was parked in and looked around them in every direction. Neither Russell nor Sheriff Silva could see a camera pointed in the direction of the parking lot that might have captured an impression of the driver. From there they had to gamble. They took as a given, that the driver was from out of town. That meant he probably got to that parking lot by taking South Coast Highway 101 or the 5 Freeway. They guessed that the driver took the 101 Highway or her companion street San Elijo Avenue. With a picture of a car that is the same brand, model, and color in hand, they stopped at every motel, gas station, and convenience store adjacent to the 101 and on San Elijo from the parking lot and as far north as Santa Fe Drive. All in all they stopped at eight motels, twelve gas stations, and five convenience stores. At each stop they asked the clerks on duty if they remembered anyone driving a similar car that may have patronized their business during the last week. More often than not they met people who wanted to help but couldn't. Either they weren't on duty during the time the driver may have come by or they just didn't remember anyone in particular. Besides, a silver Honda Accord doesn't stick out like an orange Ferrari would. Instead of giving up, they decided that they were wrong. The driver, most likely, got to town by taking the 5 Freeway. If that is the case, Sheriff Silva guessed the driver exited the 5 Freeway on Birmingham Drive. From the corner of San Elijo and Birmingham to the 5 Freeway there are two motels, three gas stations, and two 7Elevens. They checked each motel, each gas station, and the first 7Eleven, and they got the same response they received at every other location. Now they are at their last hope, the 7Eleven on Birmingham closest to the 5 Freeway. The two of them are standing in the parking lot waiting for Earl, the store manager and the person who was on duty at the time, to come back from his lunch break. Russell says, "When the idea came to me last night I was sure it was a winner."

Sheriff Silva says, "Don't beat yourself up. It was a great idea. I should have thought of it. Besides, it's been a lot of fun riding around with you and talking. From your columns I got the sense that you're a good man and now I know that's true. I feel like I've made a new friend."

"You're right. It has been a lot of fun. It hasn't turned out the way I hoped but I'm happy we did this. It has been a pleasure getting to know you too." Sheriff Silva smiles and looks at Russell with a devilish grin that he isn't trying to hide. Russell picks up on it, but thinks nothing of it until he turns away and then looks back to the Sheriff, only to find him still staring at him with the same grin. "What?"

"I saw the way you were looking at Phyllis."

Russell can't remember the last time he blushed and he's not sure he is now, but he'd bet all the money he has in his pocket that his face is beet red. All he can say is, "She's a beautiful woman."

"That she is and . . ."

"And what?"

"She doesn't have a romantic interest in her life right now. From what you've told me, neither do you. Are you going to ask her out on a date?"

"I was thinking about it."

"You should. Let me ask you a question. Do you know who Larry Mahan is?"

Before Russell can answer that question, Earl comes out of the 7Eleven and says, "I understand the two of you are waiting for me."

Finally a break. Earl remembers seeing a car like that earlier in the week. The store was quiet. There were only two people in the store at the time, and both of them were still looking around. He was standing at the cash register waiting for them to buy something. He remembers seeing that car because there was plenty of parking right in front of the store, but the driver parked the car in the spot furthest from the entrance. He remembers thinking that he must be going to a different store, but he was wrong. The driver walked directly into the 7Eleven. Other than that there was nothing strange about the car or the driver. In fact, Earl tells the Sheriff and Russell that he didn't pay any more attention to the driver until he got in line to pay for his items. Earl tells the Sheriff and Russell he doesn't remember what the driver looked like and the store's security cameras won't have an image of the car because the cameras only capture what is going on in the store and in the four parking spaces directly in front of the store, but he invites them to the back room where the three of them can review the video files from the week. Since there were only three people in the store once the driver entered, Earl is sure he can pick out which person the driver is.

2:30pm - Jessie apologizes to Lisa before she says hello. She went to her waitress job last night at 6:00pm and worked until 2:00am and then she had a photo shoot that started at 3:00am and she just got off an hour ago. There's no telling how many cups of coffee she had and the cup of Chamomile tea, she's has in her hand, hasn't taken affect yet. She confesses that she thought of asking Lisa to come tomorrow, but she figured she's wide awake now and there's no time like the present. Lisa takes the pictures out of her bag and lays them out on Jessie's coffee table. Jessie looks at all of them, one by one, but quickly. She pauses for a second look at the third picture, but ultimately decides that none of them are the guy she saw with David. Lisa separates the third picture from the rest and asks Jessie why she paused when she saw that picture.

"He looks familiar, but I can't think of why that is."

"Could he be the guy you saw with David?"

"No. He's definitely not him. This is going to drive me crazy but I'm sure I know him. Listen, forgive me but I can't sit still. We can keep talking while I wash the makeup off my face."

"OK, I'll make you another cup of tea while you do that."

"Thanks. I need it. The Chamomile tea bags are in the largest tin next to the stove."

From the kitchen Lisa says, "I spoke with everyone on the list of friends you gave me."

"That's good. Did anybody tell you anything that is helpful?"

"No. It was like you said. None of them ever saw Ronny and none of them even heard about the other guy. By the way, have you had any luck remembering his name?"

"No and I tried. On one of my breaks last night my girlfriend and I thought of every name we could think of that starts with a B or a D and none of the ones we came up with sounded familiar. I told the detective the same thing."

"What detective?"

"A Detective Morales called me and I returned his call while the photographer was setting up the scene we would shoot next."

"Did a Detective Roberts call you?"

"Yeah. He called too. He said he wanted to talk to me, but before I got a chance to call him back he left another message saying that Detective Morales would be taking over for him. Then I got Detective Morales' message, so I called him back."

Lisa thinks to herself that must be the detective taking over for Detectives Roberts just like he said. She hopes Detective Roberts told Detective Morales about their deal. She makes a note to check on that later. By the time Jessie is done washing her face, Lisa is back at the coffee table with another cup of tea. "Feeling better?"

"A little. Thanks for the tea. Luckily I don't have to work tonight. I may not have much luck but I'm going to try to go to sleep as soon as you leave."

"I just want you to look through the pictures one more time. Take your time with each one, OK?" "Sure." Jessie, feeling a little calmer now, takes her time with each picture. One by one she dismisses them all. She looks at that one, separated from the rest, last. Then she remembers. "I know how I know this guy. He works the front door at Dublin's. I'm sorry, I know that doesn't help you but if I didn't figure it out it would have driven me crazy."

"I understand."

"O'Reilly's!"

Lisa looks at Jessie with a puzzled look on her face.

Jessie explains, "I guess the Irish name reminded me. O'Reilly's is where David said he met Ronny. I'm sorry I didn't remember this before. That's why David went to North Hollywood or, at least, that's why he was there once. I've never been there but if I remember correctly it's a Sports Bar in North Hollywood. I'm sure of it now. I mean, not that it's a Sports Bar, I could be wrong about that, but that is definitely where David said he met Ronny."

3:00pm - Earl was filled with a sense of pride when Sheriff Silva explained why they are looking for the driver. He heard about the car on fire on the news Monday night, but it was one of his regular patrons, who came in for his usual cup of coffee on Tuesday morning, who told him about the body inside. Like most of the residents in this village, he stood somewhere in the gossip line. The first story that circulated was it might have been the High School's Principal's wife in the car because she drives a car like that. Truth be told, Earl got that from someone, he doesn't remember who, and he passed it on to someone else. When that story was debunked the gossip mill came up with a new one. This time it was rumored that it was Old Man Allen, a grumpy chain smoking town annoyance. That one didn't last long because Old Man does drive a silver car but it isn't a Honda, it's a Toyota. That rumor was less fact based and more rooted in someone's wishful thinking. Still, the gossip mill passed it around and Earl did his part to get the information out. It wasn't until just last night, when the Sheriff appeared on the local news to tell everyone that the person in the car was a Los Angeles resident that the gossip mill died down. The fact that the Sheriff felt that it was an isolated incident having nothing to do with Cardiff's residents put Earl's, and everyone in the village, minds at ease. So, when the Sheriff explained how Earl could help find the person responsible, Earl felt a surge of Cardiff Pride well up inside of him. He even imagined himself on the news telling the reporter how he helped the Sheriff catch the person who thought he could use Cardiff as a dumping ground to conceal a murder. Now, however, Earl is starting to wonder if that day will come. He didn't think about the day he saw the silver Honda pull into the parking space furthest away from the store. If it was any day other than Monday that would mean the person he saw wasn't the murderer. So far, he hasn't been able to identify him. As usual, the store was busy on Monday morning. There wasn't a time, between 8:00am and 11:30am, when there were only three people in the store. Then at 11:50am a silver Honda Accord pulled up and parked right in front of the store. A woman got out and came into the store. Earl recognizes her as a regular and, on top of that, he saw her in the store yesterday. However, he didn't pay attention to whether or not she was driving a different car. The three of them decide to check on that after they view the rest of the video tape for Monday. At exactly 2:39pm there were exactly three people in the store but two of them were together. Earl recalls that when the person they are looking for was in the store that person and the other two people, in the store at the same time, didn't appear to know each other. Then at 4:43pm the person they are looking for walked into the store. Earl, Russell, and Sheriff Silva watched his every move waiting for him to look directly into a camera, but he never did. While the other two patrons shopped with abandon, both of them looked directly into a camera on more than one occasion. This man, however, kept his head down the whole time. He appeared to know exactly what he wanted. He walked to it, grabbed it, got in line, paid for it, and then he left. Earl voices what Sheriff Silva and Russell are thinking when he says, "That guy seems suspicious." Russell adds, "He seems to know where the cameras are."

Sheriff Silva contributes, "And he's avoiding them."

Earl says, "Let's see if one of the other cameras got a shot of him." The three men reviewed all of the angles from each of the cameras and the best shot they could get was an over the shoulder shot from behind the man as he turned his head to the left. Earl froze that frame and printed it for the Sheriff and Russell to take with them. He also emailed a copy to both men.

That was the last time on Monday that there were only three people in the store. Before the Sheriff and Russell leave they had Earl pull up the tape from yesterday. The woman who drove a silver Honda Accord on Monday was driving that same car, and she parked in the same space, yesterday. Throughout the day, as the Sheriff and Russell went from location to location, they spoke continuously about a variety of things. They spoke about themselves and their families, they spoke about sports, and they spoke about their careers. The drive back to the Sheriff's office is different. For the first five minutes neither of them said anything. Russell breaks the silence with, "I think that's him."

Sheriff Silva responds, "I just wish we had a shot of him getting in or out or driving the car."

Therein lies the reason they are driving in silence. Both of them expected to find something or find nothing. Neither of them thought they'd come up with something and nothing at the same time.

"You're right. It would have been better to be able to tie him to the car, but he must have known that 7Eleven has cameras that capture images from the front row of parking. He's in the store just minutes before the fire is reported, and while he's in the store he did his best to avoid the cameras."

"I agree with you. In order to not be seen by one of those cameras one has to try. Still, there's too much missing for me to get excited."

Both men have been in their careers long enough to know better than to jump to conclusions. Both of them have seen the strangest of things be explained and they have both seen the seemingly normal revealed to be bizarrely strange. They are both in the business of hunches and evidence. Sometimes a hunch leads to evidence, but sometimes a hunch is just a hunch and no more than that. The unspoken rule for situations like this is to let cautious optimism rule the day. At the same time, however, when you've been in the business of hunches and evidence for as long as they have, you develop a sixth sense about some things and when that sixth sense tingles you know there's a 99% chance that you're right. That explains why, after discussing the lack of connecting evidence and all the reasons they could be wrong, Russell smiles and says, "That's him."

And, Sheriff Silva smiles when he says, "Something tells me you're right."

3:15pm - Carrying a concealed weapon, especially a gun, even if it's only a .22, makes you feel more secure. There's no doubt about it. William felt the change in him the minute he stepped out of Jarrod's shop and he's been thinking about it ever since. Now, sitting and waiting for Megan, William wonders what kind of people are on her list. He wonders if they have guns of their own and if he's going to have to use his. He wonders if things would have been different if he had this gun before he went to the house on San Juan Court. Even though his eyes are on the door, the events at the house are replaying so vividly in his head, he doesn't see Megan until she's standing right in front of him. When he does he has to do a double take because she looks so different. He remembers thinking that she is a beautiful girl the night they met. He doesn't remember thinking anything in particular about her yesterday. Now he's reminded of how beautiful she is. As he stands up to pull out her chair Megan says, "You seemed lost in thought."

William replies, "I was thinking about you. I mean, not about you but about the things you were bringing with you."

"I understand."

William asks, "Are you hungry or thirsty?"

"I would like a green tea if they have it."

By the time William returns with Megan's tea there is a sandwich size zip lock bag on the table. "What's that?" asks William.

"That's everything of Teddy's I still have in my possession. I don't think any of it will be helpful but I thought I'd show it to you, just in case, before I threw them all away."

William opens the bag. Inside there's an old utility bill with Teddy's name and address on it. There are two old receipts, both for drinks at a pub called O'Reilly's. There's a card Teddy had given to Megan for her birthday. There are two pictures. One of Teddy and Megan and the other of Teddy and a friend of his named Gino. Finally, there's a ring of Teddy's. After looking at everything William says, "I don't think I can use any of these things except, who's the guy in this picture with Teddy?"

"That's Gino. He's one of the people I put on the list. Whenever Teddy was short on cash he would run errands for Gino to make money."

"OK, I'll keep this picture. Don't you want to keep the card or the picture of you and Teddy?"

"No. I think it's time to let go. Not just of Teddy but also to the life I've been living. I thought about you and Genny all night. I remember being jealous of Genny on that night we met. Not because Teddy obviously hadn't gotten over her, but because she seemed to have everything I want. She was in love and married. She seemed so happy. Then I thought now she's gone. I know it's so cliché but it's so true, life is short. I realized that if I don't turn things around right away, years will go by and I still won't have what I want. At least Genny had it." Megan can see a change in William. Instead of looking at her, he's staring down at the table. "I hope you don't mind me talking about her like this."

"No. It's fine. Besides, you're right. That's a lesson I've had to re-learn the hard way. What's going on with you? What are you trying to get away from?"

"That's hard to say. I've made every mistake a person could make. I think my biggest problem is I have more belief in other people than I do in myself. I'm also wrestling with the fact that so much of what I've been told to believe is just untrue. I grew up believing that there was a way that a family works, and there was a way to have good relationships with friends, and there was a way to succeed at work. Maybe all of that works the way it is supposed to work for some people, but none of it has worked the way I expected it to for me. I have been feeling that the real world is underneath the world we see every day all around us, but I can't bring myself to believe in the real world. I keep believing in the world the way it is supposed to be, but the more I do that the more I lose. Long story short, I guess I'm having a crisis of faith. I'm sorry, I'm rambling on. Things aren't as bad as I make them seem. I'm healthy and happy and everything is great. I just need to believe in myself more. OK, that's enough, unless you have another question that I can answer with another ten minute rant."

William is smiling at Megan and thinking to himself, "A crisis of faith, I can understand that," but all he says, out loud, is, "No, I don't have another question right now. Maybe later. Let's talk about the list."

Megan says, "I did the best that I could. These are the five people Teddy spoke with regularly. I ranked them in order of importance. For instance, Gino is at the top of the list because I know Teddy relied on him. I've never met him but I know of him because Teddy spoke of him often. I'm sorry that I couldn't come up with a telephone number or address for the last three people on the list. I realize it might not be helpful just to have their names, but if we don't get somewhere with the first couple of people we can probably figure out how to find the others."

"You said we. I'm not asking you to get involved in this past giving me the list. You know better than I do what kind of people these guys may be."

"I thought a lot about that last night too. At first, I didn't want any part of it either, but then I thought about Genny. If I can help you find out who did this to her, I want to do that. Don't get me wrong, I'm not looking for more trouble, but I want to help you, and I think I can. I think people will be more open to me, an old girlfriend, asking about Teddy than they will be to you."

"I agree with that, but I still don't think it's a good idea."

"You said it yourself, I know better than you what kind of people these guys are. I don't think any of them are hardcore, like some other people I know, but I'm sure I'm more familiar with their world than you are. You could find yourself in real danger. At the very least, I can stay in the car and if something goes wrong I can call the police." William doesn't have an answer for that. While he thinks about it Megan grabs the list and playfully says, "No me, no list."

4:00pm - Russell is on cloud nine! Light seems lighter, colors seem brighter, even the honking of horns, the cursing of other drivers, and the drone of bumper to bumper traffic on the congested 5 Freeway seem like sweet music. When Sheriff Silva and Russell got back to the office the Sheriff could see the electric connection between Russell and Phyllis. Both of them had a sparkle in their eyes, both of them seemed to stand a little straighter, and smile a little wider. Both of them knew exactly what the Sheriff was doing when he said he left something in his car, and it would probably take ten minutes to find it. That was all the time and encouragement Russell needed. He doesn't even remember what he said. It came out of him naturally. Phyllis found it funny and they shared their first real laugh together. From there he found the courage to ask her out on a date tomorrow night, and she accepted without hesitation. Since then he could have walked outside and found that his car was towed away and it would still be a great day.

Now, sitting in traffic, somewhere between Santa Ana and Anaheim, Russell gets a call from Lisa.

"You won't believe what happened to me today," says Lisa.

"Tell me," Russell replies.

"I took a drive with Police Chief Koch."

"How'd that happen?"

"Iris must have told him that I am investigating the David Waverly murder. I get a call from Iris telling me to meet her downtown in an unmarked car. When I get in the car Chief Koch is in the driver's seat and he takes me and Iris for a ride."

"What did he say?"

"He asked me about what I've found out so far. I told him what I know about David and I told him about a guy named Ronny White, whom David's friends think had something to do with his murder." "Wait a minute. Did you say Ronny White?"

"Yeah. Why? Have you heard of him?"

"Yes. If we are talking about the same guy, he's dead. His body was found in the trunk of a burning car, in Cardiff by the Sea, three days ago. He was shot in the back of the head. I spent the day with the Sheriff of Cardiff looking for leads to his murderer. I'm on the 5 Freeway right now heading back to town. Remember last night when I told you I thought a killer had returned to LA? I think that's who murdered Ronny White."

"I think I know who he is. I mean, I don't know who he is, but David's roommate and friends said he was paling around with Ronny White and with another guy just before he was murdered. Unfortunately, none of them saw him or even know his name. The only thing David's roommate could tell me is that he definitely exists, and his name starts with a D or a B. In fact, that's who the Chief really wanted to know about. He seemed to know everything I told him about David. It was only when I told him of this third person that I seemed to get his full attention. He even gave me his business card with his cell phone number on it and told me to contact him right away if I learned anything more about that guy."

"I think I have a picture of him."

"What!?!"

"Yeah, it's a long shot but I have a picture of a man who was seen driving a car similar to the one Ronny White's body was found in. The picture was taken just minutes before that car was set on fire."

"Oh my god, I think we are looking for the same person. Jessie, that's David's roommate, said David met Ronny at a bar in North Hollywood called O'Reilly's. We should go there and ask if anyone recognizes the guy in the picture."

The last time Russell thought about what his next move should be now that he has the picture was when he and Sheriff Silva were driving back to the Sheriff's office. Even then he hadn't come up with a good idea. Since then the only thing he's thought about is Phyllis. Lisa's idea is better than any idea he's had so far, but something is telling him not to do that. Russell says, "Let's think about it first." "What's there to think about? Let me ask you a question. Did the Sheriff track the plates on the car?" "Yes, but the car was a rental and it was reported stolen a couple of days ago."

"In that case, all I have is a first initial but you have a picture. How else are we going to find out who he is if we don't ask somebody? We know of a place where he probably hung out. Someone there has to be able to tell us who he is. C'mon Russell, let's take the picture to O'Reilly's and ask around."

"I just need a minute to think about it. Let me think, and I'll call you back in a few minutes."

Starting late last night some invisible force motivated Russell. He was conscious of it, he felt it, and he even enjoyed it. It made him feel young again. Now, however, it's gone and that doesn't make sense. Taking the picture to O'Reilly's seems like a natural progression. Given the way the idea came to him, namely through Lisa and by coincidence, it seems like a gift. Russell asks himself, "What's going on? What are you feeling?" Slowly he begins to understand. It's not that the idea isn't brilliant, it is. It's not that he doesn't want to go and ask around, he does. He just doesn't want to do it tonight and he can't do it tomorrow night. He may have felt young last night and earlier today but, right now, he doesn't. He's had enough for a day and, on top of that, he wants to get some sleep tonight so he can be full of energy for his date tomorrow night. That is clearly why he isn't jumping at the opportunity tonight. He'll call Lisa back and promise her that they will go, together, Saturday night. Surely, she'll understand.

"I don't understand," says Lisa. "You're not getting old on me, are you? We have a great lead. We have to follow up tonight."
Russell wishes he could tell Lisa about Phyllis but he definitely can't. That will jinx everything. It was one thing for the Sheriff to know about him and Phyllis because he was there, where they met. Russell is superstitious and he knows the sure way to ruin a good thing is to talk about it before it happens. He'll tell Lisa all about Phyllis after their first date, but not a moment sooner. So he says, "I'm not getting old on you. I was up late last night and I didn't get much sleep, I've been driving around all day and now I'm sitting in bumper to bumper traffic. I just don't think I'll be up to it tonight."
"Fine but what about tomorrow night?"
"I just can't do it tomorrow night."
"Well, give the picture to me and I'll go tonight."
For a moment Russell entertains that idea. "If I do that you have to promise me to be careful and you have to promise to call me

if find out anything about this guy. I don't want you to get a lead on this guy and rush to follow that lead."

"I promise, I'll call you first."

"And, of course, you're going to take Tony with you, right?"

"No. Tony is working tonight."

"Oh no. You're not going to some bar to ask about someone we suspect is a killer by yourself."

"Then come with me old man."

Russell thinks to himself, "What the hell. I'll leave work early tomorrow and take a nap. That will be better anyway. That way I'll really be full of energy." He says to Lisa, "OK, I'll meet you at O'Reilly's tonight."

4:30pm - It's been a busy afternoon. After Javier stopped by, Eddie checked into the Four Seasons Marina Del Rey. He got a room on the second highest floor in the hotel. From his window he can see the entire marina. As he looked out over the marina and the ocean in the distance, his thinking was that there is no better place to spend his last night in Los Angeles. Before he left his hotel room he made two calls. The first, to an escort service he's used in the past. As always, his only request is that the woman be full figured. He doesn't like the skinny or athletic types. He prefers a woman in her mid-thirties to early forties with some meat on her bones. Once he put in his request, he made his second call. He calls the hotel's concierge and he tells that person that he'll be leaving soon, but he'd like a bottle of Dom Perignon placed in the refrigerator in his room so it's there when he gets back. Next he drove to his apartment building to do the walk through with the property manager and then surrender the keys. As he was walking out of the building he got a call from the escort service. Exactly what he wants is available and she'll meet him at his hotel at 9:00pm. Perfect. Finally, before heading back to the precinct he needs to stop at the sporting goods store. There he buys two fishing poles, two reels, and some lures. He buys extra hooks and two boxes of extra line. Finally he buys some rope and two fifty pound free weights. As he puts the last of the items in the trunk of his car he gets a call from Carl. Eddie answers the call with, "What are you worried about now Carl?"

"I just got off the phone with Pete. He's having a brunch for the partners tomorrow at his office."

"So what?"

"He asked me to invite you and I told him I would."

"Thanks but no thinks. First of all, I have to work. Even if I didn't, I'm not going to brunch with Pete Jefferson."

"I'm actually glad to hear you say that. I don't think you should go either."

"Don't worry about it. I'm not. What else?"

"I know we talked about this already but tell me one more time. How much does Bobby know?"

"For the last time, don't worry about Bobby. He doesn't know enough details to be dangerous and I'm taking care of him anyway."

"What do you mean by taking care of him?"

"What else Carl?"

"I'm just worried that . . ."

Before Carl can finish Eddie cuts him off, "No, what you are is paranoid and it's probably from all the drugs you do. Maybe I should be worried about you. Listen, it's done tomorrow. You don't have anything to worry about. Just relax."

"That's easy for you . . ."

Eddie cuts him off again, "Just relax Carl. I'll talk with you to-morrow." He hangs up and thinks, "What a pain in the ass that guy is. He's actually not a bad guy, he's just spoiled rotten and stupid." If Eddie has anything against Carl it's that he's truly a kid who was born with a silver spoon in his mouth, and he hasn't done anything with it. Still, it's hard for Eddie to stay mad at Carl because he owes everything to him. If he hadn't gotten his call ten years ago there's no telling what Eddie would be doing today. There are, at least, three things he knows for sure, he wouldn't have the boat, he wouldn't have the money, and he wouldn't be retiring. Getting rid of Carl would sure help Eddie sleep better at night. For a moment he thinks of sending Breck, but that would only call unwanted attention to everything about Carl, including his relationship with Eddie. "Follow your own advice," Eddie thinks to himself. "Tomorrow you get the money. Then you need to take care of Breck. After that, you don't have anything to worry about for the rest of your life. Just relax and take it easy." Eddie gets in his car and heads back to the precinct.

5:00pm - The second person on Megan's list is a friend of Teddy's named Tommy. On second thought, she convinced William that they should talk with him first. He's someone she actually met and hung out with a few times and, more than that, he always had a crush on her, so he should be more open to talking than Gino. Tommy lives just down the street from Teddy's apartment. On their way there Megan sees a Baskin-Robbins ice cream store she used to frequent when she was with Teddy. Megan tells William they should go there first. If they didn't drive towards Tommy's place, the way they did, Megan may have forgotten about Bash and Kamala, but luckily they did. As they walk towards the store Megan explains to William that she used to go to this store, at least, three times a week. Bash and Kamala are a middle aged Indian couple who gave up their corporate jobs to open their own Baskin-Robbins franchise many years ago. Since then they purchased two additional locations and one Burger King Franchise, but they continue to work in the location they purchased first. If anyone knows what's going on in the neighborhood it's them.

"Oh my god, look who just walked in!" exclaims Bash in his usual loud and overly exuberant manner of speaking. "Look Kamala, look who's here." Kamala just smiles. She's as quiet as Bash is loud. "Where have you been young lady? I thought you stopped loving me."

Megan says, "How could I ever do that? It's good to see you Bash."

"Of course it's good to see me. Have you seen a more handsome man in your entire life? Don't answer that question. Where have you been? How could you stop visiting your old friend Bash?"

"I broke up with the guy I was seeing and I moved to Silver Lake."

"That boy was no good for you. I'm glad you broke up with him, but that's no reason to stop seeing Bash. Let's not talk about the past. You're back now and that's all that matters. You hear that Kamala? My girlfriend is back. I'm finally going to leave you. That's it, we're through. I'm going to run away with my girlfriend Megan." Kamala rolls her eyes and smiles.

Megan says, "Hi Kamala. How are you?"

Kamala smiles and says, "Good." In truth, Bash and Kamala have one of the greatest relationships known to man. They met at work, fell in love, and have fallen deeper in love with each other with every day that passes. Their son graduated from NYU just last year and started a business of his own. Their daughter is in her last year at Columbia and she plans to stay in school to get her Master's Degree in Psychology after she graduates. Her plans make Bash and Kamala both happy and sad. They are happy because they want their daughter to be all she can be, and if this is what she wants to do next, they are behind her 100%. They are sad because they promised each other that they would take a year off from work to travel the world as soon as their kids were out of school. Now they have to wait another two years before they can do that.

"Who's this with you then? Please tell me he's your brother. Don't break Bash's heart just when we are getting back together."

"This is William. He's a friend of mine."

William says, "Hi," to both Bash and Kamala.

Bash goes on, "Are you in love with my girlfriend?"

Embarrassed, Megan pleads, "Bash!" Kamala just rolls her eyes and smiles.

"Well, are you?" asks Bash.

William smiles and says, "No. We're just friends."

"What's wrong with you? You don't like beautiful women? Are you gay? If you're gay I'm happy for you. Bash loves everybody, but that would explain why you don't love beautiful women."

William smiles, "No, I'm not gay."

"You must be married. Are you married?"

Megan pleads again, "Bash!" as she looks to Kamala for help. She should have known better than to do that. Everyone knows this is how Bash is. He's like this from the moment he opens his eyes in the morning until the moment he closes them again at night. Kamala is used to it, and her response is the same as it always is. She just rolls her eyes and smiles. This is the first time, however, that William has been asked that question since Genny died. He wants to say yes, but the answer is no. He doesn't know what to say. Luckily Bash doesn't give him time to answer.

"I just don't understand kids these days. What's your favorite flavor?"

William says, "Mint Chocolate Chip."

Bash says, "Excellent choice. Kamala give this man three scoops of Mint Chocolate Chip. Do you want it on a cone or in a cup? Never mind, take it in a cup. We can give you more that way. I'll give you a cone on the side. Kamala give him three scoops in a cup and give him a cone on the side. By the way, your money is no good here. Today, because I'm so happy to see my girlfriend again, Bash is paying for your ice cream. Now, Megan, do you still like your usual? I don't care. I'm going to make you the biggest and the best Sundae you have ever had."

William doesn't want any ice cream but there is, obviously, no stopping Bash. Besides, before he can say anything Kamala is putting the first scoop in a cup. Megan learned long ago that there's no stopping Bash, so she just goes with it. "Can I have two cherries and extra almonds?"

Bash says, "I'm going to give you five cherries and extra extra almonds."

While Kamala and Bash prepare the ice cream Megan tells Bash that she's very happy to see them again and she promises to stop by more often, but they are really there to get some information. She needs to know what happened to Teddy, the guy she used to date. Just as she thought Bash tells her he doesn't know anything about that. That's Kamala's department. By the time their ice cream is prepared there are other customers in the store. Bash services the customers while Kamala takes Megan and William to the back office to talk. From the moment they get behind closed doors it becomes apparent that Kamala is anything but the shy demure wife she appeared to be. She is as dominant in conversation as Bash is, but in her own way. She asks Megan, "So you didn't hear what happened to Teddy?"

Megan says, "No. I just found out he died yesterday. I heard he overdosed."

Kamala immediately begins to shake her head no, "He didn't overdose. Did you know that he was an informant for the police?"

"I heard that but I didn't believe it."

"Well, it's true. The rumor is he was killed by someone who knew what he was doing and the police OK'd it."

William asks, "How do you know that."

Kamala says, "Jack." She explains, "Jack is the neighborhood weed dealer. He sees everything. I'm not as involved in neighborhood gossip as I used to be, but every once in a while Jack stops by and catches me up. Anyway, he said he saw Teddy and two other men pull up to Teddy's apartment on the night he died. One of them went with Teddy to his apartment and the other one stayed in the car. Jack says he recognized the one who stayed in the car as a detective he had seen at the precinct once when he was locked up."

William asks, "Did he describe the two men or did he say who the cop was?"

"No and I didn't ask. I'm getting to old for all of that nonsense and Bash doesn't like it when I ask too many questions."

William asks, "Can we speak with Jack?"

Kamala asks, "What's this about?" Kamala sits quietly while William explains why they are there and why he's asking to speak with Jack. When William is done explaining Kamala's first words are, "I'm so sorry to hear about your wife. That's a terrible thing to have happen to your family. I'm so sorry. But, there's no way I can arrange for you to speak with Jack. He's not like that. As you can imagine, he's naturally suspicious of everybody.

Megan says, "Kamala, there must be something you can do."

Kamala shakes her head no as she thinks about it. Finally, she says, "Bash is going to kill me. I have to leave tonight at 8:30pm, so come back around 8:00pm. Let me see what I can do."

5:30pm - "Thanks for waiting. I appreciate it," says Abbey.

Julia, Abbey's assistant says, "Don't worry about it. I know it's been a crazy day. Whatever it takes, right?"

Abbey says, "Exactly."

Julia says, "You should be pleased. I have a simple update. We are green light go on all fronts. All of the paperwork has been submitted, approved, and signed off on. And, the bank will fund the loan in the morning. The Forest Canyon Mall Deal should be closed by the early afternoon."

"That's great. We worked our asses off on this one. I put a lot on your plate and you got it done." "Except for . . ."

Abbey cuts her off and says, "I'm sure you won't make that mistake again. If you do, then I'll have a problem with you, but I'm sure you won't."

"I'm sorry about that and you're right, I won't make that mistake again."

"You did a good job and I won't forget it."

Over the intercom the receptionist says, "Abbey, I have Mr. Jefferson calling for you. He's holding on line one."

Abbey says, "Thanks. Jules, I'll see you in the morning. Remember, I need you in early."

"I'll be here at 7:30am."

"Thanks. Do me a favor. Close the door behind you." Abbey watches Julia leave and she waits until the door is closed before picking up Pete's call.

"I got your text," says Pete.

Just as Abbey suspected, this call isn't about the deal or the millions of dollars Pete will make tomorrow. It's about the text message she sent to him about thirty minutes ago.

Abbey says, "Our uncle says reception was spotty but he heard enough. He's waiting for further instructions."

"Tell him to go back to the primary."

That was it. That's all Pete needed to hear and that's all he had to say. Abbey picked up her smartphone and relayed the message. The black Mercedes Benz with black tinted windows parked across the street from Carl's house started its engine and made a U-turn.

6:00pm - "Did you even go to school," asks Javier of Angela, who's sitting in the same spot on the kitchen island, on her laptop with her headphones on, just as she was this morning when he left for work.

Angela says, "Dad, you're home. What time is it?"

Javier answers, "It's 6:10."

"Yes! Mom owes me twenty dollars."

"What do you mean Mom owes you twenty dollars?"

"Mom thought you would call to postpone your date night or, at least, you'd come home late. I told her I thought you'd come early."

"You knew I'd be home early. That's part of the plan. Did you rip your Mom off of twenty bucks?" "Hey, I didn't ask Mom to make the bet. When I said you'd be home early she said let's bet on it. If I didn't say yes she would have known something was going on."

"When you put it that way, congratulations."

"Thank you."

"So you think she still has no idea?"

"You're gold Dad. She doesn't have a clue."

Just then Jay Jay comes storming into the house and he throws his book bag on the floor and asks, "What's for dinner?"

Angela says, "Nothing for you. We ate already. You missed it and it was good. We had your favorite." Jay Jay can't believe what he's hearing, "What!?!"

Javier asks, "Really Jay Jay?"

"Well, if I don't eat soon I'm going to die. I'm starving."

Javier gives him the good news, "You and your sister are going to eat out tonight."

"I don't want to go out for dinner with her."

"I'm giving her fifty dollars and she's taking you to Suzuki Sushi."

"Yes! Dad, have I told you lately how much I love you?"

"Angela, the two of you go straight there, have fun, and come straight home. Don't forget to call me as soon as you get home. I'll be expecting your call before 8:00pm."

"I won't forget Dad. OK weasel, let's go."

As the kids head out the door Javier thinks to himself, "Phase one complete. Now, phase two." He reaches into the cabinet and pulls out two champagne glasses, he takes a bottle of Moet Chandon from the refrigerator, and he heads upstairs. When he gets to the bedroom he catches Cynthia wrapped in a towel just before she's about to get in the shower. Javier says, "My timing couldn't be more perfect."

Cynthia says, "What's that you've got in your hands Detective?"

"We're starting date night right now."

"Are you trying to get me drunk already?"

"That's not beneath me."

"I know it isn't. What about the kids?"

"I gave Angela fifty bucks and told her to take Jay Jay out for Sushi."

"He must be happy."

"According to him, I saved his life." He pops the champagne and pours for two. Holding his glass in one hand he hands her the other. Cynthia reaches for the glass and says, "Oh! Look what happened. When I reached for the glass my towel fell off."

Javier takes her in with his eyes and thinks, "it's hard to believe but it's true, she more beautiful now than she was the day we met." Handing her the glass and making a toast he says, "To tonight." They tap glasses and take a sip. Then, together, they put their glasses down and embrace each other. The sight of his wife always arouses Javier and the sight of her naked sends him to the moon. Cynthia was getting aroused before Javier arrived, just from thinking about the night ahead. Their embrace turns to kisses and their kisses turn to passion. Cynthia was aroused thinking about the night, but that is nothing compared to how she feels now that Javier's hands are caressing her breasts and pulling her pelvis into his. As she reaches down to feel his hardness they both gasp with anticipation of what's coming next. Javier leads her towards the bed and Cynthia is willing, but then she stops and says, "Not yet. I want you right now. Believe me, I do. But, you know us. If we do this now we'll never make it to dinner." Javier's normal response would be something akin to, "So what? Who cares about dinner?" But, tonight is different. Dinner is phase three of four, so even though he has to deny every cell in his body, he agrees. In return for agreeing with her and in return for not pushing it, Cynthia whispers something in Javier's ear that leaves him quivering, hard as a rock, and speechless as he watches his naked wife turn and walk towards the shower.

6:30pm - From their visit with Bash and Kamala, William and Megan continued on with their original plan, but Tommy wasn't home and Megan doesn't know of another way to contact him. Instead of waiting for him, and instead of floating around town trying to kill the two and a half hours before they have to be back at Baskin-Robbins, they decided to go back to Megan's apartment, where they can grab a bite to eat, relax a little, and talk things out. The first time William was in Megan's apartment he didn't pay attention to anything but Megan. Now, he's taking the time to notice the furnishings and the pictures all around the living room. While she's in the kitchen making something for them to eat, he asks, "Who's this in the picture with you at the beach?" Megan says, "That's Yezzy or Yesenia, my roommate. She's in New York this week. I can sauté some vegetables to go with the chicken or I can make a salad. Which do you prefer?"

"A salad would be great." For some reason William feels comfortable and relaxed here. It isn't an overwhelming sensation but it is strong enough for him to notice. Certainly, it could have to do with the aromatherapy candles Megan lit as soon as they walked in. Sitting on the couch and taking the whole room in, William realizes it's more than that. He thinks it's a combination of the candles and the fixtures and finishing touches around the apartment. Many of the picture frames, and lamps, and throw pillows and so on, are similar to the ones that could have been found in his house. Case in point, the wooden fruit bowl in the center of the dining room table is exactly the same as the one he and Genny had. William gets off the couch, walks over to the fruit bowl, and stares at it.

They couldn't have picked a better day to go to the flea market in Pasadena at the Rose Bowl. As usual he and Genny shopped together for a little while, but, eventually, he would go off in one direction, she in the other, and they'd agree to meet at certain time in a certain place. After spending most of the morning browsing sports memorabilia like vintage baseball cards and jerseys and autographed bats, basketballs, and hockey sticks signed by some of LA's greatest sports legends like Magic Johnson, Fernando Venezuela, and Wayne Gretzky, William realizes it time to make his way back to where they agreed to meet. On his way there he stops for an ice cream cone and just a couple of vendors away he sees Genny paying for something. He meets her just as the vendor tops off her second large shopping bag with a wooden fruit bowl and then secures the bag with string.

Genny says, "Perfect timing. I was going to have a hard time carrying all of this stuff." She has two other large shopping bags full of knickknacks that William didn't see.

"That's a lot of stuff."

"Yeah, and I got a great deal on everything. Let's step over there so I can count how much money we have left. Can I have some of your ice cream?" William hands her his cone and grabs all four bags. They step to the side of the vendor station, out of the way of walking traffic. When he puts the bags down she gives him the ice cream cone back and she starts to count her money. "We got more than we needed and we still have eighty five dollars left."

"That's my girl," says William

"I told you I got great deals."

"It turns me on when you save money."

"Everything I do turns you on."

"That's true. Well, maybe not everything."

"Shut up and let me have some more of your ice cream."

On their way back to their car Genny tells William about all of the things she purchased and where she envisions them throughout their house. By the time they get to the car she's telling him how the fruit bowl will go perfectly on their dining room table.

Just when he puts the last bag in trunk he hears someone call his name. It can't be Genny, she's already seated inside the car. "William." There it goes again. Megan asks, "William, are you OK?"

William snaps out of it and says, "I was just admiring your fruit bowl."

Megan says, "Thanks. That's one of the few things in here that's actually mine. The food is ready. Are you ready to eat?"

They eat, for the most part, in silence. William is still caught up in the memory of Genny and Megan can tell he's thinking about something. She doesn't know what to say to him. Finally, she breaks the silence with, "Do you want to try Tommy again before we go back to Kamala."

William says, "No."

The brevity of his answer tells Megan that he doesn't want to talk, so they continue their meal in silence until she asks, "What are you going to do if it turns out that the police are involved?"

William's first thought is to tell Javier, but then he wonders if Javier will believe him. The thought of the police being involved in Genny's murder is unimaginable. Since Kamala told them about what Jack said William has been trying to wrap his mind around the idea, but it seems so far from a possible reality, it literally hurts every time he thinks of it. Ultimately, at some point on their drive back Megan's apartment, he told himself to stop thinking about it until it was time to think about it again. Megan waited for an answer for so long, without getting one, she decided to give up on the questions and she went back to eating. It takes William so long to answer that, for a second, she thought he was talking about something else. In all that time the only thing he could come up with is, "I don't know."

7:00pm - Doctor Aba has a theory. He got Bobby's lab results back this morning. After reviewing them he called Doctor Jones, Bobby's personal physician. After their conversation Doctor Aba decided to make the drive from San Diego to Los Angeles to meet with Doctor Jones in person and to re-examine and question Bobby. Now, sitting in Doctor Jones' office at the hospital, the two of them discuss Doctor Aba's theory. While an accurate diagnosis is still uncertain Doctor Jones is willing to accept, for arguments sake, that Doctor Aba is correct. For the time being, he agrees that Bobby is suffering from a form of poisoning. If that is true, then the next question is, how is Bobby being exposed to the poison? That's where Doctor Aba's theory really kicks into high gear. Of the two doctors, he's the only one absolutely certain of the what. For him, all that's left is the how. Without pointing a finger at anyone, he goes through all of the scenarios that don't make sense. For instance, it is unlikely that Bobby is exposed to the poison at work, unless other policemen from the same precinct are suffering from similar symptoms. It is unlikely that Bobby is exposed to the poison through his food, unless other people, who are eating the same food, are suffering from similar symptoms. It's unlikely that Bobby is being exposed to the poison at home, unless his wife is suffering from similar symptoms. As far as Doctor Aba is concerned, the only scenario that makes sense is that Bobby has been targeted and is being specifically and intentionally poisoned. There's only one reason to poison someone, so the question isn't why. The question is how and by whom. To try to figure that out they agree the best thing to do is to talk with Bobby. They hoped to speak with Bobby alone but Robyn is with him when they get to his room. "Doctor Aba, what are you doing here?" asks Bobby.

"I'm working with Doctor Jones to try to get you feeling better." Doctor Jones introduces Doctor Aba to Robyn and then he explains their thinking. "While we still can't say for sure, we believe you are suffering from Elemental Mercury poisoning. We don't know yet how you are being exposed to the compound but the common methods of exposure are either breathing it in or ingestion."

Robyn asks, "Breathing it in? How?"

Doctor Aba says, "We don't know that yet."

Robyn asks, "How serious is it?"

Doctor Jones answers, "In large enough doses it's deadly. We're not saying it's fatal in your case, but given the amount of Mercury in your tissues we believe you've been exposed to small doses of it for an extended period of time."

Bobby says, "Cut to the chase doctor, am I dying?"

Doctor Jones explains, "Unfortunately, we can't tell you that yet. Now that you're here you're not being exposed to it anymore, so, over the next few days, your body may heal itself, or your condition may get worse."

Robyn asks, "He couldn't be exposed to the poison at home or I would be sick too? Could he be breathing it in or ingesting it at work?"

Doctor Aba says, "We don't know. We need to talk with the other personnel at his precinct to figure out if any of them have similar symptoms. Bobby, do you know of anyone else who has been getting sick like you?"

"No, but that doesn't mean anything. I don't know what happening with everyone else."

Doctor Jones says, "The best thing you can do right now is relax. That may be easier said than done, but you need to stay as stress free as possible, to give your body the strength it needs to heal itself. Robyn, we'd like to re-examine Bobby in a few minutes, do you mind?"

Robyn says, "No, of course not. Just give me a few minutes with him alone."

Doctor Aba exchanges a glance with Doctor Jones before he responds, "No problem. We'll wait outside."

As soon as the doctors leave the room Robyn turns to Bobby and says, "That's it. I'm canceling my trip this weekend."

"I don't want you to do that. It just isn't necessary. I may not look better today, but I definitely feel better. I have no idea how I'm being exposed to the poison but, like the doctor says, now that I'm here I'm not being exposed to it anymore. I really want to spend the weekend catching up on sleep and relaxing. It would make me feel good to know that you are having a good time with your mother." "How can I have a good time knowing you're lying here?"

"Just keep in mind that I'll be here, relaxing. I won't be thinking about work, or anything else that stresses me out. I'll be thinking of the good time you are having and the good time we'll have when you get back." Robyn doesn't know what to say to that. Though she tries to hide it, Bobby notices that her eyes are starting to fill with tears. He says, "Sit next to me for a minute." When she does, he takes her hand in his. "I'm sorry."

Robyn asks, "Sorry for what?"

"I'm sorry for all the times I put work first. I know you've wanted me around the house more, and I know there are things you've wanted to do. I should have made more time for you and I should have made more time for us to do some of those things together. Like go on an extended vacation, for instance. I've been promising to take you to Europe for years but the furthest we got was New Mexico. I'm sorry about that, but I'm going to fix that as soon as I get out of here."

"I don't think you should be thinking about things like that now. I love you and I'm happy."

"I love you too and I'm happy too, but I think we can both be happier. What do you say to us driving and eating our way through Italy? We'll start in Venice, make our way to Florence, then we'll go to Rome, and finally to Naples. We'll see everything and eat every pasta dish we see. What do you say?" "That would be a dream come true but how are we going to do that? You would have to take off from work, and where would we get the money?"

"You know what this sickness has already taught me? That I'm wasting time. Don't worry about me taking off from work. I've already decided to do that. And, don't worry about the money. We'll have more money than we need. Trust me. What do you say?"

"I say yes! Let's do it."

"Good! So, have a good time this weekend and I'll get some rest. I promise, by the time you get back, I'll be feeling better. When you get back we'll start to plan our trip and we'll take off as soon as we can." Robyn, no longer trying to hold back her tears, squeezes Bobby's hand, leans towards him and gives him a gentle kiss on the lips. When she pulls away, Bobby wipes away her tears, and Robyn says, "I'd like that."

7:30pm - When Robyn steps into the hallway she's surprised to see Eddie talking with Doctor Aba and Doctor Jones. She would rather not talk with any of them, but she knows that will seem strange so she makes her way over to where the three men are talking. She gets to the group just in time to hear Doctor Jones ask Eddie to make his visit short because they want to re-examine Bobby before he gets too tired. The doctors leave Eddie and Robyn standing alone in the hallway. Robyn says, "So I hear you're leaving town tomorrow night."

"That's right. I'll be in Mexico Saturday morning."

"Lucky you. So, we probably won't see each other again."

"Probably not."

"Well, in that case, have a good life."

"You do the same."

"See ya."

Eddie watches Robyn as she turns and walks away. Then he pushes the door to Bobby's room open and says, "How are you feeling buddy?"

"Better."

"I spoke with your doctors. They said you just need some rest."

"That's not what they said."

"In a nutshell it is. They told me about Elemental Mercury poisoning. I never even heard of that. They don't know what they're talking about. All you need is what I've been telling you need for months now. You just need to take some time off. Take a vacation. Relax and enjoy yourself. Soon you'll have all the money you need to do just that. We still have a deal, right?"

"When will you wire the money to my account?"

"Give me until Tuesday, the latest, which means the money will be in your account Tuesday afternoon or first thing Wednesday morning. I'll send you an email after I've sent the money. So, there be no more talk about karma and confessing your sins, right?"

"After you send the email it might be a good idea if we didn't speak for a little while."

"I think that's uncalled for but if that's what you want, then so be it. Here's the deal though, if you take this money you better keep your mouth shut."

"Or what?"

What Eddie wants to say, he can't. He knows he has to choose his words carefully. "There is no or what, but you understand my concern. I just need to know that we have deal. I'll take your word for it." "We have a deal. Don't worry. Believe me, I want to forget everything. I think you're right about one thing. The money will help."

Doctor Aba and Doctor Jones come into Bobby's room. Doctor Aba says, "Unless you're talking about official police business we need you to wrap it up."

Doctor Jones is paying attention to the look on Bobby's face. He doesn't look relaxed like he did when Robyn was in the room. Now, he looks agitated and stressed. He contributes, "Even if it is official police business we need it to end right now."

Eddie replies, "No problem Doc, I was just leaving." He turns to Bobby and says, "Follow doctor's orders. Relax and don't worry about anything. I'm sure you'll be on your feet in just a few days." He offers his hand to Bobby and the two men shake on it. On his way out the door Eddie says, "I'll stop by tomorrow to say goodbye before I take off. Get some rest."

After the door has closed behind Eddie, the two doctors cautiously approach Bobby. Doctor Jones takes a position at the foot of Bobby's bed, while Doctor Aba pulls up a chair next to Bobby, and sits in it. What they've agreed to discuss with Bobby is extremely delicate and a little beyond the scope of their responsibilities, but they've also agreed that the best course of action is to get it out in the open sooner rather than later. Doctor Aba takes the lead. "Bobby, let me ask you a delicate question. How's your marriage going?"

8:00pm - William and Megan got back to Baskin-Robbins at exactly 8:00pm. When they arrived Bash was entertaining a family of five. Kamala led them, quickly, to the back office. Kamala tells them, "Bash is very upset with me, so after tonight I can't help you anymore. Agreed?"

William says, "Agreed."

"OK, I spoke with Jack. I told him I needed the name of the police officer he saw sitting in the car. Naturally, he had a lot of questions. I don't want to have a problem with him so I thought it was best to tell him everything."

William asks, "What did he say?"

"At first, he said he didn't remember the name, but that was before he started asking questions. I think is main concern is, he doesn't want it to get out that he said anything. He doesn't want the police to pay him any more attention than they already do. At this point, I'm not sure he remembers the officer's name or, if he does, I'm not sure he'll tell us."

William asks, "So where did you leave it?"

"He said if he feels up to it he'll stop by between 8:00 and 8:30. I'm sorry, but that is the best I could do."

Megan asks, "Do you think he'll show up?"

"I really can't tell you. After I told him everything he seemed a little more open to talking, but he also wants to protect his business and stay in the shadows as much as possible. The only thing I can suggest is that you wait here until 8:30pm and see what happens. Remember, if he doesn't show up there's nothing more I can do."

William says, "Thanks for trying. We'll wait."

"OK, I'm going to help Bash with the customers. If he comes, I'll let you know."

Megan says, "Maybe we should have brought a deck of cards."

"I'm sorry for being short back at your apartment. I was just thinking about something."

"It's all right, I could tell you had something on your mind. Can I ask you a question?"

William says, "Sure,"

"What was Geneviève like?"

"What do you mean?"

"I don't know. Just tell me about her."

"She was perfect. She was beautiful, she was sweet, she was smart, and she was funny. I loved all of those things about her, but what I loved the most was how feminine she was. She saw the beauty in things that had been around me my whole life that I never paid any attention to. She knew things that I probably wouldn't have figured out if I live to be one hundred. She made my life and everything in it better."

It takes a moment before Megan realizes she's staring a William. When she speaks, she says, "I have never heard someone describe someone else that way. I guess if I felt that way about someone I'd want to kill anyone who harmed them too."

William says, "Who said anything about killing someone?"

"Then what do you have the gun for? I saw it while we were eating."

"The gun is for my protection."

"You mean to say that you don't want to kill the person who is responsible for Geneviève's death?"

"Of course I do. In fact, I've thought about it and dreamt about it so many times I've lost count. When I think about it I always see myself shooting him, but, in my dreams, I never use a gun. In my dreams I always use my bare hands. I see myself with my hands around his neck. I just squeeze harder and harder and harder. Even after his whole body is lifeless I just keep squeezing and I never stop."

"Well, I'm glad you have a gun if you feel you need one. There are some circumstances where it's better to have one and not need it, as opposed to needing one and not having it. Killing someone, however, is entirely different from being mad enough to kill someone."

William nods in agreement, "I appreciate that."

"Can I tell you something else? I've been around people who don't have a problem with killing someone. You're nothing like them."

William doesn't have anything to say to that. Even if he did he wouldn't have had the chance. Kamala comes in the back office and says, "Jack isn't coming." William hangs his head in disappointment. Kamala continues, "But, he sent someone who gave me this." Kamala is holding a piece of folded paper. "Before I give it to you there are some rules. First, don't open it until I leave this room. Also, I don't want to know anything about it. Finally, take it with you when you leave. Again, I'm sorry to be so abrupt but Bash is about to have my head. And he's right. We've worked too hard, for too long, to be involved in anything like this. This whole episode has taught me that it's time to be less concerned with the neighborhood gossip and more concerned with my future with my family. Do you remember the three rules?"

William says, "Yes." Kamala hands the paper to him, turns, leaves, and closes the door behind her. Megan stands beside William as he unfolds the paper. In individual letters cut out of magazines and newspapers the name inside reads "Eddie Roberts."

8:30pm - Lisa got to North Hollywood first. She found parking around the block from O'Reilly's. Russell arrived ten minutes later and found a parking space about twenty yards away from the entrance to O'Reilly's. Now the two of them are sitting in Russell's car discussing the picture. Lisa says, "I think you're right. It's not the best picture but it's enough for someone who knows who this is."

Russell asks, "OK, have you ever been here before?"

"No. I've never heard of it."

"Me either. I'm sure there's a bar where people can sit and there are tables also. I want you to find a table that has a good view of the bar and sit there. If asked, say that you are waiting for friends to meet you there. Order a beer but just sip it. You don't want to drink enough to be impaired. You want to drink just enough to fit in."

Lisa says, "Got it."

"I'll wait here for ten minutes. If, for one reason or another, you can't find a table with a good view of the bar come back out before I come in. If you don't, I'll come in and take a seat at the bar. After I order a beer I'll ask the bartender if he recognizes the man in the picture. He may say no and mean it. He may say yes and tell me who he is. In that case, I'll pay my tab and leave, and I want you to wait for ten minutes and then pay your tab and meet me here. He may say no, but he does know who he is. If I think that's what he's doing I'll get up and go to the bathroom. That's when I want you to pay close attention to what he does. Once he thinks I'm out of sight he may call someone. If you can make it to the bar and act like you want to order something else you may be able to hear who he's calling and what he says. No matter what he does, don't give anyone any indication that we are together and don't give anyone any indication that you are looking for this guy either. I really need you to just observe."

"Got it. This is exciting."

"It is exciting but don't forget, if the guy in the picture is who we think he is he's a cold-blooded killer. And, cold-blooded killers, in general, aren't friends with Salvation Army volunteers, priests, or kindergarten teachers. So, keep your eyes open."

Lisa has been listening to everything Russell is telling her but she's also noticing something in his demeanor. "When we spoke earlier I thought I heard something in your voice. Now, I can see a twinkle in your eye and, dare I say, you seem happier than usual. What's going on with you?"

Russell says, "Nothing."

"I know I haven't been doing this as long as you have but I know you. I know when you're trying to sneak one by me. C'mon, what's going on with you?"

Lisa's question makes Russell think about Phyllis. As much as he'd like to, as much as he wants to, thoughts of her makes him smile, and he can't hide it. Still, he doesn't want to say anything. At the same time, Lisa is the closest thing he has to a daughter and she's been telling him for years that he needs to meet somebody. Given that, he decides to let her in on his secret but still keep a little for himself. With a smile on his face he says, "I think I met somebody."

"I knew it! Who is she?"

"I don't want to talk about it yet. We haven't even had our first date."

"OK, OK, I'll respect that but I can tell she's already making you happy. I'm so happy for you! Who knows, maybe you'll be getting some soon."

"You are out of control."

"OK, I'll stop. I'm just happy for you. You're a great man. You should have someone in your life who loves you and takes care of you in ways me and mom can't."

"I appreciate that. I promise, you'll be the first one I tell about her when the time is right. Right now, however, I need you to forget all about that and focus on the task at hand. Remember everything I told you."

"I got it. Sit at table with view of the bar, waiting for friends, order a beer, don't get drunk, if you go to the bathroom I go to the bar, when you leave wait ten minutes and meet you here."

"Good. I'll see you inside."

9:00pm - The restaurant Javier chose came as a surprise to Cynthia. Their booth is candlelit, private and it couldn't be more perfect. The service is polite, encouraging, responsive, and it too couldn't be more perfect. And, the food and wine was orgasmic. There just isn't a better way to describe it as far as Cynthia is concerned. Javier asks, "What are you thinking of having for dessert?

Cynthia says, "I don't know. I want to try the Banana Tarte Tatin. That sounds so good. But, you know I can't resist cheesecake and the Triple Chocolate Cheesecake sounds to die for."

"Try the Banana Tarte Tatin. If you don't like it, we'll just order the Triple Chocolate Cheesecake."

"Let me think about it. What are you going to have?"

"I'm going to try the Raspberry Brûlée."

"Have you ever had that before?"

"Nope. Never even heard of it before."

"Bold choice. OK, I'll join you in trying something new. I'll have the Banana Tarte Tatin."

Javier motions to their server that they are ready to order. "The lady will have the Banana Tarte Tatin and I'll have the Raspberry Brûlée. Javier thinks to ask Cynthia, "Do you want a coffee with it?" Cynthia smiles, so Javier adds, "And, we'll have two coffees with that."

Their server says, "Excellent choices. Right away sir."

Cynthia didn't notice that the server winked at Javier. She thought that when Javier smiled it was in response to their server's compliment. As soon as the server steps away from the table Javier says, "I need to talk to you about something." The seriousness in his tone of voice catches Cynthia's attention and she sits up and stares Javier in the eye. "The last nineteen years have been the best years of my life and it's all because of you. You have given us the two most perfect children on the planet, and you created the perfect environment to raise them in. You know, sometimes in my line of work, I see things no one should ever have to see, and I experience things no one should ever have to experience, but I can always count on you for two things. I know you'll always be waiting for me at home and you always remind me that life is good. You stood by my side through all of my ups and downs, successes and failures, and through it all your love, your support, and your friendship never wavered for a second or diminished in any way. After all of that, gains and losses, two kids, and a husband who can get dark every once in a while, you are more beautiful today than you were on the day we met. I don't know how I got so lucky to have you as my wife, as the mother of our children, and as my best friend, but somehow I did. I hope you feel that I have been a good husband."

"You have been so much more than just a good husband."

"Good. Then I hope you say yes." He stands up from the table, reaches into his coat pocket, and brings out a small box. He gets down on one knee.

Cynthia gasps, "What are you doing?"

Javier opens the box. Inside is a wedding band with alternating diamonds and sapphires, the exact ring Cynthia has always wanted. "Will you marry me again?"

Cynthia's eyes are like a dam that has burst. With tears of joy streaming down her face she says, "Yes!"

Their server, who was in on it and watching from a distance leads the other servers and the other patrons of the restaurant in a round of applause. He brings over a complimentary bottle of champagne and he promises to return with their desserts right away. By the time he gets back Cynthia is snuggling with Javier on his side of the booth and no matter how hard she tries, she can't get close enough to him. Javier is so proud of himself. This night took two months of planning and it went off perfectly, without one hitch. The only distraction came from his cell phone, which luckily he remembered to put on vibrate so as not to disturb them. Cynthia has no idea that Javier's cell phone vibrated several times during their dinner and that whoever is calling has left two messages. When he got the call from Angela, that she and Jay Jay made it home safely, he reminded her to call the restaurant if she needed him again. She wished him good luck and told him not to worry. She promised that she and the weasel would be fine for the rest of the night. The department knows to call Javier at the restaurant during certain hours and at home after that. He didn't explain why but he said he wouldn't be answering his cell phone until the morning. So, whoever is calling will have to wait. Tonight he is giving all of his attention to his wife.

9:15pm - William hangs up the phone and says, "He's still not answering. Did you find anything yet?"

Megan is on William's laptop in his suite at the Copenhagen. She says, "I think there are a few new faces on this page. You need to take a look." Megan checked Facebook first and didn't find a page for Eddie Roberts, LAPD. Next she checked LinkedIn and she didn't find what she is looking for there either. This is the fifth Google page of images. William didn't see the man he met earlier in the day on the first four pages. Now, he's taking a look at the fifth. While he does Megan says, "You should read some of the articles I pulled up. They mention Detective Roberts of the Santa Monica police department specifically."

"But none of them have a picture of him right?"

"No, they don't have a picture."

"I need to see a picture of him. None of these guys are him." William clicks on the sixth page and the seventh page of images but none of the pictures are of the detective he met this morning. "See if you can pull up the website for the periodicals the written articles appeared in. Search their archives for pictures. I'll try Javier again."

9:30pm - Cynthia says, "I can't wait to get home and show Angela and Jay Jay this ring."

Javier says, "Angela was with me when I bought it."

"What?"

"Yeah, she helped me plan the whole thing."

"She didn't give me a clue the whole time. She's good at keeping a secret. Did Jay Jay know?"

"Of course not. You know Jay Jay couldn't keep a secret if his life depended on it." The two of them laugh.

Cynthia takes Javier's face in her hands and says, "I love you."

"I love you too babe. Are you ready to go?"

"Yeah." Javier motions to the server that they are ready to go.

Javier gave the server his credit card in advance and instructed him to add a 30% tip to the total. The server brings Javier his credit card receipt and two slices of the Triple Chocolate Cheesecake. "These are on me. Thank you very much for your tip, it was very generous. Congratulations! Have a wonderful night!"

When Javier and Cynthia stand up from the table she turns her back to him so he can drape her scarf over her shoulders. When he does he leans towards her to kiss her on the neck. Just as he does his cell phone vibrates again. Cynthia says, "There goes your phone again."

"Yeah. I was hoping you wouldn't notice."

"It vibrated four times in the last half an hour."

"Everyone important knows how to reach me, so whoever it is will have to wait."

"If it's the same person calling maybe it's an emergency."

"The only emergency I'm responding to tonight is from the kids. Everyone else has to wait. It's all right if I take one night off to be with my wife."

"I still can't wait to get home to show the kids the ring."

"Jay Jay will say 'that's nice' and then go back to Xbox or whatever he's doing. Angela will want to hear all about the night."

"Yeah, well, we can talk about it in the morning. After I show them the ring I'm telling them to go to bed. It's all right if I take one night off to be with my husband."

9:45pm - Just as William hung up the phone again he heard Megan say, "Voila." In that moment he knows she found what he was looking for. Genny used that word at least twice a day. For a moment he thinks Megan is channeling Genny to point to her murderer. He knows that thought is a little foolish but he's going with it anyway. Another sensation tells him that Megan has found what they have been looking for. The last few times she thought she had the right picture, he was eager to look. This time he feels apprehensive. Megan continues with, "I think I have a picture of the man you're looking for. The caption says it's Detective Edward Roberts of the Santa Monica Police Department. Come take a look." He feels like he's walking in slow motion and holding his breath. He approaches the monitor with his eyes fixated on his shoes. Even when he's sure he's standing in front of it, he doesn't look up immediately. He has to talk himself into it. Finally, he does look, and that's him. That's the guy he met this morning. That's the guy who was so supportive and understanding. Now he feels like he just got the wind knocked out of him. Based on William's reaction Megan says, "Oh my god, that's him, isn't it?" Before William can respond his cell phone rings. It's Javier.

10:00pm - As planned, Lisa went in first and found a table just to the left of the bar. From her table she could see the bartender and the waitresses as they approached the bar to pick up their food and drink orders. Behind her and to her right are three pool tables, and there are flat screen televisions on almost every wall in the bar. All of them are on one sporting event or another. In front of her and to her right are a bunch of other tables for parties of two or more who want to eat and drink. Along the bar there are eight spaces for people who want to sit at the bar to eat, drink, and watch sports on the two flat screens directly behind the bar. There weren't a lot of people in the bar when she walked in, but as time went on there has been a steady stream of patrons coming in. It's easy to tell who the regulars are. The bartender and the waitresses seem to know them all by name. Russell came in shortly after she did and took a seat along the bar close to the entrance, and right in front of the flat screen on the right. Lisa watched him as he ordered a drink and made small talk with the bartender. Eventually, she saw Russell pull out the picture and show it to the bartender. He took the picture from Russell and seemed to really study it. Then he handed it back to Russell and they talked some more. That conversation seemed to last for fifteen minutes or more because the bartender would talk with Russell then make a drink for someone and then return to Russell. Judging from the expression on Russell's face he seemed to be pleased with how the conversation was progressing. Then Lisa saw Russell reach into his pocket and pull out his wallet. He held it between his legs, underneath the bar, and pulled out some money. He put his wallet back in his pocket and he folded the money so it fit in his hand. Lisa saw Russell shake hands with the bartender, who smiled and nodded his head yes. A few minutes later the bartender went into the kitchen, behind the bar, and he was there for, at least, ten minutes before he came back. He said something to Russell, who smiled, nodded his head and said something back. A few minutes after that the bartender's cell phone rang and, again, he went into the kitchen, behind the bar. He was there for another ten minutes, maybe longer. This time, however, when he came back he went directly Russell as if he was conveying a message. Russell, again, nodded his head, and then he ordered another drink. Lisa's waitress seems sweet but she is definitely nosey. She immediately found things to compliment Lisa on, but as the night went on she trended towards complimenting less and asking more questions.

As instructed Lisa told her she was waiting for friends. That held the waitress at bay for about a half an hour before she asked if her friends were coming. Lisa told her she just got a text from them and they are on their way. That seemed to satisfy the waitress for a few minutes more until she thought of another question. This time she wanted to know how many of Lisa's friends are coming. Lisa was getting annoyed by the questions until she realized the bar was starting to fill up and she's sitting at a table for four by herself. It dawns on her that the waitress may not be nosey. Maybe she's just trying to maximize her tip potential. At worst, she'll ask Lisa to move to the bar or to a smaller table if her friends don't show up. Lisa figures she'll deal with that if and when it happens. She also realizes she'll have to deal with one of the guys playing pool behind her, who seems to be looking at her and smiling at her every time she looks his way. She turns her attention back to Russell and she finds him talking with the bartender. She wished she was better at reading lips but she isn't, so she just has to wonder what they are talking about.

Russell says, "JT, I think I'm going to move to a table and wait there. So you're sure your friend Sam is coming and that he knows the guy in the picture?"

JT says, "I never said I was sure he was coming. Like I said, I tried to get him on the phone, but he didn't pick up. He's a regular, so he usually stops in, for at least one drink, on his way home. Whether he stops in tonight is anyone's guess, but I am pretty sure I've seen him with the guy in the picture. Like I said, if and when he gets here, I'll ask him if he feels like talking to you. If he's up for it I'll make the introduction. If not, I won't. That's the deal. I'll be happy to give you your fifty bucks back if that isn't cool with you."

"No. Keep the money. I appreciate that you made the call. I'll just wait."

JT gives Russell one additional admonition, "If he isn't here by 11:00pm, most likely he isn't coming." Russell says, "OK." He turns, looks around, and spots a table in the corner on the other side of the entrance. Russell takes a seat there and waits.

A minute later he gets a text message from Lisa. It reads, "What's going on?"

Russell texts her back, "The bartender, JT, believes he's seen the guy in the bar a few times but he doesn't know him. But, he says he has a regular customer, Sam, who might."

Lisa texts, "Where's Sam?"

"Might come in tonight."

"What was the deal with the money?"

"For JT to call Sam to ask if he is coming to the bar tonight."

"How much did you give him?"

"$50."

"I think you just got hustled out of 50 bucks!"

"Possible. But I don't think so."

"So, what's the plan?"

"JT says Sam likely to be here by 11:00pm if at all. We hang around until then."

"Why did you say you are looking for man in pic?"

"Told him the truth. That I'm a private investigator looking for the relatives of an old widower who just died."

Lisa texts, ":)"

10:30pm - Before the valet brought Javier's and Cynthia's car around Javier's cell phone vibrated twice more. By that time even Javier was considering taking the call or, at least, looking to see who is calling. Whoever it is obviously wants to talk with him and perhaps there's someone, who needs him, whom he didn't think of. Still, he resisted the urge until Cynthia convinced him to, at least, take a look. Javier told Cynthia that it is William, which didn't ring a bell for her. He reminded her of who William is and Cynthia, remembering the case and how bad she felt for him, convinced Javier to call him back. William told Javier that he's just learned something that could help his case. Javier invited William to meet him at the precinct in the morning. William told Javier he doesn't want to meet him there anymore. What he's just found out has to do with the Detective Roberts and Teddy. William begs Javier to meet him anywhere Javier wants, just as long as they do it tonight. Javier told William he'll call him back. Javier has a conversation with Cynthia who reminds him that they just did something William will never be able to do. Still, she doesn't want Javier to meet William someplace out of the house tonight. She told Javier to invite William to their house but with conditions. Whatever they need to talk about has to be said, discussed, and over with for the night within 30 minutes. Then, she told Javier, he's hers again. Javier called William back and gave him the address and directions.

Now, Cynthia and Javier welcome William and Megan to their home. Cynthia says, "I'm going to let the three of you speak. I just wanted to tell you how sad and sorry I am to have heard about your loss." William says, "Thank you and thank you for convincing Javier to take my call and for allowing us into your home this late at night."

Cynthia says, "It's all right but there are conditions. You get to have my husband's attention for 30 minutes and not a minute more."

William answers, "Understood. It shouldn't take that long."

Cynthia says to her husband, "I'm going to be with the kids for a little while." Her smile conveys the hidden message of, "bring your butt to bed ASAP."

Javier replies, "I'll be up in a minute." Javier waits until Cynthia is upstairs before he turns to William and says, "OK, what's this all about?"

William explains who Megan is and why he spent time looking for her. Megan explains that she agrees with William, namely Teddy gave her reason to believe that someone he knew was going to be killed and just a few days later Geneviève was killed. She also explains to Javier how unlikely it is that Teddy died the way he did. Then William explains how they came to learn about Jack and the events that happened on the night Teddy died. Finally, William shows Javier the note Jack had delivered to Baskin-Robbins. After taking it all in Javier's first thought is to remind William that he shouldn't be doing this, but his second thought is, at this point, he might as well be talking to a wall. What caught his attention when they spoke on the phone was William's assertion that this has something to do with Eddie and Teddy. That reminded him of his conversation with Eddie at Teddy's house, when Eddie said he hadn't seen or spoken with Teddy in at least a year. At that time he thought that was odd and probably untrue, but it's common for detectives to lie about their use of informants. He didn't give it any thought after that, until now. Even now, however, if Eddie had spoken with Teddy when he said he didn't that doesn't mean he had anything to do with his death, even if he assumes that Teddy didn't die of an overdose. Frankly, there's no evidence that he died from anything else. In fact, he tells William and Megan exactly that. He says, "I've seen this sort of thing a million times before. It's even happened to me more than once.

It isn't uncommon for a criminal to leak damaging information about a police officer who has busted them in the past. I'm not saying this Jack guy didn't tell you what he did. I'm just saying he's probably lying." William does his best to convince him otherwise, but Javier doesn't think this was worth the time he took out of his night with his wife. When William persists Javier runs out of patience. He says to Megan, "Listen, I appreciate you and your attempt to help, but Teddy didn't tell you anything concrete. You just got an impression. In short, that's nothing." To William and Megan both he says, "Let's talk about Jack. Again, you got nothing. Let's say we believe everything he says. Then we have the word of a known drug dealer versus the word of a detective." Finally, to William he says, "I've told you a dozen times you shouldn't be doing what you're doing. But, don't worry, I'm not going to waste my breath doing that again. But, now, you're in my house at what, 10:30 at night, talking to me about things that don't matter and that don't make any sense. I, obviously, can't stop you from doing what you're going to do, but I can stop you from wasting my time. We won't be doing this again. And, do not show up here with any other information. If you have anything else you want to tell me, make an appointment, and talk to me at the precinct." William and Megan are both disappointed but they both know Javier is right. They have nothing. William apologizes. Javier tells him it isn't a problem, but he also reminds him that if he has anything else, tell him at the precinct. After William and Megan leave, Javier wonders about Eddie but he shakes the thought off faster than it came to him. Right now, all he wants to do is get back in the mood and get back to his wife.

10:45pm - "Renting the car was a stroke of genius," Breck thought as his server placed his plate of Lobster Ravioli in Cream

Sauce with Crabs and Shrimp in front of him. What started out as a last minute business trip has turned into a mini-vacation. "I'll have another," said Breck.

"Right away," replied the server before he grabbed the empty glass that held Breck's first rum and Coke.

Breck had been to the Coastline in Manhattan Beach only once before, but the meal he had was so good he remembers it as if he had it yesterday. Besides the food, the other thing that made the Coastline a great choice for tonight is its location. Manhattan Beach may be only 30 minutes away from the Marina and a little bit more from the heart of Los Angeles proper, including North Hollywood, but it seems like a world away. As Breck prepared to dig into his Lobster Ravioli he became aware of how calm and at peace he feels. It looks like he wasn't going to be called upon to do anymore killing. It looks like he and Eddie will take off tomorrow night as planned, and without any more complications. If that is true, all that's left for Breck to do is collect his money. For the first time, in memory, he felt good about not working. Looking out on the Pacific Ocean from his table in the restaurant made him think of his new life that begins next week, as soon as he gets the money. He looked around at the other patrons in the restaurant and guessed which ones would be interested in charter fishing off the west coast of Costa Rica. He imagined entertaining the ones he thought would be interested. He realized that in each and every scenario he imagined, he and his guests were filled with happy thoughts and laughter. The more he thought about his upcoming venture the more he liked it, and the less he liked what he is coming to believe is now his former profession. At another table two rows over from his, at 2:00 o'clock from his location, there's a man and a woman enjoying their meal. Breck noticed the man first because he is one of the guys Breck imagined would enjoy a day of drinking beer and deep sea fishing. On second glance he noticed the woman, but he noticed something else as well, something more important. They seemed happy. In fact, the more Breck looked at them the more he imagined that she might enjoy a day of drinking beer and deep sea fishing too. For the next several minutes, even though he told himself not to look, Breck found himself glancing over at their table just to watch their interactions. Then he realized what he was doing. For the very first time in his life, he coveted a real relationship with a woman. He wants what they appear to have. For the rest of the night, while he enjoyed his meal, he glanced over at their table, from time to time, and tried to imagine what they were feeling. Whatever it is, it must be good because they seem to really enjoy being with each other. More than once, after turning his attention back to his meal, Breck imagined a woman sitting with him, eating, laughing, and talking with him; and he imagined that someone else was staring at them, and seeing how happy they look together.

By the time Breck finished his meal the couple that fascinated him had paid for their meal and left. He decided to pay for his meal, but move over to the bar area, and open a new tab there. Breck had just taken his first sip of his fourth rum and Coke when he got the call from JT. The noise in the bar area was too loud for him to hear JT clearly. He told JT that he'd call him back shortly, right after he finished his drink. As soon as he did, he told the bartender to leave his tab open and he went outside to call JT. The two of them spoke for about ten minutes and then Breck went back into the bar. He thought of doing nothing, except maybe ordering another drink. Instead he asked the bartender to close him out. As he signed the credit card receipt he wondered who that is. Obviously, he doesn't know who JT is. If he did, he wouldn't have asked JT to identify the guy in the picture. Standing at the valet station waiting for his car, he wondered how that guy got a picture of him. JT is sure it is him, even though, according to JT, it's just a side shot and not a very good one at that. JT said it looked like he was in a store of some kind, maybe a convenience store like 7Eleven. Breck thought back to the last time in was in a place like that. It was when he got off the 5 Freeway just before he dropped off Ronny. He thought he avoided looking into any of the cameras there. Apparently, he had avoided looking directly into any of the cameras but, obviously, he hadn't avoided them all together. Now, sitting in his car and fastening his seat belt, he wonders what he should do. "Nothing," is the thought that comes to mind. Satisfied with that, Breck pulls out of the parking lot and heads for the entrance to the freeway. As he merges into the traffic on the 405 Freeway north, he thinks that the only thing that guy has is a picture of him and, according to JT, a poor one. He probably doesn't have any other information. In short, there's nothing he can do as long Breck doesn't do anything to instigate him. Tomorrow night, by this time, Breck knows he'll be somewhere out on the Pacific heading to his biggest payday ever and a brand new life full of fishing and good times. And, if he gets lucky, he might even have a woman to share it all with. Happy with that thought his plans now are the same as they were before he left the Coastline. He'll do nothing. Surely, he can lay low for one day and he'll be gone by tomorrow night. He changes the station on the car radio, he finds something he likes on the Outlaw Country station, he merges to the far left lane, and he enjoys the drive. All he has to do now is look for the 90 west, which will take him back to the Marina and he'll call it a night. As he passes a sign that says his exit is two miles up the road, visions of him and his boat are dancing around his head. While he merges to the right he thinks of what he'll do for the rest of the night. He's had a great meal and enough to drink. He figures he'll relax, watch a movie, and go to bed. As he approaches his exit he turns on his right blinker and prepares to turn off the freeway, but he can't bring himself to do it. Instead, he turns off his right blinker and turns on his left. He turns up the music and, again, merges to the far left lane. He's going to continue up the 405 Freeway to the 101 Freeway, which will take him to the Lankershim exit and O'Reilly's.

11:15pm - Russell is starting to believe that he was hustled out of fifty dollars. He's been watching JT the entire time and it doesn't appear that any of the patrons who stopped to talk with him or order a drink were this so called Sam. He calls his waitress over, hands her a fifty and asks that she close him out and bring back his change. Then he texts Lisa, "I'm ready to leave."

Lisa texts, "Bummer but I agree."

Russell texts back, "Remember, wait 10 or 15 minutes, then pay and leave."

Lisa types, "Got it."

Russell's thoughts turn to being out fifty bucks plus another thirty for drinks and a tip, but he figures that's not too bad. The question now is whether or not Sam really exists and, if so, can he identify the guy in the picture or, as Lisa said, was this whole thing just a trick. Right now he's inclined to believe it is the latter, but that's something he and Lisa can discuss later or tomorrow even. That thought takes him back to Phyllis. Tomorrow night, by this time, he'll know for sure if she's everything he thinks she is. He smiles to himself when he thinks, "For an old man, you are sure feeling like a school kid."

He gets a text from Lisa that says, "Behind you." Lisa noticed that JT talked with the waitress when she rang up Russell's bill. She saw him take Russell's change from the waitress and come from around the bar walking towards Russell. Russell read the text and turned around just in time to see JT coming.

JT says, "I'm sorry that my friend didn't show up. Here's your change. Do you have a card or something that I can give to him next time I see him."

Russell is over the charade. "Don't worry about it. He's not the only relative I need to find and I have other ways I believe I can get in touch with him." Russell asks JT to make sure his waitress gets the tip he's giving to JT and JT says he will. The two men walk together until Russell gets to the exit and leaves and JT heads back behind the bar.

11:30pm - Breck's mind went blank the second he passed his exit. It was as if he was on auto-pilot for the rest of the drive. Now that he's arrived and parked around the corner from O'Reilly's he's regained his consciousness and he's feeling torn. Something inside of him is telling him he doesn't need to be here, yet here he is. Since he is, he decides to call JT instead of going in.

"Is the guy still there?"

"No, he left about five minutes ago." That's it. That's all the confirmation Breck needed to hear. He was worried about nothing and now he feels relieved. He was about to say goodbye to JT and head back to the Marina but JT asks, "Are you still coming? And, if so, how long will it take for you to get here?" "I'm here. I'm parked around the corner. Since the guy is gone I was just going to go back to Marina Del Rey."

"If my guess is right, you should come in."

"All right, I'll be right there."

11:35pm - Lisa thought her waitress was being nosey, then she figured she was probably asking the questions she asked in an attempt to maximize her tips. Both thoughts were incorrect. Her waitress asked the questions she asked because JT told her to. 99% of the patrons that walk into O'Reilly's think it's a bar, a place to drink, eat, maybe play a little pool, and watch sporting events on one of the many flat screens all around the room. The other 1% know that O'Reilly's is all of those things, but it is also a front for the organization's activities. This particular location dabbles a little in bookmaking, but its primary source of income comes from the monthly fees it collects from those with safe boxes stored there. Accordingly, that 1% includes all of the bar's employees. No one can walk in off the street and get a job there. You have to be nominated, approved, and voted in. That is true for everyone, from the janitor to the general manager, JT. So, while Lisa was giving the benefit of the doubt to her waitress, she had at least two sets of eyes on her at all times watching her every move. At first, it was just curiosity and caution, since it was obvious this was her first time there. She also stood out because she doesn't look like the kind of girl that normally appreciates a hole in the wall like O'Reilly's. Perhaps, if her friends had shown up the scrutiny would have passed, but they didn't, so it didn't either. JT noticed that when Russell, the other person in the bar with an unnatural purpose in being there, moved to a table a curious thing started to happen. Before that JT and the waitress noticed that Lisa looked at her phone every once in a while but she didn't seem to use it to text or email, despite her claims of communicating with her friends. But, after Russell moved to the table she did. And so did he. The curious thing is that they both didn't do it at the same time. That made JT wonder if the two stand outs were together. By the time Russell left, JT was still unsure that the two of them were together, but he had seen enough to have his suspicions.

JT explained all of that to Breck, who's standing at the bar facing the entrance with his back to Lisa's table. As the two of them talk, the waitress interrupts them to tell JT that Lisa is asking for her bill so she can pay and leave. JT tells the waitress to tell Lisa that she's going on break and she should close out her tab at the bar, with him. One minute later Lisa is standing at the bar, not six inches away from Breck, handing her credit card to JT. When JT gives her the receipt to sign he says, "I noticed you sitting alone all night. Were you waiting for someone?"

Lisa is surprised by the question. Not because it's being asked but because she knows he knows the answer to it. She saw the waitress tell JT what she had told the waitress. More than that, she caught JT looking at her on several occasions. She decides to play along, and this time, she's really going to sell it. She says, "Yes, I was waiting for two girlfriends of mine. First, there was some confusion about our meeting time. Then, apparently, there's another O'Reilly's in Hollywood, so they went there. When they finally figured out that I wasn't there, they called. That's when I told them that I'm at the O'Reilly's in North Hollywood. And then, just to add to the comedy of errors, they got a flat tire on their way here. Right now they are sitting in their car waiting for Triple A to arrive. We just decided to get together another night. But, I like this bar and I had as good a time as one can have just waiting."

"Well, I hope we see you again."

"Thanks." She signs the bar's copy of her receipt, takes hers, and leaves. JT's eyes tells Breck, who overheard the entire conversation, everything else he needed to know. He headed for the exit as soon as she walked through the door.

11:40pm - Russell is sitting in his car with the picture on his lap waiting for Lisa, when he notices her coming his way in his rear view mirror. Lisa jumps in the passenger side and says, "What a creepy place huh?"

Russell smiles and says, "Yeah. You better get used to it. Bad people never seem to hang out in places we'd like to be."

"So, what do you think?"

Now that Lisa is in the car with him and the two of them are talking, Russell hasn't looked in his rear view mirror. If he had, he would have noticed the man who walked out of the bar right behind Lisa. Breck, on the other hand, has been watching. He's sure of what JT wasn't. The two of them are together. Based on her story, she came to the bar alone, waiting to meet her girlfriends there. So, why would she get in the passenger seat of a car and be talking to what appears to be a man?

Russell says, "I don't know what to think yet. When I showed the bartender the picture his reaction seemed genuine. In fact, for a second, I thought he was going to say that he recognized the guy, but then he came up with the story of Sam."

"I don't think Sam really exists. I think he just figured out a way to get some money out of you."

"You might be right, though he didn't ask for the money. I offered it to him. You know what, let's just sleep on it tonight. We'll come up with another game plan tomorrow."

"That sounds good to me."

She was just about to give Russell a kiss on the cheek, say good night, and head for her car when there comes a knock on her window. It startled both of them. Whoever it is, is standing fully erect so they can't see his face. They just assumed it was the bartender. Maybe one of them left something in the bar. Lisa lowered her window and finally the man who knocked on the window bent down so they could see his face. It isn't the bartender, and it takes another moment before they recognize who it is. By the time they do, Breck has already noticed the picture of him sitting in Russell's lap. He asks them, "Are you guys looking for somebody?"

Russell's instincts kicked in and his only goal, right now, is to get this guy to pay attention to him and not Lisa. He's also aware of the picture sitting in his lap in plain view. While he tries to cover up the picture and remove his seat belt in one move he says, "Yeah, maybe you can help us. Let me step outside so we can talk about it."

It's too late for that. Breck shoots Russell in the forehead, and before she can react, he shoots Lisa in her right temple. Breck reaches into the car and takes the picture. Then he walks back to his car and he's on the 405 Freeway, heading south, in just a few minutes. Outlaw Country is playing one of his favorite songs and he's singing along with it. He merges to the far left lane and, again, he's looking for the entrance to the 90 west. Now, he can go back to the boat, relax, maybe watch a movie, and then go to bed.

———

Day Five

5:00am - "Are you sure you're ready for this?" asks Genny. She's lying in bed, on her stomach, with her head towards the foot of the bed watching television and talking with William, who's sitting up in bed, reading, and talking with Genny.

William says, "Honestly?"

"Of course, honestly."

"I am absolutely sure that I'm ready. I want this more than anything."

Genny turns to face William, "I only have two weeks left and then I'm done with the pill."

William puts down his papers, "I hope we have a little girl who looks just like her mother."

"That's funny because I am hoping we have a little boy who looks just like his father."

"Two weeks huh?"

"Ouais, two weeks. So, that means I'll be pregnant in three weeks, maybe sooner."

"I don't know if it will happen that fast."

"It will. My body is longing for it. I can feel it. I can't wait to have our little one growing inside of me." "Venez-vous ici."

Genny snuggles next to William as he wraps his arm around her shoulder and she wraps her arm around his mid-section. "I love it when you speak French to me."

He whispers in her ear, "Happy blood and happy oxygen."

And she whispers back, "Ten fingers and ten toes."

Later that night William wakes up in the middle of the night and looks at the clock. "Wow, it's only 2:00am." He kisses Genny, as she sleeps, on the forehead and he eases out of bed. He's in his home office looking for his bag, but he can't find it. He gets up from behind his desk, opens the door, and sees the man, dressed in black, with a gun in his hand, standing at the top of the stair-case. The man levels the gun at William and fires. Now, William is awake, startled out of his sleep by his recurring nightmare. He's lying on the floor in the living room of his hotel suite. It's

5:15am and there's no use in trying to go back to sleep. He gets up and gently opens the door to his bedroom. Megan is lying in his bed, and she's still asleep. Rather than fumble around in the kitchen, William puts on his clothes from yesterday and heads down the street. His plan is to buy some coffee, juice, and pastries and bring them back for breakfast.

5:30am - Standing in line at the bakery, trying to decide what to get, William can hear the morning local news on the television behind the cashier. Rick, the meteorologist and traffic reporter, is hovering, in the station's helicopter, over an accident on the 10 Freeway. "Yeah, thankfully it looks like the motorcyclist is moving as they put him on a stretcher. It may be an hour or two before they clear this one. Traffic is already backed up all the way to PCH. Other than this accident, however, it's been a relatively quiet morning."

Tony, the news anchor, says, "Let's hope it stays that way. OK, thank you Rick. Now, for a check on our weather I'll send it over to Maria." William has chosen a selection of croissants and muffins. He also asked for two fruit bowls and the barista is making two lattes for him.

Maria, finishing up her report says, "So, all in all, it looks like it is going to be a very pleasant day today and tomorrow, but expect the heat to turn up over the weekend. Back to you Tony."

"That sounds good to me. I like it hot."

The cashier puts William's lattes in a carrying tray and he bags William's pastries. William gives him the cash to pay for everything and now the cashier is returning William's change.

William can hear Tony, the news anchor, say, "Now, let's go to Gigi, in North Hollywood, who has today's top story. Gigi, I understand you have a very sad story to report."

"Yeah, as you said I'm in North Hollywood, just outside a local watering hole called O'Reilly's. It looks like a double homicide happened here last night. Two people, a man and a woman, were found in the car behind me. Both had been shot, once in the head, execution-style. Their names haven't been released yet and I'm waiting to speak with the police department's spokesman to find out if the police have any leads." William stops at the condiment bar to put some cinnamon in his latte and to grab some sugar and stirrers to take with him. On his way out, he holds the door open for an elderly gentleman on his way in, and then he leaves. It isn't until he gets to the corner that he replays what he's heard in his head. Though he has the right of way now he stands on the corner trying to figure out what sounded familiar to him and why. Then it hits him. Instead of heading back to his hotel, he goes back into the bakery and waits there until he hears the report on the double homicide again.

6:00am - William stayed in the bakery long enough to hear the report again but there was no new information reported. On his way back to the hotel he thought about what kind of connection can be made. The best he was able to come up with is there maybe somebody at O'Reilly's who knew Teddy, though given the events of last night, he's sure the police are blanketing that bar and, therefore, the likelihood of getting someone to talk with an outsider is probably remote at best. When he gets back to the hotel he finds Megan sitting in a robe, in the living room, on his laptop. When she woke up she checked on William and, in his absence, she figured he went for a walk or something. She washed her face, slipped into the robe, climbed back in bed, and turned on the television. She saw the same news report William watched in the bakery. Like William, it took her a moment to think of why the name of the bar sounded familiar. Unfortunately, she already discarded the sandwich bag full of Teddy's belongings, but she is sure of the name and she figures how many O'Reilly's can there be in North Hollywood? It must be the same place. She surfed through the channels to see if any other station was reporting anything new, or different, but they were all reporting the same generic information. So, she got out of bed and got on the internet with the hopes of finding any information that hadn't been reported on television already.

By the time William returned she hadn't found anything. The first thing William says is, "I saw something interesting on the news this morning."

"I saw it too. I'm online right now looking for more information."

"Great. I got us lattes, fruit bowls, and pastries for breakfast. I didn't know what kind of pastries you like so I got one of almost everything. What do you like?"

"I like blueberry muffins."

"Good, I got that."

As William stands in the kitchen putting everything on a plate, Megan says, "I'm not finding anything new yet."

"It may be a little too early in the investigation. I thought about it on the walk back. I doubt that whoever killed those two people had anything to do with Genny. At best, it's obvious that the criminal type hang out in or around that place." William continues with his thoughts as he walks Megan's latte and muffin to her. "Maybe, if this hadn't happened, O'Reilly's might have come to mind as a place to ask about Teddy. But, now that it has, I think it's the last place to go looking for answers."

"You're probably right, but I want to keep looking until I get more of the story."

William standing behind Megan leans over and places her latte and muffin in front of her. She has a short article on the double homicide onscreen and she's reading it. He bends over to read it also. Before he can get through the first paragraph something else captures his attention. He can smell the sweet scent of Megan's hair. More than that, he can smell the even sweeter scent of Megan's skin. It feels like it's been a long time since he's been this close to a woman and, in this moment, he isn't thinking about anything except the feelings he's having while he's taking Megan in. Those same feelings beckon him to do what he tries to tell himself he shouldn't, but it's too late. He's already under her womanly influence and he wants more. He allows his eyes to leave the screen. Instead, he watches her long and delicate fingers as they caress the keyboard. From there he allows his eyes to follow her hair as it cascades down the side of her neck, down her décolletage, and down, in between, her cleavage. He sees it rise and recede, on the ebb and flow of her breasts, as she breathes. By this time, Megan has become aware that William is no longer reading the article. She can hear him breathing her in, and she can tell that he's looking at her. She does nothing to encourage him and she does nothing to discourage him either. She just sits back in the chair, closes her eyes, and allows him to breathe. Now, William is aware that she knows what he's doing. Slowly and gently he turns the chair she's in until she is facing him. Their eyes meet, and they are both breathing heavily and in unison. Now, neither William nor Megan are trying to hide what they are feeling. She isn't going to make the first move. He wants to make the first move but something is stopping him. She thinks he may need a little encouragement, so she places her hand over his and she gently pulls him towards her. Her touch is stronger than whatever thoughts are stopping him, and he gives in. He leans forward and stops when they are close enough to each other for him to smell her hair and her skin again. Whatever inhibitions he had, up until that point, have now ceased to exist. His senses are fully awakened. He sees her, he hears her, he's touching her, he smells her, and now he kisses her softly on the neck, then on the cheek, and then on the lips. She welcomes and returns his kisses as if she's been waiting for them and wanting them for years. In truth, Teddy wasn't the only one caught in a fantasy on the day she met William and Geneviève. Megan found William handsome and attractive then. Part of the reason she gave Teddy a pass, for as long as she did, was because she was thinking of what it would be like to be with William while he was thinking about Genny. She, however, let go of her fantasy long before Teddy did, but it resurfaced the moment she saw William again. So, while she hasn't been longing for his kiss for years, it feels that way and she's enjoying their first kiss as much as he is. The longer they kiss, the more it becomes more than a kiss, and it continues to build until William pulls away. From there it takes a moment for them, both, to cool down from what has just happened and from what was about to happen. It feels like they are sharing an eternity without words but, in truth, just a few seconds pass before William says, "I can't."

Megan feels the urge to close her robe but she doesn't intentionally. She wants William to know that's she's ready when he's ready, so she simply says, "I understand."

William wants to find the words to tell her how much he wants her right now, and to explain why he can't, and to tell her how much he appreciates her understanding, but he can't. The only words that come to him right now are, "I think it's best if I take a shower and get dressed."

Again, Megan simply says, "I understand."

6:30am - Despite waking up to the panoramic view from Pete's bedroom dozens of times already, Abbey is more astonished by it with every new day. When she bought her business she hoped and planned to do well, but she never imagined she would make as much money, on one deal, as she is going to make today. The view from Pete's bedroom normally reminds Abbey that the sky is the limit, but today it has a different message. Today it says there are no limits. Today it reminds Abbey that what's possible lies far beyond her imagination. For a brief moment she wishes Pete was still lying next to her, but she knows that wishing for that, at this time in the morning, and especially on a day like today, is foolish. He's probably downstairs, in his gym, on the elliptical, or he's done with his workout already and he's on the phone talking business. Cuddling in bed, in the morning, is something that is rarely going to happen. Abbey has to accept that, and even encourage it, if she wants to build a life and a family with Pete. Her friends think she's crazy. She even wonders, sometimes, if they are right. The only thing standing in the way of her becoming Mrs. Jefferson is her, not Pete. He's asked for her hand in marriage twice already and both times she said, "No, but ask me again, hopefully sometime soon." On both occasions Abbey explained that he appears to have unfinished business, and that's what's standing in their way. On both occasions she went out of her way to let him know how much she loves him and how much she wants to be his wife, but she also let him know that if and when they do get married she wants him free and clear, and open and ready to start a new family. What her friends don't seem to understand is while it's often nice to marry into money Abbey prides herself on being an independent woman. She has a business of her own that she built up from next to nothing, and she has enough money on her own to live a better life than she ever imagined. Pete's money won't make her life dramatically different, and it won't make her dramatically happier than she already is. But, Pete's complete devotion and love will, if she can have them in a family setting. Like her parents and both sets of their parents, she wants to marry for life, have kids and grand-children, and with any luck grow old together. While divorce is commonplace in today's society and people seem to move on, and even flourish sometimes after it, divorce is the thing that scares Abbey the most, especially if there are kids involved. Pete was smart enough to understand what she was talking about the first time she explained it to him, and still he asked her to marry him again. Abbey is sure that he'll ask a third time. And, in light of the recent developments, she hopes that when he does she can say yes.

7:00am - Eddie feels like a king. He had a filet mignon, medium rare, with béarnaise sauce last night and it was the best meal of his life. He drank champagne and had sex with Veronica and it was the best sex of his life. After she left he took a shower, climbed into bed, and got the best sleep of his life. Now that he's awake and standing next to the window overlooking the entire Marina he feels like today will be the best day of his life. He couldn't have planned it better. He retires today with a full pension, his investment, ten years ago, of two hundred and fifty thousand dollars pays off today in the amount of two and a half million dollars, and he'll use part of that to make the final payment on "Miss Behavin." Tomorrow at this time he'll be just off the shore of Northern Mexico and on his way to a life of leisure in Costa Rica. Right now he feels that he can run a marathon and still have energy to spare. He's so excited he doesn't know what to do with himself. Then he reminds himself that he has to get through one more day of work. With that in mind, he calms down and prepares to shave, jump in the shower, and get dressed. He turns on the television and tunes in to CNBC. The market has gotten off to a choppy start but his next thought is, "who cares." He's not going to stress out about that or anything else today. Next he tunes into ESPN. Nothing special is happening in the world of sports or, at least, there's nothing going on that he's concerned about. Finally he tunes into the local news to get the weather report for the day. He laughs to himself when he thinks the reporter couldn't have been more accurate when she said today would be a perfect day. With that, he's seen and heard enough. It's time to shave. Over the drone of his electric razor he can hear the rest of the weather report, he can hear the traffic report, and he can hear the news stories of the day. Normally, a report of a double homicide would catch his attention but not today. Today, he'll sleepwalk through the work day. In effect, he's already checked out. Now that he's done shaving he packs up his toiletries, except for the last couple of items he'll use just before he gets dressed. He turns on the shower and walks to the bed to get undressed. While he's doing that he listens to the day's top story and, as he does, a knot starts to form in his stomach. He starts to seethe with anger. He tries to calm himself down but he can't. He doesn't have any reason to believe what's making him so mad, but he heard the words, murder and O'Reilly's and he's as certain that Breck had something to do with it as he is of his first name. He thinks of calling Breck, but he puts the phone down before he dials. He's convinced himself that there's no way Breck could be that stupid. Besides, knowing what he knows of O'Reilly's and its clientele, anyone who frequents that establishment could be the one responsible. The fact that the police haven't reported who the victims are is probably procedural. They will after they notify the next of kin. It took just that long for Eddie to go from happy to furious and back to happy again. Now that he's back to being light on his feet, he jumps in the shower so he can get on with his day.

7:30am - The waking public, as they enjoy their morning coffee while watching the morning news, may be just getting wind of the double homicide in North Hollywood last night, but the top brass in the LAPD has been working on the case since 3:00am. That's when Chief of Police Koch was awakened and told of the news. Normally, a murder in the City of Angels wouldn't get the Chief's attention until he got to the office, but this event is different. First, a high profile and upstanding member of the Los Angeles Journalist and Crime Prevention communities was killed. That, alone, would have those in the chain of command wondering if they should inform the Chief in the middle of the night. But, in addition to that, two .45 caliber shells were found at the crime scene, more specifically, they were found on the floor, in front of the passenger seat of the car the two victims were murdered in. When that information reached those close enough to the Chief to know what he's been most interested in over the last few days, the call went out immediately. Now, assembled in the Chief's office are the Chief, his second in command, Police Commander Stevens, Captain Ramirez, captain of the North Hollywood Precinct, and Captain Upton, captain of the Santa Monica Precinct. Chief Koch says, "I can't believe no one saw this happen."

Captain Ramirez informs the Chief that, "We have ten uniforms going door to door right now. If someone saw anything we'll find him."

Chief Koch asks, "What about the bar? Do they have any kind of surveillance system?"

Captain Ramirez answers, "None."

Chief Koch asks, "Is that the same O'Reilly's I get reports on every now and again?"

Captain Ramirez says, "One in the same."

Chief Koch says, "Ok, play time is over for that place. I want you to turn up the heat on that place. I want cops crawling all over that bar every day and every night. And, I want you to keep the heat turned up on that place until we put them out of business. If you get stretched out too thin and you need to take men off that detail let me know before you do. I'll find a way to get you more men. Let me be absolutely clear, the heat stays cranked up on O'Reilly's until they are out of business. I don't care how long it takes. You got it?"

Captain Ramirez replies, "Got it."

Chief Koch continues with, "Each of us, in this room, knows who Russell Armstrong was. He was a great man and a personal friend. And, Lisa Becker was like a daughter to him and she was following in his footsteps. I met her, for the first time, just yesterday afternoon for goodness sake. These murders are not going to go unsolved. We are going to catch this son of a bitch no matter what it takes. There has to be a reason the two of them were there at the same time. They could have been in that neighborhood visiting someone, but I don't think so. I think they were there working. Captain Ramirez I want you to send two detectives to the Los Angeles Times and find out what Russell was working on. Captain Upton, I know Ms. Becker was working on the David Waverly murder, a case you and your detectives have the lead on. I want you to send the detectives assigned to that case to the Malibu Journal, the paper Lisa worked for, and find out everything you can on what she was working on."

Captain Upton adds, "Just for full disclosure, one of the detectives I had on the case is in the hospital. I replaced him with another detective, but the other original detective on the case is retiring today, and I don't have anyone else to spare."

Chief Koch says, "OK, I'll get someone else assigned to you for this case by the end of the day, but tell the detective that's retiring he has to put in a full day today. I want him working this case every minute of the day he's being paid for. No excuses. Got it?"

"Got it."

"Listen, push your people today. If they need a break tell them they can take it tomorrow. If they need to eat tell them to eat while they're working. If they aren't turning up anything then you better hit the streets and find something yourselves. I want us all to reconvene here tonight at 7:00pm and you better have something to tell me that I don't know already. Got it?"

Captain Ramirez and Captain Upton, in unison, "Got it."

8:00am - Eddie was as happy as could be when he pulled out of the Four Seasons in Marina Del Rey on his way to his last day of work. Two minutes later he almost crashed his car into the back of a bus when he got the news from Breck. Eddie screams into the phone, "Who were they?"

Breck says, "I don't know."

Eddie screams again, "How the hell can you kill two people you don't even know? What if they were cops?"

"They weren't cops."

"How do you know that?"

"Trust me. They weren't cops. That much I know."

"Trust you? Are you out of your mind?"

"Yeah, trust me. You should be happy that I did what I did."

"How the hell do you figure that?"

"Like I said, they had a picture of me and they were already asking questions at a place I've been known to be."

"How did they get a picture of you?"

"That's not important any more. What's important is they are no longer looking for me, which means they aren't, eventually, going to look for you."

"I should have never brought you back to LA."

"Maybe not, but now I'm glad you did and you should be too. If I hadn't taken care of those two there would be people still looking for us after we left. Who knows, maybe they would've caught up with us at some point."

"I didn't bring you here for those two. I'm not paying you for them."

"You know, somehow I knew you'd say that. It's OK just as long as our current deal stands."

"Where are you now?"

"I'm on your boat."

"Good. Lock yourself in your stateroom and don't come out until I get there tonight."

"I still have a couple of things to do before we leave."

"Breck, listen to me, lock yourself in your stateroom and don't come out until I get there tonight. If you stick your head above deck for one second today I'm not going to pay you for this trip. I'm only going to pay you for the work I hired you to do on your first trip. So, tell me now, are you going to do those things and forfeit your money, or are you going to follow my directions, to the freaking letter, and get your money?"

"They won't take long. One of the things I need to do is return the rent a car, for instance."

"Breck, don't take one step off that boat or else I'm not paying you for anything."

"That's twice now you've threatened not to pay me. I don't do what I do for free. You know about my resume. You better re-think what you're saying to me."

"Look, you've earned a lot of money. Do you want us to get to Costa Rica so you can get paid or do you want us to go to prison?"

"All right."

"No. Say it."

"I'm not going anywhere until you get here."

They hang up on each other. Breck remains unapologetic for what he's done and he's sure, once Eddie calms down, he'll realize that he did the right thing. Eddie's final thought is, "As if I needed another reason."

8:30am - In part because they both wanted to get out of the hotel room as soon as they were dressed and in part because it was the best idea they had at the time, William and Megan decided to try Tommy again. Since he wasn't home either of the times they tried yesterday they hoped, by stopping by in the morning, they'd catch him before he left his apartment for the day. Unfortunately, he still wasn't home and a neighbor of his told Megan he hadn't seen Tommy for a few days. That leaves Gino Moreno as the next person on the list. Megan explained to William that Gino sells marijuana, by delivery only, but he also has a legitimate computer systems and repair business. She says, if she remembers correctly, he owns a small apartment build-ing in West Hollywood. He lives in one apartment and runs his businesses out of another. They decide the best way to get to him is through his computer business. Sitting in William's car, still parked in front of Tommy's apartment building, they call Gino's business. It isn't open for the day yet, so William leaves a message.

9:00am - Detective Jackie Webb and Detective Kirsten Reynoso, both from the North Hollywood Precinct, arrive at the Los Angeles Times Building and find the flag, outside the building, at half mast. Despite their youth they have both already proven to be accomplished detectives. Given their youth, however, neither of them are familiar with Russell or his work. They notice two things immediately upon entering the building. The interior of the building is magnificent, but the mood inside the building is somber at best. That dovetails with what they were told about Russell, namely he was one of law enforcement's best friends. They are met, by the Globe in the lobby, by Giovanna Templeton, the liaison between the Los Angeles Times, the Media Group that owns it, and the public. She leads them to Russell's office and tells them that she's available to them all day if they should need anything. For the first few minutes Detective Webb and Detective Reynoso take all of Russell's office in. Reading the articles hanging on his walls and the captions underneath the various pictures hanging beside the articles is like getting a quick history lesson on law enforcement in Los Angeles for the last thirty years. Detective Reynoso notices the pictures on Russell's desk of him and Lisa, and she shows them to Detective Webb. Though they didn't need any more motivation, seeing the picture of Russell and Lisa sharpens their focus and resolve to find a lead. The whole time they are in Russell's office they are aware that they are being watched by his co-workers, several of whom were bold enough to tell the detectives that they would be glad to help them in any way they could. To that end, Detective Webb commandeered a conference room just steps away from Russell's office and started her interviews of his co-workers. At the same time, Detective Reynoso started going through the papers and files on Russell's desk.

An hour into their investigation Detective Webb hasn't been given any information she thinks is helpful, but Detective Reynoso thinks she has the lead they are looking for. She shows Detective Webb the file, labeled "LAPD Issued," she found on Russell's desk. The two of them sit down to read and reread the contents of the file. They learn about the gun's history. They learn about the three murders that happened six years ago. It's clear to them that the same person is suspected to be the perpetrator of all three murders because all of the murders were committed in the same way with the same gun. Then they read the newspaper clippings of a man named Ronny White, who turned up dead in the trunk of a burning car in a small village south of Los Angeles called Cardiff-By-The-Sea. Russell highlighted a section of the article that reported that burning the car, with Mr. White in it, turned out to be an attempt to cover up evidence. In fact, the cause of Mr. White's death was a single gunshot to the back of the head with a .45 caliber pistol. Given that the article was just printed earlier in the week, Detective Webb agrees with Detective Reynoso that this was, most likely, what Russell was working on last. It doesn't escape them, either, that the preliminary report on last night's double homicide is that both victims were killed by a single shot to the head with a .45 caliber pistol. Detective Reynoso calls Captain Ramirez to tell him what they've found. Detective Webb calls Sheriff Silva, in Cardiff-By-The-Sea. She got his name and number from a piece of paper found inside the file she just read.

9:30am - Nine days out of ten the marine layer that hovers over the Southern California coast denies the sun long after the sun has conquered the inland. Today is that tenth day. Despite Breck and despite being told that he has to work a full day, nothing seems to be able to get in the way of Eddie's happiness. The sun is shining brightly along the coast as he and Javier drive north on Pacific Coast Highway on their way to Malibu and to Lisa's office at the Journal.

Javier says, "If you leave tonight it will be too dark for you to see any of this as you coast down the shore, and isn't it more dangerous to boat at night? Why don't you wait until the morning to leave?" Eddie says, "I thought about that but I decided what I want most, on my first day of retirement, is to watch the sun rise from the top deck of my boat a mile off shore. Yeah, boating at night is slightly more dangerous but I'm not in a rush. Even during the day, I plan to take it slow and easy."

Javier asks, "Are you still planning on stopping in Cabo?"

"Yeah, but just to refuel and restock supplies. From there I'll be able to make it all the way to Costa Rica."

"What's the first thing you're going to do once you're there?"

"Nothing!"

The two men laugh and Javier says, "Now that sounds like a good plan." A moment goes by before Javier says, "Let's talk shop for a minute."

"OK but I have to admit, I'm having a hard time concentrating."

"I can understand that. Let me ask you a question. Do you think there is any way Teddy could have been killed as opposed to overdosing himself?"

"Teddy? Teddy Gallo?"

"Yeah."

"I don't want to spend my last day talking about him." Before Javier can think of a way to re-approach the subject Eddie asks, "Why would you want to talk about him anyway?"

Javier explains, "Do you remember William, the guy you met yesterday whose wife was killed? He says he heard that Teddy was murdered."

"You have to be kidding me, right?" Javier doesn't respond. Eddie asks, "What do you mean he says he heard? Who is he? Did he recently join the force? What is he a street detective now, doing his own investigation? Come on Javier, you're smarter than that. You're letting his sob story get to you."

"Maybe. You said yesterday that you thought his story could make sense."

"I was just telling the poor guy what he obviously wanted to hear. I didn't mean any of it. What do I know about his wife's murder? That's your case, not mine. As far as Teddy goes, he was a low life. I don't find it hard to believe that he overdosed. In fact, I'm surprised he lived as long as he did. You know more about that guy's, what's his name again, William, you know more about that guy's wife's murder than I do. Do you see any connection?"

"No, but if Teddy was murdered that would raise some suspicion and make William's theory a bit more credible."

Eddie looks a Javier in disbelief and shakes his head. Finally he says, "Listen, if you want to follow up on William's fantasy, be my guest. Just leave me out of it. If you ask me, you're letting the guilt of not finding his wife's killer get to you. Like I said, you know more about his wife's case than I do. If you turn up a real lead or some real evidence let me know. Actually, don't let me know. Frankly, I don't care anymore. But, if you find something worth following, do your thing. As far as Teddy is concerned, he OD'd. That's all to it. I don't want to talk about this foolishness anymore. Let's just get to where we're going and do what we have to do."

The rest of the ride is done in silence. Along the way Javier is wondering if he is letting William get to him, or if there is more to the story. At this point, he really isn't sure. Eddie, in contrast, is wondering what or how much does Javier know and if this guy, William, is going to be a problem.

10:00am - All of Pete's guests are assembled in the waiting area just outside the main conference room. When the curtains and the doors to the conference room swing open there is a collective and audible gasp. Pete's caterers have done a magnificent job. The space is decorated with large vases of flowers strategically placed around the room. To complement the floral arrangements there twenty large ice buckets placed around the room, each containing a three litre Jeroboam of Moët & Chandon's Dom Perignon White Gold. In between the floral arrangements and the buckets of champagne there is a buffet of every kind of breakfast food and drink imaginable. There's even a chef in the far left corner who will cook any omelette a guest desires.

As the festivities get started Pete makes his way around the room. While speaking with one of his partners he finds out that that man plans to retire from the business world and spend the remainder of his days consulting with his sons on their business ventures, and babysitting his grandchildren. Another of Pete's partners, a married couple, tell Pete that they plan to do a 1031 exchange with their proceeds into another shopping mall in New Mexico. Still another of Pete's partners says he isn't sure what he's going to do with the proceeds, but he's taking his family to Scotland for the summer. While he's there he plans to meet with several investment managers and investment bankers based in Glasgow. That's the way the party goes for Pete. He spends his time talking with each partner, getting a gauge on their future plans, and answering questions about his. All of his partners, however, have two things in common. First, they all express their appreciation to Pete for putting the deal together and including them. Second, they all want to know what Pete is doing next and they all want in. The best Pete can tell them for today is that he's working on buying something even bigger than the Forest Canyon Mall but it's too early to speak of it yet.

Intentionally Pete waited to speak with Carl towards the end of making his rounds. Pete looks around the room and doesn't see anyone he doesn't know already. Obviously, Mr. Roberts chose not to attend. Finally he makes his way to Carl and says, "Congratulations. Without your contribution, this deal would have been that much harder to pull off."

The two of them shake hands and Carl says, "That's very flattering, but the truth is you would have found a way. I'm just happy you gave me the opportunity to be a part of it."

Pete asks, "Do you have any plans for your proceeds?"

"Why, are you working on something?"

"In fact, I am. If you're interested, I'll tell you more when the time is right."

"You know I'm interested. I'm looking forward to it."

"Did you extend an invitation to Mr. Roberts? I don't see him here."

"Absolutely, I did. He said he'd try to make it, but he also said it was unlikely that he would attend because he had to work."

"Carl, are you in any kind of trouble?"

"No. Why do you ask?"

"When I saw the name of his company pop up on the settlement statement I thought it was odd, at least for that stage of the game. Maybe I'm too paranoid, but it made me wonder if you were being blackmailed or something."

"Is that what you thought?"

"Yes, of course. What you do with your money is your business. It's just that you hadn't mentioned him ever before and then all of a sudden he's line for a big pay day. My interest in him was really my interest in you. Is everything all right?"

The weight off of Carl's shoulders would have been obvious to anyone watching him at the time, even if that person were standing on the other side of the room and couldn't hear a word the two men were saying. Carl says, "Pete, I truly appreciate your concern but everything is great. Mr. Roberts is planning to develop some land, in Costa Rica, into a resort hotel and I'm just one of his investors."

"That sounds good. As long as you're all right. That's all that matters. Let me catch up with you a little later. Enjoy the party."

Carl feels ten times lighter and, at the same time, silly for letting his guilty conscience get the better of him. For the rest of the party he mingles freely with the other partners, and he eats and drinks until his heart is content. After an hour had gone by Pete tapped his champagne glass with a fork to get everyone's attention. He makes a passionate speech about the hurdles they had to jump to get the deal done, and about how lucky they got when the companies they targeted agreed to be the anchors for the mall. At the time, they thought the three companies they chose as anchors would do well but, he admits, no one, not even he, thought they would do as well as they have. Finally, he says the words that everyone wanted to hear. He tells everyone that all of the wire transfers should be complete by 1:00pm. That last bit of information was met with thunderous applause and no one clapped louder than Carl Davies.

10:30am - No one could put their finger on what was going on with Phyllis this morning, but everyone sensed something. It wasn't that she came to the office this morning in a happy mood, she usually does that. It was her attire. Having worked at that the Sheriff's station for so long as she has, she considers it her home away from home. While she is always dressed well, her style could be described as business casual or, as she likes to call it, business comfortable. She has a saying for people who are dressed very well. She likes to call them, 'dressed to the nines.' Today, Phyllis, herself, would have to say that she's, 'dressed to the nines squared.' She made Sheriff Silva promise that he wouldn't tell anyone about her date with Russell and he hasn't. He hasn't even told his wife. So, when her co-workers asked, she simply smiled and said, "a girl feels like dressing up every once in a while." About an hour ago Sheriff Silva called her into his office and told her the news. He was prepared to console her. He was prepared to tell her to take the rest of the day off. But, none of that was necessary. She took the news as if he asked her to work late tonight. She accepted it, without any emotion, and went back to her desk. Anyone paying attention, however, could tell that something had changed for Phyllis. She, of course, still looked fabulous, but gone was her smile, and along with it went her cheerfulness. In their place there was only a somber quiet and a more intense focus on her work. Her new front was just a facade masking her thoughts and feelings. She tells herself, repeatedly, that she only met the man once. They hadn't even gone out with each other yet. While what happened is definitely tragic and sad, there's no reason for her to have the feelings she's having. She kept up appearances for as long as she could until, finally, she asked Sheriff Silva if she could use his office to call Detective Webb back. She claimed she wanted to make the call to confirm that the detective got the picture. Though she could have made that call just as easily from her desk, Sheriff Silva understood right away, and left her alone in his office.

Phyllis's' call was put through to Detective Webb at Russell's desk. While Detective Reynoso and Detective Webb have spent the morning figuring out what Russell was working on last, during that time, they also found out how much Russell meant to so many people. One co-worker after another stopped by to see if what they heard was true, and when they found out that it is was, many of them left Russell's office crying, even some of the men. As further testament to his worth, now Detective Webb is on the phone speaking with Sheriff's Silva's assistant, who confessed that she and the Sheriff had only met Russell yesterday. Still, in the short time of their acquaintance, he had made enough of an impact that Sheriff Silva's assistant, Phyllis, is on the other end of the line weeping. Detective Webb wishes she knew what to say to Phyllis, but everything she thinks of saying doesn't sound genuine since she never met the man. The only thing she can think of offering to Phyllis, as consolation, is that she isn't alone. She tells her that everyone at the Los Angeles Times, who knew him, appears to feel the same way she does. The only other thing she has to say is that, yes, she did get the email with the picture attached. She tells Phyllis thanks and she asks her to pass on that same message to the Sheriff. She says she'll call them back if she has any other questions. Finally, she tells Phyllis she hopes she can find peace and she hopes she feels better soon.

While Detective Webb is on the phone with Phyllis, Detective Reynoso is on the phone with Captain Ramirez discussing the picture and discussing what Sheriff Silva told her and Detective Webb about his outing with Russell yesterday. The possibilities, being as remote as they are, aren't lost on either Detective nor on Captain Ramirez. Nor is the poor quality and camera angle of the picture. Still, it's better than nothing and, more than that, it is a lead. Captain Ramirez instructs Detective Reynoso to make a couple dozen copies and distribute them to the uniforms in North Hollywood that are going door to door in the neighborhood surrounding O'Reilly's.

11:00am - William finally hears back from Gino, who apologizes for taking so long to return his call. He explains that he would have returned it sooner but he was working on the system of a long time client who lives in Beverly Hills, and the job took him all morning. William, in an effort to seem authentic, tells Gino he's happy he caught him when he did. He was just about to call someone else. Gino says, "Great. So, what's going on with your laptop?"

William says, "My fan is making a lot of noise and the laptop seems to be overheating. It shut down once and I was afraid I might have lost everything but, luckily, once it cooled down I rebooted it, and it was fine. Since then, however, I shut it down as soon as it starts to overheat."

"What kind of laptop do you have?"

"A Toshiba Satellite Pro 6100."

"Oh, I have one of those as well. Have you tried to shoot compressed air into the vents?"

"Yeah. I keep a can of compressed air next to the laptop. I spray the keyboard regularly. I did shoot some into the vents. A lot of dust came out and it seemed to have done the trick for a minute, but then the fan started making noise again and the laptop started to overheat again."

"Where are you located?"

"I'm in West Hollywood but the laptop is in Santa Monica."

"I asked because I was going to come to you, if you were closer, but I'd have to go back to my shop anyway to get the piece I need."

"It's OK, I'm moving around a lot today. It's probably easier for me to get the laptop to you."

Gino says, "OK, my shop is on North Kings Road, just above Sunset, but I won't be there until 12:30pm. I need to stop and get something to eat before I get back to my desk. Do you want to bring it by sometime this afternoon?"

"Yeah, I'd like to get this fixed as soon as I can so I can use it without worrying. I can meet you at your shop at 12:30pm if that's all right with you?"

"OK, how did you learn about my shop?"

"An old friend recommended your shop a while ago, but I went to someone else instead. But, I remembered your name and, this time, I found you on the internet."

"So you have my address right?"

"I didn't notice it, but if it's on your website I can get it from there when I get back to Santa Monica." "Great. I'll see you at 12:30pm."

11:30am - Though Eddie has one foot out of the door and claims to have trouble concentrating today, Javier found him to be as thorough a detective as any. Together they interviewed Iris, the owner of the Journal and several of Lisa's co-workers. Understandably, they all found it truly difficult to concentrate.

Everything Iris told them was exactly as Eddie told Javier yesterday and exactly as Jessie had told Javier as well. The only new piece of information they got from Iris was that Lisa had a reason to speak with Jessie again, and she planned to do that yesterday. Most of Lisa's co-workers didn't have anything useful to say with regard to their investigation. Mostly, they spoke about how nice she was and how unimaginable it is that she's now dead. One co-worker pulled up Lisa's blog and the detectives read all of Lisa's recent postings. The only story with teeth was about David Waverly's murder. Even then, she apparently chose not to include many of the facts that she learned from Jessie and shared with Iris and the detectives already. Her other postings were benign stories about car crashes and domestic disputes in Malibu. Another co-worker, however, did provide some useful information. She told the detectives that Lisa asked her to get copies of the California driver's license for everyone named Ronald or Ronny White. She told the detectives that she did, and that she gave Lisa a folder containing approximately ten pictures yesterday morning.

On their way out of the Journal the two detectives agree to stop at the Starbucks on Cross Creek to get a coffee, and discuss what they've learned before calling in an update to Captain Upton. From a comparison of all of the notes they've taken over the last few days, and the notes they took today, it's obvious that Lisa believed that Ronny White had something to do with David Waverly's murder or, at least, she believed he knew something about it. They combined that with what they learned about Ronny White this morning from Captain Upton. Namely, that he turned up dead Monday afternoon. Apparently, Lisa didn't know that or else she wouldn't have been looking for him yesterday.

None of what they've learned explains why she was in North Hollywood last night or who wanted to see her dead. Javier calls Captain Upton to give him the update. After listening to everything Javier has to say, Captain Upton tells Javier that he's just spoken with Captain Ramirez and he's learned something. The Captain tells Javier that Russell spent yesterday with the Sheriff of the town Ronny White's body was discovered in, and that the Sheriff and Russell believed they found a picture of the person who killed Mr. White. So, if Lisa was looking for Mr. White, surely Russell would have filled her in on what he found out. The Captain tells Javier that detectives from the North Hollywood Precinct have a copy of that picture and that they are following up on that lead. He instructs Javier and Eddie to follow up with Jessie to find out if she and Lisa did speak for a second time, and, if so, find out what in addition, if anything, did Lisa get from her. After hanging up with the Captain, Javier calls Jessie but gets her voicemail. He leaves an urgent message asking her to call him as soon as she gets the message. Then he tells Eddie what the Captain just told him. Together they try to put the pieces together. Eddie says, "Based on my conversation with Lisa, I know she thought Ronny White was somehow affiliated with David Waverly, maybe she came to believe that he was responsible for or knowledgeable about David's murder."

Javier adds, "Jessie definitely thinks he was a negative influence, at the minimum, on David."

Eddie offers, "If Lisa then spoke with Armstrong, who believed he had a picture of the person who killed Ronny White, she must have assumed that the three of them, David, Ronny, and this new guy, were connected somehow. Lisa told me that Jessie said that there was another man David was hanging around with when he was hanging around with Mr. White."

"Yeah, Jessie told me the same thing. But, she was really vague about it. She said she never met him and she couldn't even remember his name. She said she only knew of him from conversations she had with David."

"Did the Captain say he has the picture of the man Armstrong and the Sheriff discovered?"

"He didn't say but I'm sure he does. I guess he's leaving that lead to NoHo."

"Then I think the best thing we can do is track down Jessie and find out what she and Lisa talked about yesterday."

12:00pm - The police presence is palpable. Detectives Reynoso and Webb see two black and whites circling the neighborhood, and there are four more parked in front of O'Reilly's. They walk directly to the car the victims were found in. Detective Webb says, "The report says one of the victims was found in the driver's seat, the other in the passenger seat, and there was no sign of a struggle." Detective Reynoso offers, "That means they either knew the person who shot them or they were taken by complete surprise." Standing side by side on the sidewalk next to the passenger side of the car the Detectives try to imagine how the killing happened. Detective Webb continues, "I don't see a place where the killer could have laid in waiting and not been seen. Maybe he or she was sitting in another car and approached after they got in theirs."

"That's possible. They are so close to the entrance of the bar. I wonder if they were in the bar and were followed out by the killer."

"That's possible, but since there was no sign of a struggle and since they were found sitting in the car with the engine off I don't think they were running from anybody."

"I think you're right. So, if they were in the bar and followed, or even if the killer was sitting in a different car waiting for them, they didn't see it coming until it was too late. The report says the driver's side window was up and the passenger's window was down, and we know they were shot from the passenger side. It's possible that they were sitting in their car talking, either just getting here or preparing to leave, when someone walked up to their car on the passenger side."

"If the killer came from the front they would have seen him or her, if the killer came from behind they might not have."

"Either way it appears that they didn't feel threatened. The passenger side window was probably down so they could talk with that person. None of their possessions were taken so it was all about killing them. The questions are what were they doing here? What was going on? And who benefited from their deaths?"

A uniformed police officer, Officer Warren, approaches the two detectives, and asks, "Are you Detectives Webb and Reynoso?"

Detective Reynoso says, "Yes."

Officer Warren explains, "I was told to look out for the two of you. I understand you have a picture of a person of interest that I need to distribute."

Detective Webb says, "Yes, we do. We have them in the car."

As the three of them walk towards the car Officer Warren says, "Unfortunately, we haven't found anyone who saw or heard anything yet, but there's still a lot of people we haven't spoken with. The dishwasher came back earlier and his statement was taken. He says he was in the kitchen all night so he doesn't appear to know anything. But, one of the waitresses that was working last night, Aimee Donovan, is here. And the bartender that was working last night, James Thomas, got here just a little while ago as well. We were going to take a statement from them but then I was told you would be here shortly. So, I have them sitting in the bar waiting for you. I also asked them to compile a list of everyone that was here last night that they could remember. I told them to use their memory and their credit card receipts to make the list." Detective Reynoso says, "That was good thinking Officer. Well done."

Detective Webb says, "Here's the picture. We made thirty copies. That should be enough for now." Officer Warren takes all but two of them. The detectives keep one a piece. Officer Warren says, "I'll distribute these now if the two of you are going back to the car. Otherwise, I can take you in the bar and introduce you to the waitress and bartender, and then distribute them."

Detective Reynoso says, "Why don't you take us in the bar. We'd like to speak with the waitress and the bartender now."

"Excellent. Follow me." Walking behind Officer Warren, Detective Reynoso and Detective Webb share a glance and a smile. They like Officer Warren. He's eager, smart, and decisive.

12:30pm - Gino was visibly put on guard by the presence of a second person. William's explanation that she is his girlfriend, who is just tagging along with him as he runs his errands for the day, does nothing for Gino. He assumed William was coming alone, and he doesn't like surprises, no matter how large or small. Still, he invites her to have a seat and he asks William to see his laptop. William takes out the laptop and hands it to Gino. While Gino turns it on, William explains that it will only take few minutes before the fan turns on and the computer starts to overheat.

William and Megan discussed their strategy before they showed up at Gino's place. Given his side business and the fact that he doesn't know them, they knew he'd be on edge. So, the plan is to make small talk, get Gino to relax, and then ask about Teddy. It's obvious to William that Gino is still bothered by Megan's presence. On the phone he seemed very open and conversational, but now it appears that Gino would be happy to sit in silence until the problem resurfaces. Then he'll fix it, take his pay, and hope they leave as soon as possible. William starts operation "Gino Relax" with, "You know I've had that laptop for over two years now, and I'm sure I still don't know how to use it super efficiently. Didn't you say you have the same model?"

Gino says, "Yes. I do."

"Can you show me some shortcuts or tricks that I probably don't know?"

"I don't know what you know."

"I know the basics. You know, turn it on, and turn it off, stuff like that. Oh, I also know how to defragment the C drive." William turns to Megan and say, "I learned how to do that, what four months ago?"

Megan's contribution is, "I think it was more like six months ago."

William turns back to Gino and says, "OK, I learned how to do that six months ago, but that's about as sophisticated as I get."

"Sure, I can show you a few things, but let's take care of the fan problem first."

William continues with, "Let me ask you another question. What do you think about the anti-virus software I have on there? I mean, is that good enough to protect me from all the threats I hear about on the news?"

"Right now, you're using Norton. That's probably good enough, though you could find better and less expensive software. If you really feel the need to upgrade you should look into Bitdefender or Webroot. They're both slightly better than Norton and they're both less expensive."

"That's good to know. Thank you."

Megan chimes in with, "Maybe I should do that too."

William says, "Yeah, you should. But, wait, you have a Mac." Turning back to Gino, William says, "She has a Mac. Does that make a difference? I remember reading somewhere, when I was shopping for a new laptop, that Macs don't need anti-virus protection."

"That's both true and false. The OS-X system is much more difficult to bring down, so in general you're pretty safe with a Mac, but you could still be subject to attack. I have anti-virus software on my Mac too. You can also look into Bitdefender for Mac."

Megan says, "Thanks. I will."

"OK, your fan just turned on. It sounds normal to me."

"Of course it does. That's just like my car, which stops making the noise I've been hearing for two weeks as soon as I take it to the mechanic. Give it another minute. I'm sure you'll hear it. By the way, how much is this going to cost?"

"If I have to replace the fan the whole job will cost $200.00."

"That sounds reasonable. I wish I had come to you sooner. I wonder if you remember my friend, the one who recommended your shop to me in the first place. His name is Teddy Gallo. Do you know him?"

That question combined with William's laptop, which is working perfectly, confirms for Gino what he suspected when they first walked in. He doesn't know what their visit is about but it's not about his computer. Gino says, "Your computer is fine. I think you should leave."

William says, "Listen, we just need to ask you some questions about Teddy."

"So, there really wasn't anything wrong with your computer?"

"No. I'm sorry about the deception, but I didn't think you'd talk to me if I asked you about Teddy outright."

Gino shuts down William's computer, stands up, and hands it to him. "You were right and I'm not going to talk about him now either. Take your computer and your girlfriend and leave."

Megan stands up and says, "I'm not really his girlfriend. I was Teddy's old girlfriend. I'm sure you heard of me."

Gino grabs her by the arm, pushes her towards the door, and says, "I don't care who you are. It isn't cool for you to come at me that way. Now you both have to leave."

William stands between Gino and Megan to make sure he doesn't touch her again, and to try to calm Gino down so they can talk. Gino grabs William by his arms, spins him around and pushes him towards the door. William bumps into Megan, who trips over her feet and falls down. William turns to Gino and again tries to calm him down. "Listen, I'm really sorry for coming at you the way I did. You're right, that was wrong. But, this is really important. I just need to ask you a few questions."

Gino pushes William in the chest and says, "Am I not speaking English?" Gino takes another step towards William and pushes him in the chest again. "Get the hell out of my shop." Gino continues taking steps towards William and Megan, who are almost at the door. Gino reiterates, "Get the hell out!" This time he grabs Megan and tosses her towards the door. Again, William stands between Gino and Megan. This time when Gino goes to grab William, William punches him flush on his left jaw, knocking him out cold.

1:00pm - "Bring your sexy," was the only direction the director gave to Jessie. She auditioned for this music video a week ago, and since she hadn't heard back, she thought she didn't get it. In fact, the director chose her for the lead before she walked out of the casting session, but the production was pushed back a week. The producer thought the casting director told her, and the casting director thought the director told her. So, when she got the message about her call time she was surprised and confused. But, after speaking with the director she was happy and excited. She heard the track during the casting session and she's sure the song will be a hit. So, getting the lead in the video is a dream come true. The job pays well and hopefully it will be another stepping stone in her career. When Eddie and Javier arrived at her apartment they found her dressed in sweat pants and a tank top tee shirt. Her girlfriend, Sky, whom Jessie asked to come over to help her select which outfits to take, is dressed in skin tight yoga pants and a sports bra, as she went directly to Jessie's apartment right after her morning yoga session. As if watching two beautiful and scantily clad women isn't titillating enough, the two detectives, while trying to conduct their interview, had to watch the two women lay out one sexy outfit after another in an attempt to select the sexiest of the sexy. They were even asked, on more than one occasion, for their opinion. Javier is aware of what they're doing, but his attention is on the interview. Eddie is aware of the interview but he's imagining what Jessie would look like in each of her outfits. Jessie apologizes for not being able to sit down and talk. She explains that this job came as a surprise to her and she only has a couple of hours before she has to be on set. So, in between visits to her closet and try-ons she tells the detectives mostly what they know already. There's nothing about David that she can remember, that she hasn't already told them. There's nothing about his friend Ronny White that she can remember, that she hasn't told them. She takes the news about Mr. White's death like water off a duck. She allowed herself to give that information two seconds of her time. Just long enough to think, "Who cares." But, when she hears the news about Lisa, everything stops. She tells her friend to hang on for a minute, she sits down, and she gives the detectives her full attention. When they tell her where it happened she feels sick. She tells the detectives that she told Lisa about O'Reilly's yesterday. She explains that Lisa brought several pictures of men named Ronald and Ronny White to her apartment yesterday, hoping she would be able to pick one of them out as the man she met. None of them were the man she met, but one of the pictures reminded her of someone else and that reminded her of O'Reilly's. She says she told Lisa, just before she left, that David mentioned O'Reilly's as the place he met and, at times, hung out with Ronny. While Javier and Jessie are surmising that Lisa must have gone to O'Reilly's to find Ronny, Eddie is congratulating himself. He's thinking how remarkable it is that he's the one who put all the players together, he's the one who set this drama in motion, and no one is the wiser. He snaps back into the conversation just in time to hear Javier ask Jessie if she can recall anything about the other man David would hang out with when he was with Ronny. Unfortunately, Jessie can't recall anything about him. She told Lisa and the detectives that she thought his name started with a D or a B, but now she's not even sure about that. That conversation gets Eddie to thinking that maybe someone could become the wiser. Javier met Breck on Eddie's boat and now there's a picture of him circulating in the precinct. The same picture Breck mentioned when he explained why he killed Russell and Lisa. Right now, all he can hope for is that the picture is as bad as Breck said it is and then, hopefully, Javier won't recognize him. Now, Eddie snaps back into the conversation just in time to hear Javier say he thinks they are done. He asks Eddie if there is anything he can think of that they haven't discussed already and Eddie says there isn't.

On their way back to the car they discuss the two new pieces to the puzzle. Now they know why Lisa, and presumably Russell, were in that neighborhood last night. And, they know that Ronny was already dead when Lisa went looking for him. That, however, makes Javier and Eddie, outwardly at least, wonder who Lisa and Russell met there last night. Again, Javier calls Captain Upton to give him the latest update. While he's doing that Eddie is wondering if they will be able to get through the day without seeing the picture that's circulating. Then it wouldn't matter if Javier recognizes Breck because once they leave Los Angeles, Breck won't ever be seen again anyway. Excited by this new possibility Eddie feigns interest in Javier's conversation with the Captain until he gets an email. If life really does come down to just a few moments, then Eddie is having one of those moments right now. The email is from Eddie's banker. It was sent to inform Eddie that a deposit has been made into his account. Per Eddie's instructions, his banker has wired enough to Viking to cover the balance for the boat, and the remainder of the deposit is sitting in his account.

1:30pm - The way it is supposed to work is not the way it's working. Normally, when someone gets knocked out and wakes up, only to find that they have been tied to a chair at their wrists and ankles, they are the one who's supposed to be afraid. Normally, they are the one apologizing for whatever they did that got them there. In this case, however, it's William and Megan who can't apologize enough. Admittedly, William didn't intend to hurt Gino. His only intention was to stop him from physically pushing them around. Because the two of them won't stop apologizing Gino isn't suffering from fear. William says, "Really, I didn't mean to hurt you and I'm sorry we had to tie you up. We just really need to talk."

Gino says, "OK, OK, OK already. Would it help if I say I accept your apology?"

"Only if you really mean it."

"Really? You guys must be new at this sort of thing. Well, since you have a captive audience why don't we just get to it. What's this about?"

"My wife was killed recently."

Gino interjects, "I'm sorry to hear that."

"She dated Teddy many years ago."

Again Gino interjects, "And you think Teddy did it? That's absurd. Teddy was too much of a wimp to do something like that. He couldn't even do what you've done here today."

Megan adds, "You're right about. We don't think Teddy did it. We think whoever killed Teddy had something to do with it."

Gino turns to Megan with a renewed interest. "You said your name is Megan right? I have heard of you. I didn't think you'd be as attractive as you are. You're hot. What did you see in Teddy? You certainly could have done better than him."

William isn't pleased with Gino. He, obviously, isn't taking this as seriously as he should. William says, "We need to stay focused on why we're here."

Gino ignores William and continues his play with Megan. "I'll give you credit though. If what I heard is true, you left Teddy and broke his heart. You finally woke up huh?"

William, trying to refocus the conversation, says, "We want to get out of here as soon as possible so we can go about our business, and you can get back to yours. So stop playing around and just answer the few questions we have for you."

Gino turns back to William and says, "I'll tell you what. Why don't you untie me and leave, and I promise I won't call the police."

"So, we're back to square one. Is that it?"

"No, too much has happened already for us to ever get back to square one, but if you're asking if I intend to answer your questions, the answer is no. Now, untie me!"

For a moment time stops for William. Everything has come down to this. Why can't people just be helpful? Why don't people take him seriously? And then it hits him and he knows why. He reaches into his pocket and he pulls out the gun. Instead of recoiling, the sight of the gun makes Gino more brazen. He asks, "What are you going to do with that pop gun?" William never intended to shoot Gino with it. He didn't even intend to threaten that he would. He did exactly what he thought of doing with it. He slammed the side of the gun into Gino's left temple, almost knocking him and the chair he's sitting in, over. Megan's eyes are as wide as they have ever been. She would say something or, at least, gasp, but she's too shocked to move a muscle. That's for the best anyway. At this point William isn't aware that she's still in the room. His entire attention is focused on Gino, who says, "What about you saying you didn't mean to hurt me?"

William replies, "Maybe you didn't hear me. I said my wife was recently murdered. I didn't say she was hurt or that she was killed in an accident. I said my wife has been murdered. I am looking for the person who did it, and I think you can help me. If you think I'm here to play with you, you're wrong about that."

"If you don't untie me . . ." He doesn't finish that sentence because he sees William raise his hand preparing to hit him with the gun again. Instead he says, "Alright, alright, what do you want to know?"

"Did Teddy ever mention a detective named Edward Roberts?"

"The name sounds familiar but I can't be sure."

"Did you know that Teddy was an informant for the police?"

"Yes. I found that out not too long ago."

"I have reason to believe that Teddy was killed. The police say he overdosed but I think his death was made to look like an overdose to cover up what really happened."

"Overdosed on what?"

"Heroin."

"In that case, my guess is you're right. There's very little chance Teddy tried heroin. That wasn't his thing. He was strictly a pothead. He was one of the biggest potheads I've ever known, but strictly a pothead. Here's something I can tell you. I know that Teddy hated the cops he was working with. He felt that they owed him money. He felt that they screwed him by cutting him out of some deal and not paying him the share he thought he would receive."

"Did he say why they owed him money?"

"Yes and no. He said he gave them some information that they profited from. He was under the impression that he'd get a piece but, apparently, he didn't. But, before you hit me with that gun again, I can tell you right now, I don't know any more about that than what I just told you."

"Don't you sell marijuana on the side? You let Teddy work for you even though you knew he was an informant?"

Gino looks over to Megan to let her know he knows where that bit of information came from. Then he turns back to William and fills him in, "My business is so small, I don't qualify as a snack. As long as I remain the tiny fish that I am, I'm protected. But, since you've brought that up I can think of a way to really help you. I had to stop using Teddy when my supplier told me that he was off limits. If you really are the big man on campus, and if you really want to know about Teddy and the police, you should talk to my supplier. You've proven you've got the balls to come in here and rough me up, but I'm just a computer geek trying to make a little extra money on the side. If you really want to know what's going on, go speak to my supplier. But, because I like you, I'm going to give you one more piece of information. If you go to talk with him the way you came to talk with me, you won't have to wonder, anymore, about who killed your wife. He's going to make it so that you can ask her personally." William takes down the information about Gino's supplier. He puts two hundred dollars on Gino's desk. He asks Megan to untie Gino's right wrist, and then the two of them back out of Gino's apartment.

2:00pm - Detective Webb and Detective Reynoso are sitting in Captain Ramirez's office bringing him up to speed and trying to make sense of what they've learned so far when the Captain takes a call from Captain Upton. Detective Webb decides that's a good time to grab a cup of coffee. When she gets back, the Captain and Detective Reynoso are taking what they know and combining it with what Captain Upton just told him. Captain Ramirez is saying, "Upton's detectives say that Lisa was looking for Ronny White. They say a source of hers told her that she might be able to find him at O'Reilly's." Detective Reynoso says, "Then she didn't know that he was dead already."

Captain Ramirez hypothesizes, "Maybe not when she spoke with her source, but she had to know that before she went to O'Reilly's last night because Russell knew he was dead. At some point yesterday they must have figured out that while she was looking for Ronny, he was looking for the person who killed Ronny. They must have gone to O'Reilly's looking for that guy."

Detective Webb asserts, "Aimee, the waitress, said that Lisa got to the bar around 8:00pm and she stayed until around 11:00pm. She said Lisa sat alone the whole night, waiting for friends that never showed up. She doesn't remember seeing Russell at all last night. James, the bartender, said that Russell got to the bar around 8:00pm and he left around 11:00pm as well. He said Russell sat at the bar alone most of the night watching a game, but he moved to a table later. He said Lisa and Russell never sat together or talked with each other. In fact, he said they were seated at opposite ends of the bar and he didn't have any reason to believe they were together."

Captain Ramirez asks, "Did he say if Russell asked him anything?"

Detective Reynoso responds, "We asked him that more than once. He swears that other than polite small talk and taking his orders, he and Russell didn't speak at all."

Captain Ramirez asks, "Did you show them the picture?"

Detective Webb adds, "Sure. Both the waitress and the bartender said they didn't recognize the person in the picture and neither of them remember seeing anyone who resembles it in the bar last night or any night for that matter."

Captain Ramirez professes, "I find it hard to believe that Russell worked as hard as he did for that lead and then he sat on it. If he and Lisa went to that bar and just sat around for three hours, without talking to anybody, then why are they dead? We know nothing of theirs was taken before or after they were killed. So, if they were just two separate individuals sitting in a bar, who would have a reason to kill them? It doesn't make sense."

Detective Webb says, "If they didn't speak to the bartender or the waitress maybe they spoke with some of the other people that were there. We have them compiling a list of the people that were there based on their memory and their credit card receipts."

Detective Reynoso adds, "By the way, we gave the rest of the pictures to an Officer Warren. He distributed them to the other uniforms. By the time we left the bar, no new leads had turned up on that front yet."

"Yeah, I told Officer Warren to look out for the two of you. What did you think about him?"

Detective Webb says, "We liked him right away. He seems really smart and a step ahead."

"Yeah, I'm hearing that a lot about him. I think he's on the fast track for making detective." Captain Ramirez's assistant interrupts their meeting via the intercom. She says she has a call for the detectives. It's Officer Warren calling for them and he says it's important. The three of them smile at each other and the Captain tells her to put the call through. The Captain answers. He explains that the detectives are sitting in his office, and tells the officer that he's putting him on speaker phone.

Officer Warren announces, "I think we may have gotten lucky. I just spoke with a man named Charles Clarke. He was at the bar last night. He stopped by the scene when he heard about it on the news. I think you're going to want to talk with him."

2:30pm - Megan and William are on the same page for the same reason, but neither of them are speaking of it. Both of them recognized the address on San Juan Court when Gino gave it to William. Without discussing why, both of them think that it's best to find someplace where they can eat and talk before making their next move. While they wait for their food, they take out the list of Teddy's friends hoping to find someone they prefer to talk with, other than Gino's supplier. Quickly, however, it becomes apparent that, of the people on the list, Gino was their best bet. They could stop by Tommy's apartment again, but they both know that's just a waste of time. Even if he's there, he's likely to know less than Gino. With no other workable options, William decides he has to go back. Megan admits, "Lexi told me what happened to you the first time you went to that house."

"Did she tell you that the fat guy who appears to be the boss promised to kill me if he ever saw me again?"

"Yeah. And, he might."

"You obviously know him. Who is he?"

Megan concedes, "He's a bad seed. I've thought a lot about him, and the best explanation I've been able to come up with is that he was born without a conscience."

"How do you know him?"

"That's not really important."

"I don't think you should come with me. I think he's too dangerous."

"I have been avoiding that place for months now. The last thing I want to do is go there. But, believe me, if you are going to go back to that house you want me to go with you."

"What does that mean?"

"I don't want to talk about it. Let's just finish our food. If we are going to that house, then let's just do it and get it over with."

3:00pm - "I think we have a problem," Officer Warren says to Detective Webb and Detective Reynoso when they pull up in front of Charles Clarke's house.

Detective Webb asks, "What's the problem?"

Officer Warren divulges, "I just knocked on his door to tell him you'd be here shortly, and now he says he doesn't want to talk to the police."

Detective Webb asks, "Why? What happened?"

"I don't know," claims Officer Warren.

Detective Reynoso asks, "Where were you when you took his statement?"

Officer Warren explains, "We were standing across the street from the car. If I had known what he was going to tell me I would have taken him somewhere else to talk. Still, I didn't see anyone from the bar watching us talk. And, as soon as I finished taking his statement I told him to go home and wait for us there."

Detective Webb tells the young Officer, "Get in the car. Let's talk for a minute." Once Officer Warren gets in the car they drive around the block and park so they could talk there. Detective Webb continues, "OK, so tell us again, exactly what he told you." Officer Warren retells the story, "I was standing close enough to him to overhear his conversation with someone else. He told that person that he was in the bar last night. Apparently, he's a regular because the person he was speaking with said something that made me think he wasn't surprised to hear that. I approached Mr. Clarke and asked him if it was true that he was in the bar last night. He said yes. I asked him what time he got there. He said he got there around 9:00pm and stayed until closing. I showed him the picture and asked if he had seen anyone in the bar that resembles the person in the picture. He said no, but that's when he said he saw a man show JT, the bartender, a picture. He said JT took the picture from the man, to look at it, and then he gave it back to him. He said he saw the two of them talk for a while. He assumed they were talking about the picture because he remembers thinking to himself, that that guy must be looking for somebody. He said that was all he thought about it. He said later, when he went back to the bar to order another drink he had to wait for a minute because JT was talking with man, who, at that time, was still sitting at the end of the bar. Later, in the night, he noticed that the man moved to a table by the entrance. After that, however, he doesn't remember seeing the man in the bar for the rest of the night. I asked him to describe the person he saw talking with the bartender and he described the deceased. I know the bartender claims that he didn't talk with the deceased, except to take his orders, so I thought I should let you know what I found out."

Detective Reynoso voices, "Not only does he claim he didn't talk with Mr. Armstrong, he also claims that Mr. Armstrong never showed him a picture or asked him any unusual questions."

Detective Webb volleys to Detective Reynoso, "Maybe somebody from the bar got to him and told him to keep his mouth shut?"

Officer Warren remembers, "You know what, when I first started speaking with Mr. Clarke the person I overheard him talking with told him to shut up because he didn't know what he was talking about. I asked that man to excuse us so we could speak, and he went away. I assumed he said that because it's apparent that Mr. Clarke has a drinking problem. I mean, while we were speaking earlier he wasn't slurring his words or exhibiting any other signs of intoxication, but when you see him you'll see what I mean. Do you think he told someone that Mr. Clarke is talking with the police?"

Detective Reynoso responds, "It's possible. There's only one way to find out. Let's go have a conversation with Mr. Clarke."

Officer Warren worries, "What if he doesn't want to talk with us?"

Detective Webb declares, "Watch and learn kid. Watch and learn."

3:30pm - Their meeting started in Captain Upton's office but it never got off the ground. Before they were all seated comfortably the Captain's stomach started to growl, and he realized he hadn't eaten anything all day. He suggested they walk to the diner just down the street and have their meeting there. Now, having placed their orders, the Captain is ready to get back to business. The first topic up for discussion is last night's double homicide. The Captain tells Javier and Eddie that after he spoke with them he spoke with Captain Ramirez. He says, "So far, what we've have been able to piece together is that Lisa probably spoke with Russell at some point yesterday afternoon. We all think that he filled her in on the fact that Ronny was already dead, and he told her about what he had spent his day doing. Captain Ramirez says they have proof that Russell and Lisa were both in O'Reilly's last night together." Javier asks, "If they already knew that Ronny was dead why would they go there?"

Captain Upton explains, "According to Ramirez, O'Reilly's is a known underworld hang out. His thinking is that they went there either hoping to find the guy in the picture or hoping to find a lead on who he is."

Eddie asks, "Didn't you say that Ramirez's people have copies of the picture, and that they are following up that lead?" Before the Captain can answer, two detectives from their precinct stop by the table to congratulate Eddie on his retirement and wish him well.

When they leave the Captain continues, "Yeah, they do have copies of the picture. They've been going door to door in the neighborhood, and they've spoken with some of the employees of the bar. So far, no one recognizes him. That reminds me, I have a copy of the picture as well." The Captain looks through the file he has with him, but before he finds the picture their food arrives. "I'll show it to you after we eat."

While they eat their conversation spans several subjects. They discuss the homicides a little further, they discuss other cases the department is working on, they discuss Bobby, they discuss Eddie's plans for retirement, and they discuss how their unit will work after Eddie leaves and, if and when, Bobby returns. The whole time Eddie is dying to see the picture, but he doesn't want to call any more attention to it than it deserves. So, he waits, hoping the Captain will forget. And, he almost did. They got through their meal. The Captain had a cup of coffee after. He gave their server the money to pay for their meal. But, while he was waiting for his change, he remembered. He searched through his file again and this time he finds it. The Captain gives the picture to Eddie first. His immediate, out loud response is, "This isn't much to work with." Inwardly, however, he's thinking that the picture is good enough for someone who knows Breck to recognize that it's him. He hands the picture to Javier, who looks at it without a comment. Without trying to appear that he's doing so, Eddie studies Javier looking for any reaction, but none is forthcoming. Javier hands the picture back to the Captain, still without any comment.

While taking the picture back from Javier the Captain says, "I'll make sure the two of you get a copy of this picture when we get back but, like I said earlier, Ramirez's people are following this lead.

Truthfully, Javier, you're the only who's going to need it. Our boy here is almost done."

Javier already has a question in mind, he just has to figure out how to get to it without tipping his hat. The Captain may have just given him a way in. As the three men get up to leave, Javier begins with, "So how does it feel to have your money in the bank and about an hour of work left?"

Eddie declares, "It feels great. And, I have to spend this last hour filling in paperwork so I can get my pension."

Captain Upton says, "Ouch, now you're just rubbing it in."

As they walk back to the precinct Javier keeps Eddie engaged in conversation about his plans. He asks, "So, are you still planning to set sail tonight?"

"Yeah, that's the plan."

"Tell the Captain about your route."

Captain Upton, unwittingly, plays along. "Yeah, I'm all ears. What's the plan?"

"It's simple really. I'm going to go from Marina Del Rey to Cabo San Lucas and from Cabo San Lucas to my slip in Marina Papagayo, Costa Rica."

Javier adds, "And, Cap, I know you saw the pictures of his boat but they don't really do it justice." "Yeah, I wish I had been able to find the time to see it for myself but we've been so busy."

Javier asks, "Did you always want to have a boat and how did you decide on that one?"

Eddie answers, "I always fantasized about having a boat, but I wasn't ever sure I would have one. I chose "Miss Behavin" because she was the most boat I could buy for the money."

Javier says to the Captain, "I met one of Eddie's boating friends while I was on his boat." Then he turns to Eddie and says, "What kind of boat does he have and what was his name again?"

Eddie didn't see that one coming though he recognized Javier's sudden interest in his plans as suspect. Javier may have thrown him a curve ball when he was looking for a fast ball, but he's confident he can handle it. Confidently he states, "His name is Breck. He isn't a friend of mine. He has a boat a few slips away from mine, or so he says. I have never seen it."

Javier got what he was looking for. He didn't really care whether or not that guy had a boat or what kind of boat was it. So, his reply is, "Oh, I'm sorry. I thought he was a friend of yours."

"No, in fact, I hardly know him."

Just to keep the charade going Javier continues with, "And then once you get to Costa Rica, are you going to live on your boat or buy a place down there?"

"I haven't really thought that far ahead. I plan to live on the boat for a while. I'll look into whether I want to buy a house, a month or two, or more, after I get there."

As the three men walk into the precinct Javier finishes up with, "You're a lucky man."

The Captain adds, "You sure are."

Eddie wraps it up with, "Don't I know it."

As soon as they enter the building the three men go their separate ways. As soon as Eddie is out of sight Javier goes to the Captain to get his copy of the picture. Eddie can fill out the forms he needs to complete in the personnel office, but he decides to complete them at his desk so he can keep an eye on Javier. By the time he gets back to his desk Javier isn't anywhere to be found. Eddie, nonchalantly, looks for Javier in the bathroom.

Not finding him there, Eddie hastily makes his way to the parking area and, sure enough, Javier's car is gone. Eddie takes out his cell phone, thinking to himself that Breck better pick up the call.

4:00pm - The look-out's normally intimidating stare is replaced with disbelief. By the time William and Megan are across the street from the house the look-out has seen enough, and he goes inside to tell the others. Megan and William haven't said a word to each other since they got out of the car and started their walk towards the house. Both of them are as unsure as the other of what awaits for them there. By the time they reach the front gate on the fence that surrounds the house, Lexi is standing on the porch waiting for them. When they get to the top of the porch stairs she opens the door without saying a word to either of them and as if she's never seen either of them before. Neither Megan nor William make any attempt to speak with Lexi because they both know that would only cause trouble for her. Up until now William has been calm and steady, but as he steps foot inside the house he can feel himself battling anxiety. To make matters worse Wade and KiKi are standing in the living room, obviously waiting for him. They are accompanied by two other young men and by two young woman, whose breasts are the only indication of their gender. The additional men and the two woman are as bald and as tattooed as Wade and KiKi. Immediately, William and Megan's senses are overwhelmed. There is the strong scent of burning cedar wood incense throughout the house and each of the nine televisions hanging on the wall are on. Some are showing television stations and others are showing video games, but all of them have their volumes up. It's impossible to make out what any one show or game is saying. The volumes aren't loud enough to be deafening, they're just loud enough to mask any noise coming from inside the house. Both William and Megan find the noise disturbing. Music is also playing in the background just to add to the confusion. Once William and Megan are in the house Lexi closes the door behind them, from the outside, and she walks away. For the briefest of moments it appears to William that Wade and KiKi want to talk instead of fight, but that thought lasted just long enough for Wade and KiKi and the four others to get into position. Then all hell breaks loose. The six people surrounding William and Megan start screaming at them simultaneously. None of their questions are meant to be answered. They are delivered to disorient the two of them further. At the same time Wade lands the first punch to William's mid-section, and one of the women does the same thing to Megan. Before they know it they are both on the floor being slapped around and stripped of their clothing. The slaps and the punches aren't designed to hurt either of them, rather they are thrown just to let William and Megan know that resisting is pointless. Once both William and Megan are stripped down to their underwear they are stood up, blindfolded, and dragged down to the basement. The screaming and the insults keep flying at William and Megan, but their captors seem less intent on causing bodily harm and more intent on getting them into position. In the basement each of their wrists are tied to a beam across the ceiling and each of their ankles are tied to rings on the floor, so that Megan and William are hanging from the ceiling, side by side and spread eagle. The six people who got them there retreat and go upstairs, but not before KiKi is able to sneak in one good punch to William's side, just for good measure.

William waits to hear KiKi reach the top of the stairs before he asks, "Are you OK?"

Megan answers, "Yeah, you?"

William confesses, "Compared to my first visit, they were gentle."

Megan warns, "I wouldn't let my guard down if I were you. We are far from being out of trouble."

The two of them hang there for a few minutes more until they hear the unmistakable sound of him laboring down the stairs. The closer he gets the more the sounds of his footsteps gets drowned out by the sound of his heavy breathing. William and Megan can tell that he's standing right in front of them, but they can't see or hear what he's doing, and that makes them tenser than they have been since they first walked in. The longer nothing happens the more anxious William becomes. Soon he's flinching, as if he's preparing himself to be hit, each time the heavyset man makes a sound other than breathing. Finally, he removes their blindfolds, first Megan's and then William's. The heavyset man with the Fu Manchu mustache and the ponytail stands before them and his eyes are blood red.

"What the fuck are you doing here?"

William speaks first, "I know you . . ."

The heavyset man barks, "Shut the fuck up! I'm talking to her."

Megan capitulates, "You know I wouldn't come here unless it is really important. We need your help Kevin."

William, under his breath but loud enough to hear, repeats, "Kevin?"

The heavyset man reaches into his pocket and pulls out a reverse double action, out-the-front knife. He exposes the blade, and then he walks over to William and promises, "Say my name one more time and I'll cut out your tongue and put it with the others."

Megan trumpets, "William, don't ever say his name again. He will cut out your tongue. I've seen him do it. You'll be lucky if that's all he does. I know the two of you have met already but Kevin, that's William and William, that's my cousin Kevin, the genius who set me up with Teddy."

4:30pm – Luckily, Breck did answer his phone and he was off the boat and through the side gate two minutes later. There's a Coffee Bean and Tea Leaf directly across the street from Viking Motor Yachts. It's the perfect place to watch the boats come and go, in and out of the Marina, and it's the perfect place to sit and watch who goes in and out of Viking. Breck makes it to the coffee shop with enough time to order an espresso and to take a seat against the window. He takes his tablet out and pretends to be on that while he sits and waits. Eddie was right. Breck watches as Javier pulls into the parking lot, parks, and walks towards the entrance with a large envelope in hand. As Breck watches Javier enter the building he's comforted by the fact that he followed Eddie's instructions for getting on and off the boat to the letter. He's not sure if anyone has seen him, but he knows he hasn't spoken with anyone or even made eye contact with anyone with the exception of Javier. He wishes he could share Eddie's belief that they have nothing to worry about, but he doesn't. Maybe it's true that no one at Viking can tell Javier anything that he doesn't know already, but he does have a picture of Breck and he's obviously looking for him. Breck decides to stay right where he is, to sip on his espresso, and wait. In the meantime, he calls Eddie to tell him that his suspicions were correct. Again, Eddie tells him not to worry. His only instruction for Breck is to keep an eye on Viking until he sees Javier leave. He tells Breck not to go back to the boat for the rest of the day. Finally, he tells him to stay out of sight, and to call him back as soon as he sees Javier leave. A few minutes later Breck sees Javier exit the building. He watches him as he walks back to his car. Almost as if Javier can hear Breck thinking his name, Javier turns towards the coffee shop and looks directly at Breck. Just as quickly as he looked in that direction, he looked back in the direction he is walking.

Javier, while walking back to his car, is thinking about Heidi who said she didn't recognize the man in the picture, not as a visitor and not as a client. Javier is wondering what that means when he glances over to the coffee shop across the street. Suddenly he stops in his tracks and looks back to the window where the man, who was watching him, was sitting. He's no longer there but something in Javier is beckoning him to take a closer look. As he walks towards the coffee shop he keeps his eye on the doors to get a good look at everyone who exits. He doesn't see anyone leave who resembles the man he thought he saw. Once inside he takes a good look at everyone inside. None of the people sitting around resembles the man either. Next, he waits on line for the bathroom. There's a lady in front of him so he waits his turn. The person who comes out isn't the man and once the lady leaves he enters and finds no one, other than himself, in there. He exits the coffee shop and looks in the parking lot, and up and down the street. Still, he sees no one resembling the man he thought he saw. He would have felt better if he saw someone inside who resembled the man he thought he saw. That way, at least, he could have convinced himself that he was just seeing things. But, since no one looked like the man who was watching him his senses are tingling. Had Eddie noticed that he was missing and given this guy the heads up or is he off base in thinking that the man in the picture resembles the man he met on Eddie's boat just yesterday? As Javier walks back to his car his head is swirling with conflicting ideas. Has William gotten to him and made him suspicious of Eddie, or is Eddie somehow involved with Teddy's death and, thereby, somehow involved with Geneviève's death as well? Javier thinks he's crazy to think that Eddie is involved with any of it. After all, here's a man with the world in the palms of his hands. Doing anything to destroy the life he's just been delivered is crazy. Yet, the minute he saw that picture he was certain he had seen that man before, and he knew exactly where. But, then again, Eddie explained that he wasn't a friend, just someone with a boat close to Eddie's. But, Heidi says she doesn't recognize that person at all, which makes sense if he's a visitor, but it doesn't make sense if he's a client. Javier doesn't know what to think. He hopes the drive back to the precinct will bring some clarity.

Breck watched from across the street as Javier searched the coffee shop looking for him. He watched Javier check the parking lot, and look up and down the street. Finally, he watched Javier walk back to his car and drive away. He called Eddie and recounted all of Javier's actions for him. After a short silence Eddie reiterated that they have nothing to worry about. He tells Breck that that's what detectives do. They have a hunch and then they follow it. Eddie tries to convince Breck that if they were to be in town for a few more days there might be cause for concern, but since they are leaving tonight there's nothing that Javier can turn up, between now and then, that could cause them any harm. He tells Breck all he has to do is stay away from Viking until it is time for them to leave. Breck tells Eddie that he agrees.

5:00pm - Megan was right. Having her along on this visit is what made it entirely different. This time the initial beating was a lot less violent than the first one he took. It was more like an aggressive search for recording devices. Having them tied spread eagle was done, it seems, for their amusement more than anything else. There was no apparent reason for it. After Megan explained that they needed his help the heavyset man had them untied, and he had their clothes returned to them. Those two things he did of his own free will. Talking with Megan and William, about anything, particularly Teddy, was something else altogether. The heavyset man was more than reluctant to do it. He had zero interest. His claim was that he didn't see any way it would benefit him. What he wanted was for Megan and William to leave and be happy that they could. Megan, however, begged and pleaded with him. When that didn't work, she begged and pleaded some more. Somehow she got through. The heavyset man granted them a five minute conversation.

Gino was right. The heavyset man knows almost everything there is to know about Teddy and not by coincidence. It turns out that he was the one who gave Teddy his start in the drug selling business. He knows about all of Teddy's friends and girl-friends, including "William's bitch." The first time William heard the heavyset man refer to Genny that way it stung, but he was able to talk himself out of reacting. The heavyset man seems to refer to all women that way, including Megan. He went on to tell William and Megan that he found out that Teddy was a rat about a year ago. Yeah, he heard about Teddy's beef with some cop. He doesn't know the cops last name but he's sure his first name is Eddie. But, that's all he has to say about that. He tells William that he doesn't know anything about why, "your bitch got killed." This second sting hurt more than the first. On one hand, he's sitting face to face with someone who would kill him and not think twice about it. On top of that, there are several people upstairs, all of whom would like the chance to do the same thing, especially KiKi. On the other hand, listening to this fat bastard refer to Genny that way, without saying a word, is making William feel like a dog with his tail between his legs, and he doesn't like that feeling. Still, William thinks the better thing to do is to keep quiet. Megan explains that they think that Geneviève, William's wife, was killed because of something Teddy did or said. She explains that they believe that the cops Teddy was working for killed him. And, they believe that they did that to silence him from exposing what they had done to Geneviève. The heavyset man's response is, "Why the fuck would I care about that? I didn't know that bitch. I don't give a shit about her."

"Stop calling her that," escaped from William's lips before he thought about it. He said it with his head down and almost to himself. It was like he didn't want to say it, but he couldn't help himself. Still, he said it loud enough to be heard. And, just as he suspected, the heavyset man took it as a challenge. Formidably he asks, "What!?!"

"Is this how it ends," is William's exact thought. There's no backing down from what he just said and there's no telling where it will go. But, if this is the end then so be it. William raises his head and looks the heavyset man in the eye and repeats, "I said, stop calling my wife a bitch."

The heavyset man stands up and towers over William. He exclaims, "Man, fuck you and fuck your bitch. I dare you to have one more thing to say about anything I do or say."

The moment isn't lost on William. He's not looking for a fight, at least not with him and certainly not here. But, there's only one thing to do now, and he does it. He stands up, looks up so he can stare the heavyset man in the eyes, and dares to say, "Call my wife a bitch one more time."

Before the heavyset man can respond Megan jumps in between the two men. To her cousin she requests, "Kevin, calm down."

To which he responds, "Bitch, don't think I won't have that tongue too."

Megan offers, "I'll make a deal with you. You don't call his wife a bitch anymore and I promise I'll never say your name again. If I do, feel free to make me suffer the same fate that the others have. Deal?"

The heavyset man counters her offer with, "I'll tell you what, it's time for you to take your shit and go." It's obvious that the conversation is over. Megan just has one more thought she feels the need to share. "I won't ask you again what happened. We've been through that a thousand times and you, obviously, don't want to talk about it. But, I remember the happy little man I used to babysit. I remember playing hide and go seek and red light green light one two three with him. I remember cutting the crust off your peanut butter and jelly sandwiches, just the way you liked. Most of all, I remember that you used to love me. I really miss that little man. I really miss you. No matter what, you're family and I will always love you."

As she's done a hundred times before, Megan searches his face and his eyes for any sign that something she's had to say has gotten through to him on some level. She's desperate for any sign, no matter how small, that little Kevin is still in there. But, the heavyset man says, "Take your shit and leave before I change my mind about the two of you."

Megan turns to William and says, "Let's go."

The heavyset man watches as the two of them climb the stairs. For a moment, Kevin remembers playing hide and go seek and red light green light one two three. The brief memory almost makes Kevin smile. But, the heavyset man thinks to himself,

"That was a long time ago. Everything is different now." This is the life he has chosen, and the people upstairs are his family now. Emotions are for civilians. Maybe if life had been different, he would be too. But, it wasn't, so he isn't, and he has no regrets about any of it.

5:30pm - Javier makes it back to the precinct just in time to have the last piece of Eddie's retirement cake. Eddie teases Javier about almost missing his party. Javier explains that he just had a couple of errands to run but he always planned to make it back in time to see him off. One of the other detectives at the party tells Javier that they have all done a celebratory shot of tequila, and he has to catch up in that arena as well. Egged on by the others, Javier takes his shot of tequila. Then Eddie goes back to telling the story he was in the middle of telling before Javier walked in. As Javier takes a bite of his cake his cell phone rings. It's William. He excuses himself and walks to the far side of the room so he can take the call.

William petitions Javier, "I know you don't want to hear this but I really believe Detective Roberts had something to do with Teddy's and Genny's death."

To William's surprise Javier's reply is, "I glad that you called. I thought about calling you. You're actually the perfect person for something."

Just then the small crowd of people gathered around Eddie, listening to his story, simultaneously burst out in laughter. Eddie looks around and sees that Javier is on the other side of the room on his cell. Just then his cell phone rings. It's Breck. Eddie excuses himself and walks to the opposite side of the room so he can take the call. While Eddie talks with Breck, he's keeping an eye on Javier, who appears to be telling someone to calm down.

In fact, he's saying to William, "Calm down. Even if he leaves, if we develop enough evidence against him we'll find a way to have him arrested."

William argues, "It's not that I don't believe you, I just think that once he's gone that will be the end of it."

"Listen, I have to be clear with you. I don't have any proof. I just have a suspicion. It could turn out to be absolutely nothing, which means we are right back to where we started."

"Yesterday you thought I was out of my mind. Today, maybe I'm not. I don't have anything to lose. What do you need me to do?"

Javier tells William he can't go into the details now, but he needs him to meet him at the Coffee Bean and Tea Leaf on Admiralty Way, across the street from Viking Motor Yachts at 7:00pm. William agrees to meet him there. Javier hangs up and turns around to rejoin the party. He sees several people talking in groups of two and three but he doesn't see Eddie. Finally, he finds Eddie on his cell phone on the opposite side of the room. It looks like he's having a spirited conversation with someone.

In fact, Eddie is saying to Breck, "Calm down. I'm telling you there's nothing to worry about. He followed a hunch, but he obviously came up empty. He standing just a few feet away from me having some of my retirement cake."

Breck concedes, "OK, so what's the plan?"

"I need to finish up here. From here I'm going directly to the Marina. They are having a small reception and a handing over the keys ceremony for me. It should be over by 9:00pm. So, what I need you to do is to stay away from Viking until exactly 9:30pm. Unless you hear differently from me, I'll have everything in order by then and I'll have the engines running. At 9:30pm, exactly, I want you to come through the side gate, jump on the boat and we'll push off."

"OK, I'll see you at exactly 9:30pm."

"Breck, go have a nice dinner somewhere. Or go watch a game and have a few beers. Relax. Let's not blow it now. We're just hours away from no more worries." Eddie hears someone calling his name. The others are motioning for him to get off the phone so they can say their goodbyes. "Listen, I have to get back to the party. Just relax. Don't do anything except have a nice dinner. Just stay away until 9:30pm and then we're out of LA."

Eddie hangs up on Breck and rejoins the party. One by one, Eddie's co-workers say their goodbyes and they all wish him well, including Captain Upton and Javier.

Breck will be on the boat at exactly 9:30pm, but as for dinner or watching a game and having a few beers, no. He already has other plans.

6:00pm - Pete's BMW stretch limousine pulled into his hanger on the west side of runway 16R at Van Nuys Airport at exactly 6:00pm. Michael, his Head Mechanic, was waiting for him there as instructed. Pete says, "It's good to see you Michael. Is she ready to go?"

Michael says, "It's good to see you too Mr. Jefferson. Yes sir! She's fueled and all systems are greenlight go."

"This is for you." Pete hands Michael an envelope. Michael opens it and finds a check for $50,000.00 inside.

"What is this for Mr. Jefferson?"

"The company did extremely well today. It's a bonus for your hard work."

"Mr. Jefferson, you don't know how much this means to me. The wife and I were talking, just last night, about how much we'd like to remodel our kitchen, but we really can't afford it right now. With this we have enough to do the things we want to do and we'll have plenty left over to put in the bank. Thank you sir. Thank you very much."

"You earned it."

"Well, that explains the sudden trip to Jamaica."

"Yes, it does. It wasn't my idea but I didn't need to have my arm twisted."

"Whose idea was it?"

Pete doesn't have to say a word, the answer to Michael's question can be found in one of the three Lincoln Town Cars that just pulled into Pete's hanger. In the first Town Car is Aunt Sarah and Uncle Rameez. Aunt Sarah is Pete's father's youngest sister and Uncle Rameez is her husband of twenty years. In the second car, is Canon, Aunt Sarah and Uncle Rameez's daughter and Pete's cousin. If Pete had a daughter of his own he wouldn't treat her any differently than he treats Canon. Also in the second car are Melissa and Elham, Canon's best friends. In the third car is Abbey, the person who dropped the hint that a family vacation would be a good idea. With her are Rocco, Canon's younger brother, and Alvin, Abbey's younger brother. Rocco and Alvin met each other and became fast friends before they knew about the connection between their families. The final person to make it into the third car is Adam, Canon's older brother, Pete's nephew, and the closest thing Pete has to a son now. Adam has shown a considerable interest in following in his uncle's footsteps. He's worked in the company, during his summer vacations, since he turned 15. Initially he turned down the invitation to spend a week in Jamaica, citing previous plans with his friends. But, when he found out that Elham was going, for some reason, he changed his mind. While Michael's staff loads the family's luggage into the luggage compartment, Canon, Melissa, Elham, Rocco, Alvin, and Adam climb aboard and jockey for seats. Aunt

Sarah and Uncle Rameez stop to talk with Michael briefly. They tell him how nice it is to see him again and he returns the compliment genuinely. While Aunt Sarah and Uncle Rameez climb aboard Abbey stops to talk with Michael. To say that he adores her would be an understatement. He thinks she's a fine woman and she's always treated him like family. Secretly, he wonders what is taking Mr. Jefferson so long to ask for her hand in marriage, but he knows better than to propose that subject as a topic for conversation. Still, if he was a betting man he'd put his money on that happening sooner rather than later. After Michael and Abbey exchange pleasantries, Michael turns to Pete and says, "It looks like you have everybody with you except Uncle Eli. Isn't he going?"

That question caught Abbey's attention and she waits, along with Michael, for Pete's response. Pete says, "Uncle Eli is attending to some unfinished business. I'm pretty sure he'll meet us in Negril within the week."

For Michael that's just an answer to his question. For Abbey, those are the exact words she wanted to hear. Twenty minutes later, Pete's Dassault 900LX was approaching cruising altitude and headed Southeast, on course for Montego Bay.

6:30pm - Given the omnipresent coverage the killings are receiving from the media, Breck is certain that the cops are engaged in a small manhunt for him. With each car that has gone into or come out of the Santa Monica Precinct's parking lot he wonders what they would think if they knew that he's been parked just across the street, for the last hour. Somewhere along in his career his opinion about the police changed. First, he wanted to be one of them. When that became impossible he seized an opportunity to become one of the people that makes them necessary. Early in his career he feared them. No matter what country he traveled to for work, he was always worried that he'd be discovered. But, with each job successfully completed, he started to worry less. He started to learn what they look for and how to be the opposite of that. Like now for instance, instead of hiding, he's sitting in his car, in plain sight, and he's as invisible to them as he could possibly be. He laughs to himself and says, "Case in point," as he watches Eddie pull out of the station and head south. No doubt he's heading for his boat and the reception at Viking he told Breck about. Eddie even looked in the direction of Breck's car, but he didn't see him. Spotting Eddie was easy because he's familiar with his car. Spotting Javier will be more challenging. Breck has gotten a good look at everyone who's left the precinct since he hung up with Eddie, who said that Javier was standing close by at the time. Two more cars leave and still no Javier. Just when a doubt crept into Breck's mind, there's the car he saw Javier in earlier today. And, yes, that's Javier. He starts his car and jumps into traffic just one car behind his target. As soon as Javier turned left on Lincoln Breck thought he had a bead on where Javier is going. If Breck is right and if Javier plans to stay there that could be trouble. Breck can't think of when or where he'd have an opportunity to carry out his plan. For now, he's going to have to be happy with continuing the stalk. The closer Javier gets to the Marina the more Breck worries. "What if he's going to Eddie's reception?" "What if he plans to stay long enough to see Eddie push off?" In that case there'll be no way he can get on the boat. Then it dawns on Breck that Eddie could always postpone leaving until later. Javier surely has to go home at some point. The simplicity of the solution is comical to Breck, who's staying just close enough to keep Javier in sight. To Breck's surprise Javier doesn't park in the lot at Viking. Rather, he parks in the lot of the coffee shop directly across the street. Breck parks close enough to see Javier get out of his car and walk into The Coffee Bean and Tea Leaf. He waits in his car for several minutes thinking that maybe Javier is buying a cup of coffee and will come back out and get back in his car. But, ten minutes later still no Javier. Breck considers driving by to look for Javier, but it might be too conspicuous to drive by as slowly as he may need to. He decides to take a look on foot instead. It turns out he could have driven by just as well. It doesn't take long to spot Javier. Luckily, he has his back to the window Breck is looking through. Breck thinks to himself, "OK, he's there for a meeting." Breck wonders if it's odd that Javier is there, or if it makes sense. "Maybe he lives in the neighborhood." Breck also wonders who the two people Javier is talking with are. It doesn't matter right now. He walks back to his car to wait for Javier to leave.

7:00pm - "You're going to get yourself killed if you keep this up," is Javier's warning for William. William's reply is, "Let me worry about that. The point is I have one person saying they saw Eddie and another man with Teddy the night he was killed, and I have another person saying that Teddy and a cop named Eddie were working together before they had a falling out over money." Megan adds, "And I can say for sure that Teddy knew that someone close to him was going to be killed. So, unless you know of someone else who has been murdered recently that had ties to Teddy, it had to be Genny."

Javier grants, "I'm not saying that what you've told me is worthless. I'm saying your sources are. First of all, neither of them have given you a fact we can build a case around. Let's agree for a moment that what you've said is true. What does it matter that

Eddie was seen with Teddy the night that he died. That doesn't prove anything. What does it matter that Teddy and Eddie had a falling out. Cops and informants often do. That doesn't prove Eddie had him killed. Most of all, none of what you've said, even if it's all true, even if both of your sources are willing to testify, and even if a jury was inclined to believe the word of drug dealers over a cop's, has any provable connection to your wife's murder. I'm sure you've heard this before because it's true. Cases build on what we know and what we think we know. But, whether a case gets brought before a grand jury depends on what we can prove and that depends on the authority of our sources."

William submits, "OK, so why are we here?"

Javier responds, "I asked you to meet me here because something is bugging me and if I brought it to the attention of anyone in the department they would think I'm crazy. Before I tell you what I think I know, I have to tell you two things. One, we don't have much time. If what Eddie says is true, he'll be leaving Los Angeles in an hour or two. And, two, our chances for success are one in a million if they are that good."

William mumbles, "We're listening."

Javier takes out the picture he's carrying with him and explains. "This doesn't have anything to do with Genny's case or Teddy's for that matter, but bear with me. It all started with the murder of someone named David Waverly."

Breck has done everything he can think of doing to keep himself busy. He's sure Javier is still in The Coffee Bean and Tea Leaf because it only has one entrance, which is also the exit, and he's kept a close eye on it. But, just to make sure and stretch his legs at the same time he decides to take another walk and peek in. Just as he thought, Javier is still seated at the same table talking with the same two people. The guy he's talking with seems vaguely familiar to Breck, but he doesn't think of it any more than that. What has caught Breck's attention is the item Javier has in his hand. A devilish grin surfaces on Breck's face and before he knows it, he's acting on his idea. As long as Javier's attention is on the people he's speaking with and on the entrance to Viking he should be able to get close enough to see what it is. He enters the coffee shop and makes his way closer to the window and Javier's table. He positions himself right behind Javier but he keeps his back to him, pretending that he's looking towards the entrance of the coffee shop itself. He gets close enough to hear Javier talking and what he hears alarms him. He decides to leave, but not before taking a quick glance over his shoulder to see what's resting in the middle of their table. Half way back to his car it hits him. The guy Javier is talking with is the marks husband. He only saw him once, standing outside his house, when he, Ronny, and David were driving by, but now he's sure that's him.

Javier explained how David's death led to the name Ronny White, and how Ronny White's death led to the picture. He explained how certain and uncertain, at the same time, he is of meeting that man on Eddie's boat, but he also confessed that a person who works at Viking told him that she didn't recognize that man at all. Finally, he explained that he thought he saw that man sitting in the very chair next to them at the bar along the window. Now, he's asking them to keep a look out while he crashes Eddie's reception in one last attempt to satisfy his gut feeling. He tells William and Megan, "I know what I'm asking isn't along the lines of what you were thinking but it's, literally, all I've got. After this, unless some credible evidence turns up, I don't know what I'll be able to do to help you."

William asks, "What happens if you find this guy or if we see him?"

"At the very least we can question him."

"What happens if neither of us see him?"

"In that case, we are right back to where we are now."

"As far as you're concerned that means we've got nothing and Eddie sails away without being asked a single question."

"We've been here before. I understand your frustration. Frankly, with all of your efforts you've come up empty too. I know you don't want to hear this but not every case gets solved."

William says, "This one will."

7:30pm - Breck watches Javier leave The Coffee Bean and Tea Leaf. He was about to start his car but he notices that Javier doesn't go to his car. Instead, he watches Javier cross the street and walk into Viking. He doesn't see the two people Javier was speaking with leave so, again, he gets out of his car to take a look inside the coffee shop on foot. He finds that the man and the woman have moved from their table and are now sitting along the bar facing the window. He decides the best thing to do is to go back to his car and wait. He only had to wait for ten minutes before he sees Javier coming out of Viking and heading back to the Coffee Bean and Tea Leaf.

Javier says to William and Megan, "Unfortunately, he wasn't in there. I'm sorry I got you guys involved in this. At the time I really thought I had something but obviously I didn't." William is reminded of how he felt when Javier stopped by his house to tell him that he has to turn his attention to his other cases, but this time he refrains from saying how he feels out loud. Instead, the two of them shake hands and promise to keep each other informed of any new and credible developments. Breck watches

Javier exit the coffee shop and this time he appears to be headed for his car. Breck starts his car. When Javier pulls out of the parking lot, Breck follows.

Megan feels deflated for William. To watch him go from sad, when they left the house, to excited, after they spoke with Javier, to sad again is depressing. Now he seems lost in thought. She wants to ask what he thinks they should do next but she doesn't have to. William says, "Let's ask him ourselves."

The truth is, it didn't take a lot for William to convince her to come along. She agreed with William's assertion, "What have they got to lose?" Their first obstacle was the doorman at Viking, but they got past him easily by telling him they are friends of Detective Roberts. They didn't spot the detective right away but they wouldn't have approached him first anyway. William needs a dose of liquid courage first. He drinks his first glass of champagne in one gulp before wrapping his fingers around the next. With his second glass in hand he and Megan begin their search. They find the detective in the corner of the conference room talking with two other people. Before they get to him he notices them, but it takes a second or two before he realizes who the gentleman is. It's obvious that they are making their way towards him so he decides to meet them half way. Eddie says, "Mr. Flowers, right? What are you doing here?"

William wastes no time, "What do you know about my wife's murder?"

"What?"

"What do you know about my wife's murder?"

"Are you out of your mind?" The question and the volume at which it was asked gets the attention of those standing close to the two of them.

William continues, "I know that Teddy worked for you. I know that the two of you had a falling out over money he felt you owed to him. I know that he knew someone close to him was going to be murdered. My wife was murdered. I don't know who did that, but I do know that you and another man drove Teddy home on the night he was murdered. You sat in the car while the other man did the dirty work." Now, there's a small commotion in the conference room as the guest get an earful of William and Eddie's conversation.

Eddie leans close enough to William so that only he can hear what he's about to say. "If today wasn't the day it is I'd beat the crap out of you just for insinuating that."

William yells, "Do it." Now, the doorman and another man, who's a little larger, are making their way to the conference room. "What happened? Why was my wife murdered? What did she see or hear or what did Teddy tell her?"

Eddie insists, "You don't know what you're talking about. I think you should leave." Now, the doorman and the other man are standing on either side of William. Everyone at the reception is giving their full attention to the event in the conference room.

The doorman grabs William by the arm and says, "It's time to go buddy."

William shakes his arm free and says, "No! Not until he answers my question." That makes the two men more determined to re-move him from the party. As they take hold of William and drag him out Eddie smiles and winks at him. Megan is close behind as the two men drag William out of the building and to the edge of the property. They throw him to the ground and they stand over him daring him to take another step on the premises. Megan kneels next to William and tells him that it's best if they leave now. Perhaps they have had enough for one day.

Inside Viking, Eddie is addressing the situation. He explains, "I'm sorry that happened. It's a part of my job that I won't miss. I feel bad for that guy. His wife was murdered a few months ago and we weren't able to solve it. When that happens sometimes loved ones and friends come to think that the police are holding some information back. Their frustration with the lack of answers causes them to do things like that. It's a sad thing, but today is a special day for me so I hope you won't hold it against me if I don't let that spoil my mood. More than that, I don't want that to spoil this party." He reaches for a glass of champagne, raises it, and offers a toast to his boat. "To Miss Behavin!"

A few of the guest bought his story hook, line, and sinker. They raise their glasses and repeat, "To Miss Behavin!" Some of the other guests aren't quite as boisterous. That was a bit disturbing and they aren't sure what to think. Eddie can pick out the doubters, but he couldn't care less. In about an hour all of Los Angeles, and everything in her, will be a memory.

8:00pm - Having lost sight of Javier twice and then regaining it Breck is starting to view the hunt as a game. He thinks to himself that he should be better at this given his profession. But, when he thinks about it he realizes this is truly the first time he's actually tracked someone. In all of his other assignments, information was fed to him with regard to the habits and whereabouts of his targets. All he has ever had to do was set himself up and wait. Now, three cars directly behind Javier, Breck is worried that Javier is on his way home and he won't get a chance at him. His only hope is that Javier makes one more stop before he gets home and, even then, a number of factors have to all fall in place in order for him to have an opportunity. His wish is granted when Javier turns into the parking lot of a neighborhood convenience store. Breck got the stop he wanted, but the other factors aren't cooperating. The parking lot is well lit and the store has a flow of customers going in and out of it. On top of that there are four teenagers lingering in front of the store drinking soda and eating snacks as they take a break from skateboarding. The only thing Breck can do is circle the block, park his car down the street from the entrance to the parking lot, and wait for Javier to pull into traffic again.

Inside the store Javier is on the phone with Cynthia. "I'm drawing a blank. What was it you asked me to bring home again?"

"Two cans of condensed milk."

"Condensed milk, that's it."

"You know what, don't worry about it. I can get it tomorrow. Just come home. I want to show you the beautiful ring my husband got for me."

Javier smiles and promises, "I'm in the Harvest right now, so I'll pick them up. I'll be home in five minutes."

"Hurry. I miss you. I love you."

"I'm on my way. I love you too babe."

From where he's parked Breck can't see the door to the convenience store. So, he keeps his engine running and he keeps an eye out for Javier's car. His cell phone rings. He thought about not taking the call, but it's JT calling so he answers it. JT, in a calm, cool, and collected voice, tells Breck, "The police have flooded the neighborhood. They've already interviewed me twice and they've been in and out of the bar all day."

"Yeah, well, that's to be expected. It will blow over."

"Yes, I'm sure it will, but I've been instructed to rely a message to you. The boss has confiscated and destroyed everything you had in storage. This is the part you need to pay close attention to. Your membership has been revoked. You are no longer welcome at this establishment or at any of the others in our network. Do you remember what membership revocation means?"

Breck's mind flashes back to when he became a member and the rules and responsibilities were explained to him. He can hear the boss telling him that for a member to have his membership revoked means he committed an offense to the organization that was potentially lethal. If Breck remembers correctly his exact words were. "Should a member commit such an offense he would be seen as an enemy to our way of life, and the organization would be left with no choice but to defend itself." That was all the boss said and that was all he needed to say. Breck knew that meant if he showed his face again he would be killed and he'd be lucky if they did it quickly.

To JT's question Breck answers, "Yes, but . . ."

JT stayed on the phone just long enough to hear yes. The finality of the conversation was a bit disturbing, but Breck feels, at the end of the day, it doesn't matter. After this job he doesn't have any plans for returning to the States and much less Los Angeles. If anything, the phone cemented his plans to get out of the business and into the Charter Fishing trade. Right on cue, as soon as Breck reconciled his thoughts, Javier pulled out of the parking lot. Breck follows him for three blocks along a major thoroughfare before Javier turns down a side street. The one sided conversation he just had with JT is still replaying in his head. Breck figures Javier must be close to home. Maybe the better thing to do is give up the hunt and just get out of town while he's ahead. If Javier had just driven one more block Breck would have turned off the trail and made his way back to the rental car agency. He figured he could return the car and then hang out in the Applebee's until 9:20pm, when he would start walking towards the Marina. But, Javier didn't. Javier pulled into his driveway in front of his house. Breck pulled over at the end of the block and watched, much the same way a predator watches his prey get away after the predator decides not to chase any further. From his vantage point he can't see Javier's garage, but it appears to Breck that Javier is waiting for the garage door to open before he pulls in further. Finally, he does exactly that and Breck says to himself, "Game over." Before Breck pulls out of the parking space he sees Javier walking down his driveway. At the end of the driveway are three garbage bins. Javier grabs two and rolls them up the driveway. Breck can feel a wave of excitement rush through him. Without giving it a second thought he springs into action. He lowers the passenger side window, grabs his gun, and drives slowly in Javier's direction. He timed it perfectly. Just as Javier makes it back to the curb to retrieve the third garbage bin Breck is driving by the front of the house. The speed the car, or lack thereof, caught Javier's attention. He looked up just as Breck was directly in front of him. Their eyes met for the second time in one day. Breck drives away, leaving Javier lying on his back, in his driveway, with a bullet hole in the middle of his forehead.

8:30pm - The street is lined with cars filling every available parking space. The candlelit house that sits in the middle of the block has a steady flow of people entering it. Gita, Lisa's mother, and her second husband, Jonas, are bravely welcoming everyone who arrives, and graciously thanking them for coming. They invite their guest to eat and drink, all the while doing their best to keep a stiff upper chin. Once inside the house the guests can view dozens of pictures of Lisa. The pictures visually document

Lisa's entire life, from birth to death. The pictures that provoke the most emotions are the pictures of her, as a child, with her father. One after another each guest comments on how incomprehensible it is that two of this world's most lovely and loving people are now gone, entirely too soon. The other pictures that are just as provoking are the ones with Lisa and Russell. Those pictures are moving exhibitions of how much he loved her. He's in her graduation pictures, her recital pictures, her team pictures, and he's in the pictures of her at the beach, at Six Flags, and at Disneyland. On the walls are hung many of the articles he's written over the years. Hung most prominently, however, on the wall just beside the entrance to the kitchen is the article that Lisa and Russell wrote together. It was her first published article. Clearly, there is as much love in this house for Russell as there is for Lisa. It's only nervous energy keeping Gita upright. She goes from the front door to the kitchen to make sure everyone has enough to eat and drink, and then back to the front door again to greet more guests. Her friends ask what they can do to help, but Gita won't hear of it. She just wants everyone to eat, drink, and be happy. For now, this is how she's dealing with her grief. As she leaves the kitchen for the fourth time her guests comment on her display of strength. Only seconds later they hear a loud, haunting wail followed by deep, continuous, and increasingly disconsolate sobbing coming from the living room. There they find Gita and Tony locked in an embrace, and Jonas standing outside their embrace with his arms draped over both of them.

9:00pm - Eddie's smile and wink seared itself in William's mind indelibly. That smile and that wink are like colliding hydrogen atoms in the core of the Sun. The only thing stopping William from exploding is gravity; the gravity of Genny's death and the gravity of William's determination to follow the path he's on until it leads to a rightful conclusion. In truth, he has Eddie to thank for his renewed energy. Having turned up nothing but remote speculation over the last few days and with Eddie leaving the country, William, before the smile and the wink, was running out of ideas, running out of support, and running out of energy. Now, the probability of William collapsing has gone from 80% to zero. Replaying that smile and that wink is William's endless source of self-sustaining energy. Megan was right when she said they had enough for one day. After the excitement of the quarrel with Eddie and the excitement of flap with the two gentlemen who escorted William off the property wore off, William settled back into his right mind, and the ride back to the hotel was calm and peaceful.

Rumors about William, among the hotel's employees, started the day he moved in. If any of them had bothered to read about the current events, either on paper or over the internet, they would have found out exactly who he is and what brought him to their hotel. But, none of them did. If they had that would have taken all the fun out of it. They preferred to create scenarios. Some were outlandish and others were reasonable. That's not what mattered. The fun of the game was the constant guessing and the constant reinventing of possible explanations. The game went into hyper-drive with the appearance of Megan. For, at least, one of the employees, Gael, the game became less fun because there appeared to be evidence that William was heterosexual. Gael developed a crush on William the minute he met him. Before Megan showed up Gael was quick to attend to each of William's requests personally. After Megan, he became a lot less interested. Today, however, his interest is peaking again. It isn't because of his sexual attraction to William this time. It's because the two of them returned to the hotel looking disheveled, and now his curiosity is getting the better of him. So, when the request for ten large buckets of ice came through for room 107, Gael, again, saw to it personally. When he gets to their room he finds the door slightly ajar, but he knocks anyway. It's Megan's voice that invites him in. He finds her in the kitchen area preparing food. She tells him the ice is for William and she asks Gael to take it to the bathroom where he will find him. Gael finds William sitting in the bathtub, in chest high water, with just enough suds to cover that portion of his body that is beneath the water line. William opens his eyes just long enough to see that it is Gael who brought the ice. He asks him to pour all of it into the bathtub and Gael happily obliges. Seeing William naked in the bathtub excites Gael enough to throw him off of his game. Instead of looking around their suite for clues, or instead of being more direct by asking questions, all he did, on his way out, was say to Megan, "You're a lucky woman."

The minute those words came out of his mouth he regretted saying them. Clearly he just crossed the line between employee and guest. What's done is done. All he can do now is hope that she wasn't offended enough to bring what he said to the attention of his superiors. Unbeknownst to Gael, Megan wasn't the least bit offended. Initially she thought the sentiment was kind of funny. It's obvious, at least to her, that Gael is homosexual. Her second thought is, "I wish." Sure William is handsome. She knew that when she met him. But, now, having spent the last few days with him she knows he's everything, and more, she wants in a man. She feels torn for thinking selfishly of how to make him hers, especially while he seems to be thinking of nothing but

Genny. Still, she doesn't want him to get away. She wants him for herself. She decides right there and then that tonight, if need be, she'll be the aggressor. Tonight the two of them will make love, hopefully, for the first time of many.

9:30pm - Everything that's happened over the last ten years have led to this very moment. Getting the email from his banker, informing him that the money had been deposited, was the appetizer. Now, it's time for the main course. And like a guest in a five star restaurant, Eddie savors the moment before taking his first bite. When he pushes the ignition button his inboard, dual, 550 HP diesel engines purr to life. The sound of the engines combined with the churning water beneath the boat and the accompanying vibration are euphoric for Eddie. It's not like he hasn't heard this sound or felt this vibration many times before. He has. But, this time, the boat is officially his and that makes the same sound and the same vibration even more satisfying. He can't think of a single thing he hasn't double checked twice. He's fully stocked, fully fueled, his navigation system is engaged, and he's ready to go. The only thing keeping him in place are the last two ropes that are still tied to the cleats on the slip. Right on time he hears someone jump onto the boat. He looks down from the fly bridge and tells Breck to untie the last two ropes. Eddie hoped Breck was, at least, smart enough not to ruin the moment. Thankfully, Breck stayed below deck while Eddie navigated through the Marina. He only came above deck when Eddie started to turn southward. He came up to the fly bridge, stood behind Eddie, and he didn't say a word until they were well past the Jetty and headed for the open ocean. If any tension existed between the two men it was gone for now. The two of them are all smiles and laughs now. Eddie tells Breck to get a bottle of champagne from the galley. Soon the two men are toasting to the boat, toasting to getting the job done, toasting to their new adventure, and high fiving each other relentlessly. They both feel like the weight of the world has been lifted off their shoulders. The breeze and the sea air are more intoxicating than the champagne. They both wish this moment could last forever.

Of course it can't and it doesn't. As soon as the celebration dies down the two men's thoughts turn to what's next for each of them. For Eddie, the next thing he's looking forward to is watching the sunrise from his Captain's Chair on the fly bridge. For Breck, the next thing he's looking forward to is collecting his money. The two men engage in small talk for a few minutes more. When they run out of things to say Breck excuses himself, telling Eddie he's going to go to his stateroom to lie down for a minute. At the risk of ruining the moment and against his better judgment Eddie asks, "So, what did you do with yourself while you waited."

Breck invents, "I took your advice. I want to Applebee's, watched a game, and had a few drinks." Eddie's natural inclination is to disbelieve almost everything Breck says, but, for now, that's good enough. His reply is a simple, "Thanks."

"No problem," says Breck, and then he leaves Eddie alone with his thoughts and his boat.

10:30pm - If she's told herself once, she's told herself a thousand times, "Expectations always lead to disappointment." And, for Megan, disappointment is like quicksand. Whenever her hopes of escaping the life she knows get high, they always come crashing down to a new and deeper low. It's not the disappointment that she's afraid of. What frightens her is the pain of reality that accompanies each new low. Only that pain is severe enough to make her second guess every step she has ever taken and every word she has ever said. It's times like this that make her think about all of the little things she could have done and should have done differently, and what her life might be like now if she had. Little things like homework and studying for tests, like listening to her mother when she said Megan partied too much, like saying no to drinking and smoking to appear cool to the friends she didn't even like having. All of those things, and more, seemed so uncool at that the time but each time the pain of reality blankets her, she can hear the friends she thought were uncool then, ask, "Who's uncool now?" Making matters worse is the one thing she has always been able to rely on has failed her this evening. No man, or woman, has not noticed Megan when she wants attention. Her looks and her body, when used with a certain intention in mind, have always gotten her the results she sought. But, tonight they didn't. As she lies in bed, alone, and crying, her tears aren't a release from not feeling wanted. Though she had hoped that she and William would be enjoying the ecstasy of making love at this very moment, she understands that it's still too soon, and she can live with that. Her tears fall for the uncertainty that is her life.

Something in William changed after his encounter with Eddie at the Marina. On one hand, he seemed at peace. She even noticed that he was smiling on the drive back to the hotel. But, on the other hand, he's barely said ten words to her since. He took three, maybe four, bites of the food she prepared for him. And, most troubling to Megan, immediately thereafter he got up from the table and lied down on the living room floor, without saying a word, and went to sleep. He acted as if she wasn't there. Right now she doesn't know what that means. She's worried that they could be done before they had a chance to get started, but that only leads to her kicking herself for thinking there could ever be a "they." She's worried that since Eddie is gone William may want to move on and start a new life someplace else. If that's the case, he probably won't want her to come along. Given the distance she felt between the two of them tonight, she's worried that soon he won't want to see her again. That leads to her kicking herself for getting involved in the first place. Before she met William, she was sleeping on the couch at Yezzy's, looking for a job, and trying to think of a way to get to a better life, with better friends. To her credit she had already come to the conclusion that she needs to be better herself in order to get those things. She thought she was doing that by helping William. Now, she's worried that she was just fooling herself again. If she can think of what to do next she would feel better, but she can't. She can't get past William not speaking to her and she can't get past the uncertainty of not knowing what that means.

Between sobs she hears William talking. Thinking that he must be awake and calling for her she jumps out of bed and goes into the living room. There she finds William still asleep. As she stands over him she can see discomfort register in his face as he tosses and turns, but when he finally settles down again she sees him smiling. That's when she realizes that he wasn't talking to her. He was talking to Genny.

11:00pm - The compass reads that the heading is fifteen degrees south-southeast, and they are cruising along at ten knots. The boat is on course at a snail's pace, but that's just the way Eddie wants it. As he pours himself another cup of coffee, he realizes he hasn't heard from Breck in a while. That too is just the way he wants it. Hopefully, he thinks, Breck is asleep and won't bother him until sometime tomorrow morning. Eddie thinks of all the times he's flown into LAX at night. It's unlike flying into any other city. Where other cities may have a cluster of lights here and there, Los Angeles is a carpet of lights that extends out in the distance for as far as the eye can see. That has always been one of Eddie's favorite things to do and see. Now, however, he's witnessing something just as beautiful. The lights along the coast are mesmerizing. Though they aren't as concentrated as they are from above, they have a different and just as alluring quality. They seem to dance or, at the very least, they seem like notes along one long and continuous bar of music. The lights, the smell of the ocean, and the gentle sway of the boat are more relaxing than anything Eddie has ever experienced. He can feel the burden of his thoughts and his worries slipping away minute by minute. Without the constant din of his internal dialogue, he feels his mind journey to a place that's wide open and free. Now that he's alone and on course, with no obstacles ahead of him; and now that he has all of the time in the world, he doesn't fight his mind's desire to travel through space and time. Rather, he settles back in his Captain's Chair and enjoys the ride.

The journey begins in the future. Eddie imagines what he might do upon arriving in Costa Rica. He sees himself living on his boat, entertaining the friends he's yet to meet. He sees himself riding a horse through a meadow and then he sees himself riding that same horse along a beach. In both scenarios the ride comes to an end when Eddie gets to the house he's bought for himself. The house is the same whether he sees it in the middle of a meadow or on a beach. It's white with glass windows from the floors to the ceilings. There's so much sunlight coming into the house he only has to turn on his lights at night. There's a fireplace in the living room and another, even larger, one in his bedroom. There are paintings, and sculptures, and pictures everywhere. In his marble tiled bathroom, on the sink, next to his toothpaste is the picture he cherishes most in the world. It's a picture of himself when he was sixteen. He's handsome, tall, and cock strong. More than any other day since taking that picture, he feels he resembles that guy today. Still, he thinks about the day that picture was taken. He thinks about growing up in Simi Valley and he thinks about his family and friends. He remembers high school there. He remembers being a second string quarterback on the football team. He remembers Heather, his first love, and their first kiss. He remembers the night they had sex for the first time. It was the first time for both of them, and they both found it more comical than romantic. He remembers joining the police academy, when some of his friends were joining the fire department, others were looking for jobs having no sense of career, and others went off to college. He remembers his first and only wife, Dorothy, and how happy they were for five years. But, after five years he remembers feeling trapped in a bad dream. He thinks about having to downsize everything after their divorce. The only thing he was grateful for, at the time, was that they didn't have any kids. Though, as the years went on he changed his mind about Dorothy and he changed his mind about being thankful for not having kids. By the time he was smart enough to want her back, she was engaged to a fireman that had gone to the same high school as Dorothy and Eddie, though he was in the class one year ahead of the two of them. He already had one kid and it was rumored that Dorothy was pregnant with their first child on the day they got married. Last he heard they were happy. It was during his downsized life that Carl came to him looking for money. He remembers that, at that time, he wasn't what civilians would call corrupt, which he calls opportunistic. But, he was already a detective, he was familiar with the street, and he knew a lot of the players. The stars must have been aligned that night because Carl came asking and Eddie knew where they could find. Had he not heard of the drug deal that was about to happen there would have been no way he could have come up with that kind of money. But, he did and it came with a price. Eddie thinks to himself, "What happened, happened." That's all he's allowed himself to think of it then and, despite this free and open space he's enjoying, that's all he'll allow himself to think of it now. "Suffice it to say that after that I became very opportunistic." He smiles with that thought because he doesn't feel an ounce of remorse. Not for any of it. Not even for killing the girl. With that thought Eddie's mind wants to go back to Marina earlier in the night, but Eddie won't let it. That's not what this journey is about. This journey is about good thoughts and all the things that got him to this point. He doesn't want to think about the unpleasantness of earlier in the night. So he re-directs his mind to skip ahead in the story. When it does it directs him to open his eyes and look at the reflection of himself in the glass of in front of him. Despite his explicit directions his mind journeys back to the thing he did to get the money and the thing he had to get done in order to receive it. Eddie finds that funny and, just for good measure, he decides to let his mind know who the boss is. He tells the man in the reflection staring back at him that, "given all that I have now, this boat, the money, and the freedom, I'd do everything I've done again, and if I had to do it all again, I'd do it without hesitation. I'm not sorry about any of it." He takes a sip of his coffee and checks his instruments. He smiles and thinks to himself, "Steady as she goes."

———

CHAPTER FOUR

Day Six

6:30am - Megan couldn't be happier. She woke up feeling rested and refreshed, and when she checked on William she found that he wasn't there. She almost danced back to bed to wait for William to return with coffee and pastries just as he had done yesterday. As she curls up underneath the comforter she hopes that, like her, a good night's sleep was all William needed. She tells herself that if she had just realized that last night, that would have insulated her from her fears. On the other hand, she knows she needs a good cry every once in a while and she got one last night. Maybe that's why she's feeling so parched this morning. Given her choices of going to the kitchen and getting something to drink or lying in bed and waiting for William to return, she chooses the latter. The news is still covering the double homicide from yesterday but not as prominently. The rest of the news, sports, gossip, and weather is par for the course in Los Angeles. She flicks through the channels ultimately deciding to watch music videos. A half an hour goes by and still William hasn't returned. Megan is sure that he must have left just before she woke up and, accordingly, he'll be back any minute now. Since she told him that she prefers blueberry muffins, knowing William, he'll probably come back with two just for her. She's longing for that muffin and a tall glass of orange juice. That would be perfect. Another fifteen minutes go by and still no William. Now, she's starting to get concerned. She calls him on his cell phone and her call goes straight to voicemail. Now, she's really concerned. She jumps out of bed hoping that William is still asleep and that she just didn't see him, but he's not there. And, what she didn't notice before but sees now is that everything is folded away neatly and there's a note on the kitchen table. Megan's tears start to flow again as she reads the note William left for her. First, he apologizes for not speaking with her last night or this morning, but he doesn't give her any explanation. He asks her to return the gun he's been carrying and he leaves the address and the name of the person to give it to. He tells her that he paid for the room through the end of the month, so if she wants to stay she can, but she has to pay for her meals. Finally, he says he doesn't know if he'll be back. He hopes he will and he hopes to see her again, but he doesn't know when that will be, if ever. He thanks her for all of her support and help, and then he signed the letter. Megan is so shocked and confused she has to read the letter twice to be sure that it's not a joke. If this had happened last night it would have devastated her. Although she's crying now it's not like last night. She's sad, but she understands exactly what William is telling her. She leaves the letter on the kitchen table and she prepares to jump in the shower. Her first order of business is to get that blueberry muffin and orange juice for herself. Then she plans to return the gun just as William asked. Then she'll figure out what to do next.

7:30am - The sun rose over Ensenada, Mexico at exactly 7:17am. Before that Eddie saw things he had forgotten existed. In the dark of the early morning night he gazed at the stars shining brilliantly against the black back drop of space. It was easy to find The Constellation Orion, as Orion's Belt seems to always be shining brightly in the night sky. The harder task was finding the Big Dipper. Looking north, however, Eddie was able to find it. From there he used the two stars that form the edge, furthest from the handle of the cup, to point to the North Star. As much as he enjoyed that exercise it paled in comparison to watching night give way to light. As the darkness of space mixed with the blue of the atmosphere and the bright yellow of the rising sun, the sky took on a hue of Magenta. The stars seemed to be the most incandescent and the most beautiful in the Magenta sky, just before they retreated and gave way to the sunshine. From atop his fly bridge, seated in his Captain's Chair, Eddie felt he had the best seat in the house for the main event. Only once before, in his entire life, had he stayed awake all night for the sole purpose of seeing the sun rise. On a family vacation, in his youth, to Virginia Beach he sat in a life guard's chair all night to watch the sun rise. He remembers that even as a young kid he felt something indescribable in that moment, and he's hoping for a repeat performance. Given that the sun would rise from behind mountains and hills, as opposed to from behind the horizon over the ocean as it had done while he was in Virginia Beach, Eddie was prepared for a slightly less impressive experience. But, the sun didn't disappoint him. In fact, it outdid itself. Despite being partially blocked as it rose, the power of the sun was, again, unmistakably indescribable. What made this experience better than Eddie's first, was this time it seemed to rise directly on and solely for him. He took the sunlight as a sign that all he had done has been forgiven and that everything, from this moment forward, will be great. After the moment had passed Eddie started the boat and headed into the Marina at Ensenada.

Breck can't remember ever getting a better night's sleep. His first thought was that he had never slept on a water bed but that he'd have to look into it. If it was anything like waking up on the ocean he would have to get one and he will never go back to a spring mattress ever again. Just as he convinced himself to lie in bed a little longer he felt the boat bump into something. It didn't feel hard enough to cause a problem, but the boat also came to a stop and he knew that they still had to be a long way from Cabo San Lucas. He decided to get up, though not in a rush, and go on deck to see what's going on. When he got on deck he finds Eddie tying the boat's stern to a cleat on a slip. "Morning," he says to Eddie. "What's up? Where are we?"

Eddie replies, "Ensenada, Mexico."

"I thought you said our first stop would be in Cabo?"

"That's still the plan but I need to stop here first."

"What for?"

"I need to pick up something."

"Well, let me get dressed and I'll go into town with you."

"No. I need to do this alone. I need you to stay on the boat. I'll be back in a couple of hours and then we'll take off again."

"If I have a couple of hours maybe I'll just take a short walk around town. I'll make sure I'm back before you get back."

"Do me a favor and just stay on the boat. I might be back sooner. Whenever I get back I'm going to want to leave right away."

Breck is a little put off by Eddie's request and he not a big fan of being told he can't do something, especially when there doesn't appear to be a good reason for it. On the other hand, however, having breakfast, climbing back in bed, and watching a movie isn't unappealing to him. While he fixes himself something to eat, Eddie comes below deck and goes to his berth. Breck can hear Eddie's shower being turned on and he can hear Eddie moving around in his cabin. Just as he climbed back in bed and popped in a movie he got a knock on his door. It is Eddie telling him, again, to stay on the boat, that he is leaving now, and he'll be back as soon as possible.

8:30am - From the Hotel Coral Marina Eddie takes a short walk along De La Villa and then over to Teniente Azueta where the pharmacy he's looking for is located. He has a half an hour to spare before he needs to be at their meeting place, and that should be more than enough time to get what he needs and maybe have a cup of coffee after. The pharmacy was right where his internet search said it would be. "Buenos Dias," he says to the woman behind the counter.

"Buenos días señor! ¿Cómo puedo ayudarle?"

Eddie responds, "Necesito una botella de Viagra por favor."

"¿Veinte, cincuenta o cien señor?"

"Veinte por favor."

"Sí señor! Un momento por favor." A few moments later Eddie walks out of the pharmacy, he takes two blue pills, and he walks back in the direction from which he came. He thinks about getting a cup of coffee but, surprisingly, he's feeling a little nervous, so more coffee is the last thing he needs. He wants to avoid the hotel until it's time, so he heads back to De La Villa to pass time looking at the other boats in the Marina. At 8:55am it's time to start heading for his meeting. Her text messages gave him the layout of the hotel and the best way to get to her room without calling any unwanted attention to himself. Just as instructed he entered the hotel and walked directly to the bank of elevators to his left, just to the right of the check in desk. He takes the elevator to the fourth floor and turns left off the elevator. The closer he gets the more excited he feels, but he can't deny that he's feeling nervous as well. He gets to room 421 and he hesitates for just a moment. The nervousness he's been feeling has stopped him in his tracks, and it's forced him to take an inventory of the line he's about to cross. This moment has been more than a year in the making and now that the moment is here he needs to collect his thoughts before he goes on. To push himself, he says out loud but to himself, "Well, here you go," and then he knocks on the door. Robyn opens the door wearing a full length white terry cloth bathrobe and she invites Eddie in. She asks, "Did you have any trouble getting here?"

Eddie answers, "No. Your directions were perfect." There's an awkward silence as Eddie walks deeper into the room.

Finally, Robyn asks, "Are you as nervous as I am?"

Eddie, who was looking out of her window down on the Marina, turns to her and says, "I was feeling nervous when I was walking here, but now that I'm here and now that I see you, I'm not feeling nervous at all." They are standing face to face and three feet apart. Robyn takes one step back and unties her robe. She's wearing a pink sheer Daisy Apron Babydoll. She can tell, by the look in his eyes that he likes what he sees.

She asks, "What about now?"

"No. I'm still not feeling nervous, but I am feeling something else." Robyn drops her robe to the floor and Eddie takes a step towards her. They stare each other in the eye until the animal nature of their scandalous rendezvous takes over. From the beginning their kisses are open mouthed, deep, and wild. They only stop kissing when continuing to do so gets in the way of them taking off their clothes. He removes her top immediately so he can feel her full breasts and lick, and kiss, and suck, and nibble on her erect nipples. By the time they fall on the bed they are both completely naked. He lies her on her back and kisses her on the mouth, then on the neck, then on her nipples, then on her breast, then on her stomach, and then on each inner thigh. Now, he has her lying on her back and he's lying on the bed with his head between her legs. He lifts up both of her legs and holds them both in the air to expose her flower even more. She throws her head back, let's out a sigh, and her eyes roll to the back of her head when she feels the pressure from his tongue on her inner lips and then on her clit.

10:00am - Lying next to each other, drenched in sweat, Eddie and Robyn are both completely spent.

Robyn speaks first, "That was worth the wait."

Eddie speaks next, "It certainly was. And, we have the rest of the weekend for plenty more." "Remember, I have to be on my flight Sunday night so I can be back in LA by late Monday morning." "I remember, but let's not think that far ahead."

"Deal."

"Remember, Breck doesn't need to know who you are. All he needs to know is that you are a friend of mine and that you're coming along."

"Got it."

"Speaking of Breck, did you bring the stuff I asked you to bring?"

Robyn gets out of bed and walks over to the closet. She retrieves her suitcase and then she retrieves a smaller bag from inside of it. From that bag she withdraws a vile containing three ounces of a clear liquid. She shows it to Eddie and says, "Here it is."

"Are you sure that's enough?"

"It's odorless, tasteless, and this is three times the amount we need to get the job done." Then she puts the vile back in her bag, and that bag back in her suitcase, and her suitcase back in the closet. She climbs back in bed and snuggles underneath Eddie's arm. She asks, "Should we shower and check out?"

"Yes but let's do something else first." He rolls over to face her and he kisses her on the mouth again. This time foreplay is out of the window. The Viagra is kicking in again and he wants to get the most out of it. After a brief visit to her re-erect nipples, he flips her over, lifts her to her hands and knees, and her enters her from behind.

11:00am - The story of an off duty police officer killed last night was on the news as Megan showered and got dressed, but it didn't catch her attention. At the time, if she was interested in anything it was the weather. On the drive to the Valley the music station she was listening to reported the story with more developments. Apparently, the off duty officer was killed in front of his home and his body was discovered by his family. Megan thought to herself about how evil someone has to be to do something like that. Jarrod was surprised and annoyed when Megan returned the gun he lent to William. She didn't know why and he didn't explain, but he assumed the deal he had with William would stay between them. But, he did find some comfort in the fact that the gun was returned and it hadn't been fired. Having surrendered her key to William's hotel suite, Megan was on her way back to Yezzy's when she heard another report about the off duty officer. This report released the officer's name and Megan almost crashed into the car in front of her when she heard it. Instead of driving to Silver Lake she drove to Culver City, to the house she had just visited, because she couldn't believe what she heard. Now, standing across the street from Javier's house she's doing the very thing she promised herself she wouldn't do anymore today, she's crying again. If her guess is right William's phone is still off and her call will go directly to voicemail. Still, she tries and she was right. So, she sends him an email to let him know that she checked out of his hotel room, that she returned the gun, and that Detective Morales was killed last night.

12:00pm - Breck hadn't given any thought to the purpose of Eddie's excursion into Ensenada, but if had, the last thing he would have thought was that Eddie was there to pick up a woman. After two hours had gone by without Eddie's return Breck intended to give him a hard time about it as soon as he got back. That plan fell by the wayside. Instead he was introduced to Robyn and told that she would accompany them for the rest of the trip to Costa Rica. Breck finds her to be extremely attractive and friendly, but he can't stop wondering what's behind the farce. Clearly, Eddie didn't just run into her in town. Clearly, this stop and pick up had been planned. What would be the harm in giving him a head's up? Why hadn't Eddie mentioned it? And, who is she really? Just as Eddie said earlier, as soon as he got back he was ready to leave. Eddie gave Robyn a quick tour of the boat that ended in the Captain's Berth. She remained in there while he climbed the companionway to the deck and the next one to the fly bridge. Breck untied the knot on the slip's cleat at the bow and the other one at the stern and jumped onboard. Within fifteen minutes of Eddie's return they were navigating out of Hotel Coral's Marina. Breck is happy they are back underway, but he has an unsettling feeling about the new situation.

2:30pm - Thick as thieves the three of them have quickly become, but especially Breck and Robyn. The last couple of hours have been filled with drinks and laughter. At some point Breck convinced Eddie to put his fishing gear to use. They detoured from their heading of south-southeast to head west about a mile past the continental shelf. Breck took one rod, reel, and a lead-head jig and Robyn to the others. They positioned themselves on opposite sides of the bow while Eddie stayed atop the fly bridge allowing the boat to drift. Breck got a few nibbles right away, but Robyn was the first to get a fish on the line. Whatever she hooked was big enough to make it difficult for her to reel it in. Breck reeled in his line and set his pole down so he could help Robyn, who is battling a fish that, apparently, likes the life it is living and doesn't want anything about it to change. For Robyn, this moment, right now, is one of the most exciting moments of her life. She's never been fishing before and, frankly, she never understood the fascination. But, now, with a fish on the line she's the one that's hooked. She can't wait to reel this fish in so she can drop her lure and catch another. For Breck, the excitement he's feeling stems from the future he sees in his mind. He's so looking forward to doing this very thing for a living that, in his mind, right now, Eddie and Robyn are a couple that's chartered this boat, his boat, for a fun afternoon of fishing. As he talks Robyn through releasing and reeling the fish in, he's imagining that he's the Captain of this boat and no reality can tell him different. He offers to take the pole from Robyn and do the rest of the work, but she isn't having any of that. This is her catch and she doesn't want to miss any of the fun of reeling it in. After a fifteen minute battle Robyn is victorious. She reeled in what Breck is estimating to be a thirty pound Grouper. Breck extracts the hook from the fish's mouth and shows Robyn how to hold it by the gills. She takes hold of the fish and turns towards the fly bridge to show Eddie her catch. He had been smiling and enjoying seeing her so happy, though he would have preferred to be the one helping her reel in it instead of Breck. Still, he applauds her efforts and he's truly happy for her. His display of approval is muted only by the fatigue that's setting in. He stayed up all night and then, on top of that, they had two torrid sessions of sex. There isn't enough coffee in the world to keep him from taking a nap soon. If Breck didn't believe in beginner's luck before, he believes in it now. He and Robyn both lowered their lures into the water again at the same time. He hasn't gotten as much as a nibble this time and she has already hooked another fish. This fish must be smaller because the fight in it isn't as ferocious as the first. A tinge of jealousy prevents Breck from abandoning his efforts. It's enough for him to watch Robyn struggle with her fish while he continues to try to hook and reel one in for himself. Five minutes later Robyn has her second but smaller Grouper onboard. She, like an expert now, extracts the hook and holds her trophy over her head for all to see. They continue fishing for a little while longer. Breck did finally catch a fish, but Robyn caught another one as well. The fun only stops when Eddie asks them both up to the fly bridge. He needs to take a nap, so he needs Breck to take control of the boat.

After getting the boat back on course in a south-eastwardly direction Eddie gives Breck a quick tutorial on the navigation equipment and on controlling the direction and speed of the boat. While the two of them are talking Robyn goes to the head in the Captain's berth to wash up, now that the fishing is over. When Eddie is confident that Breck understands the equipment he tells Breck not to go any faster than they are going now and to keep the boat on course. He says he just needs two or three hours of rest and then he'll return, and take over. As far as Breck is concerned Eddie can sleep for the rest of the journey. The fantasy of this being his boat and Eddie and Robyn being his guests hasn't left his mind yet. When Eddie makes it to his berth he finds Robyn inside, crying. Apparently, she's missed several calls and she just checked her voicemail. Bobby has died.

Despite this being the outcome she was hoping for she's still despondent. Her sadness, however, isn't over Bobby's death as much as it's over the timing. This means she'll have to cut her trip short so she can go back to Los Angeles, feign being the grieving wife, and make funeral arrangements. Eddie comforts her over her loss, but he also reminds her of the insurance policy she can now collect. It's surprising to her that she didn't think of it before he reminded her. That was the whole purpose of poisoning Bobby, to collect the money. Now that she's thinking of it, it hits her that now she's what she's always wanted to be, a millionaire. That thought turns her depression into excitement and she turns Eddie's comforting hug into a passionate kiss and groping session. Eddie wants to have sex with her, but he's too tired. Robyn, however, is too turned on to be denied. She drops to her knees to take Eddie into her mouth hoping that will arouse him enough to give her whatever he's got left. And it does. The two of them have an abbreviated form of what they shared earlier. This time Eddie falls asleep the moment he climaxes, but Robyn hadn't gotten there yet. So, while he sleeps, she lies beside him, fingering herself and rubbing herself, while she thinks of the things she can, now, afford to buy. For the first time in her life she climaxes while seeing herself as the naked center of attention for several people, male and female, and all at the same time.

5:00pm - The fantasy of this being Breck's boat left his mind an hour ago. In its place is envy. For the last hour, sitting alone in the Captain's Chair, Breck has been stewing. It started with him thinking of the beginning. He's the one who enlisted Ronny's help. He's the one who took the guy Ronny found, David, and held his hand as he talked him through what had to be done and how to do it. He's the one, when Ronny couldn't find David after the murder, who found him. He's the one who killed David and along with Ronny dumped David's body. He's the one who tricked Ronny into believing he was having car trouble on that deserted road in the middle of the night. And when Ronny turned his back, he's the one that killed him. In other words, he's done all of the dirty work and now he's feeling that the payment he's owed, alone, isn't enough. His mind is warped enough to think that he deserves this boat more than Eddie. And then there's the girl. The fun they've had since she came aboard is leading Breck to think that maybe she likes him too. He overhead them having sex when Eddie said he was going to take a nap. Breck wants to have sex with her too. More than that, like the boat, he wants her for himself. It's like he has a devil on one shoulder and bigger, badder devil on the other. Both are trying to get him to see things their way. The bigger badder devil says he's right to be thinking the way he is. He earned this boat, not a smaller one, and he earned the girl. The devil says he should be happy with what he's getting. In just a couple of days he'll have more than enough money to retire without ever having to worry, and the charter fishing idea is a good one, and that will make money too. Breck's greed wins the day. The only thing that relieves him of the torture of going back and forth is the resolution that once he gets paid, he'll kill Eddie and keep his boat. That way he won't have to use his money to buy a boat of his own. And regarding the girl, the jury is still out on that. He doesn't know enough about her to know what to do. That they started to have drinks and party when she got onboard, detoured him from following through with his initial plan of finding out who she is and finding out about her relationship with Eddie.

By the time Eddie reappears on the fly bridge, after his nap, Breck has already decided his fate. Robyn reappears just few minutes after Eddie and the three of them don't skip a beat. They pick up right where they left off, with Eddie taking control of the boat and Robyn offering to make the drinks. Breck keeps Eddie company while Robyn goes to the galley. She returns with a pitcher and three glasses and they all toast to their continuing trip and to their continuing good fortune.

6:00pm - The party, at least for Robyn and Breck, has moved to the galley. While Eddie keeps the boat on course, Robyn and Breck have started to prepare dinner. "The closest I've ever come to camping was staying in a Holiday Inn," says Robyn. "I'm just not that type of girl."

Breck replies, "Don't worry about it. I'll talk you through it. The first thing you want to do is chop off the head."

"Yuck," but with one forceful chop the head is gone.

"Good. Now you don't want to cut the tail off yet. Just make a shallow cut across the skin just before the tail. Good. Now hold on to the tail and run the knife just below the skin from the tail to where the head used to be. Good."

"Should I take the skin off now?"

"Not yet. First, let's do the same thing on the other side." Breck watches as Robyn repeats the steps. "Good. Now, take the skin off this side. Then cut slowly across the body until you feel the backbone." Robyn says, "I feel it."

"Great. Now, staying above the bone cut the fish from back to front. There you go! You just cut your first fillet. Now you just need to do the same thing on the other side."

After Robyn fillets the other side of the fish she admits, "Thanks for the filleting lesson and I really mean that, but that's not my thing. You can do the other fish. I'm going to wash my hands and make the salad."

Eddie can hear the two of them laughing and having a good time, and it's getting on his nerves. He calls for Robyn and when she's standing next to him he tells her, "The two of you are having too much fun together."

"If I didn't know better I'd think you are jealous."

"I think tonight's meal is the perfect opportunity to leave him behind." It's obvious to Robyn that Eddie didn't find her comment funny and that he's talking business now.

"I agree. We're having the fish we caught with rice and a salad. Do you have a bottle of Chardonnay to go with the fish?"

"Yes. There are three bottles in the refrigerator."

"Perfect. I'll put it in his wine."

"And I'll make a toast before we eat."

"He'll be dead in minutes."

"In that case don't start eating until he is. We'll have to warm up our food later but that's all right, worse things have happened."

"In that case, let me get back to having a good time with him. That way he'll stay as comfortable with me as he is now." She gives Eddie a kiss and then heads back to the galley. She finds Breck filleting the final fish. She asks Breck, "Chardonnay goes perfectly with fish. Do you know if we have any?"

Breck answers, "I'll take a look." He washes his hands, looks in the refrigerator, and says, "Yeah, there are three bottles in here. They are all the same."

"Good. We just need one. Let me have it and I'll put it one ice."

"It's pretty cold in here. I think it will be fine if we leave it here until dinner."

"Even better."

7:30pm - Dinner is ready. Robyn has set the table and told Breck where he, she, and Eddie will sit. All that's left is for Eddie to come to the dining area and then she'll plate the food. She asks Breck to let Eddie know it's time for dinner. While he does that, she pours the wine. When Eddie makes it to the galley Robyn says, "Wow. I didn't think we'd be able to get you out of that chair. I thought you were going to ask us to bring your dinner to you. This is your place, I'll sit here, and Breck will sit there."

"Sounds good. Let me wash up a little bit. Don't start without me."

While Breck and Robyn wait for Eddie, Robyn plates the food. When that is done the two of them take their places and wait. Breck tells Robyn, "You're in for a treat. Fresh fish tastes better than anything you can buy in a store and better than anything you can get in a restaurant."

"I'm looking forward to it."

"What's taking him so long?" Breck reaches for his glass of wine and Robyn playfully slaps his hand. "If I can wait so can you. Let's wait until we are all together."

"OK, in that case, I'm going to the loo for a quick minute. I'll be right back."

Sitting alone at the table Robyn's mind drifts to the thought she didn't allow herself to think while she and Breck were preparing dinner. She's never seen someone die before. She watched her husband deteriorate over time, but even in his case, she wasn't present when he died. The picture she has in her mind is of the fish she caught when she took it out of the bucket, just before she chopped off its head. She saw the fish trying to wriggle itself free from her grasp and hopelessly gasping for oxygen. She imagines Breck's fate will be a lot like that. She felt sorry for the fish, but she doesn't think she'll feel the same for Breck. She's had a good time with Breck today, but, at the end of the day, he doesn't matter. Finally, she realizes she's looking forward to watching him die. If she had to admit her true feelings, right now she'd have to confess that she's feeling curiously excited.

Eddie is furious. He can hardly contain himself. He tries to tell himself to ignore it, the problem will take care of itself in just a few minutes. But, that's not enough. He has to do something. When he exits his berth he sees Robyn sitting at the table but not Breck. Just one moment later he sees Breck coming out of his stateroom. Eddie walks directly to Breck and punches him in the face, knocking him to floor. A moment later he's on top of Breck swinging wildly but connecting only twice more as Breck has his hands covering his face in defense. The beating only stops when Robyn pulls Eddie off of Breck. "What the hell is wrong with you?" asks Breck.

Eddie says one word, "Javier." Eddie checked his email while he was in his berth and found out that Javier was killed last night in front of his house. Eddie barks, "You didn't have to do that!"

Breck, standing up and wiping the blood from the corner of his mouth, says, "What do you care?"

Both men are aware of Robyn's presence so both are careful about what they say.

"You sat at a bar and watched a game, huh?"

Breck's only response to that is a slight shrug of his shoulders. The truth is out now so there's no use in carrying on with that fiction. "You know I had to, for the same reason as the others. Believe me, I did us both a favor."

"When we get to Costa Rica we'll settle up, and then that's it for us."

"I understand that you're mad now, but when you think about it you'll realize I'm right and that I did what was best for the both of us."

Robyn, standing between the two men, says, "OK, OK, whatever this is let's just try to get past it." She looks Eddie in the eye and reminds him, "Let's just calm down and have dinner."

Eddie walks back in his berth to pace until he's calm enough for dinner. Robyn follows him in there. When she closes the door behind them Breck plops down at the table, in the seat designated for Robyn. He sits there feeling his jaw for any loose teeth and thinking that Eddie will understand and feel better after he's had a chance to digest the news. He reaches for the glass of wine in front of him and he drinks it all in one big gulp. That's when he thinks of Robyn slapping his hand and telling him to wait. He takes the glass of wine from his place setting and replaces hers with his. Then he pours himself another glass of wine in the glass he just drank from, places it where his sat just a moment ago, and goes to the head in his stateroom to double check his jaw and teeth.

Inside Eddie's berth Robyn is consoling Eddie without asking what that was about. In truth, she doesn't want to know. She just wants him to realize that if he can calm down for just a few minutes, whatever problems he has with Breck will be over soon. Eddie tells her he just needs a minute alone to collect his thoughts, and then he'll be right out. Again, she finds herself sitting at the table alone, but this time she's unaccompanied for no longer than a few seconds. Breck comes out of his stateroom first, having washed the blood from his face and straightened himself out again. Eddie is right behind him. It's obvious that there's still a lot of bad blood between them, but the two men sit across from each other, ready to have dinner. Robyn turns to Eddie and says, "Don't you want to make a toast?"

Eddie responds, "No, let's just eat."

"Oh come on guys. Never mind, I'll do it. Even though my trip got cut short . . ."

Breck cuts her off to ask, "What do you mean?"

"An emergency came up at home. I have to leave you guys in Cabo and fly home from there. But, let's not talk about that right now. This is a beautiful boat and I've had a beautiful day. I even caught my first fish, in my life, today." She raises her glass and says, "We have the rest of the day together. Let's enjoy it." Both Breck and Eddie raise their glasses in a half-hearted gesture, and then the three of them drink from their wine glasses. Finally, Robyn says, "OK boys, let's dig in!" With a devilish grin on her face Robyn takes her first bite of the fish. Immediately she thinks that Breck is right. It surely does taste fresher than any fish she has ever had. She wants to say that out loud, but she can't. All of a sudden she feels confused. She's not sure of where she is or of what she's doing. Eddie is waiting for Breck to show signs of the poison taking effect, and Breck is enjoying his dinner. Robyn, however, is starting to panic. Something is wrong. She grabs her shirt at her chest but that doesn't relieve any of the tightness she's feeling. Then she grabs her throat. If she can just dislodge whatever is stuck in her throat she'll feel better. Breck is the first to notice that something is wrong with Robyn. To him it looks like she's choking on something. Eddie notices next and he thinks the same thing. Just like the fish as it sat on the cutting board, waiting to have its head chopped off, Robyn is wriggling in her chair trying to free herself of whatever it is that has a grasp on her, and she's gasping for air. Breck jumps up from his place, lifts her from her chair, stands behind her, and starts to employ the Heimlich maneuver. Robyn is convulsing uncontrollably now. Breck figures out that she isn't choking. Rather, something else is happening, but he doesn't know what. Eddie doesn't know how, but he thinks he knows what. Breck lowers Robyn's convulsing body to the floor. He can see the terror in her eyes as she desperately tries to regain control of her body. As Eddie stands above the two of them looking down, his emotionless eyes meet Robyn's crying eyes just before she starts to vomit violently. Breck is screaming that they have to get her to a doctor while he cradles her in his arms, but Eddie doesn't move one inch. Robyn's body continues to convulse and she continues to vomit for another minute. Then she takes one last gasp for air before she goes silent, still, and finally limp. Breck feels for a pulse for on her wrist and then on her neck. There's none he can find. He lowers her to floor and kneels beside her in a state of shock. He stays still for a while trying to figure out what just happened. A list of possibilities quickly run through Breck's mind, but none of them explain what just happened, except for one. But, as far as he can tell she only had one or two bites of her fish, and he knows he had just as much as she did and he's feeling fine. He thinks, "If it wasn't the fish then what was it?" The answer comes to him as soon as he asks the question, "It had to be the wine." But, with that answer comes more questions. "If it was the wine then why isn't he or Eddie sick?" Sensing that he's close to solving this riddle he tells himself to, "Wait a minute." He wants to slow his thoughts down in an effort to do the math right. It takes just a few seconds for him to realize that the poisoned wine Robyn drank was originally meant for him. But, she was the one who poured the wine. Why would she want to poison him? That's when the uncomfortable feeling he had when she boarded the boat comes back to him. That's when he knew that she and Eddie planned to kill him. As soon as that thought registered he turned around to see where Eddie is. Still on his knees, beside Robyn, Breck turns towards Eddie who's holding a gun in his hand with the barrel pointed at Breck's forehead. Breck didn't hear the gun go off. He saw a quick flash of light and he felt a slight burning sensation on his forehead, but that only lasted for the shortest fraction of a second.

8:30pm - The first thing Eddie did was wrap Breck's head in three layers of towels. Then he poured the rest of the wine down the drain. Just to be safe Eddie threw all three wine glasses away as well. Having done those three things Eddie sat down at the dinner table to take a break and think. This was not the way it was supposed to happen. His emotions are mixed over the event. On one hand, he's sad about Robyn's death. He waited so long to have sex with her, and when he finally got the chance it was better than he expected. He wouldn't have been opposed to her flying down to Costa Rica, after she buried Bobby, to spend a few weeks with him. In fact, while listening to her and Breck laughing in the galley, he decided to talk with her about that very thing as soon as he got a chance. At least he had her three times, but he wanted more. On the other hand, he's happy about Breck. He owed Breck a lot of money and now he doesn't have to pay him one cent. That's a very good thing. But, what pleases

Eddie more than keeping Breck's money, is now he's truly home free. There's no one left to tie him to Geneviève's murder, no one can tie him to David's murder, and no one can tie him to Ronny's murder either. He didn't realize how much he worried about those loose ends until just this minute. Eddie laughs to himself when he thinks about the surprised look on Breck's face just before he pulled the trigger. Breck should have seen it coming. Eddie thinks to himself, "Did he really think I would let him live knowing that he had information and proof that could bury me. Knowing him, he would have burned through his money and then come back to me for more with threats of blackmail if I didn't pay him." Eddie turns to Breck's dead body, lying next to Robyn's, and says out loud, "What did you expect, you idiot?" Eddie smiles when Breck doesn't respond, and says out loud, "For the first time you don't have something to say." After the excitement of the event passes, Eddie turns his attention to the unpleasant things that need to be done next. It's still too light outside to dump the bodies, so that will have to wait. Right now, he needs to find some rubber gloves, a mop and a bucket, and the cleaning supplies he stocked up on. The cabin is starting to reek of the stench of Robyn's vomit and urine combined with Breck's blood. Also, there seems to be specks of Breck's blood and pieces of his head on Eddie's cabinets, so he has to get to those things as well. The whole point of asking Robyn to bring the poison, besides the fact that she'd developed a bit of expertise on the subject over the last year, was so that he could kill Breck without having him bleed all over the boat. To that thought Eddie thinks, "It is what it is." After he cleans up all of the bodily fluids he puts everything he used, including the rubber gloves, in one bag. He washes his hands, and then he looks for the list of items he needs to purchase in Cabo San Lucas. He adds rubber gloves, sponges, and ammonia to the list. His next thought is that he's starving. He throws away all of the food that was on their plates and he makes a plate for himself with the food that wasn't plated. He throws it in the microwave for a couple of minutes, and then he sits down and has his dinner.

10:00pm - At this distance Eddie is far enough outside Cabo not to run into any recreational boaters. He shuts down his engines and returns to the galley. His only concern now are the weights he brought with him. His plan was to use both fifty pound weights to take Breck's body to the bottom of the ocean. Now, he has to use one for Breck and the other for Robyn. He just hopes that they are enough to do the trick. To that end he decides to scrap his plan of wrapping the bodies in sheets before dumping them. He works on Breck first. He ties a rope around Breck's neck, and then he loops it down around Breck's chest underneath both arms, and then back up around his neck. He ties the other end of the rope to one of the weights. He drags Breck's body to the top of the companionway but not on deck until he makes sure the coast is clear. Having done that, he lifts Breck's body over the railing and watches as it sinks to the bottom of the ocean. Relieved that the weight was enough to sink Breck he does the same thing to Robyn's body and it watches that sink as well. He pours himself a glass of champagne and he heads back to the fly bridge. He's close enough to make it to the marina and sleep there tonight, but he decides to anchor just outside the marina for the night. Cabo is a popular destination for Southern Californians because you can get there and back in no time. Eddie, however, has never been there and now he's excited to finally be going. He considers spending a day or two there, especially now that's he's fully unencumbered, but on second thought, given what he's just done, it's probably best to get what he needs and then get out of town. Besides, Cabo is just a distraction. The real prize is Costa Rica. Everything, from the rainforest, to the wild life, to the surfing, to the food, to the nightlife, to the gorgeous Central American and South American women, is great in Costa Rica. Eddie has the same thought he's had almost daily for the last three months, "A guy like me, with my boat and my money, can live like a king there." He decides definitively that he'll be in and out of Cabo as quickly as he can. Costa Rica is where he wants to be, and he's just a few hours away. The sooner he gets there, the sooner the coronation can begin. He drops anchor less than a mile outside of Cabo and he retires for the night. If he feels up to it he'll get up early and watch the sun rise again.

———

Day Seven

7:30am - Friday nights in Venice Beach, and especially at Chaya, is the sweet juice of life. There are people everywhere, everyone looks great, and laughter and romance is in the air. In the sea of people hovering around the bar it takes a minute for William to spot his party. He finds Andy, a college friend of his, at the bar, and he sees Erica, Andy's wife, standing at a waiting table just off the bar area. As he walks past Andy to get to Erica, Andy says, "You got here just in time. We finally have the bartender's attention. Tell me what you want so I can tell him when he comes back. Otherwise it will be twenty minutes before you can get a drink."

William answers, "Vodka Tonic."

When William gets to their waiting table Erica says, "You look very handsome. This is going to be perfect."

William confesses, "I can't believe I let you guys talk me into this."

"You have to trust me. I'm good at this."

Andy puts two drinks on their table and says, "A Kir Royale for you and here's my JD and coke. I'll be right back with your Vodka Tonic."

"If she's so perfect why is she available?"

Erica reminds William, "You're available aren't you?"

"Touché."

Andy, back at the table with William's drink chimes in, "You're brushing up on your French. That's good." Erica and William look at each other and laugh. For the next few minutes they enjoy their drinks while they talk about old times, work, family, and mutual friends. As the time draws near Andy says, "I hope you have sown all of your wild oats my friend. Erica is two for two at this."

Erica adds, "Yeah, the first couple I hooked up are married already, and the second couple are engaged."

William says, "I'd hate to be the one to spoil your record but I wouldn't hold out much hope for me getting married any time soon."

Andy smirks, "Famous last words."

Erica announces, "Here she is." Squeezing by one person at a time Geneviève is making her way to their table. With all the people coming and going William isn't sure which girl she is until he sees her wave at Erica. Erica and Geneviève greet and hug each other. Then Geneviève says hi and hugs Andy. Finally, Erica says, "William, this is Geneviève. Geneviève, this is William."

Erica couldn't get a read on Geneviève at first but it was easy to read William. He couldn't take his eyes off of her. He tried to seem less impressed and less interested, but every time he looked at Geneviève he smiled and then looked away. Erica could tell he was fighting it, but as they walked to their table for dinner she thought to herself, "Three for three."

When they were all seated the conversation went on as to be expected. Erica spoke more often with Geneviève and William spoke more often with Andy, but every once in a while the four of them would discuss something together. As the night wore on, however, the pattern of conversation changed. William and Geneviève spoke, almost exclusively, with each other. It got so apparent that at one point Andy whispers to Erica, "I bet if we got up and left right now they wouldn't notice."

Lost in her thoughts but hearing Andy as well, Erica reveals, "I thinking of starting my own dating service."

By the time dessert was served what started out as a party of four, consisting of a couple and two individuals, had become a party of four, two couples. There was one more sign that Erica was looking for before she was truly ready to claim success. She gets that sign right after the bill was paid and they were all ready to part ways. She asks Geneviève what she is going to do for the rest of the night and Geneviève says, "William and I are going for a walk. We might find a new place and have another drink."

As they all head for the door Erica whispers Geneviève's and William's intentions in Andy's ear, and he turns around to give his wife their secret handshake and a kiss. Just outside of Chaya, Geneviève hugs and says goodbye to Andy and then she hugs and whispers, "Thank you," in Erica's ear.

William then hugs Erica and he too whispers, "Thank you," in her ear. Then he turns to Andy to say goodbye. The two of them shake hands, and as they let go Andy smiles and winks at William.

William wakes up angry, on the floor of his hotel room overlooking the Marina in Cabo San Lucas. The dream he had was so vivid, he can feel what he felt when he saw Geneviève for the first time. He can feel what he felt while they sat at the table talking. He remembers that they went for a walk together after dinner with the intention of finding another bar and having more drinks. But, they never went to another bar. They just walked and talked until their feet hurt and their legs got sore. He can feel what he felt when he walked Geneviève back to her car, and they kissed for the first time. He remembers containing himself until she was out of sight, and then he remembers being so happy that he ran all the way to his car. But, he was so full of joy and energy he ran past his car and around the entire block. Only when he got to his car, for the second time, had he burned enough energy to be able to sit still and drive. Even then he couldn't stop smiling. The dream, the memories, and the feelings make William happy up to a point. When Andy smiles and winks it isn't Andy he sees, it's Eddie, and the happiness he was feeling is replaced with anger. He grabs his binoculars and looks down on the Marina, replaying Eddie's smile and wink in his mind the whole time. There are no new boats in the Marina. He knows there's no way Eddie made it to Cabo before he did. He just hopes that Eddie hasn't changed his plans. It's too early to know if he has or hasn't. All William can do, now, is wait.

8:30am - Eddie backs his boat into the slip he's rented for the day. His night didn't go the way he thought it would. Robyn's death haunted him and prevented him from getting a good night's sleep. While he lied in bed she was all he could think about. When he did finally fall asleep it was 5:00am. But, sleep was no reprieve from the thoughts that kept him awake. In fact, sleep only exasperated the haunting. While he slept he dreamt about the sight of her gasping for air and about the terror and hopelessness in her eyes as he stood over her and watched her die. Those things were unsettling but they weren't what kept Eddie awake or what frightened him out of his sleep. It was the picture, in his mind, of her body floating to the surface that bothered him. In his dream her dead body was recovered from the ocean and her corpse kept repeating his name. His sleep only lasted for two hours. He woke up feeling tired, cranky, and destabilized, so he decided to stay in bed. He figured he has plenty of days to watch the sun rise again. When he finally did get out of bed it was just to get the boat to the marina. Once he tied his boat to the slips cleats he went back below deck. The last day has been super eventful and super hectic and he needs to catch up on his rest so he can continue on his journey. The plan now is to sleep for a few hours, and then restock, refuel, and be on his way.

9:00am - Checking the marina every ten minutes was starting to drive William crazy. He decided to take a break. He ordered breakfast and then jumped in the shower and got dressed. William needed the shower and breakfast more than he expected. Feeling full reminds him that there are other things happening in the world and that, maybe, he should be concerned about some of them. He retrieves his cell phone and his laptop from his travel bag. He checks his messages first and then his emails. The sound of Megan's voice makes him happy even though she sounds worried and she's pleading with him to return her call. He feels bad about not telling her that he was leaving, but he was unsure and panic stricken enough of his plan and he didn't want to run the risk of being talked out of it. The only way he was going to follow through, for sure, was to just do it. He thinks of calling her now, but he decides against it. He can't think of anything he wants to say to her and he can't think of anything she could say, right now, that would mean anything to him. He's tempted not to open her email, thinking it's more of the same, but he does and his heart hits the floor. It's good that she returned the gun, that's one less thing to worry about, but he can't believe that Javier's dead. Hoping that Megan has made a mistake, he goes on the internet to read the story for himself. He sits in front of his laptop in shock, confused, and dumbfounded. No matter how hard he tries to wrap his mind around the news he can't make any sense of it. It makes him reflect on the world as he saw it before Genny's death, as opposed to the world he's seen since. It's one thing to hear about someone being murdered on the news. It's such a distant event it almost doesn't seem real. It's another thing when murder comes to visit close to home or, worse yet, when it comes to visit one's family. He wonders what his friends and co-workers would think of him now if he articulated what he's come to believe. Better yet, what would they think of him if they knew where he is and of what he's planning to do? They'd probably label him cynical for his beliefs and crazy for his actions. The funny thing is, if he were standing in their shoes, he'd probably think the same thing. William's thoughts turns to Javier's family and the anguish they must be feeling. He thinks of Cynthia and of how kind and understanding she was towards him. He thinks that she must be suffering through some of the same anguish he's been living with, and maybe more because she and Javier have two children. William doesn't have a sense of whether Javier's death is related to Genny's or Teddy's. But, he does know that there can be no good reason for it. There's no reason on Earth that Javier, a good man and a good police officer, should have died where and how he did. It sickens and maddens William to think that he's been flushed into this underworld, where corruption and depravity have no limits. In truth, he's afraid of this world and he doesn't want to be here. He was a hair's breadth away from letting go and leaving, but a smile and a wink renewed his convictions and gave him the strength to finish what he started. Again, he's replaying the smile and the wink on a continuous loop in his head. That's enough to take him away from thinking about Javier and refocus him on his mission. No doubt, he wants out of this world but not until someone answers for Genny. He grabs his binoculars and scans the marina. He counts three slips that were empty before that now have boats in them. It's time for him to take a walk and see if any of them are the boat called "Miss Behavin."

10:00am - William makes the five minute walk from the Wyndam to the marina. The three slips in question are on docks three and four. The boat in the first of the three slips is too small and is obviously not Eddie's. William didn't have to check the third. The second of the three slips housed "Miss Behavin." William feels a heightened sense of anxiety as he stands frozen in front of the boat waiting for the owner to show himself. When Eddie doesn't appear William gets closer to the boat hoping to hear any sound that would indicate that someone is aboard, but he doesn't hear anything. Then he whirls himself around as he hears someone walking along the walkway in his direction, but that person isn't Eddie. William figures that climbing aboard in search of Eddie is too risky, and, if Eddie isn't aboard, waiting there for him would put William at a disadvantage. He wants to confront Eddie in public as much as possible. That way, if the unimaginable happens, at least there will be witnesses. He scans the marina area looking for someplace where he can wait for Eddie without being seen by him, at least initially. He picks the La Taverna GastroBar, an open air bar and restaurant that faces the marina. From there he can see everyone that goes and comes to and from docks three and four.

12:00pm - Eddie wakes up from his nap still feeling a little tired and cranky but with his mind at ease. No visions of Robyn entered his mind while he slept and though he's reminded of her because some of her belongs are still in his berth, he doesn't feel one way or another about her. In fact, the only thing he thinks, upon seeing her stuff, is that he needs to get her belongings, and Breck's, off his boat before he leaves Cabo. Good sleep, a quick shower, and a strong cup of coffee are doing wonders for Eddie. Where once he felt he should get out of town as soon as he took care of his business, now he's thinking why not extend his stay and enjoy Cabo, at least for today and tonight. He's even considering finding a pretty girl he can strike a bargain with, because if he does miss Robyn for one thing, it's the sex. He's tempted to go online to read if there are any further developments into Javier's death, but he dismisses that idea with a chuckle as he thinks to himself that the person the police are looking for has a bullet in his head and his body is at the bottom of the ocean. He pats himself on the back with the thought that maybe he should include that among the cases he's solved during his career. With that thought he can feel his mood darkening. He promises himself to think no more about Javier, or Breck, or Bobby, or Robyn. He wants to remember his life in Los Angeles fondly for being what it was. He wants to remember the LAPD fondly. After all, he enjoyed being a cop and it got him to where he is. But, most of all, he wants to think about tomorrow from now on. Having the money, the boat, and the freedom is going to take a little getting used to, but he smiles to himself as he thinks there are worse problems to have in the world and, besides, he's up to the challenge. Yesterday was supposed to be his first new day, but it turned out to be a false start. Like a sprinter, he decides to climb back into the blocks and allow today to be the restart. Now the plan is take care of his business first, and then enjoy the rest of the day and night drinking and, hopefully, having sex with a pretty girl with meat on her bones. He emerges from below deck to a perfect day. The Sun is shining brightly, but there's a nice breeze in the air and the sounds of the seagulls and the sound of small waves in the marina lapping up against the boats are comforting. He goes, first, to the Marina's business office to make arrangements for an overnight stay. After that is done he considers having lunch at the restaurant across the way, La Taverna GastroBar, but he decides to push himself and get some of the shopping out of the way before stopping for lunch. Besides, from the look of that place it seems very commercial. He's sure, in town, he can find a small mom and pop restaurant where he can get authentic Mexican food and have a more authentic experience. The things he needs most, other than more fuel, are the cleaning supplies, especially the ammonia. So, from the Marina's business office he makes a right as instructed by the girl in the office and heads for the Boulevard Paseo de La Marina. On the other side of that boulevard is where she said he can find several stores that sells the things he's looking for. Eddie is walking on air as he saunters around the Marina completely oblivious to fact that he is being followed.

1:00pm - The walk so far has been fun. Eddie quickly realizes that Cabo is a party town. There are hotels, motels, restaurants, and bars everywhere. And there are more than a few strip clubs and working girls around. The promise of a fun night makes Eddie want to get his work done right away so he can get to playing sooner. He was surprised to hear that there are three Walmarts in town and a Costco, but all of them are too far away for walking, so he stops in local stores to get what he needs. The first supermarket he goes to doesn't have everything on his list, so he has to make another stop at the Super Disemex on Vincente Guerrero. With two bags of supplies in his hands all that is left is to stop for lunch, get back to the boat to refuel, and then he is free until it's time to leave. He walks along Lazaro Cárdenas looking for the right restaurant and he finds one just off Lazaro Cárdenas on Calle Cabo San Lucas. Mi Casa Verde is exactly what he's looking for. It's small, with only ten tables, and those that are occupied have locals as patrons. It is obviously family owned and operated, and from what Eddie can see the food is inexpensive and the plates come full of food. The server is an older man, perhaps the father or grandfather of the family that owns the restaurant. He hands Eddie a menu and says, "Buenos Dias Señor."

Eddie takes the menu and responds, "Buenos Dias. Una Tecate por favor." Eddie is paying so much attention to the menu that he doesn't see the man who enters the restaurant until he sits at his table directly across from him.

William carefully chose where and when to confront Eddie. By keeping the confrontation in public William hopes that will diminish the possibility of the worst that could happen from happening. Barring that, he prepared himself for any reaction that Eddie might have, except for the one he got. William is the last person Eddie imagined ever seeing again, so he's surprised to see him. Instinctively he knows this isn't a good thing, but his first reaction is to laugh. He sits up straight in his chair and he pushes back from the table just enough to give himself room. The server returns to the table just then and says, "La cerveza, señor."

Eddie, keeping his eyes on William says, "Gracias."

The server turns to William and asks, "¿Cualquier cosa para usted señor?"

William, keeping his eyes on Eddie, answers, "Nada, gracias."

To Eddie, the server asks, ¿Está dispuesto a pedir su comida, señor?"

Eddie responds, "No, necesito un minuto." Finally, Eddie asks William, "What are you doing here?"

"I need you to tell me everything you know about my wife's murder. I know you know why it happened and I need to understand."

"I already told you. I don't know anything about your wife's murder."

"It should be obvious to you, by now, that I will follow you anywhere you go on this Earth until I get what I need from you."

Eddie pushes his chair back a little more and stands up. He walks around the table to William and starts to feel up and down his chest and up and down his back. The frisk has a dual purpose. He's checking for weapons but, more importantly, he's checking to see if William is wired. Satisfied that William has neither a weapon nor a recording device Eddie asks, "What makes you think I know anything about your wife?"

"I know, for a fact, that you and another man murdered Teddy, and I know you did that to silence him about my wife's murder."

Eddie can feel his blood start to boil, not because he's being questioned by someone he considers insignificant, but because he's a little too close to the truth for comfort. And, more than that, if he's willing to show up in Cabo, completely unexpectedly, he'll surely make it to Costa Rica. The last thing Eddie wants to do is spend his new life running from this guy. "I don't know where you're getting your so called facts but you're wrong. Teddy overdosed. Check the coroner's report."

"What about Javier? Did you have him killed as well?"

Eddie's response to this inquiry is immediate and forceful, "I had nothing to do with Javier being killed."

William knows immediately that that's the first truthful thing Eddie has said. That emotion was genuine and, by contrast, that reassures William that everything else Eddie has said is a lie. Now he sees his way in. He thinks if he can get on Eddie's nerves enough, he can get what he needs out of him. William continues on that line of questions, "Why would you have Javier killed? Is it because he was starting to realize that you did have Teddy murdered?"

Eddie has had enough, so he asserts, "You should be thankful that you're still alive. If I were you I'd let this go. You need to go on with your life and stay out of mine before you end up just like your wife." William thinks to himself, "Now we're getting somewhere," but out loud he says, "You're not me, and you, obviously, don't know anything about me. You're right, I do need to get on with my life, but in order to do that I need to know about my wife. You don't have to worry about the police being involved. I just want to know why her."

Mentioning the police did exactly what it was designed to do. It impacted Eddie emotionally, bringing out the grandiose arrogance in him. Eddie leaned in over the table so that what he has to say can only be heard by William. "I'm telling you for the last time, I had nothing to do with your wife's murder. From now on, I'll consider you a threat. If I see you again I'll kill you myself."

It is William's turn to laugh. He leans in even closer to say, "I've been told that twice in the last week by someone much scarier than you. This isn't over."

With that William stands up and leaves the restaurant. Eddie's first thought was to pay for the beer and leave as well. But, on second thought, he came there for lunch, and he decides to eat as planned. Outwardly it appears that he's enjoying his meal, but this new threat is on his mind the whole time. For the first time, Eddie feels less like the hunter and more like the hunted.

2:00pm - Before paying his bill Eddie tried to map out the fastest way to get back to his boat. He remembers that he walked along the marina past the parking lot. From there he made a left and then a right on the Boulevard Paseo de La Marina until he got to Vincente Guerrero, where he made another left. The last store he went to was on the corner of Vincente Guerrero and Lazaro Cárdenas. From there he walked two blocks west, along Lazaro Cárdenas, to Calle Cabo San Lucas, where he is now. He figures if he walks along Calle Cabo San Lucas in the same direction he was going when he found Mi Casa Verde he should hit the Boulevard Paseo de La Marina right at the parking lot. He can cut across the parking lot and be back at his boat in a few minutes. While he paid his bill he looked for William, but he hasn't seen him since he left the restaurant and walked in the opposite direction of the route Eddie plans to take. Now, with his bags in hand, Eddie makes a right out of the restaurant and walks along Calle Cabo San Lucas. He makes it past the church and all the way to the roundabout at the corner of Calle Cabo San Lucas and the Boulevard Paseo de La Marina without seeing William, but William has been standing behind the trees in the roundabout, and he sees Eddie coming his way. Just as Eddie steps onto the

Boulevard to cross he sees William step from behind the trees, walking towards him. When the two men are face to face Eddie asks, "So what are you planning to do now?"

"I'm not letting you leave Cabo until you tell me what I need to know."

Again, Eddie laughs as a vision of him shooting William and leaving his dead body in the middle of the street dances in his head. He tells William, "Get out of my way. I don't have anything else to say to you."

But William doesn't back down. As the two men cross the Boulevard side by side William continues to harass Eddie. "Why did you have my wife killed? Why did you kill Teddy? And, why did you kill Javier? Is that how you got the money for your boat? I bet there aren't many police officers who can retire with so much money. Speak up you coward. I told you, there's no place you can go that I won't follow you to. You should just deal with me now. Like I said, I don't want to involve the police. I just need answers to my questions. Why did you kill my wife?"

The two men have made it across the street and are now entering the parking lot. Two young Mexican men have noticed the budding fracas and they follow Eddie and William waiting to see what happens next. As soon as the two men are off the street and in the parking lot William stands directly in front of Eddie and continues to berate him with insults and questions. "How did you get your money? Speak up you coward. What are you afraid of? You know I'm not wired. Just tell me what I need to know. Why did you kill my wife?"

Eddie is determined not to say anything else, but the barrage of questions and, more than that, William's insistence of standing in his way is starting to wear on his nerves. Each time he tries to walk around William, William gets back in front of him.

And, with each try William is becoming increasingly aggressive. It started with William just standing in his way but now William pushes Eddie back each time he repositions himself. William is starting to worry because it appears that Eddie is going to be closed mouth about it from now on. It appears that he will be content to take one step forward at a time until he gets to his boat. In truth, William knows he can't spend the rest of his life following Eddie around the globe. If he's going to make something happen, he has to make it happen here and now. So, he steps up his attack. The next time Eddie tries to walk around William, William knocks one of Eddie's bags out of his hand. The two young Mexican men are still following Eddie and William, but they are keeping a distance. Others have noticed the commotion and a small crowd is forming around Eddie and William. Knocking the bag out of Eddie's hand did two things. It pushed Eddie past the limit of his patience and it freed up one of his hands, which Eddie clinched into a fist and he used to that punch William on the right side of his head. The punch staggered William but he quickly recovered and sprang for Eddie. Eddie dropped the other bag and met the oncoming William with another punch to his stomach this time. William crumpled, but there is so much adrenaline coursing through his body, he is back on top of Eddie in a second. He wraps both of his hands around Eddie's neck and Eddie instinctively brings his arms underneath William's and breaks the hold William has on him. As the two men break away from each other they both throw a punch at the other and both punches land. Eddie's is, by far, the most effective. William is standing in front of Eddie with his hands on his knees trying to catch his breath. As soon as he stands upright Eddie becomes the aggressor. He takes a step towards William and punches him in his mid-section again. As soon as William bends over Eddie drives his elbow into William's back, knocking him face down on the parking lot pavement. As he attempts to walk back to his bags, to collect his things and leave, William tackles him from behind. During his fall Eddie hits his forehead on the pavement. He can see his own blood trickling onto the pavement and he can feel it flowing down his forehead and into his eyes. He turns over and wrestles William off of him. Knowing, now, that William won't quit, Eddie feels he has to do more than beat him. He has to finish it. He grabs William and throws him to the ground. Then he mounts William and delivers one punch after another to William's face, which is cut in three places and covered in blood. William does his best to keep his hands up, but Eddie has connected with too many blows and William is out matched and out of energy. When he lowers his hands and stops defending himself, Eddie punches him twice more in the face. William is lying on his back, bloodied, dazed and confused, and completely at Eddie's mercy. Eddie grabs William's hair and pulls his head up so he can hear what he's about to say. He whispers in William's ear, "You want to know what happened to that cunt you called your wife? That whore was fucking Teddy at the wrong time. I should have paid to have you killed as well. I thought you'd eventually get over that bitch's death and go on with your life. I guess I was wrong. I told you this before, but this time I mean it. If I ever see you again I'll kill you. Now, are you satisfied?" With that Eddie slams the back of William's head into the pavement. William lets out a sigh and then his eyes close, his body goes languid, and his head rolls to one side.

The crowd surrounding the two combatants are being held at bay by one of the two young Mexican men. As Eddie collects his belongs a police officer walks by, but he makes eye contact with one of the two Mexican men and he keeps on walking. When Eddie has all of his supplies bagged again he walks past William and pushes through the crowd on his way to his boat and the rest of his life. When he is far enough away, one of the two Mexican men says something to the other one. Then he walks over to William, who's conscious again and struggling to sit up. Most of the gathered crowd dispersed when Eddie pushed by them, but there are still a few onlookers. While the first Mexican man keeps the remaining crowd at bay, the second helps William to his feet.

2:30pm - Despite being cut, bloody, and sore Eddie is thankful that his luck is still holding. As he makes his way back to his boat he's thinking of how lucky he is to have gotten out of that situation without calling the attention of the police. Though he might have been able to identify himself as a retired detective and explain away the incident, there was a chance that a police investigation into the matter could have led to an inspection of his boat. Then he would have to explain having Breck's and Robyn's clothing and other items onboard without Breck and Robyn. There were witnesses to the fight so he's sure, at least, one of them would back him up when he explained that he did everything he could to avoid it. And, he's sure he could come up with a story to explain why he has Breck and Robyn's clothing, but if either or both of their bodies ever surfaced he would be remembered, and immediately become a person of interest. After all he's done, it would be nothing short of a calamity if he lost everything, including his freedom, over a fight with William. As far as Eddie is concerned the worst part about today's event is that he feels compelled to change his plans. Cabo is beautiful, colorful, alive, and fun. Eddie was having a good time just walking along her streets people watching. Now, however, he thinks the best thing to do is to get out town as soon as he refuels. He'll let a few weeks go by and then he'll come back and stay for a week instead of a night.

Now, back at the boat, Eddie hesitates before climbing aboard. He has a premonition that William's onboard waiting for him. But, that's impossible. He left William unconscious and lying in the street. His hesitation dissolved when he thinks to himself that he wishes William is onboard. That way he could shoot him, claim he was there to rob him, and get away with it. He climbs aboard enthusiastically. He takes his bags of supplies and drops them on the table in the galley. He doesn't want to waste time putting the items away. He'll get to that when he's out in the ocean. Right now, he wants to start her up, refuel, and be on his way. But, the boat won't start. Being new to boat ownership he's not sure what he's doing wrong, so he withdraws the ignition key and tries again. She turns but she won't start. There's a first time for everything, and this is the first time that Eddie is frustrated and angry with "Miss Behavin." He tries again, but he gets the same result. His frustration and anger is building. He can't think of a reason why she wouldn't start and of all the times this could happen, now is the worst time of them all. He tries again, and again, and again, and he gets the same result each time. The only thing he can think of doing is going to the office and getting someone from the maintenance staff to come and tell him what he's doing wrong. He storms off his boat and walks tentatively towards the office. William is nowhere in sight, but Eddie can't escape the feeling that this has something to do with him. He makes it to the office without incident and explains his dilemma to the receptionist. He's more than happy to hear that the marina has a full time maintenance staff working at the marina every day of the week. However, the receptionist informs him that it may take thirty minutes to an hour, if not more, before one of them has the time to take a look at his boat. That sends Eddie through the roof. He yells at the receptionist for not having someone available immediately. Eddie knows that what he's yelling about is unreasonable. Somewhere in the middle of his rant he realizes he's just blowing off steam, and taking out his frustrations on the receptionist. She handles him professionally. When he finishes his rant, she assures him that she'll put a rush on his request and she'll have someone there as soon as possible. On top of that, she offers to refund the money he paid to stay in the marina overnight. Those two things, combined, have a calming effect on Eddie. Though she doesn't show it, the receptionist is happier than Eddie is that he is taking her up on her offer. She has been instructed to keep him in the office for at least fifteen minutes, and longer if possible, and she didn't know how she was going to do that. Even if she rushes, refunding the money is a fifteen minute process. So, she plans to stretch it out for, at least, ten minutes longer than it normally takes. She pretends to make the call to the maintenance office, but there isn't anyone on the other end of the call. Then she starts the refund process. As soon as she as she begins she gets a call. She apologizes to Eddie and asks him to fill out a couple of forms while she deals with the person on the telephone. He still seems anxious but more relaxed than he was a minute ago. While she speaks with the person on the phone, she watches Eddie, with an undetectable smile on her face, give his full attention to completing the forms. She's sure now she'll be able to keep him in the office longer than the time that was asked of her, and she feels good about the five hundred dollars she just earned.

3:00pm - The news doesn't make Eddie happy. After spending twenty five minutes in the office just to get a refund he still has a thirty minute wait for maintenance. At this point he just accepts it, and he walks back to his boat to wait for the technician. As he heads back his walk isn't as cautious as his walk to the office, but he still keeps an eye out for William. With William nowhere in sight and nothing else to do while he waits he resigns himself to stowing away the supplies he picked up today.

From behind the closed door to what was Breck's stateroom William hears Eddie return to the boat. Each step Eddie takes down the companionway seems to echo as throbbing in William's head. Just making it to Eddie's boat exhausted all of William's energy. That Eddie wasn't onboard when he got there was divine intervention. William needed all the time he could get just to stop seeing two of everything, and to muster up what little energy he has left. There is no place above deck to hide where he wouldn't be seen so he went below to find someplace else. The largest of the three staterooms he knew was Eddie's. He didn't want to hide in there because chances are good that Eddie would go in there as soon as he returned. William chose one of the smaller staterooms hoping that would give him more time to recuperate. Now, as he listens to the noise coming from the galley he imagines that Eddie is taking the items from the two bags he saw on the table and putting them away. At this point he realizes that even if Eddie had returned two hours from now, he'd still be feeling a minute away from defeat. In the parking lot, Eddie proved to be stronger than he is and, obviously, more accustomed to fighting. The only thing William has going for him is that he hasn't yet answered Eddie's question. No, he isn't satisfied yet, and he wants to tell Eddie that personally. In a flash, he thinks of Genny and of all the things that have happened and of all the characters he's encountered since her death. But, his thoughts don't linger there. His thoughts turn to the story of his father as a young man, who kept going back to the bank even though the manager labeled him irritable and deranged, and even though the security guard took delight in violently throwing him out of the bank at the end of each day. He can hear Aunt Ernestine retell the story and he imagines watching his father, as if he's one of the people standing in line at the bank while the entire incident plays itself out. Surely, the other people standing in that line were wondering what's wrong with that kid. But, as William sees himself watching his father, all he can think of saying to that young man is, more power to you. Looking down at his own hands he imagines that he has, now, some of the same scrapes, cuts, and bruises his father had then. He hopes he lives long enough for someone to think as highly of him as he thinks of his father. Through the blood and the pain William finds it in himself to smile when he thinks that it has all come down to this. The only choice remaining now is should he wait for Eddie to open the door and then attack or should he just go for it?

Eddie has had an ominous feeling since he returned to the boat. It could stem from the reverberation of the fight he just had, or to a persistent sense of uncertainty about William's whereabouts. But, given all of his choices, he attributes it to the frustration of his new boat not starting when he needed it to start the most, and to having to wait so long before he can get help. Though he feels safe now that he's back on his boat, the sense of foreboding he's feeling continues to grow. Just before he puts the last item away he stops what he doing to stand still and listen. He waits long enough to convince himself that he's letting his mind play tricks on him, and then he goes back to doing what he was doing. Just as he does, out of the corner of his eye, he sees the door to the stateroom aft swing open. He turns just enough for William to grab him by his waist and push him back against the cabinets. William lands a punch to Eddie's head before Eddie can defend himself. The two men wrestle against the cabinets until Eddie knees William in the groin. The force drives William back and the pain folds him in half. Eddie scans the room for something to hit William with, but there isn't anything within reach. He turns his back in an attempt to walk to the other side of the galley where there are pots and knives, but before he knows it William his on his back trying to wrap his arm around Eddie's neck. Eddie takes hold of the arm William has around his neck, bends over, and tries to flip William over his back. The only thing that saves William from being flipped is there isn't enough ceiling room below deck to pull off a maneuver like that. Instead William's body goes flying sideways against the cabinets, hits the countertop, and then falls to the floor. Again Eddie tries to make his way to the other side of the room but this time he's hindered by William, who's grabbed his feet. Eddie breaks free of William's grasp, turns, and tries to kick William in the face, but William grabs Eddie's foot, which destabilizes him just enough to cause him to lose his balance, and join William on the floor. William uses Eddie's body like a rope and climbs on top of him until he is on Eddie's back. Again, he tries to wrap his arm around Eddie's neck. Eddie throws an elbow that connects with William's temple, which loosens the grip William has on Eddie. The two men wrestle on the ground, neither of them able to get a dominate position on the other, until Eddie lands a punch on the same temple where he just delivered an elbow. That takes just enough steam out of William for Eddie to pin his arms to the floor with his knees and beat William in the face mercilessly.

Though William manages to get both of his arms free and up to his face, to block some of Eddie's punches, it's too little too late. Eddie delivers one more blow to William's face and William's arms go completely idle and fall to the floor. Eddie climbs off William and looks around the room trying to get a sense of where he is in relation to the knives on the galley's countertop. He gets his bearings, but he needs a moment or two to catch his breath. He's not worried about William anymore. He isn't going anywhere, and in a minute he'll be dead. While he sits just across from William he sees William coming to consciousness again. Lying on his back, completely at Eddie's mercy and with a mouth full of blood, William says something but he says it so faintly Eddie can't hear him. "What?" asks Eddie.

William spits as much blood out of his mouth as he can, but he doesn't have enough strength for the spittle to make it to the floor. It drips down the side of his face instead. Then he repeats what he said before, "This isn't over."

Eddie laughs and disagrees, "I told I would kill you if I saw you again." Eddie lifts himself off the floor to get to the knives, but then he thinks about all of the blood that he'd have to clean up. He realizes the easiest thing to do is choke William to death. That way there'll be no blood and he can hide William's body in the shower of one of the staterooms until he gets out to the open ocean, where he can dump it like the others. As William lies on the floor he isn't feeling any physical pain, but he's full of sorrow. He knows that Eddie will finish him off any minute now, but he isn't sorry about the life he's about to lose. He uses his last few moments on this Earth to apologize to Genny for not having the strength to see it through. He apologizes for not keeping her safe that night, and he apologizes for not stopping the person who's responsible for her murder from getting away with it. He can barely open his eyes because they are filled with his own blood, sweat, and spittle, but he can see Genny clearly now. She's standing on the Champs-Élysées looking down on him as he asks for her hand in marriage on bended knee. He sees her smiling and saying yes. That's the picture he wants to take with him. He wants to remember how happy he made her once and of how happy they were together. Before he can stand from bended knee he feels Eddie's elbow slam into his ribs. Next he feels Eddie climbing on top of him, again pinning both of his arms to the floor with his knees. He finds the strength to say once more, "This isn't over."

Eddie smiles and affirms, "It will be in a minute." Eddie takes hold of William's throat firmly with both hands and squeezes while thinking of the pleasure he's about to get from watching William's eyes roll to the back of his head. The sound of a single shot bounces off the walls of the galley. It registers as a popping noise to William, but he doesn't know what it truly is or where it came from. All he knows is Eddie's grip around his neck is loosening, and then he feels Eddie let go entirely. The next thing he knows is that Eddie's body has rolled off of his and is lying on the floor across the room. William can hear someone walking down the steps of the companionway and he can hear Eddie moving. He hears Eddie ask, "Who are you?"

William can turn his head just enough to see this person with the one eye he can barely flicker open and closed. He can see that the man standing over him has a gun in his hand, but he can also see that the gun isn't pointed at him. It is being held with a purpose, and it's pointed in the direction of where William thinks Eddie's body is. The man is just staring at William, who's trying to keep his one eye open long enough to get a good look at him. William guesses, "Cyrus?"

With that the man smiles and turns his attention to Eddie, who's sitting up and holding his hand on his stomach trying to slow the bleeding. Cyrus levels the gun at Eddie's head and says to Eddie, "Pete Jefferson sends his regards."

Eddie begs, "Please don't shoot! Please don't . . ."

"Heta dlia Ryki Džefiersan" and then he puts two bullets in Eddie's head.

———

EPILOGUE

Two Days Later

10:00am - William's driver woke him up, as requested, when they got to the outskirts of Negril. A few minutes later the driver pulled off Norman Manley Boulevard and onto the Moon Dance Villas property. A security guard escorted William to Pete's office, where Pete and Cyrus are waiting for him. William says, "Mr. Jefferson, it's a pleasure to meet you."

Pete insists, "The pleasure is all mine. I hope you had a good flight."

"Thank you for the use of your jet. I wish I could say I enjoyed it more, but I was asleep before we took off and the attendants had to wake me up after we landed."

"That's entirely understandable. Have a seat. Let's talk for a little while."

William waves to Cyrus, and Cyrus smiles and waves back.

Pete admits, "I have to start by saying I'm sorry. I am responsible for your wife's death."

Confused, William asks, "How's that?"

Pete explains, "Ten years ago my company was negotiating for the purchase of the property that would become the Forest Canyon Mall. The owners were an unscrupulous bunch. At the last minute they demanded a higher price for the property. We agreed, but that sent me and my partners into a mad scramble to raise the extra cash. I just found out, very recently, that one of my partners enlisted the help of a dirty police officer who knew about a drug transaction that was about to take place. That police officer hijacked the buy money, two hundred and fifty thousand dollars, and unfortunately, my son, the buyer, was shot and killed during the hijacking. I spent years looking for the person who killed my son, but I couldn't find anyone who knew what happened. About five months ago, a private investigator I hired turned up a lead. He found out that there were only three parties that knew about the transaction before it took place. Those three parties were the buyer, my son, the seller, and the man who introduced the two of them. It turns out that the man who introduced them was also a police informant. We know that because he thought he was going to get a cut of the hijacked money. When he didn't, he felt cheated, and he started to complain out loud. My private investigator never found out who the cop was, but he got the name of the person doing the complaining. His name was Teddy Gallo. Apparently, when this police officer went to Teddy's apartment, to talk, he thought they were alone, but Teddy's girlfriend was in the bathroom and she overheard their entire conversation. The first mistake I made, that cost your wife her life, was I put all of my resources into finding her when I should have found Teddy first. I did that because I thought she'd be more credible, and I didn't want the police officer to know that I was close. My guess is, she never told you that we spoke." William answers, "No. She didn't."

Pete continues, "We only spoke once. She agreed to speak with me again, but not until she spoke with you first. She said she just needed time to figure out how to tell you about what was happening."

William asks, "If you only spoke once, who else knew that you contacted my wife?"

Pete looks at Cyrus, and then he hangs his head before lifting it up again to continue, "That's the second mistake I made. I was having lunch with Cyrus and, coincidentally, one of my partners was seated at the table next to us. He overheard me tell Cyrus about finding and speaking with your wife. Unfortunately, he happened to be the same partner who enlisted the help of the dirty police officer to come up with his share of the money."

William asks, "Who is he, and where is he now?"

Pete reveals, "His name was Carl Davies and you don't have to worry about him."

William asks, "Why?"

Pete is seated in his office in Los Angeles and Cyrus is in the room with him. His receptionist announces over the intercom, "Mr. Jefferson, I have Mr. Davies on the line. He says it's the third time he's called and he says it's urgent."

Pete replies, "OK, I'm ready to speak with him now. You can put him through." Pete picks up the phone and says, "Carl, I already know why you're calling, and I've already fixed the problem."

Carl demands to know, "How did this happen? I thought we had all of our ducks in a row. I've asked around. I'm the only one who didn't get my money transferred to my account."

Pete concedes, "I know, I know. I've been over it with escrow. There was a mix up when they added the company that got part of your proceeds. They should have had you sign an additional waiver but they didn't. I've already sent Cyrus to your house, with the waiver, to get your signature. He'll notarize it and take it to escrow. You'll have your money before the end of the day. Are you at your house?"

Carl answers, "Yes."

Pete says, "Good. Wait there for Cyrus. Don't worry. It's just a minor glitch. You'll get everything before the end of the day."

When Cyrus arrives at Carl's house, Carl let's him in, but he hasn't calmed down any. When he turns his back to lead Cyrus to the kitchen, Cyrus hits him in the back of the head with the butt of his gun. When Carl comes back to consciousness he's seated in a chair, and he's bound to that chair at his wrists and his ankles.

Pete says to William, "We got a suspicion about my partner's involvement so we had a heart to heart conversation with him. He admitted everything. He told us the name of the police officer who killed my son and stole his money. He admitted, that money was the money he put into the deal. And, finally, he told us about overhearing our conversation at lunch. He said he told the police officer about my conversation with Cyrus and the two of them came up with a plan to silence my witness, your wife." William asks again, "But where is Carl Davies now?"

The garage door at Carl's house opens and inside, with the remote in his hand, is Cyrus. He backs his car into the garage and then he pushes the button on the remote to close the garage door again. He lifts the trunk door open and goes back inside Carl's house. When he returns he's carrying Carl, whose ankles are duct taped together, his arms are duct taped together behind his back, and there is a row of duct tape going around his head covering his mouth. Cyrus throws Carl in the trunk of his car and then, unceremoniously, shoots Carl twice in the head.

Pete officially discloses to William, "Nobody knows what happened to Carl, but we are pretty sure we won't see him again." Pete gets up from his chair, walks around his desk, and sits in the chair next to William. He goes on to say, "You've lost someone that can never be replaced. I am truly sorry for my involvement in that. I hope you can forgive me."

William grants, "It wasn't your fault."

Pete is truly thankful that William feels that way. Though he already decided to make the following offers, given William's grace and understanding, he now makes them with added enthusiasm. He says, "There are a couple of things I want to do for you. First, I want you to have Carl's share of the deal. That's fifteen million dollars and I'll pay the taxes on that, so you'll get that amount and every cent of it. I was going to make sure you got the boat, but I figured once you knew the whole story you wouldn't want it."

"You were right about that."

"Good! Then you'll be happy to know that the boat sank to the bottom of the ocean with Detective Robert's body in it. Listen, when we all get back to Los Angeles I want you to come by my office so we can talk about future business together, but before that, I think you've earned a vacation. I've arranged for you to have a three bedroom villa on this property for two weeks, all expenses paid."

"Is it alright if I go back to Los Angeles first and then come back in a couple of days?"

"Of course it is. We'll be here for a few more days, I hope you make it back before we leave. Remember, after you've had some time to heal and rest, let's talk again."

William and Pete stand, face each other, and shake hands. William walks over to Cyrus, who stands as William approaches. William shakes Cyrus' hand and then he hugs him. As he pulls away he says, "Thank you for saving my life."

Cyrus just smiles.

One Day Later

5:30pm - There isn't a single cloud in the sky. The gentle breeze combined with the setting sun, whose rays are being partially blocked by the hills to the west, are turning what must have been another hot day in the valley into another day in paradise. William is lying on his side, in the perfectly manicured grass, facing the bouquet of red roses he just laid over Geneviève's final resting place. The two of them have been talking and laughing for the last thirty minutes. William laughs and says "I know, I do look like a raccoon with my two black eyes. Do you remember how many times I used to tell you that you don't need make up? I wish you were here because now I need some."

William pauses to hear, in his mind, what he imagines Genny would say.

Then he responds, "I know, I know, you're not here. Believe me, nobody knows that more than I do. I miss you so much. I know you know that, but you're going to have to get used to hearing me say that." Again, only William can hear Genny talking to him. "Thanks, I know you do. Well, I'm going to get ready to leave now, but I'll be back soon. I'm glad you like your flowers." Up until this point William kept it together, but the anxiety of saying goodbye again is more than he can handle. He starts to cry. While he gathers himself and wipes the tears from his eyes, he laughs and says, "You gotta admit, I held on for longer than either of us expected. I love you babe. I will always love you. I hope I live a long life but, at the same time, I can't wait to be with you again. Listen, I'm not going to say goodbye. Let's make a deal. Instead of goodbye, let's just say I'll see you later, OK?"

In William's mind, Genny agrees.

"Good!" William stands up and looks down at the name on the tombstone, Geneviève Flowers, and he says, "OK, my love, I'll see you later."

The Next Day

10:00am - The chauffeured limousine pulled up in front of the house at exactly 10:00am just as William said it would. The driver wanted to get out and then help with the bags, but William insists that he wait with the car instead. William wants him to pop the trunk and wait there until he returns. William walks to the front door which is already open. He goes in the house. Ten minutes later he comes out carrying two suitcases, and he has Aunt Ernestine on his arm. She can sense that William is walking awkwardly trying to take care of so much at the same time, so she tells him to go ahead with her bags. She says she can make it to the car just fine by herself. Before they get to the bottom of the porch steps the back passenger door of the limousine swings open. Megan jumps out and rushes up the walkway to help Aunt Ernestine. The driver meets William at the trunk to help load Aunt Ernestine's luggage. By the time Megan and Aunt Ernestine make it to the car the two of them are laughing and talking about taking walks along the beach, and about how much oxtail, jerk chicken, and ackee and salt fish they are going to eat. Megan helps Aunt Ernestine into the car and then she gets in the car behind her. The driver closes the trunk and walks to the passenger side of the car to close the door behind William. But, William asks that he goes ahead and take the driver's seat. He wants to take a minute for himself before he gets in. When he turns to look at the house he sees a bluebird washing his wings in the bath. William smiles and allows himself to fantasize that that is the same bluebird of his youth, even though he knows that isn't the truth. Still, it's a comforting thought to have, so he takes that thought with him as he gets in the car. As they pull away from the one story pink house with a terracotta tiled roof on Orange Avenue, he watches and listens to Aunt Ernestine interact with Megan. As he watches and listens to Aunt Ernestine, he realizes how much of an impact she's had on his life, and he realizes how much he'll need her in the future. He thinks to himself, "There's a woman who's had more than her share of life's trials and tribulations. She lost her parents at an early age, she lost her sister, her best friend, to breast cancer, she was struck with diabetes, and eventually that disease would claim her eye sight. Yet, she's still here, fighting, and squeezing as much happiness out of life as she can. That reminds William of what she's told him many times, at her kitchen table, when he asked where she gets her strength from. Aunt Ernestine always says, "Life goes on, Son. And, you gotta go on with it."

THE END

Daniel Alexander studied Literature at Syracuse University. He is a native New Yorker living in Southern California. *Seven Days* is his debut novel.

Made in the USA
Columbia, SC
25 April 2023

15787216R00281